Save
Your Own

Save

Your Own

Elisabeth Brink

HOUGHTON MIFFLIN COMPANY

BOSTON • NEW YORK

2006

For Robert, Ben, and Ellen

For information about permission to reproduce selections
from this book, write to Permissions, Houghton Mifflin Company,
215 Park Avenue South, New York, New York 10003.

Visit our Web site: www.houghtonmifflinbooks.com.

Library of Congress Cataloging-in-Publication Data
Brink, Elisabeth, date.
Save your own / Elisabeth Brink.
p.   cm.
ISBN-13: 978-0-618-65114-6
ISBN-10: 0-618-65114-4
1. Women graduate students—Fiction. 2. Drug
addicts—Services for—Fiction. 3. Women—Drug use
—Fiction. 4. Halfway houses—Fiction. I. Title.
PS3602.R5318S28 2006
813'.6—dc22   2005024017

Book design by Melissa Lotfy

Printed in the United States of America

QUM 10 9 8 7 6 5 4 3 2 1

"Hungry Heart" by Bruce Springsteen. Copyright © 1980 Bruce
Springsteen. Reprinted by permission. International copyright secured. All rights reserved.

"The Pickaxe" by Rumi. Translation copyright © 1995 Coleman
Barks, *The Essential Rumi*.

Save
Your Own

one

LET ME BEGIN by describing my physical self. I am a full-grown woman who looks like a ten-year-old boy, and not even a very handsome or cute one at that. At four feet nine inches, I stand in an awkward relation to most countertops, and there are chairs from which my legs will exuberantly swing. The features of my face are pinched and asymmetrical. I have no figure worth mentioning, my bones are thin, and my pale hair frizzes out from my head like cotton candy that has been pulled as far as possible from its cardboard cone. The truth is that I am quite remarkable in my unattractiveness. I use the word *remarkable* in its most literal sense, as in *able to be remarked upon* or *provoking notice* or *calling forth attention*. I doubt that I shall ever be allowed to forget that nature endowed me with not even one of the charming physical attributes with which the human female has been attracting friends and lovers for thousands of generations. Apparently, it is a once-in-a-blue-moon kind of thing to have been so genetically unlucky so consistently, without being actually deformed.

My mind, thankfully, has more to recommend it.

The following events took place in the fall of 1984, when I was a graduate student in my fourth year at Harvard Divinity School. My goal that year was simple: I was to write my dissertation. The work went smoothly at first. I submitted a detailed prospectus at the end of April, according to schedule. Then, for reasons that will soon be clear, the process stalled. An unproductive May became a futile June that stretched into a wasted summer. I spent the empty months loitering in coffee shops, dozing on park benches, wandering through grocery stores, getting lost in art museums, and dawdling in the back rows of planetary shows and public lectures—often while entertaining vivid, highly nuanced sexual fantasies that featured either a man with greeny-brown eyes whom I had crashed into on my bike over two years before or a handsome waiter named Ravi who had served me keema mattar once at an excellent Indian restaurant I could not afford to frequent as much as I would have liked. (I was a twenty-five-year-old virgin, and I was determined to shed this sad and troubling condition as soon as humanly possible.)

A slender fellowship provided by the Zephyr Foundation was my only income at the time. These fellowships, which also covered tuition and fees, were awarded annually to three or four carefully selected students who showed exceptional promise. They were coveted prizes; the fact that I had been a recipient for three consecutive years had made me an object of the starkest envy among my highly competitive colleagues. The continuation of the fellowship from one year to the next, however, was by no means assured. One needed to be progressing at a rather accelerated rate through the several stages of study that culminated in the Doctor of Philosophy degree, and one needed to demonstrate the highest level of scholarly achievement at each stage. Even when those conditions were met, the Committee for Graduate Studies (hereinafter referred to as "the Committee") might simply change its mind and bestow the fellowship on a more favored student.

Given the quiescent—or shall I say, comatose—state of my academic affairs in the fall of 1984, I was flooded with dread but not really surprised one morning in late September to find that an official-looking white letter had fluttered into my Divinity School mailbox. It read,

Dear Ms. Gillian Cormier-Brandenburg:

The Committee for Graduate Studies regrets that starting in January the Zephyr Foundation Fellowship that funds your monthly stipend will be revoked. Should you wish to continue your graduate studies, tuition and fees for the spring semester are payable in full by the first of the year.

Sincerely yours,
Dr. Henry T. Trubow
Dean of Graduate Studies

My thoughts flew immediately to Thomas More, whose head was severed from his body by legal decree in 1535. I often wondered what he'd thought and felt as he approached the chopping block and saw the executioner's blade. I was coming closer than ever to imagining his suffering when my reverie was broken by a neatly groomed, pale-skinned Methodist who stepped into my peripheral vision.

"Bad news?" he asked unctuously. He would not have been the least bit sorry if it was.

"Not at all," I replied airily, balling the letter in my fist.

He took a big stack of mail out of his assigned slot. "How's your dissertation going?"

"It's been a stimulating adventure."

He flipped through several notes and announcements, picked out a 5" x 7" card with colorful balloons around the rim, and smiled delightedly. It was clearly a party invitation—the design was rather childish, I thought. For a minute I feared he would ask whether I had been invited.

"You must be almost finished by now." He slipped the invitation into his jacket pocket and stuffed the rest of his mail into his backpack.

"I'll be done soon," I assured him.

As soon as he was gone, certain words began to reverberate: *stipend will be revoked . . . tuition and fees . . . payable in full*. I had less than one hundred dollars in my checking account, and no savings. My parents were college professors; they couldn't afford full tuition either. What was more, they were atheists who disapproved of my interest in religion, a subject they considered at best squishy and ornamental, and at worst an impediment to scientific progress and a threat to global political stability. Those were two good reasons not to ask them for help. The third was this: I had no stomach for the kind of criticism—thorough, incisive, accurate, perpetual—an unrenewed fellowship would provoke.

Dean Trubow's office was just down the hall. A few steps took me to his open doorway.

"Oh, it's you, Gillian. Come in. And close the door behind you," he said.

Altogether unexpected at a citadel for higher learning, not to mention a sanctum for the story of God, was Henry T. Trubow, who chain-smoked menthol cigarettes and had a laminated I'D RATHER BE TROUT FISHIN' bumper sticker affixed to the front of his enormous mahogany desk.

I pressed the letter into its proper shape and laid it face up on his blotter. "I would like you to reconsider this decision."

He sighed and leaned back in his chair. "It's not my decision. It's the Committee's."

"Of which you are a member."

"Of which I am one member."

"You could persuade the others."

He pulled a squashed pack of Salems out of his pocket. "Have a seat."

I sank into a leather chair that by itself could have funded the rest of my education.

"Since your prospectus was approved in April, you've missed three deadlines in a row. Brass tacks, Gillian: You're not Zephyr material anymore."

"I'm due for a breakthrough. I think I'll be having one soon."

"That's what you told me the last time we talked."

I sighed raggedly, averting my eyes.

"Tell me you have a chapter. Tell me you have an outline at least."

I glared at the bumper sticker, detesting its coy apostrophe.

Dean Trubow slowly lit a cigarette, and his eyes narrowed in the swirl of smoke. "It's worse than that, isn't it? You don't have a methodology."

"I *do* have a methodology. I told you already. My plan is to find and interview nonreligious individuals who have had true and lasting spiritual experiences. From the case histories so compiled, I intend to analyze the psychology and spirituality of what I am calling the 'secular conversion experience.'"

"So what's the holdup?" he asked.

"It's just that . . . well, it's been kind of hard to find truly converted nonreligious individuals. By definition they don't go to churches, mosques, or temples. And no one has answered my ads in the newspaper."

"Have you ever wondered whether these people—and this phenomenon of 'secular conversion,' as you call it—actually exist?"

"Of course they exist," I said staunchly. But I was beginning to doubt.

He laid his cigarette in an ashtray. "Gillian, listen carefully to what I'm about to say: Your writing has stalled because your topic is bunkum."

Bunkum? I thought I knew all the words in the English language, but this little one must have slipped by me. I guessed it to be United States slang, probably early nineteenth century, possibly from the same hinterland where Dr. Trubow himself originated.

"Nonsense, poppycock," he clarified.

I actually liked Dean Trubow. When he demolished a student, it was fast and clean. The other faculty members took a lot longer and left a bloody mess.

He continued, "You ought to throw away that foolish topic and get back to doing the kind of scholarship that will get you a job."

"I understand your concern, Dean Trubow," I replied evenly. "My topic *is* unusual. But I can't possibly dispose of it because I am convinced in my marrow that the secular conversion experience holds the key to our species' survival. You see"—and here I leaned forward to make my point—"*secular conversion obviates religion!* It proves that one doesn't have to belong to any particular group or hold any particular belief to enjoy all the benefits of religious life. A scholar who could find a simple, reliable method for demonstrating the validity of a secular conversion experience would in effect be ushering the human race to the brink of an unprecedented possibility. By working backwards from the conversion event, we could formulate a new, one-size-fits-all, experience-based, anti-religion religion!"

"And what on earth would be the sense in that?" Dean Trubow fairly bellowed.

I sat back, chagrined by his tone. "Isn't it obvious? The global community is emerging. Different religious sects are finding themselves in closer proximity. Greater and harsher conflicts are inevitable. A secular religion would render wars, slaughter, and tribal prejudices completely unnecessary. It would save us before we killed each other off!"

Dean Trubow let out a low whistle. "That's one heck of a leap. But I have to give you credit. In all my years of teaching, you're the first graduate student I've had who thought a dissertation could change the world, much less save it. You're not afraid of big ideas. I like that in a scholar."

I blushed furiously, as I did whenever I received a compliment, and the embarrassment of blushing furiously made the temperature of my cheeks rise even higher, so that my face must have looked positively inflamed. "Thank you very much, Dean Trubow."

"But I'm willing to bet that's not the only reason you're so excited about this topic."

"Excuse me?"

"Look, I respect your noble purpose. It's always heartening to see idealism in the young. But I've been in this business long enough to know that a student usually has a personal reason for picking a topic. They don't always want to tell you about it, but it's there."

"I don't think I do," I answered. Having a personal reason had never even occurred to me. It was obvious he *wanted* me to have one, though, so I said, "But I'm sure I'll find a personal reason if I keep going, Dean Trubow. Look, the topic's not my problem. What's holding me up is finding suitable subjects. If I could just locate a dozen nonreligious people who've had deep and lasting spiritual experiences, I'm sure this project would take flight."

He sighed. I could see that he wasn't completely convinced, but he decided to relent. "Try a halfway house," he said.

"A what?"

"There's one right here in Cambridge. It's for drug addicts and alcoholics. A friend . . . well, a child of someone I know went there. I forget what it's called. But don't just waltz in spouting academic claptrap and expect to get anything done, Gillian. These are people who've been battered by their passions and by life. You have to spend time with them and earn their trust before they'll be likely to share their deep inner lives with you."

"Are you suggesting I go to this place and just linger in the hallway chatting?"

He shrugged. "Work there, maybe. Get a job."

"Dean Trubow, I'm in a high-pressure graduate program. I can't afford the time!"

He gave me a pitying look. "What exactly have you been doing with your time?" He stood, signaling the end of the interview.

"What about my Zephyr?"

He paused, sighed, stubbed out his cigarette. "Look, I'll tell you what." He consulted a calendar on his desk. "This is Monday, September twenty-fourth. I'll give you till October thirty-first. If I don't see some progress from you by then—either a first chapter or a few completed interviews from residents at the halfway house—your fellowship will most certainly be revoked."

I stood up and almost yelled, *You want me to do in one month what I haven't been able to do in five?* But I bit my lip. "Thank you, Dean Trubow."

"If you were anyone else, I wouldn't give you another chance. I'm only doing this because you're one of our best students and you've got your heart set on this thing. But I can't say I'm optimistic, Gillian. Secular conversion experiences, a new secular religion—it still sounds like bunkum to me."

Pretty, plump Gretchen O'Neil sat beneath a halo of strawberry hair. "Your academic qualifications are impressive," she said, though with a small furrow disturbing her brow. On the desk behind her, the string of a tea bag descended from a handmade ceramic mug. From where I was sitting, I could read the tag. IN-FUSION OF SERENITY.

"Yes," I said.

She leaned back in her chair, folding dainty hands over my curriculum vitae. "But what I'm really interested in is who you are as a person."

"As a person," I repeated. What a pointless, pedestrian phrase! In different circumstances, I might have chirped, As opposed to what? But since any chance I had of becoming a scholar seemed to depend on my acing this interview, I merely straightened my wool vest and tried to imagine what the perfect candidate for a job in the social services would say.

"I guess you could say that I . . . I . . . want to help people," I said.

Gretchen smiled encouragement. "Why?"

Why? This question was worse than the last! *Res ipsa loquitur*, I wanted to say. The thing speaks for itself. But I bit my tongue and smiled as best I could. "Well, because . . . some people need to be helped."

Gretchen nodded sagely. "And what brings you here?"

What indeed. Responsibility House was a state-subsidized residential treatment program for female alcoholics and drug addicts. About half of the twelve residents had formerly been housed at the women's correctional facility in Framingham. They were undoubtedly ignorant, frightening, and unsavory; the wage was probably minimum; and the duties were likely to be thankless and dull.

Gretchen looked at me with innocent expectancy as I tried to formulate an answer. The wall clock ticked. The tea cooled. The smile on my face was becoming too arduous to maintain. Finally I had to admit to myself that I was simply incapable of fabricating the large number of lies that would be necessary if I were to continue pretending to be altruistically motivated.

"I, ah . . . Actually, I'm here to do research for my dissertation." I cringed, imagining (or hoping?) that she would see how completely uninterested I was in the job for its own sake.

"Mmm. What's it about?"

I groaned inwardly. Experience had taught me that talking

about one's dissertation to nonacademics was a bad idea. The vast majority of listeners were likely to find one's topic, whatever it was, excruciatingly boring and would tune out posthaste. A scholar probably had between ten and forty seconds to get a few salient points across before his or her audience was drifting in a private sea of mental distractions. But what choice did I have, under the circumstances?

So, rising to the challenge, I defined a conversion experience as "the direct sensory apprehension of a supernatural power followed by the complete and lasting reorganization of the life and mind on a new and morally higher plane." I mentioned a few famous examples from well-known religious texts, then went on to describe a *secular* conversion experience as the same kind of thing happening outside an established religious tradition. Having covered this ground in what I believe was half a minute, I took a much-needed breath and looked closely at Gretchen to see whether she was following. Her eyes were red-rimmed and, to my horror, she acted exactly like a typical undergraduate by lifting two fingers to pursed lips in an attempt to stifle a yawn.

"Excuse me," she said. "With the shortage of help I've been working a lot of overtime. Please go on."

"Anyway, Ms. O'Neil, my fundamental research questions are these: Do secular conversion experiences share the features of traditional conversion experiences, or are they different in identifiable ways? Are there recurring settings, themes, and narrative patterns? Are they as profound and lasting as the conversions recorded in religious texts? And, the most provocative question, which I'm sure you've guessed by now, is this: Can they be induced?"

Gretchen had innocent blue eyes, a button nose, and a sweetly bowed mouth. She screwed these features into a painful-looking squint. "Responsibility House?" she prompted.

"Yes, yes, I'm getting to that," I said, barely able to conceal my annoyance. As hard as I tried to reconcile myself to intellectual apathy, it was always wounding. "I thought about these issues night and day, but as exciting as the possibilities were"—I almost added, "to me *as a person*"—"I began to feel hopeless. A thorny methodological problem stood in my way. Where would I find a goodly number of nonreligious converted people? I'll be honest, Ms. O'Neil: For the last five months I've made little headway, and I was beginning to wonder whether my goal was even attainable. But something kept telling me that it could work, that the answer was close at hand.

"It just so happens that the laundromat I bicycle to has your flyer taped in the window along with other community announcements. I must have read it dozens of times—Responsibility House, a Halfway House for Chemically Dependent Women—without thinking anything of it. Then everything came together in a big *click*. I fell off my bike and just stared at the sign. It was like Saint Paul falling off his horse!"

Gretchen looked a little startled.

I think I may have looked startled, too. Such a colorful lie popping out of my mouth was a bit of a shock, especially when I had committed myself to honesty moments before. But what kind of applicant would admit she'd been all but ordered to the interview by her dissertation advisor on pain of losing her fellowship? And isn't it true that including dramatic events such as falling off horses in one's stories often does recapture an audience's flagging attention? A similar effect can be achieved by varying body position and tone of voice.

I leaned forward and continued in a stage whisper, "Ms. O'Neil, I've heard that there are women inside these secular walls for whom the miracle of salvation is not an empty phrase but a living, breathing reality. They come here from prison or the streets and achieve sobriety. They mend their family relations and become useful citizens of the commonwealth. And they begin speaking of spiritual things. How does that happen, I wonder?"

Gretchen placed a pink finger on her tender cheek and mused, "Well, we do encourage positive behaviors."

"Whatever the catalysts are, the change in lifestyle is dramatic, is it not?"

"I guess you could say that," she admitted.

"And wouldn't you agree that the validity of the conversion is easy to determine? Either your residents maintain sobriety or they do not. Either they become workers and worthy citizens or they return to lives of thievery and prostitution. Either they exude peacefulness and serenity or they blame, rationalize, and complain the way they they always did. Don't you see? It's so simple! The proof is in the pudding, so to speak."

"Does this mean you're going to write a book about us?"

"A dissertation first. A book later. I hope." I almost blushed, imagining myself as a published author.

Gretchen looked away. "This conversion thing you're talking about . . . it's not like flicking a switch."

"Of course not. I'm sure it's nothing like that," I said, backpedaling quickly. I was worried that I had gone too far. I sometimes forget that religion—like money, sex, and power—is a subject best approached obliquely.

Gretchen reached behind her for the cup of tea. "Do you have any idea how unusual a candidate you are?"

"I imagine I'm not the typical applicant."

"I almost always hire social workers, young ones, just graduated, but they don't last long. Six months is average. Once they figure out that they can get third-party payments for private addictions counseling, they're gone. They usually walk out in the middle of a shift." She made a snorting noise, which surprised me. There was something incongruous about a sound like that emanating from her lightly freckled face.

"You won't have to worry about me," I assured her. "I'm very reliable. I don't even take sick days. I was the only student in my hometown who had perfect attendance through eight years of elementary school and four years of high school." This was very close to being true.

"The job pays minimum wage." Her face twisted into a childish grimace of apology.

"I expected no more."

"Good. I'll start you with the easy stuff—house supervision and some office work. No special training required. We'll see how you manage with that."

"Thank you very much, Ms. O'Neil."

"Call me Gretchen."

I'm not sure which emotion was primary in that moment—relief that the interview was almost over, pride in my rousing success, or terrible, wrenching dread. You see, I had never actually worked before. In fact, I had spent most of my life shunning social activities of any kind. While other kids were waitresses or sales clerks, I enrolled in special summer courses or independent studies. Even as a youngster, I preferred the air-conditioned library, with its exquisite smell of leather and dust, to the beach or summer camp.

But a timid, cerebral temperament wasn't the only cause of my social discomfort; there was a darker reason, too. All through childhood and adolescence, day after day and year after year, I had withstood barrages of jeers and taunts directed at my body and mind. The insults were sometimes physical as well as verbal: I was pushed into mud puddles over and over again. In the cafeteria, I was a repeat target of pudding-followed-by-popcorn throwers. My labia majora were pinched in the locker room, a picture of my naked body next to my name was spray-painted on the field house, and my glasses were stolen so often I carried a spare pair. Though I tried to hide the damage, even from myself, this treatment had occasionally pushed me from the realm of shy bookishness into an abyss of terror and profound aversion to other human beings. I'm sorry to say that, even in my adult life, there were times when I simply was not capable of social interaction at all.

"When would you like me to start?" I asked, trying to cover the quaver in my voice with a look of bright optimism. I was hoping for several weeks to psychologically prepare.

"Right away, actually. Tomorrow night." Gretchen swirled in her chair and began rummaging through a messy file drawer. "I just hope I can find a W-4 before then."

The next afternoon at 4:45 I firmly set my jaw and rode my bike down Massachusetts Avenue. I turned at Summer Street and there, at the end of a row of Depression-era three-deckers, every one some shade of pukish green, stood Responsibility House.

It was a rambling, pukish pink, three-story Victorian surrounded by a sickly waist-high hedge and a tiny balding lawn. Real estate in Cambridge being what it was, it might have sold for a hefty sum to an upwardly mobile couple who would have painted it a happy medley of coordinating colors and lovingly restored the bow windows and leaded glass, the carved posts and curved railings. As the house was owned by the state of Massachusetts and dedicated to purely functional purposes, however, maintenance was kept to a minimum. The concrete walkway was cracked and lumpy, and the brick foundation had sunk unevenly into the ground. The wide front porch sagged, and a north-facing turret seemed to have only a precarious relationship to the rest of the house. An added-on side room had all the allure of a hitchhiker's thumb.

Gretchen O'Neil met me in the bare-bones kitchen. A short, round woman in black was tending a steaming pot, and a few other residents—recently returned from work, I supposed—were milling about. I glanced at them nervously. One of them kept her head down so that her dirty hair fell forward and camouflaged her face. Another woman, many-ringed hand on hip, was pouring a Diet Coke into a plastic glass of ice. She looked at me briefly and without apparent interest; her dark eyes showed a mix of boredom and defiance. Gretchen did not introduce me to these individuals and talked as if they were not there, which gave me an uneasy feeling about the job, as though I had been charged with shepherding a flock of ghosts.

Leading me to the second-floor office where I had been interviewed the day before, she explained my duties. I was to do whatever filing was necessary, join the residents for dinner at six, and supervise the cleanup and chores. After that I could read, write, chat with the women, or watch TV. At precisely 10:30 I was to turn off the television, lock the doors, and click off the downstairs lights. If a resident was missing, I was to make a note of the fact in a logbook provided for that purpose. In the same book, I was also to record my comments and observations and report any unusual or noteworthy incidents. (Gretchen would read the logbook every morning and respond briefly in writing.) Then I would have another block of solitude until midnight, when I would be relieved by Dolly, a former house resident who made extra money working the graveyard shift.

Gretchen directed my attention to a list of emergency numbers posted on the wall above the desk: Fire, EMTs, Police. Then she pointed to a three-ring binder bearing the title *Responsibility House: Handbook of Policies & Procedures*. It was a messy affair, with loose pages haphazardly inserted and yellow Post-Its peeping out everywhere. She said it would tell me how to handle virtually any issue or problem that might arise.

I looked at it dubiously. "May I call you if I need assistance?"

Sighing noisily, she wrote her number on an index card and taped it to the wall. As if her grudging manner were not enough to dissuade me, she said, "You might have a hard time reaching me. I'm seeing someone, so I'm hardly ever home." Then she added, "By the way, don't let them play the radio during dinner. They can never agree on a station and it's unfair to force people to listen to music they don't like."

I nodded, but my blood ran cold. I was an only child; even in college I lived alone. I had never battled with a sibling or traded insults with my peers or fought and won a single turf battle with another human being. I didn't know *how* not to let people play the radio. Was one supposed to plead, cajole, tease? Should I ask politely or issue ultimatums from on high? And what if the residents ignored me? Should I threaten retribution, pretend not to notice, or call the police? I might have quit the job right there, confessing my inadequacy, but by the time I found my voice, the heels of Gretchen's sensible shoes were plunking down the un-carpeted stairs.

I watched from the window as she emerged into the driveway and slid into the driver's side of her Civic. In another minute, the car had backed into the street beyond my angle of vision, and the fear that Gretchen's presence had kept in abeyance snaked through my body and constricted my throat. Was this really happening? Was I really alone and defenseless in a modern-day version of Sodom and Gomorrah? Hyperventilation began. It felt as if the edges of my mind were smoldering to ash. I collapsed into a shabby, bedspread-covered armchair, put my head between my legs, and took deep breaths.

I was still in this vulnerable position when a small vibration pulsed through the floorboards and bubbled up the legs of the chair. Though I willed it to do anything else, the tremor swelled into the unmistakable reverberation of thumping bass that was superseded by the piercing wail of a throaty female voice. The artist screamed her lyrics at such a pitch of rage and desperation that they were almost indistinguishable, but I could make out two words—*nail* and *baby*—which spiraled around each other nauseatingly in a forced conjunction horrific to any feeling human being.

The *Handbook of Policies & Procedures* was instantly in my hand. Chapter headings listed Schedule, Medications, Cooking and Chores, Laundry, Telephone Privileges, Weekend Passes, and Visitations. There was no heading for Radio or Stereo and none for Dinner. I flipped to the back in search of an index, but in my haste I failed to notice that the metal rings were not firmly shut, and the entire first half of the book slid out of the binder and fell across the floor in a perfect arc like a suddenly opened fan. I dove to retrieve the pages, believing (absurdly, as I now realize) that they would contain specific instructions for me, that there would be a heading titled something like Managing Conflict Vis-à-Vis Meals and Music Selections.

But I did not have time to complete my search before the situation escalated. Angry voices rose even over the sound of the deafening music. I thought I heard some kind of wooden crack or crunch coming from the room beneath me. Obviously, the residents were about to riot. There was no time for study or preparation. Gretchen had said, "Don't let them play the radio." In imperative sentences the *you* is understood. Thus, it was clearly up to me to intervene before the frustrated tempers of drinkless alcoholics and drugless addicts led to the destruction of property or assault. With dread choking my throat and the heavy-metal beat shaking the already compromised structure of the house, I opened the office door and proceeded down the stairs.

The dining room was off the front hall to the right of the stairway. I could see shadows flitting. The sounds of banter and complaining were discernible through the jarring drumbeat and guitar whine. I reached the threshold of the room and got a good look at several of the individuals whose behavior I needed to modify. One had blue-black hair raised in a ponytail that descended from the apex of her head; another wore a stack of silver bracelets on the lower half of a muscular dark arm. A third was obese, which forced one out of delicacy to notice nothing more, except the oxblood color of the tentlike dress she wore. There were others gathering around the table, and three or four milled around the radio deep in either conversation or argument. As I watched, the door from the kitchen swung open and the black-clad woman I had noticed earlier entered, bearing a platter of spaghetti (in halfway houses one does not call this meal *pasta*) crowned with steaming tomato sauce. Behind her tagged the dirty-haired woman carrying a large bowl of unadorned iceberg lettuce. The woman with strong brown eyes entered last, tossing napkins and silverware on the table heedlessly.

At first no one noticed me. Then, gradually, eyes began to find me. In time I garnered the attention of the entire room and, in what I assumed was deference to my authority, the volume of the radio was reduced so that the music seemed tame and only re-motely annoying, like a vacuum cleaner in someone else's house.

At that point I cleared my throat and attempted to speak. I intended to notify the women in a simple, respectful way of the rule forbidding radio play during the dinner hour, but I am sorry to say that my voice was so small and broken, it came out as a squeak. Several of the women craned forward in what I guessed was a game attempt to hear me better, but I noticed that sev-eral began to smirk, and I was instantly covered in a hot flush of shame. A seated woman in a fuchsia turban raised her hand in a warning gesture and screamed "Shut the fuck up!" to the room at large. Silence descended. All eyes were on me. But alas, it was not the background noise that had prevented me from be-ing heard but the mutiny of my vocal cords.

I squeaked again.

A woman burst out laughing.

I pushed my glasses firmly onto the bridge of my nose and ran to the haven of the second-floor office, where I stood trembling against the accidentally slammed door. I'm sorry to say that I had not learned to be free of the desire to make a good impression, even though I so seldom did. On that particular occasion my fail-ure of nerve stung me bitterly and brought to mind *as justified* all the cruel taunts I had ever received.

Eventually my trembling ceased. I shed a few tears of self-loathing, removed my glasses, and dried my eyes with the sleeve of my shirt. I was supremely grateful that there was no more noise or thumping coming from downstairs.

After a time of numbness, I heard a soft knock on the door. I opened it to find the stout woman dressed in black. She was carrying a dinner tray.

I had not noticed how old she was, and I was as much surprised by that as by her thoughtfulness. I did not know that addicts could be so aged. Her liver-spotted skin had deep vertical creases that sharpened and elongated her arching Roman nose. Her mouth was a thin brown dash. Bushy white eyebrows seemed, unlike her bones, to have grown thicker with time. Her eyes were hidden so deeply beneath them that whatever expressions they bore were fated to remain a mystery. She passed the laden tray to me wordlessly and disappeared down the stairs. It did not surprise me that she had not spoken. She looked like a gypsy stolen from another land.

After I had wolfed down the food, I felt much better and applied myself to the work of tidying up the *Handbook of Policies & Procedures*. When that was finished, I began to read it. I noticed repetition, ambiguity, awkward phrasing, and numerous examples of completely undecipherable prose. However, in spite of its poor quality, I enjoyed reading the *Handbook of Policies & Procedures* very much and was quite sure I would retain virtually all of the information contained therein.

Soon it was ten-thirty, time to execute my closing-up duties. I fought down a wave of panic, faced the door resolutely, and prepared myself to meet for the second time that evening whichever residents might be lurking in the common areas downstairs. However, as my hand curled around the doorknob, I was overpowered by debilitating fatigue and had just enough time to sink into the armchair before I fell asleep. I was awoken at midnight by my co-worker, Dolly, who wondered with rough impatience why the television was blaring, the doors were unlocked, and the downstairs lights still burned.

two

FIRST THING THE NEXT MORNING I considered quitting. But the prospect of losing my Zephyr—and, by extension, my career as a scholar—was too much to bear. So I told myself that I was not unequal to the task at hand, only that I'd had a few adjustment jitters. The discerning reader may have noticed, too, a touch of narcolepsy.

I had been treated unsuccessfully for this condition by a high school guidance counselor named Mrs. Bandolini, who described it as a maladaptive response to stress and overstimulation combined with deep-seated feelings of personal inadequacy.* In college, on the advice of several professors who found my habit un-

---

* I remember her diagnosis well because it was delivered in early spring of my senior year, just around the time her son, Bernard Bandolini, and I began to vie in earnest for the title of class valedictorian.

Bernard and I had identical 4.0 GPAs and were slated to be co-valedictorians. But apparently Bernard did not wish to share the crepe-strung graduation dais with anyone. One day he announced his intention to get perfect scores on the math and physics finals, a feat that would raise the bell curve enough to put him squarely in the lead. My initial reaction was slow and befuddled: I actually had been hoping Bernard would invite me to the prom. This delusion dissolved in the glare of the new development. I realized that a gauntlet had been thrown in my general direction, so I squashed my dream of romance and pledged myself to honorable battle. Longer-than-usual nights of study followed, and I began to fall asleep at inconvenient times throughout

settling, I agreed to try medication. But the amphetamines I was prescribed made my brain race at warp speed, and in order to keep up, my speech got so high and rapid that I sounded like the offspring of a chipmunk and an auctioneer. Not surprisingly, my illness only grew worse. Pent-up exhaustion began erupting in dramatic cataclysms during the day, and cataplexy (sudden loss of voluntary muscle control — i.e., swooning) was added to my narcoleptic symptoms. In frustration I threw away the drugs, and a few months later, all on my own, I stumbled upon a simple, occasionally successful strategy to ward off sudden naps. Whenever I found myself about to nod off (it was sometimes difficult to catch myself), I would repeat the phrase *I am not unequal to the task at hand* many times over in a commanding voice with great (faked) conviction. Within minutes, provided I was not too far gone, my chest would start to puff out and my spine would straighten and I would start half believing what I said. I found that if I could get to that point, I would usually stay awake. *And* I would behave with more courage and confidence than if the narcoleptic attack

---

the day. Soon my problem was brought to the attention of Mrs. Bandolini, who fell on me in a fiendish fervor of helpfulness.

At that time in our cultural history, the concept of self-esteem was gaining wide appeal; it was thought that everything from poor grades to unwanted pregnancy could be attributed to it. Mrs. Bandolini was an ardent devotee of the self-esteem movement, and I admit that I was drawn to the Emersonian romanticism of the theory. Wouldn't it be wonderful, I gushed to myself, if the I-me relationship really was the one true bedrock of felicity? If that were the case, it would be so easy to set oneself on a pleasant course of ever-ripening maturity! After all, the only two parties to the deal were housed connubially in the same body, presumably sharing interlocking goals of health and happiness. What force could impede such a self-contained system? What foreign agent could foil its well-laid plan?

So I willingly submitted to Mrs. Bandolini's suggestions, which included loving myself and liking myself (these two not to be confused), taking time for myself, indulging my whims, asking for what I wanted, being good to myself, being on my own side, and being my own best friend. As a bonus, Mrs. Bandolini selected styles of hair, makeup, clothing, and eyewear from a teen magazine. A small nod in the direction of fashion, she said, would make it easier for me to integrate socially. Finally, she warned of the dangers inherent in "hostage situations," relationships with dominating individuals who were prone to exacerbate, even unintentionally, one's poor self-image.

Logic eventually dictated that I apply this last skill to Mrs. Bandolini her-

had not been imminent at all! I was proud of the fact that, with nothing but this quaint remedy, I had managed to mitigate the effects of both a shockingly timid disposition and a potentially debilitating medical condition.

But back to my story. My second evening at Responsibility House went much better than my first. I passed briskly through the kitchen, greeting several women at once with a brief professional nod, ascended the stairs without incident, and finally achieved the office, where I repeated my anti-narcolepsy sentence frequently and fervently until, with all the muffled chanting they heard coming from behind the door, the residents must have assumed I was a practicing Buddhist. I am glad to say that I fulfilled my locking-up, shutting-off duties with rapid efficiency that night and stayed fully conscious until midnight, giving Dolly no new reason to complain.

On my third evening at Responsibility House I added a new element to my ritual vocalizing—the numbers 4-6-2-9-9-7-1. These comprised Gretchen O'Neil's phone number. Knowing that I could dial those numbers at any time and either request assistance or resign my post, and repeating them in a relatively quiet patter, helped to lessen my deep anxiety, even as the block letters someone had printed anonymously below the phone number, FOR USE IN TRUE EMERGENCIES ONLY, and the sentence

---

self, who was soon recommending padded bras and expensive manicures. By then, a grueling schedule of relaxation regimens had me all but exhausted, and the casual way my mentor kept referring to my psyche as "damaged" had shaken my confidence (such as it was) to the core. I had begun to believe that I was a sorry specimen indeed, that I had barely survived my ghastly seventeen years, and that the only luck I'd ever known was landing in the surreal oasis of Mrs. Bandolini's office, where I could safely address the issue of being horribly and incorrectably maimed. One day I managed to wrest myself free of the turgid weightiness of it all. I fired Mrs. Bandolini, but the damage had been done.

I went to the math and physics finals inadequately prepared. Bernard soared above me on the bell curve. His tailwind forced my grade to an earthbound A minus and my GPA to 3.95. And so it was that on a beautiful Sunday in early June I sat wide awake among my snoozing black-robed classmates (where is narcolepsy when you need it?) and was forced to listen to the younger Bandolini deliver himself of a ponderous and tendentious speech. I managed to retain a shred of dignity by refusing to rant affirmations of self-worth.

scrawled under that, DON'T FORGET 9-1-1, tended to restore the original stress.

Anyone who has suffered from phobias or anxiety disorders knows that they tend to diminish in intensity with repeated exposure to the instigatory object or situation. Such was the case with me. I managed to open the office door on my fourth night at Responsibility House, and by the middle of the following week I was joining the residents for dinner. My progress was rapid after that. In mid-October I began uttering brief salutations (So good to see you, Did you have a sober day?, Such a colorful tattoo!, etc.), and it was not long before I was sprinkling a few witticisms of my own into the generally lively conversational brew.

To my great surprise the residents seemed to like me. They took to calling me the Professor. I told them I had not earned the title yet, but they replied they were giving it to me ahead of schedule. They said I deserved it for actually reading the heavy books they saw stacked on the desk in the office, which they knew I tackled during the latter part of my shift.

Of course I knew that their goodwill was unreliable. After all, they were women of low character who had spent most of their addicted lives lying, cheating, and stealing. So I was not particularly surprised or offended when their generally respectful treatment of me was accompanied by teasing remarks and guffaws, or when I overheard uncharitable references being made to my unusual size, my serviceable but unattractive and generally unvaried clothing, and my odd personality traits. These remarks hurt me less than you might imagine. Insults flew so freely in that house that a recipient had no reason to feel singled out. And the fact that the residents were willing to include me at all in their rough-and-tumble banter touched my heart. In sum, I felt a strange mix of threat and merriment in their presence — as if I had been thrown in with a band of pirate-survivors who were setting out together for parts unknown, trusting irrationally in the benignity of the same blue sea that had swamped their previous boat.

One evening, Gretchen O'Neil pulled me aside. "Gillian, I think you're working out really well. You're dependable, and your notes in the logbook are very thorough and detailed."

"Thank you very much, Gretchen," I said, my cheeks aflame.

"How's your dissertation going? Are the women cooperating when you ask them for interviews?"

Oh, dear. The interviews. They were the reason I had come to the house, yet in all the stress of social adjustment I had almost forgotten them. "Actually, I'm not quite ready to begin that stage of the research yet. I need a little more time to establish trust."

Gretchen gave me an odd, wobbly look. "You've been here over a month."

"Yes, of course. Well, you see, the problem is compounded by the fact that I sometimes don't feel comfortable, especially in large groups of people with whom I have nothing in common. But this job is providing me with a rare opportunity to improve my social skills."

Gretchen's eyes went gooey with the kind of bottomless but rather bland sympathy that therapists are famous for.

I disliked it when people felt sorry for me. It seemed unjust that they should view me as weak or impaired when in fact I wrestled with demons on a daily basis and therefore, in my own way, had as much grit and courage as anyone else. Besides, Gretchen wasn't even aware of the true extent of my problems, my squeaking, chanting, and falling asleep, behaviors that, in any case, were diminishing. In fact, I was well on my way to forging trusting alliances that I intended to make use of very soon.

"Your deadline is only a few days away," Gretchen said.

"I don't foresee a difficulty. My advisor simply asked to see progress by October thirty-first. He said that an introductory chapter would suffice, and for the last few weeks I've been working diligently on Chapter One."

"Wonderful." Gretchen pulled an attractive autumnal scarf from the sleeve of her trench coat and draped it fetchingly across her shoulders. "Are you almost done?"

"The chapter is finished. All I have to do is check the footnotes, which, by the way, are extensive."*

---

* Needing to remind the Committee of my academic prowess, I had taken special care with the footnotes. Not a single paltry *ibid.* had bled from my pen. Instead, I had composed more than a dozen notes of truly staggering length and complexity. Citations grew from citations like branches from a spreading chestnut tree, then (what an elegant surprise!) fused back into one another

"Good for you." Gretchen fluffed her strawberry hair.

"In case you're wondering, Chapter One is a seventy-page history of conversion experiences in the three monotheistic religions."

"Really?" She put on her coat, adjusted the collar and sleeves, and tightly cinched the belt.

"My research turned up some interesting things. Did you know that the Puritans documented hundreds of sudden, dramatic conversions right here in the Boston area? Who knows? There may have been one or two close to where we're standing now!"

"Is that so?" Gretchen unzipped her pouchy leather purse and fished around for her keys.

"What I found really fascinating is that on their deathbeds, Puritan children would rise up, their faces would turn pale and shine with inner light, and they would either murmur or shout such things as 'Yes! I see Him!' or 'The Kingdom is at hand!' or 'The Truth, at last, is revealed!' Their parents would weep in gratitude, because in Puritan New England, to die unconverted was to be doomed to hellfire. Most of us can only guess how painful it would be to lose a child of two or three or four years old, or indeed a child of any age, but can any of us imagine the anguish of parents who believed that their deceased darling was destined to burn eternally in hell? Of course in those days children were not seen as 'darling'; they were seen as reprobates, a fact confirmed by their universally bad manners—"

"Gosh, I wish we had all the time in the world to talk," Gretchen interrupted, keys in hand, "but we don't." She slung her purse over her shoulder and was just about to head out the

---

like the interdependent branch-root system of the swampy banyan. In keeping with the latest trends in deconstructive hermeneutics, I drew attention to the unintentional lies, contradictions, poor analogies, bad jokes, and horrendous puns of every author whose pages I touched. I deftly reiterated rumors and possible rumors about the sex lives of ancient men and performed what I believed to be one of the first analyses of slant-rhyming in the titles of secondary sources. I wrote a thousand words on the symbolism of mountaintops, finding therein a mix of phallic and vulvar imagery that, in the ongoing rhythms of their alternating emphases, mimed the sex act itself!

door when she turned and said, "It's good for the residents to know serious women who lead high-functioning lives. You're an excellent role model for them, Gillian."

Me? A role model? I was too surprised to blush.

But when I dropped my paper in Dean Trubow's mailbox on the thirty-first, the idea didn't seem so strange. After all, I appeared to be succeeding at my new job and had made some headway on my dissertation after months of writer's block.

On the evening of Friday, November 2, I started my shift at Responsibility House the way I always did—by removing the electrical cord to the radio in the dining room. This was my simple, nonconfrontational way of enforcing the rule forbidding music during the dinner hour, and I was proud of how well it worked. Dinners on my shift were generally quiet, harmonious affairs.

There was a message from Gretchen O'Neil in the logbook that evening. We had a new resident, a parolee from MCI Framingham. I needed to do nothing special—all her intake forms had been completed, her schedule for the first week had been discussed and agreed upon, and she had signed a form agreeing to abide by all the rules of Responsibility House. However, I was enjoined to "keep an eye" on her. She was a "tough character" who would need an "extra-firm hand." No sooner had I read those words than the skin on the inside of my arm began to itch. I willed myself not to scratch, and scratched anyway. *Ice*, I thought with mounting panic. Applying ice sometimes halts the spread of those little red bumps.

I flung open the office door and rushed downstairs. As I turned the corner into the kitchen, I heard a husky voice from the dining room. "Hey, where's the cord to this friggin thing?" I stopped to listen. I could make out laughter and mumbled conversation and then the voice again. "What do you mean she takes the cord? Jesus, why doesn't she just tell us not to play it?" More mumbled conversation; then, "You mean the mousy one with the glasses who just came in? You're kidding! *She's* the counselor here?"

Not wanting to let this situation go any further, I entered the room. Almost all of the women were there—some sitting, some just milling around or helping to carry in plates.

"Is there a problem?" I asked. I felt surprisingly assured before I spoke, but once my voice was in the air and I recognized its squeakiness, my confidence drooped.

A woman stepped forward to meet me. She seemed twice my size in both height and weight—although *bulk* would be a better word. Clearly, she had made good use of the prison weight room. Her biceps seemed (I admit that fear may have led me to overestimate this) as large as my thighs. Her quadriceps bulged out so far from her femurs that they seemed poised to embark on separate lives. She was wearing a muscle shirt and sweatpants. Her bosom, which was substantial, did not seem like a normal womanly bosom but like an extra layer of muscle bulking across her chest. From where the shoulders of the shirt had been cut away, a bra strap peeked. It was a demure ecru with slight scallops at the edge, and the sight of it relieved me more than I can say. If it were not for the bra strap, I would have sworn she was a man.

Her face was more friendly and receptive than I expected. A touch of innocence in her expression was a refreshing change from the looks of guardedness or hostility or passivity often worn by the other residents of the house. When I came to know her better, I realized that its charm lay not in any particular feature but in the synergistic expressiveness of its parts. Her eyes, for example, were a changing mixture of green and brown; which hue predominated was keyed to her emotions. Humor brightened them; sadness tempered them; anger darkened them; at equilibrium, they flickered with practical intelligence. Her mouth was fluid and sensitive, almost always ready to speak, laugh, or curse. When she listened, her lips pursed in purposeful silence; her smiles were easy and wide. Her sandy hair was cut in the style favored by American boys (cropped close at the neck and sides and fuller at the top), and one lock crested across her forehead in a spirited cowlick. She often had to shake her head or rake the lock back with her fingers to clear her line of vision, but this gesture turned out to be just another way to express different emotions —adventurousness, pleasure, impatience—without the distortion of words.

"Ain't no problem here," she quipped. She turned her head

blithely as if looking for one in the room. "Nope, don't see a problem." A few of the women smiled.

The reader will forgive me for balking at this point. The woman had the vivid energy of a wild animal — a bear, perhaps, or a lion — and I had never stood so close to one before. What was more, I had no stomach for confrontations, which was why I had taken to confiscating the electrical cord in the first place. And hives were popping out all over my body like the grand finale of a July Fourth fireworks display. However, I very much wanted to acquit myself well in this situation, so I attempted to conquer my emotional and physical discomfort by conjuring a mental image of my stern, judgmental father, who seemed able to control people with nothing more than a change in his facial expression or tone of voice.

"Janet," I said, with what I hoped was my father's innate dominance. I had read her name in the logbook. I had no idea what to say next.

"Yeeeeesss?" she proffered with sweetly mocking patience, like someone who can't wait to hear what funny nonsense might be coming next.

"It is against the rules to play the radio during the dinner hour. Dinner is for pleasant, superficial conversation, which I think you will find helpful in reducing the stress of the day." A few of the women tittered, whether in response to the fluctuating octaves of my voice or the awkwardness of my lexicon I could not say.

"When I need to chill, I play Bruce Springsteen *loud*." Janet pantomimed a guitar player by shifting her hips forward, bending her knees slightly, and rocking from the waist in a lateral motion. Her bicep pulsed rhythmically in the imaginary strumming.

"You like the Boss?" she asked me.

Well, I couldn't say whether I liked Bruce Springsteen's music, but at least I had heard of him. It was my guilty secret that on many dateless nights across the years, when my eyes were too tired to read, I had sat alone in a darkened room in front of a flickering television set absorbing the sights and sounds of what can only be called a cultural wasteland. The truth is that these hours had accumulated to such a degree that I was rather well versed in late-twentieth-century American popular culture.

Not waiting for my answer and persisting in her gyrations, Janet proceeded to belt out the words, *"Like a river that don't know where it's flowin'* . . ."

The women started laughing, and someone yelled, "Sing it, Jan!"

"I took a wrong turn and I just kept goin'. . ." Janet's voice was rich and deep; it filled the room effortlessly. She did not appear to be the least self-conscious, which saved the spectators from the embarrassment that would otherwise attend an impromptu amateur performance. I actually got the impression that she'd had some training in voice or drama, but I learned later that this was wrong. The women were watching with shining eyes.

"Everybody's got a hungry heart . . ." She motioned for the group to join, and to my amazement the often irritable, bored, defiant, and vacant-faced residents raised their voices one after the other. In time, they were all singing, *"Everybody wants to have a home* . . ."

The line of women seated at one side of the table began to sway together, some who were standing clapped the slow rhythm, a gospel voice was raised in harmony. I had no idea Bruce Springsteen could feel so biblical. There were wide smiles and hurrahs to Janet at the end of the song.

I was standing stiffly by the door to the kitchen. Janet winked at me with the happy confidence of someone who thinks she's come out on top. Then she reached over and flicked a switch on the radio's dusty façade, whereupon raucous music exploded like a sonic boom into the room.

"It also runs on batteries!" she yelled to me over the noise. Several women hooted with laughter, some were doubled over holding their sides, and one began to jerk her neck in an ugly motion like that of a rooster crossing a barnyard.

I knew immediately that this was the second real test of my authority. I had miserably failed the first, and it had taken me weeks to recoup my dignity. I could not lose face again or I would become a permanent laughingstock, and the stream of lovely compliments I hoped to keep receiving from Gretchen O'Neil would dry up.

I was also beginning to understand that my loss of authority would have pernicious effects on the recovering women of Responsibility House. Such institutions rise or fall on the degree to which they can hold their residents to an even higher standard of behavior than is generally practiced in the population at large. That is how they guard their clients against the reemergence of the unsavory element that lies temporarily dormant within each of them and that is constantly in danger of being prodded awake by the unsavory element in any of their neighbors. At places like Responsibility House, the rules are more than rules; they are the blueprint for a New Way of Life. Women who follow the rules are demonstrating their commitment to a substance-free future of personal humility and cheerful service, while women who cheat and gripe are revealing the presence of unresolved emotional issues and dangerous backsliding attitudes. That is why staff members are enjoined to record even the most trivial of infractions and to report hastily any portents of insurgency among the ranks. One does not wish to let the unredeemed (i.e., residents who flout the rules) remain in residence long enough to challenge the newly converted or corrupt the merely confused.

So, convinced I was acting for the good of the many, as well as in the interests of my own job security, I uttered the following words: "Dinner will proceed without music, thank you. Afterward, I will see you in my office."

"Oooooooohh," the women intoned with dramatic sarcasm, almost as a single body.

"Watch out, Jan, the Professor is one tough screw!" someone called out in obvious amusement.

"Don't let her fuck with you!" a less friendly voice yelled.

I made a mental note to remember which individuals had brazened these remarks, but my heart was beating so fast I could barely keep my gaze steady on the offending person. She loomed, as I have said, a head, shoulders, and half a torso taller than myself.

"Come on! Whad I do?" Janet whined, her voice all injured innocence. No doubt she knew that a call to the office meant some kind of disciplinary action. "What, I was just pretending to be Bruce Springsteen!"

I thought it best not to respond but to leave the scene immediately. Passing quickly through the swinging doors into the kitchen, I nearly collided with several women standing about holding plates of the ubiquitous sauce-crowned spaghetti. One of them, a newer woman, looked at me in alarm. The others, more seasoned veterans, hid their smirks unsuccessfully.

I went straight to the office, not bothering to pick up a plate of my own dinner on the way, and sat down at the desk. Though the evening was still early, it was dark outside; the windowpane next to me, framed by a frilly unwashed curtain, was completely black. I looked into it, and it returned a distorted image of a tiny, austere woman trembling in a chair.

Why are you shaking like a withered leaf? I asked my reflection. You did nothing wrong. You were merely doing your job, which is to enforce the rules of Responsibility House for the benefit of all. Why did the confrontation unnerve you so much? Do you lack strength? Willpower? Were you afraid of being hit?

No, my reflection seemed to answer calmly. I am not a traditional coward, though I am afraid. I fear something I have never dared name and which now for the first time I begin dimly to perceive, something so simple and profound that it is only with the greatest self-conscious reluctance that I am willing to admit it at all. I want to be loved. Failing that, to be liked. Failing that, to be tolerated kindly. Or failing that, not to be overlooked. I fear rejection. Especially casual rejection. The scorn of strangers, the spontaneous derisive glance. In point of fact, nothing terrorizes me as much as the specter of a dismissive hand raised and waving in thin air, speaking in lazy wordlessness the syllables *You are unimportant, beneath notice. You are of no account.*

No sooner had this strange conversation taken place in my head than I became conscious of another source of unease concerning the situation in which I found myself. I didn't like enforcing the rules of Responsibility House. I didn't like the rules themselves. They were trivial and nonintuitive, like trick questions on the SAT. They were also patronizing and too numerous.

A resident risked breaking one at every step. I had written this potentially inflammatory criticism in the logbook a few weeks before, but I buried it in a lengthy paragraph favorably critiquing the method of trash removal, so even though I half hoped that Gretchen O'Neil would concur with my analysis and appoint me to revise the bulky *Handbook of Policies & Procedures*, discarding half the rules therein, I would not have been surprised to learn that my dissatisfaction with the excessively legalistic environment she created had not actually come to her attention.

Gretchen had told me that if I didn't hand out the occasional punishment the women would not respect me. "Give punishments whenever you feel they are needed," she had counseled. "That's how the women get to know you. You'll be amazed at how quickly they'll smell out your limits. In a few weeks they'll know exactly how far they can push."

Much as I hated to admit it, it seemed I had gotten myself into a situation where I would have to dispense a punishment. If Gretchen was right, this punishment would serve as a message to all the women. It would be saying something (although I couldn't imagine what) about me. Sitting at that metal desk, still itching mightily, I suddenly felt the burden of creative freedom. It was as though the punishment was about to become a signed work of art. I wanted it to be so many things: Ordinary, yet elegant. Obvious, yet original. I wanted it to burn like a hot stove without being cruel, to have teeth enough to be considered sharp, and yet to embody the quality of mercy, which, as Shakespeare said, "droppeth like a gentle rain."

I wracked my brain, but nothing came to me. The minutes ticked by. Janet would be knocking soon. No doubt she belonged to the type who wolfed her food and leapt from her seat, eager to prowl about. I broke into a sweat of performance anxiety. Surely there is some book or study that can guide me, I thought. My eye fell upon the wire basket labeled TO FILE on a little table next to the desk. Resting on top was Janet Tremaine's Confidential File. Gretchen had not given me permission to peruse the women's files. Then again, she had never said that I could not.

———

That manila folder contained the most thorough profile of a human being I had ever read. There were official papers concerning her sentencing and parole process, a long medical history, four years of annual psychiatric evaluations commissioned by prison authorities, and detailed reports from Janet's prison counselor, who had met with her weekly during her incarceration. To this mountain of paperwork Gretchen had added the ten-page Resident Intake Form used by Responsibility House. It included family, educational, sexual, and criminal histories, as well as a detailed history of drug and alcohol use.

After a mere twenty minutes (I am a highly skilled speed-reader), I had learned more about Janet Tremaine than I'd ever known before about anyone save myself. I knew details about her I suspect some married people don't know about each other. I was familiar with episodes from her past she herself had probably forgotten. What's more, I had read evaluations *of* her that she probably didn't know existed and would never be privy to. There was something exhilarating about having such a vast, unobstructed vista of a life. It was like coming suddenly to a high mountain crest and gazing down upon a heretofore hidden valley stretched out below. One possessed it from such a superior angle that one was tempted to think of oneself as its owner and master rather than its accidental voyeur.

Conscience and space limitations prohibit me from sharing the entire breathtaking view. But as some of the details figure in my story, I will summarize in narrative form (highly colored by my own fantasies, imagination, and literary style, I admit) the tragic history of a life derailed by lust, cocaine, and rage.

Janet Tremaine was born in the poor hill country of western Massachusetts. She grew up unsupervised, poorly educated, and gay. She knew by the time she was ten that she wanted to marry a woman. The love of women seemed as natural to her as breathing and, while she clearly knew she was different, she grew up without a flicker of worry or self-doubt. She became a contractor. Most of her clients were suspicious of female contractors, but she looked them in the eye, had a firm, dry handshake, completed work according to the promised schedule, and finished every job with a thorough cleanup. They could find no reason to complain.

Recession hit. Tensions ran high. In a lumberyard a competing contractor accused Janet of deliberately underbidding jobs, and her truck was stoned on the way out of the parking lot. A while later a group of toughs in a barroom challenged her to a fight. Obscenities were spray-painted on her mobile home in fluorescent pink. She responded to these threats by stowing a pistol under the seat in her truck.

She fell in love. The girl was only nineteen, a sad blond wisp of a thing, not the full-fleshed Italianate beauty she had always fantasized. Perhaps it was the girl's small sorriness that drew her. Perhaps it was because, next to her, Janet was more conscious than ever of her physical strength. In any case, the girl agreed to come home with her, and Janet felt the way she had so often before when, as a child, she'd carried a small wounded bird or animal out of the woods, cradling it in her arms.

Janet, age twenty-six, had never loved physically before. Rich sensations stormed her abstinent senses like barbarians at the gate. They beat upon her skin, mouth, eyes, and fingertips and skirmished along her neural pathways until she felt as if her body and brain were joined by trails of fire. In short order she was taken, conquered, done in, prostrate to the feathered moisture of breath, the curve of a white instep, the damp palm, the brown beguiling nipple, the warm dish of the hips.

But problems soon cropped up. It was not clear, for example, whether Patrice was truly, innately oriented toward members of her own sex or whether her attraction to Janet was a temporary thing, born from a long-standing hatred of scurrilous men and the newly discovered pleasures of social nonconformity. Conversations on the subject—on any subject, in fact—tended to be one-sided. While Janet posed open, nonintrusive questions designed nevertheless to gauge her lover's deepest feelings and motivations, Patrice stared silently out the trailer window. She sighed, she combed her hair, she toyed with the saltshaker. Talking gave her a headache, she said.

Janet wanted to ignore the implications of Patrice's emotional reticence, but she could not, and in her lonely moments she took to pondering the relationship's likely course. She felt anger because she suspected that her passion—the brute, honest beauty of it—was being toyed with as a trivial thing. She adopted a stance of staunch, quiet defiance, vowing to take as much as she could get of what her heart longed for and would ultimately lose.

Patrice enjoyed cocaine. Janet, for her part, needed no further trigger to bliss than the sight of her lover's turned-out thigh, but she allowed herself to be cajoled into use. Under the drug's influence, Patrice became ardent and passionate, so it was not long before Janet was willing to rationalize increasingly larger amounts of the drug. It worked. Gone was the semi-smirk, the averted posture, the reluctantly unbuttoned blouse. Patrice loved Janet now with equal fear and trembling, with fervor worthy of a goddess from the bottom of the world, and with deep, wet, shining eyes. Janet, ashamed of herself, proffered the mirror and the dollar bill thinking, I didn't really know myself till now.

They began to argue. Patrice resented the way Janet hid the coveted vial before she went to work. And for all the splendor of their loving, Janet felt mean, like a cur neglected on a chain. The source of her ugly moods lay hidden even from her. Their flow could be frightening. At times one would swell inside her like a flooding stream, and she would find herself riding down rivers of resentment into fat tributaries of anger and into a roiling ocean of rage. Her passion for Patrice seemed at the heart of everything. She drank to thwart herself sexually and failed.

Patrice started spending afternoons at a barroom called the Clover Club. Soon she was not allowed to drive home for drunkenness. Janet had to pick her up. Janet would carry Patrice to the truck, a bundle far heavier and more troublesome than a fledgling bird. Carry her home and undress her and, hating herself, make love to a flaccid body that bewitched her less and less. Once she carried Patrice to the detox unit of a hospital, another time to the police. She dreamed of returning Patrice to her habitat but did not know where or what it was. She was full of guilt and washed herself with pity for Patrice. She did not know the difference anymore between love and pain.

One night they were driving home from the Clover Club under a bright winter moon. Patrice was slumped in the passenger seat, spewing swears and heaves of burp. Behind them a pickup truck, with flashing beams, gave notice of its intention to pass. Janet pulled to the shoulder, but the road was narrow from stacked snow and her truck did not completely clear the lane. The truck following hers pulled to a stop behind her, and two men got out. They were upon her door before her wits sniffed danger.

"We want Patrice," one of the men said. "She don't belong to you."

In her rearview mirror, Janet saw two more men exiting the truck.

"You ruined her," the other man said. He gestured crudely to the passenger seat. "Look what you done."

Janet smelled alcohol and figured they were drunks from the bar. She put the truck in gear and pressed the accelerator to the floor.

They piled into their truck and pursued. The vehicles skidded and careened around the snow-swept country roads. Terror sobered Patrice somewhat. She began shouting, "Stop it, you crazy dyke!" and "Let me out." Janet made for the highway interchange where there was a gas station and other human beings. The truck in the rearview mirror gained and fell away, gained and fell away.

They entered a curve slick with invisible black ice. The back wheels slid forward at such an odd angle to the rest of the truck that Janet had a momentary sensation that she could reach out the window and touch her tailgate. With a jarring crush, the truck broadsided a snowbank and bounced back into the road. It came to rest blocking the lane, and the vehicle in pursuit crashed at full speed into the passenger door behind which was Patrice.

All was silence. The moon shone bright over the hills. Janet got out of the truck unsteadily and walked around to the other side. She meant to carry Patrice to the hospital, but she could not possibly have opened the door. She walked back to the driver's side and got in. A moment later the body of Patrice was in her arms.

A flashlight shone into the dark interior of the truck. Four men stood behind it. "What you gonna do with her now?" one asked.

"Oh God, I think she's dead." Janet held Patrice's limp wrist and felt no pulse.

"Couldn't leave her alone. Corrupting her."

"Oh God, please. Oh God."

"Almost killed us, too."

The ugly river inside Janet swelled and began to flow. She pushed Patrice's body into a sitting position. The head rolled sideways and blood trickled out of the mouth onto the sleeve of Patrice's parka. Janet stared at it.

"Unnatural woman," one of the men said. The four turned and started to walk away.

Janet took her pistol from under the seat and a cartridge from the glove compartment. They came together with a loud metallic snap. The head of one of the men swiveled around as Janet got out of the truck. She walked to where he had stopped, frozen in his tracks. She pointed the gun at his chest but found she couldn't pull the trigger. So she turned the gun around in her hand and smashed the side of his head with the gun butt instead. He acquired a dazed expression and then lay sprawled under the moon, arms and legs akimbo.

Janet got back in the truck. She removed the cartridge and put it in the glove compartment. She put the pistol under the seat. She cradled Patrice's body and buried her face in the matted blond hair.

The men huddled over their fallen comrade and finally dragged him away. They did not approach the truck. At the hospital that night it was determined that he had a fractured skull.

In the courtroom four men told a single story that was only partly true. Janet Tremaine was convicted of driving to endanger, vehicular homicide, and aggravated assault. During her incarceration, she came to terms with a substance-abuse problem and, after completing four years of a seven-year sentence, was paroled to Responsibility House.

———

Shortly after I finished the pages a knock came on the door. I quickly slipped the folder into the desk drawer and relaxed in my chair, opened a book to make it look as if I was studying, and called out in a voice artificially deepened by a transient flush of power, "Come in."

Janet edged her bulk sideways through the door—somewhat sheepishly, I thought—and sank into a folding metal chair next to the desk. Her thighs flowed over the narrow seat. I felt embarrassed but also faintly excited by the intimate things I knew about her, especially what I knew about her sex life.

In a soft voice she said, "Why are you doing this? You know I didn't mean nothing. I only asked where the cord was. How was I to know it was such a big deal?"

"That's not the point," I replied, as evenly as possible. "You created a scene. You got the women agitated to make yourself look good and me look bad. *And* you turned on the radio *after* I requested silence in the dining room."

"Oh hell," she said. "What if I did? Do you really want us kissing your ass all the time?"

"Observing quiet during the dinner hour is hardly a case of kissing my ass." The vulgar words felt odd in my mouth.

"What I *mean* is, if we can't pull your chain once in a while, how can we stand being here? How can we stay human?"

I smiled briefly at her sophomoric attempt to raise the issue to a philosophical level. "The other women manage to retain their humanity without flouting authority. Besides, this wasn't 'once in a while'; this was your first day in residence." I paused to let her know I was choosing my next words carefully. "I happen to know that the terms of your parole are very strict. In essence, if you fail to complete this program, you'll return to Framingham for another three years. I think a person in your position might want to be . . . careful."

A chastened Janet stared at the floor. "I was just having a little fun. I wasn't hurting anyone."

I confess that something in me responded to this argument. After all, what damage had been done? The whole situation was, frankly, ridiculous. I had an urge to let the matter rest, but I worried that the women would see me as soft. Besides, hadn't Gretchen warned that Ms. Tremaine needed an "extra-firm hand"?

My deliberation was rudely broken by Janet muttering, "Screw—"

"I am not a screw," I interrupted promptly. "And this is not a prison. And you are not an inmate who needs to perform infantile actions to stay sane. Please believe me, Ms. Tremaine, I am sympathetic to the indignities you must have suffered during your incarceration. But now you are at Responsibility House, a place where we all take responsibility, and I think you will find, if you stay with us long enough, that there is no mileage in shenanigans. If you find that you are unhappy, remember that the doors here are not locked. You are free to leave at any time."

It shocked me to hear how much I sounded like my father. With the cold imperiousness that could have been his, I gestured expansively toward the office door, offering it as evidence for my argument. Then I raised my arms from my sides to show that I carried no gun, handcuffs, billy club, or other tool of domination, though I'll admit that in the minutes immediately preceding Janet's arrival I had felt the absence of these things keenly and in an entirely different spirit.

Janet, gazing at the floor, began to turn her head slowly from side to side like a dog trying to see itself in a puddle. "Oh, I have free will, is that what you're telling me?" She seemed sadly disappointed.

"Yes," I insisted. "You are free to make this experience as pleasant or unpleasant as you wish." Of course I knew it was not as simple as that. Technically, participation in our program was a voluntary affair, but if a woman on probation or parole chose to depart, we were obliged to notify her parole officer immediately. In short, Janet Tremaine could leave Responsibility House, as long as she left the state and country as well and never came back.

"In any case, the transgression was minor," I continued. "That is why I'm giving you a relatively light punishment. I'm taking away your weekend privileges."

"Oh Jesus, oh shit," Janet said. "Shit shit shit." Her fist curled and swung into her chest. Her neck seemed to swell half an inch. Clearly this upset her more than I had thought it would.

"Is something wrong?" I asked, trying to disguise my unease.

"You're wrong. You're wrong. You don't know what you're doing. This is my first weekend in four years. *In four years.* It's everything I've been waiting for. Do you know that? Do you know that?" She reared up, looking entirely too much like the bear she had first reminded me of. I thought about reaching for the phone, but she sat down quickly, resuming her hunched, subservient posture, and I sighed in relief. It seemed she was aware of how frightening her body could be. But she could not keep her anger from spilling out. "Do you *know* that?" she said for the third time.

I shook my head.

"Some friends of mine are coming in from Springfield Saturday night. They're bringing my motorcycle, which has been sitting in a barn for four years. They didn't forget me. I still have friends. And I'm gonna get to ride my motorcycle again. In prison I used to dream about getting on that thing and just going; it didn't matter where. Just riding, you know. That's what I've been waiting for all this time."

I sat rigidly.

"I'll do anything. Any fuckin thing you want. Clean the bathrooms. Do the lawn, the cooking, all the laundry. I'll paint the friggin house for you. But you gotta let me out this weekend. I just . . . I gotta go."

I didn't know what to say. I didn't have a plan for this contingency. I stared into Janet's earnest, spluttering face and felt inadequate. The room around us got small and tight.

She leaned so close I could have counted her eyelashes. "Please, Gillian," she whispered. The green and brown specks in her irises seemed to swirl together and apart like the filters in a kaleidoscope. Looking deeply into my own eyes, she repeated, "Please, Gillian."

The proximity of her impressive body, the intimacy of her beseeching eyes, the heady fact that in that moment I and only I held the key to her perfect happiness—such an intense interaction was more than my official persona could withstand. I felt it dissolve until there was just me sitting there, just flawed, naked Gillian, fellow traveler in this vale of tears, just another lonely human being who wanted to be touched.

I don't know how many times she spoke my name before something in her lap came toward me—it was her hand. With thrilled horror, I realized she actually intended to touch me. My first instinct was to pull away, but a second, less familiar instinct caused me to leave my hand just where it was, lying without guile on its side in my lap. I held my breath. Her fingers brushed the area between my thumb and index finger. Immediately the skin began to tingle. An image of her with her lover rose before my eyes. Would I ever know what it felt like to be with someone that way, to be touched all over, to be the object of another person's passion? In mere seconds the sensation in my skin faded, and I remembered with dismay that I was sitting at a metal desk being paid very little to do an unsavory job. I shook my head slightly to clear my thoughts. Obviously, the woman's physical magnetism was considerable, but I had to resist it as best I could. I certainly could not allow any of the residents to take advantage of my various types (social, professional, sexual) of inexperience.

"Please, Gillian, do unto others what, uh . . . you know . . ."

That remark sealed her fate. It was clear that she'd asked the other women for information about me while I was reading her file, and now she thought that an appeal to religious values would be persuasive. Little did she know that my Christianity was nonexistent and that I had no tolerance for people who could not remember simple quotes. Yes, Janet Tremaine was charismatic, very good-looking, and capable of heroic acts like leading women in song, flouting authority, and throwing herself on the altar of doomed romantic love. But to those traits there must be added a wide swath of manipulativeness, which it was my clear duty to thwart.

"One weekend," I said coolly, swiveling my chair to face the window. "That's all now. You may go."

"Oh fuck," she whispered. I felt her bulk rising from the chair and braced myself for something, perhaps a blow or wire garrote, coming from behind. But there was nothing. Instead, she paused in the doorway for a moment, saying in a slow, sad voice, "God, I hate new screws," before pulling the door shut.

All that time I had managed to keep my fear and anxiety at bay. Now they emerged and engulfed me. Within seconds, I was asleep.

three

ON THE SATURDAY MORNING of Janet Tremaine's first free weekend in four years—the one I had so blithely stolen from her—I was thinking of taking a machete to the hydrangeas on my wall. I rented a room on the third floor of a Harvard professor's Depression-era, book-strewn manse. My landlord was a classics scholar—I'd been told to call him Lawrence—who took a distracted, fatherly interest in me. For three years I'd been living in his garret, enjoying the fact that its sloping walls made it inhospitable to anyone over 5'6". I didn't enjoy the wallpaper, however—faded bunches of pink hydrangeas that crawled up to the ceiling and seemed to dangle over me as I lay in bed. In addition to being ugly, they had a way of morphing into other shapes—cows and fungal growths and bunched sticks of dynamite, for example—which changed according to my state of mind.

On this particular morning, the hydrangeas looked like sullen groundhogs preparing to attack. A machete, I thought, would nicely decapitate them all. Of course I knew that this was projection and that the real turmoil lay within myself. I was worried that the chapter I'd given Dean Trubow was pointless and long-winded, I felt guilty for incarcerating a woman for doing a Bruce Springsteen impersonation, and I was waiting for the obligatory birthday phone call from my parents.

My parents were by all accounts impressive people. My father, an astrophysicist, had spent years studying the convergence of gases in supernovas and had recently gained international renown by using measurements of stellar spectra to estimate the amount of helium in the universe. As a young geneticist my mother had been pushed into the national scientific spotlight for producing dozens of startling mutations in fruit flies by manipulating their DNA. Her latest work on telemeres was touted as a promising breakthrough in anti-aging research. Peerless scientists themselves, my parents saw no reason to depend on psychologists for the latest in child development theories, especially when they had their own undoubtedly brilliant ideas and a subject (me) to test them on. After some consultation, they developed a working hypothesis. A child, they believed, would ascend naturally and quite rapidly to the highest level of cognitive functioning as long as he or she was set completely free in a stimulating, unobstructed environment. It was only the modern culture of childhood (exemplified by Disney characters, didactic stories that mixed fantasy and reality, wading pools, birthday parties, plastic baby dolls that passed streams of tap water from tiny holes between their legs, and *Goodnight Moon*) that made children so helpless and irrational. Twentieth-century infants were being, well, infantilized. Excessive amounts of adult interaction usurped toddlers' opportunities to practice independent decision making, and youngsters were routinely denied the long hours of solitude that stimulate creativity. Eager to right these wrongs, my parents swore to eschew babble, pablum, and sentimental gush. They vowed to treat me like a fully equal colleague they lunched with once a month. They also decided never to repeat anything, thus helping me to develop a keen memory. In keeping with their philosophy, I received (once only) nothing but scientifically demonstrable answers to all of childhood's important questions.

"Why do we die?" I asked one day. I was wearing madras shorts on my head and smearing fluffernutter on tree bark.

"Because we are carbon-based biochemical compounds."

"What happens to us when we die?

"Our flesh rots like uncooked meat and is eaten by maggots and worms."

And, a year later, hopefully: "Mommy and Daddy, what happens to us when we die?"

"Stop calling us Mommy and Daddy. Our names are Bertram and Joan."

"OK, Bertram and Joan. What happens to us when we die?"

"We told you that already. Don't you remember what we said?"

Bertram and Joan's fondest hope was that I would grow up to be a Nobel Prize–winning scientist. When an IQ test administered in high school showed that I was not a Genius, but merely Superior, they were devastated. (My score fell into the middle of the Superior range. This was another blow. If only I could have been High Superior instead of Average Superior, they might have been consoled.) The fact that I went into the humanities in college was a third bitter shock. And my decision to study religion in graduate school finally crushed their dream. Nevertheless, my parents had learned the value of adaptability from studying evolution. So when it became clear that I would not be a Nobel Prize–winning scientist, they flexibly shifted their focus to my becoming a Pulitzer Prize–winning anything.

At exactly nine A.M. the telephone on the second-floor landing shrilled. I trudged down the stairs. "Hello, Bertram and Joan," I said.

"Happy twenty-sixth," they said. And got to the point. "How are you doing in school?"

"Fine." Torture would not have made me divulge the threat to my Zephyr.

"Are you almost done with your dissertation?" Joan had her heart set on coming to Cambridge for the gala graduation weekend in June. I suppose she imagined herself and Bertram snuggling the way she said they used to in the laboratories of MIT, where they had met.

"Not quite," I said.

"Well, you'd better get a move on," Bertram said heartily. "We agreed that you would finish in January so you could spend the spring interviewing at universities and start your first job in the fall." Bertram often used a hearty tone to camouflage his iron will, which, in turn, covered deep anxiety. He had long suspected that my dedication to arbitrarily imposed schedules was not as strong as his.

"Well, there is some good news," I dodged. "Just last week I turned in Chapter One."

"That's nice, dear. I'm sure you'll have the rest done soon," Joan said.

"Only Chapter One?" Bertram smelled the rat. "You've been working on this for months. You ought to be much farther—"

"I think you'd find Chapter One very interesting. It's a summary of two thousand years of conversion history. It treats both famous and lesser-known conversion events. In it, I pay special attention to—"

"OK, that's enough." There was nothing like talking about religion to throw Bertram off the scent.

"I saw Bernard Bandolini at the grocery store the other day," Joan said. "He was squeezing eggplants with his mother."

"How charming that must have been for them," I said.

"Bernard is studying mechanical engineering in graduate school at Berkeley. He's still single," Joan informed me.

What I said was this: "Oh." What I didn't say was this: Dear mother, I deeply regret having told you years ago that I wanted Bernard Bandolini to invite me to the prom. Since then you have acted like a bloodhound or CIA agent, tracking his whereabouts with gritty determination and reporting back to me here at what you think is marriage headquarters so that I might take followup steps. I am supremely grateful that you don't know, nor ever will be told by me, that I am not interested in the constricting conventions of marriage but only in what I imagine is the wild liberation of sex and that, acting on a tip of yours, I actually went to my fifth high school reunion, where I sat stiffly among the preening, hilariously laughing classmates I had always hated until, near the stroke of midnight, Bernard finally exited the building and I shadowed him into the parking lot, where, without fanfare or coyness, I offered him my virginity and he refused.

She continued, "I told him you'd be coming home in a few weeks, and he seemed mildly interested."

"It was your imagination, Joan," I said.

"You will be coming home at the end of December, won't you?"

"Not if she's as far behind in her work as she appears to be," Bertram said.

"Did I tell you that I got a job?"

Silence.

"A job?" Joan said finally. "What for? Isn't your Zephyr Foundation Fellowship enough?"

"I bet that's what's holding up her dissertation," Bertram said.

Who is he talking to? I wondered. "Actually, the job is part of my research. And I only work at night."

"Well, in that case . . ." Joan's relief was palpable.

"I'm glad to hear that you're conducting research. Is it yielding the desired results?" Bertram asked with actual interest. The word *research* had reestablished a tenuous rapport.

"I'm sure Gillian will tell us all about it when she comes home," Joan said. Translation: This call is getting expensive. Time to wrap it up. "You will be home, won't you?"

"With bells on," I said dryly.

I hung up and went back to my room. I felt the way I always did after talking to my parents—as if I were mired in a subtle but epic skirmish I couldn't possibly win. But I was an adult now. I didn't live with them and didn't rely on their money, so why did I persist in half-truths and evasions? A really mature person would simply have reported the facts: *My work is significantly behind schedule and my funding might be cut.* What could they do about it anyway?

I sat on my low bed with my hands in my lap and my two feet flat on the floor and admitted to myself that I was not a mature person yet. I still wanted their approval, and somehow, some way, I was determined to get it, even as I did things I knew they would never accept. Maybe that was why, invariably, the moment I hung up the phone after talking to my parents, I felt as if my entire life was a juvenile farce.

This day was no exception. Self-hatred swirled in my stomach like a tapeworm. What was I trying to prove by going to grad school anyway? And why on earth had I, an agnostic, enrolled in a program of religious studies? Yes, I had always envied religious folks. I admired the way they swaggered through swamps, urban jungles, and third-world countries with the same fearlessness as first-world armies, remarkably unbothered by the metaphysical confusions that drive the rest of us insane. Everything in their world seemed bright, clear, and parallel: there was light and dark, right and wrong, men and women, the saved and the damned, and all those other important things that come in pairs. But envy, I realized now, had not been the really decisive factor. It was watching my parents' faces go green whenever I mentioned the words *Divinity School.* The fact that I could so thoroughly disappoint them while simultaneously pursuing their oft-stated dream for me—an advanced degree from a top-ranked university—had been an irony too sweet to pass up.

You're right. That was not a good reason. But I was not always unhappy with the result, and in any case it was too late to undo it now.

I crawled into bed and pulled the covers over my head. The hydrangeas drooped over me, withered and torn, as though they'd survived a gale.

When I got to work on Monday, I opened the logbook right away and skimmed the latest entries by Dolly and the weekend staff. I was relieved to see that Dolly had not reported the fact that on the night of my confrontation with Janet I had fallen asleep on the job again, that when she let herself into the house at midnight, the doors were unlocked, the television was blaring, and all the lights were on. From the way Dolly talked to and gestured at me, I knew that she considered me dim. But she apparently had too much pride to lower herself to the level of a common tattler.

I learned that Saturday and Sunday had passed without incident. Per my instruction, Janet had stayed indoors. Her motorcycle was delivered as promised early Saturday night, but it sat in the driveway all day Sunday without a rider. With several residents off to visit friends or family, the house had been fairly calm.

Gretchen said she was pleased with the way I had handled the incident. "The women need discipline," she reiterated in her mild voice before she left that evening. "That's what they're here for."

Maybe so, but I wanted to do something positive for the residents after the tense incident. Remembering that Gretchen saw me as a role model, I tried to think of a way I could use my talents to help the women achieve high-functioning lives. Finally I hit upon a strategy. Since my first day at Responsibility House, I had been dismayed by the residents' poor language skills. A simple program of study would surely help.

Vocabulary building seemed a good place to start. The more words a person has at her disposal, I reasoned, the more she can say. The more she can say, the more she can affect her world. I took twelve index cards from the desk drawer and wrote across the top of each a nuanced and muscular word, along with its pronunciation and definition. Here are the words I picked: *Rogue. Insurrection. Acclimate. Confound. Tranquility. Confabulation. Insouciant. Disingenuous. Caterwaul. Troubadour. Antidisestablishmentarianism. Sinkhole.*

I folded the cards and decoratively propped one beside each of the twelve glasses at the table. When they sat down to eat, I asked each woman to say the word in front of her, read its definition, and, if possible, use the word in a complex sentence. A few stalwarts did make the attempt but dissolved in gales of laughter halfway through the exercise, and the rest politely or not so politely demurred. The experiment sputtered out from lack of interest and, as I finished my spaghetti, I couldn't help feeling the glum self-pity that sometimes afflicts even the most determined and optimistic people. This feeling returned frequently over the next few days, as I found my carefully printed cards cast away in various places—dropped into a potted plant, left on the coffee table to be treated as a coaster, and, in a particularly wounding case, used as a doodle pad for a remarkably detailed pencil drawing of several ancient, hairy, horned beasts—possibly bison—in a conga line of sexual humping.

The following night I concocted what I thought was a very

creative strategy to eradicate profanity, but it proved to be well beyond the residents' abilities.* Reluctantly, I decided to set aside my pedagogical hopes for the time being. Then a more profound avenue of influence opened before me. Gretchen asked if I would like to try my hand at counseling.

Me? Counseling? I was thrilled and incredulous. With that came a flush of terror, so I briskly told Gretchen that although I had read a great deal in the field of psychology, as I had in all the humanities and social sciences, I had no training in counseling per se and thus felt that, for the women's sakes, it would be most conscientious of me to decline.

She countered by bemoaning the extreme shortage of qualified personnel willing to work at the house for the wages she could pay. She was managing the entire enterprise virtually by herself, she said, and she was near exhaustion. The paperwork alone was a full-time job, not to mention the bookkeeping, the upkeep of the building and grounds, and the supervision of the few untrained staff members she was lucky enough to have. She barely had time to think about therapeutic issues, the ostensible business of the house, and felt that without help in this area, the entire enterprise was likely to close down. "What a pity that would be," she concluded. "Then where would they go?"

---

* I shouted a simple two-word phrase—"Remember Eliza!"—whenever I heard a vulgar or offensive word at the dinner table. I quickly realized, however, that profanity was not the only problem that plagued the residents. They also suffered from a host of grammatical deficiencies, so I started calling out "Remember Eliza!" at ungainly predications, double negatives, dangling participles, improper agreements, and other less obvious errors. Soon, with all the yelling I was doing, there was little chance that anyone at the table could finish a sentence, so it really was a small miracle that the women were able to communicate their feelings about the situation at all. After repeated (interrupted) attempts to do exactly that, they went off to huddle in a corner of the dining room, engaged in some uncensored rantings, shrieks, and guffaws, and finally turned to face me. "Who the fuck is Eliza?" they cried out in unison.

I was dumbfounded. "Eliza *Doolittle*?" I sputtered. "Rex *Harrison*? Julie *Andrews*? In the Broadway hit *My Fair Lady*?"

I had purposefully chosen a character from popular culture, rather than the rarefied world of high art, thinking that the women would surely recognize a sufficiently pedestrian reference. But no one had heard of Eliza Doolittle! So, clearing my throat sadly and trying not to dwell on the horrible dumb-

Besides, she explained, the kind of counseling that took place at Responsibility House was not psychotherapy in the pure sense. It was really just a chance for the house to "touch base" with people "on an individual basis" and "keep tabs" on their progress—to find out how their new jobs were going, for example, and whether they needed help with any particular problems. It was vitally important for the women to have a safe place to express their feelings about the many changes they were going through. Their feelings could be intense, Gretchen warned, ranging from joy and exhilaration to paralyzing fear and dangerous rage. Without dependable emotional support, many of these women would derail themselves.

"I would only give you two to start with," she said, pulling two folders out of the file cabinet and tossing them on the desk. "Stacy and Florine." Stacy was the nondescript woman I had seen on my first day at the house. She was a humorless, no-frills, cheap-beer alcoholic from a hardscrabble farm in Washington County, Maine. Florine was the one with the long black ponytail. A streetwalker and dope fiend from Fall River, Massachusetts, she had begged for treatment from a judge after nearly every accessible vein in her body collapsed.

"I don't know," I answered. I could afford to act dubious be-

---

ing effects of our video culture and the pathetic failure of American public education, I told them the famous story.

Eliza Doolittle, I said, managed a spectacular class transition by learning every jot and tittle of English grammar, as well as the correct pronunciation of many words in the dictionary. By this simple expedient, which any impoverished person can emulate, she made the enviable journey from "rags to riches." Yes, it's true, I told the women, Eliza escaped her drunken, bawdy, though really very charming father and saw her way to marrying a sexless prig with the very degree I myself was working toward. She rose from the grimy gutters of London to the best drawing rooms of English society, where we can be sure that she whiled away the rest of her days making really nice flower arrangements and expressing her hostilities in the kind of tepid though nonetheless biting sarcasm that the English aristocracy enjoyed.

Finishing this summary, I looked around the table expectantly, trusting that Eliza's story would inspire the residents the way it had inspired millions of Broadway viewers. But the women's faces were blank and incredulous. One woman appeared completely stunned. At that point, I decided not to follow up the lesson with a staged reading of *Pygmalion*.

cause it was clear at this point that Gretchen intended to talk me into it.

Gretchen fixed me with her pale blue eyes and asked whether I could imagine what it felt like to *be* Florine.

I squinted into the wall. With help from the house, Florine had gotten a job as a receptionist at an insurance company. At the dinner table nearly every night, she complained about her boss, who randomly checked her handbag for filched office supplies and expected her to address him and every male caller as *sir*.

"What does Florine feel right now?" Gretchen asked after a suitable pause.

"Anger, restlessness. She's wondering whether coming to the house and getting a legal job was a huge mistake."

"Exactly." Gretchen shook her head sadly. "Florine needs a lot of help right now. She needs someone to help her talk *through* her negative feelings so she doesn't act them out."

I nodded sagely. I was flattered by the seriousness of the subject and the fact that Gretchen was confident enough in my abilities to initiate me into the inner circle, the sanctum sanctorum, of Responsibility House. And I certainly understood the larger point she was trying to make: Unless Florine developed an entirely new arsenal of behaviors that artfully disguised who and what she really was, her absorption into the mainstream of society would remain largely theoretical. She needed more than a makeover, although that would be a good place to start. She needed a thorough gutting and renovation, her engine entirely rebuilt. For starters, she would have to relinquish all of the déclassé habits she had acquired during the nearly two decades she had spent standing under a train bridge selling her body. The vivid, vulgar language had to go, and she had to cease threatening or cajoling people by promising to perform any of the acts for which she was used to being paid (at an hourly rate substantially higher than what semi-skilled office workers make).

Gretchen smiled, correctly presuming her case to be closed. "Don't forget to write a brief report of each counseling session for the file. I'll read your notes, and if I have any comments I'll let you know." She gathered up her things. "Call if you have questions," she tossed over her shoulder, but a moment later her heart-shaped face reappeared in the doorway, bearing an apologetic frown. "Although, as I said before, I'm spending a lot of time with my boyfriend these days, so I'm hardly ever home."

She gazed at me thoughtfully, her haste apparently run out. "You know, I think you're a really sensitive and perceptive person, Gillian. You're going to be good at this." She left without noticing the pink blossoms of pleasure appearing on my cheeks.

I saw Stacy in counseling for the first time that night. Stacy was a young woman who appeared old. She seemed to exude decrepitude, so that in her company one felt that one was aging rapidly. Her bony frame stooped even when she was sitting down, and her voice, like a postmodern symphony, alternated between the acute, metallic shrill of criticism and the flat, flaccid whine of discontent.

But Stacy, for all her superficial unpleasantness, was one of the most remarkable successes the house had ever seen. She was avidly conscientious in her chores, desperately worried about the welfare of her two sons, who had been left with relatives, and abjectly grateful to the people who had helped her get on the road to, as she called it, "just a plain, ordinary life."

During a meeting at an employment agency some months before, Stacy had owned up to having some bookkeeping experience and was given a job as office manager at a local karate academy. Within a month she streamlined the billing system, introduced a half dozen cost-cutting measures that uncorked the cash-flow problem, and pulled off a few simple publicity gambits that upped enrollment dramatically. Soon the school was profitable for the first time in its history, and a happy feeling of rejuvenation reigned within its walls. At a well-attended Chinese New Year celebration that Stacy organized, the beaming shihan awarded her a modest bonus check and spoke heartfelt words of praise and appreciation.

Stacy arrived at her first counseling session with me a passive-aggressive quarter hour late. This was surprising behavior for one so punctilious. I took it to mean that she was not pleased at having been assigned to an inexperienced, lower-ranking officer. Flopping into the upholstered chair in the corner of the office, she proceeded to light up a cigarette. I pointed to a dainty card on the bookshelf that read THANK YOU FOR NOT SMOKING. Little did I know that this simple request would become Stacy's excuse (or pretext?) for making a troubling allegation about Janet Tremaine.

"Why shouldn't I smoke," she said sullenly, "when some people drink in their rooms?"

"Who's drinking in her room?" I asked casually as my throat constricted in panic. Drinking was an Immediate Automatic Expulsion offense.

"God, how could you miss it?" Stacy said disgustedly. "Some of the girls were trying to liven up Janet's weekend. Ha!"

"Go on," I prodded.

Stacy alleged that Florine and Varkeesha, in an effort to make Janet's confinement more palatable, had smuggled two six-packs of Budweiser into Janet's room on Friday afternoon and hidden them under her bed. Apparently, the fact that Janet was able to get a little tipsy on both Friday and Saturday nights imbued the three of them with a celebratory sense of having won something or put one over on the staff, though how an admitted alcoholic's consumption of twelve cans of beer in a two-day period can be construed as a victory I will leave to the reader to ponder.

"She was sitting up there all night burping in her earphones and singing off-key," Stacy concluded. She looked at me slyly. "I don't know, but I think it was Bruce Springsteen."

"Did you actually see her drinking?"

"I didn't have to, I could smell it on her when she went to the john. I bet you could find the empties in her room, but you better do it soon since she'll probably sneak them out with the trash tomorrow morning."

The next day was indeed trash day in this section of town.

"Thank you, Stacy. I appreciate your reporting this offense. It is said that the good man is never afraid to do what's right."

"Oh, come on. There's nothing right about me. I'm a kiss-ass and a snitch. That's how I get along." She seemed oddly complacent.

"Is that right?" I asked, happy to have hit upon what seemed to be a suitable therapeutic topic. "Perhaps you'd like to tell me about it."

I soon had reason to regret that blithe invitation. For the rest of the hour, Stacy railed against five or six residents who had not completed their housekeeping chores with due diligence. Several more, she said, had used house funds to purchase food items at the supermarket that were not on the official Responsibility House Shopping List.

"Hmm," I said, not caring.

Her eyes narrowed. "You're not going to do anything, are you?"

"Not at this precise time," I hedged.

"Then when?"

"Leave that to me," I said mysteriously. In fact, I had absolutely no intention of dispensing eight or nine punishments for exceedingly trivial infractions that probably couldn't even be proved.

"Well, you're going to have to do something about Janet right away," Stacy warned.

"I am?"

"Yeah. You have to kick her out."

After Stacy plodded down the stairs into the television room, from which emanated rowdy whoops and caterwauls (a particular subset of these women watched sporting events, especially professional boxing, with the same bloodthirstiness as men), I glanced through the second-floor bedrooms and, seeing no one about, slipped quietly into Janet's room.

It was surprisingly neat. I could identify Janet's side of the room immediately, because the other bed was covered with a cavalcade of cheap stuffed animals that could belong only to her roommate, Meg, a quivering, harelipped woman with a penchant for Peter Pan collars and lemon lollipops. Janet's bed, in contrast, was simply made up. A worn plaid blanket was folded neatly at its foot.

I looked under the bed, behind the night table, and in the wastebasket. No beer cans. I hesitated long enough to be shocked at how blithely I was invading another person's privacy; then I opened the top drawer of Janet's dresser. It glided quietly and contained nothing to arouse suspicion—just a few aged, curling photographs, a silver chain with a cross on the end, and some neatly stacked full-cut briefs and several large-cup bras. I closed the drawer in embarrassment.

I went to the closet and slid open the plywood door. The closet was much messier. Jackets and sweaters were stuffed over a rod already sagging from the weight of hanging garments. I ran my hand quickly through the jeans, sweatsuits, flannel shirts, and nylon jackets, but I found nothing amiss.

I was about to move on when my eye glimpsed something shiny and anomalous behind the wall of clothes. I separated the hangers carefully. A plastic garbage bag hung from a nail positioned at such a height that the bag would not be visible from above or below. I shook it gently, and the unmistakable sound of aluminum tinkled through the room. I pulled out the bag, opened it, and spied red and white cans. I counted twelve. After replacing the bag in its former location, I returned to the office and softly closed the door.

For the rest of the evening I neither opened my books nor wrote my observations of the women copiously in the daily log. I sat in the armchair and looked around the room, wondering what to do. In every direction was a wall.

Point 1: The use of banned substances was the most dire of all offenses, warranting Immediate Automatic Expulsion.

Point 2: The successful completion of Responsibility House was a condition of Janet Tremaine's parole. If for any reason she failed to complete the six-month treatment program, she would be sent back to Framingham to serve out the term of her original sentence.

Conclusion: If I expelled Janet Tremaine, she would, in essence, pay for twelve beers with three years.

My duty was clear. The no-alcohol-or-drug policy was the most important and well-advertised feature of Responsibility House. Indeed, it was the institution's *raison d'être*. A resident who smuggled alcohol into the building and imbibed it on the premises threatened the safety, sobriety, and peace of mind of every member of the community. As the only functionary currently on site, I had a responsibility to enforce the policies of the institution exactly as they were written in the *Handbook of Policies & Procedures*. Nothing less than speedily kicking Janet Tremaine out the door would do justice to the egregious error the empties testified to.

But the more I thought about doing my duty, the more horrified I became. The action seemed entirely wrong, especially when I considered the fact that, while drinking alcohol was clearly a poor choice for Janet "as a person," it was not actually illegal in any state. Then there was the roundabout manner in which the incriminating evidence had been unearthed. For starters, the tip had been tattled in a counseling session. Catholic priests are under oath not to report what they hear in the confessional, and it is understood that psychiatrists will not divulge what they are told in the fifty-minute hour. Didn't I have a similar obligation to keep Stacy's disclosure about Janet a private *therapeutic* matter between Stacy and me, or, given the exigencies of life in a halfway house, had I been right in treating it as information to be acted upon? And what about the problematic nature of my subsequent behavior? The Fourth Amendment protects citizens from illegal search and seizure. Hadn't my search of Janet's room been a violation of her rights, or had she abrogated those rights when she signed into a halfway house? It occurred to me that by treating the situation from the vantage point of religion, psychiatry, or law, I might in good conscience be able to ignore the beer cans.

A deep sigh escaped my lips. Yes, that was what I would do. Nothing at all. And what difference would a small dereliction of duty really make?

If I kept quiet tonight, Janet would most likely get the empties out in tomorrow's trash. Life at Responsibility House would churn on as it always did, and no one would be any wiser. Except, of course, Stacy. Stacy would see that nothing had happened to Janet. She would suspect that I was protecting her, and it would enrage her to think that Janet was a favorite among staff as well as residents. Like a jealous sibling or spurned mistress, she would come to me demanding answers. She would be unimpressed with any excuses I might fabricate and would emblazon the double standard as proof of administrative corruption. At that point, she would probably go to Gretchen O'Neil directly. And then, of course, my name would be mentioned as the staff member who was notified first and who failed to act.

In short, if I kept quiet, I would lose my job.

My head, throbbing with the thorniness of this dilemma, fell into the crook of my arm. Oh, Janet, I moaned, how could you? After everything you've been through, how could you trade your freedom for two six-packs of Budweiser? The upholstery on the arm of the chair was dusty, and I sneezed. Why couldn't whining Stacy have been the culprit instead? I thought miserably, reaching for a tissue. I wouldn't mind giving Stacy the old heave-ho.

Clearly, it would have been better to have left off deliberations at this low point, but I was young and compulsive, so I heedlessly went on to consider several murky emotional issues, and in this way I managed to advance from a simple, if painful, indecision to complete rigor mortis of the will.

Ever since I had deprived Janet Tremaine of her first free weekend in four years, I'd been aware of cool receptions from the residents. Conversation during the dinner hour had become quite stiff. At times I felt that superficial discussions were staged for my benefit and that what the women really wanted to say to one another was saved for more confidential settings. In short, the lovely feeling of camaraderie with which I'd been favored not long before had passed as quickly as springtime in New England. The house had become cold and frightening to me again, and I often had to resort to private chanting to retain my vagrant consciousness.

What hurt even more than the residents' coldness, though, was being shunned by Janet herself. Janet, who had sat so close to me that evening in my office, who had reached out (inappropriately) and touched my hand, and whose greeny-brown eyes I had entered intimately in a moment I often replayed, was obviously avoiding me. That fact filled me with desperation. I wanted to hunt her down and tell her in no uncertain terms that she had misjudged and misunderstood me, that I personally did not agree with the punishment I had meted out, that all through that horrid interview a part of me had wanted to cry, "Go ahead, ride your motorcycle! And have a damn good time!"

How could I send Janet Tremaine back to jail when I believed that I had put her, through foolish pride and ineptitude, into the very situation that spurred her "crime"? Or was that line of reasoning merely an elaborate rationalization to hide the fact that I didn't have the guts to do the job I was hired to do? Or was I waffling because I was afraid of earning even more of the residents' enmity? Or (the most disturbing possibility) had my professional objectivity been undermined by Janet Tremaine's impressive physique and considerable charm?

At this point my eye chanced to fall on the wizened houseplant on the windowsill, the one whose soil was as hard and dry as a concrete block. There was a glass of water on the desk (in the frenzy of study I often became quite parched), so I gave the plant a little water and heard it gurgle.

But that was the only droplet of grace that evening. The rest of the night wore on without relief for me. In a desultory manner, I thumbed through the *Handbook of Policies & Procedures*, looking for an entry that might describe how the process of Immediate Automatic Expulsion was to be carried out. In truth, the phrase annoyed me. It made me imagine the roof of Responsibility House retracting smoothly, a button being pushed somewhere, and a surprised Janet hurtling through the blue sky, yelling in diminishing decibels, "What the fuuuu . . . ?"

There was no index that might have directed me to a specific point in the handbook, so I was forced to peruse each page individually. My speed-reading skills mysteriously petered out, so this process took a long time. Shortly after ten, I put down the book in defeat. How bureaucratic it was, I thought, that the procedure I was supposed to enforce was nowhere explained in its particulars. Apparently the choice was mine. Should I call the police and have her taken away in handcuffs? Or allow myself an angry fit, tossing her full-cut briefs and large-cup bras with much invective out the window? Or would I prefer stealth, smiling as I always did and letting her go unwittingly to work the next day, only to find her bed stripped, her bags packed, and her grim-faced parole officer waiting in her room when she came home?

I couldn't make the choice. I didn't have the heart.

At ten-thirty I went downstairs and dimmed the lights and flicked off the television, as my job description required. I returned to the office and listened to the women settle into their rooms with a clamor of doors, footsteps, flushings, running water, and chatter that grew ever more subdued until the house was quiet as a tomb. By then, I had lost my chance to expel Janet, unless I was prepared to rouse her from her bed. Now the issue I had to decide was whether to report the incident in the logbook or forget it and plead ignorance later. If I took the former course, there was a good chance I would arrive at work the next day to find an empty bed.

The hour of midnight approached. It had become my unconscious habit to gaze at my reflection in the night-darkened window, and as usual I was perplexed at the indeterminacy of what I saw: the fuzzy outline of a slight, bespectacled woman toying with a pen. At ten minutes before twelve Dolly's car turned in to the driveway. My time was up. Hastily I opened the log, dated the top of the page, and wrote what may be the shortest paragraph I ever penned:

> Conversation with Stacy indicated that alcohol was smuggled into Janet's room over the weekend. Stacy reports having smelled the substance when Janet went to the bathroom. Twelve empty cans are hidden in a garbage bag in Janet's closet. I have said nothing to anyone, thinking it best to leave the matter in your hands.

Under that I wrote, *Do what you think is right*, then crossed it out, fearing that it would only reveal my own misgivings. I closed the book and cordially greeted Dolly, who gave me her usual look of disgust.

The night was cold and dark. An awful sorrow stole over me as I bicycled home.

four

THE NEXT DAY I found this note in my mailbox at school:

Gillian,
> Please stop by my office at your earliest convenience.
>> Dean Trubow

It was understated, which I found ominous. But I tried not to have any negative thoughts as I walked to his office. Really, he might have loved Chapter One.

He was on the phone but motioned me in. He swiveled his chair so his back was to me until he finished his conversation. I found that ominous, too. When he turned around again, his face wasn't friendly. He put his elbows on the desk and hunkered down behind cupped fists. He needn't have said anything at that point. I already knew.

"Gillian, I'll cut to the chase. The Committee voted to reject the chapter you recently handed in."

No response came readily to mind.

"The paper is unnecessary historical summary that merely rehashes some well-known facts. It is significantly below this university's standards—or yours, for that matter."

My eyes filled. "Didn't you think the footnotes were good?"

He paused. I could see he was considering how blunt to be.

He must have thought I was stronger than I was, because he answered calmly, "I didn't read them. They were monstrous."

Monstrous. My admiration for Dean Trubow rose as my self-regard plummeted. Academics do not usually use such colorful words.

"Why don't you sit down?" he asked.

A good idea, since my legs were giving out.

"The Committee discussed your topic, too," he continued, "and it was decided that the 'secular conversion experience,' as you term it, is not a suitable topic for a dissertation in our department. The Committee feels that it doesn't fit in a traditional program of religious studies such as ours. Let's face it, Gillian, they've got a point. The subject is unfocused and experimental. God is everywhere, God is nowhere, God is whatever anyone wants Him to be. The whole thing's just too darn New-Ageist. You know as well as I do that scholars are judged according to the contribution they make to their fields. The Committee feels that your study—provided it was ever completed, which seems unlikely at this point—would not make a contribution."

I had stopped breathing during this speech. Now I wheezed, "You could have told me this before."

"That was my fault. I had my doubts about your project, as I told you. But I believed in you, Gillian, and I talked the others into supporting you. Now, of course, the situation is different. It is clear from this chapter that you're incapable of getting the project off the ground, much less bringing it to completion. We have no choice but to withdraw our support.

"So, Gillian . . ." His tone softened. He knew that the fatal blows had been struck. "You know how things work around here . . ."

The tenderness in his voice so moved me that I thought fleetingly (forgive me) of falling in love with him.

". . . You know I can't fund a student who is producing inferior work when there are other promising candidates out there."

"It's because I'm a nonbeliever, isn't it?"

"You mustn't think that. The department's policy has always been inclusive."

"But you can't stand it when people treat religion as cultural studies. I mean, no one else here is agnostic."

"Maybe your agnosticism is a factor. Frankly, I sometimes wonder whether you respect the world's religions. You seem more interested in poking holes in them."

"You probably want me to write a life of Saint Teresa of Ávila."

"A new biography on that figure wouldn't be a bad idea. It's almost thirty years since Grant Thomas wrote his."

"But I would use an interdisciplinary approach to look at the overlap between religious ecstasy and psychosis, and you probably wouldn't support that project either."

"Gillian, no one would read it. No university would hire you. Whoever heard of a religious studies professor who treats religion as a mental illness?"

"Literary critics do things like that all the time. They proudly problematize inherited truths."

"And look where they're at. The laughingstock of academe. They can't even understand each other. Students are fleeing from their department toward ours, Gillian. People need truth. They need religion to be sacred even if it is false."

"Then you admit the possibility."

"Doubt is the flip side of faith. There is no journey without doubt. I choose faith over doubt. That's what makes me a happy man."

Anger made me blunt. "And the fact that I choose doubt over faith is what makes me threatening to you."

A watery glint came into his eye. "You don't rise to such a grand level as that. You are a confused young woman who is doing shoddy work. Perhaps you should take some time away."

"I don't have much choice now, do I?"

"Not unless you're independently wealthy." He smiled faintly.

I stood up, feeling frozen and nauseated. A tremor of rage passed through me. "This is totally unjust and irresponsible on your part, Dean Trubow. I'm a fourth-year student. I have three and a half years of my life tied up in this. You may not realize it, but you . . ." — and here the reader will forgive me for letting a sob escape — "you are destroying *my entire life!*"

Dean Trubow stood up, walked to the front of his desk, and perched on its rim. For an anguished moment I thought he was going to offer me a tissue, which would have been the worst humiliation. But instead he tapped a Salem out of its cellophane pack, lit it carefully, and, after a leisurely exhale, directed these remarks to the air about a foot above my head: "Look, if I'm the manager of a baseball team, I put the best outfielder in the outfield, the best pitcher on the mound, the best first-base man on first base. That's my job. What seems heartless to you is simply the way the game is played. You struck out, kid. You're being benched."

There was a teak god on the desk behind him, some relic of an ancient Indonesian rite, probably a fertility god, as the figure held a giant engorged penis in its hand, pursuant, one imagined, to discharging its potencies. Smoke curled around Dean Trubow's forehead and for a confusing moment I thought of him in the arms of his frizzy-haired wife, whom I had seen at functions doling out yellow macaroni salad, and tried to imagine him in the moment of climax, tried to hear what words would escape his lips. Would it be *Hallelujah!* or *Another run batted in!*

"Wait! The inning's not over," I said. My mind had started to race. I was having a horrible vision of myself in ragged clothes pushing a wire cart around my hometown of Lublin, Ohio, while my parents drove by, smirking and listening to *Einstein, Part 3: The Photoelectric Effect* on tape. My voice rose higher and higher as this sentence progressed: "What if I submitted a new prospectus — an entirely new one, with a new methodology, on a new topic?"

"I believe that's what I suggested the last time we talked."

"Well, what if I did it? Threw away secular conversion. Found something much better, more traditional, something the Committee would really like?"

"An excellent idea — necessary, in fact, if you still want to be awarded a degree. But I don't think there's much hope of saving your fellowship at this point. The Committee will start selecting next year's recipients soon. At the very latest, we'd have to receive and approve your new prospectus before the end of the semester."

"I can do it!" I leapt from my seat. "I know I can. The end of the semester is December fourteenth, right? That's five weeks from now—plenty of time!"

"Let me finish, please. Given your recent troubles, any new proposal would have to be . . . well, *dazzling* for your Zephyr to be renewed."

"I can do that, too. You said yourself I'm one of your best students. Isn't that why the Committee gave me a Zephyr for three consecutive years? So come on, Dean Trubow. Don't lose faith in me now. I ran into an obstacle, that's all. You'll have a new topic from me before the semester ends. And I guarantee it will make a contribution—a dazzling one."

Dean Trubow was kneading his forehead as if it were cookie dough. I felt sorry for him, I really did. He didn't like withdrawing my funding. The others had put him up to it.

"All right, Gillian. There's no harm in letting you try. But I'll tell you something right now: The absolute deadline is December fourteenth. There'll be no more favors for you after that date. And the bar is very high this time, higher than it was before. Do you hear me?"

"I hear you," I said staunchly. "You won't regret this, I promise."

His eyes turned a dim tawny color as he watched me go.

That was four o'clock on Friday, November 9. The air outside was darkening quickly, as if a bottle of ink had been spilled across the sky. Flame-colored leaves swirled along the walkway. In the distance I could see my bike—blue and chrome and altogether homely—leaning against the trunk of a fat black maple.

You'd think I would have been happy that I'd won a stay of execution, but I wasn't. I was upset. I rode without my helmet on. That's how upset I was. I had no clear idea of what I'd promised or what besides fear had made me promise it or what I was going to do. As I pedaled along Massachusetts Avenue, through dangerous, honking rush-hour traffic, I thought about myself, what a pitiful future lay ahead of me, how I had known all my life there was something shriveled and decrepit at the heart of me, something horribly maimed and unworthy, which I had spent a life-time trying to hide, and which now had been found out.

I bicycled as far as Belmont in my funk and showed up for work thirty minutes late. It wasn't until I walked into the kitchen at Responsibility House that I remembered the beer cans and the note I'd left and dreaded what might have transpired. Would I see a stripped-down, sour mattress and anemic walls where once had been the cheerful plaid blanket and posters of Janet Tremaine?

Gretchen whooshed past me with an annoyed, supercilious air. "It's five-thirty, Gillian," she said, nodding at the clock above the stove as if to establish my infraction beyond the possibility of debate. I got only a blurred glimpse of her as she disappeared out the door, but I could see that her lips were rhododendron pink and a gauzy purplish scarf was floating after her. She was obviously up to her neck in romance, so I forgave her her pique and the awful getup. Love makes fools of us all, I said to myself. Well, not everyone, I thought sourly. Not me.

After Gretchen left, I lingered in the kitchen. Maria's broad rump undulated beneath a sagging apron bow as she plodded from refrigerator to counter to stove and back again, like a workhorse in its well-worn round.

An odd recklessness made me ask (and the clearness of my voice surprised me), "Maria, why won't you speak?"

She froze for an instant before resuming her slogging pace, and something in the way her back straightened and softened again, an infinitesimal movement of tension and release, made me think that she had appreciated the question. But after my unsettling day I was so in need of a kind signal from the universe that I might have imagined that response. It was more likely that she simply didn't hear me, either because she was at the beck of her own crazed, ancient voices or because her ears were clogged with sixty years of unexcavated wax.

"May I have a piece of bread, Maria?" I asked in a louder voice.

She glanced at me out of the corner of her eye, which proved that she could hear. Her eyes were narrow to begin with, so her sideways look was a decidedly furtive affair. I had never spoken to her so forthrightly before; her silence had always made me feel that I ought to be silent myself, or else sigh, mime, whisper haltingly, or sign—anything that might bring me into a sympathetic orbit. I was suddenly curious to find out how she would behave in the glare of my direct question, but I was not prepared for what happened next.

Maria slipped a loaf of Italian bread out of its paper wrapper and commenced cutting it into pieces of proper spaghetti-sopping width with a large, curve-bladed knife. Somehow she managed, in the rapid *thunk, thunk* of her chopping, to pick up one of these chunks and hurl it over her shoulder. It hit me squarely in the forehead, where, as if to prove her marksmanship, the crust left a dainty smattering of light brown flakes that fell into my fingers when I touched the spot. I yelped in surprise and indignation, but she didn't even turn around, and because I could think of nothing to say and was hungry after so much bicycling, I picked the bread off the floor and went upstairs, tearing the rubbery crust in my jaw. Having closed the office door behind me, I sank into the armchair, munched my bread, and reflected on the fact that, in the murky world of social relations, it is sometimes better to leave well enough alone.

The sight of the logbook open on the desk jolted me back to Janet and the beer cans. Under that day's date, Gretchen had written in fuchsia ink:

Gillian—No beer cans in Janet's closet. What gives? If you found them, you should have acted immediately. Possession of alcohol is a serious offense requiring instant expulsion, as I'm sure you know. See if you can find out what's going on. Stacy might be able to help with this. Glad things with her are going so well. Your counseling notes are excellent by the way—very thorough! From now on, keep a close eye on Janet T. That one's a troublemaker. If she is drinking in the house, we need to nab her ASAP!—Gretchen.

Relief flooded me. Janet was still in residence. If I opened the door and looked across the hall, I would see her bear named Leslie, her posters of Che Guevara with his fist in the air, and the monkeys hanging upside down. I went ahead and took this action and have never been so grateful for the sight of such pedestrian décor. I closed the door thinking that we had "dodged a bullet" and did not even notice, in this first instance, the Westernization of my idiom or the fact that I had partnered myself with her.

My glow was short-lived. I soon started reacting to the implications of Gretchen's note. *If you found them, you should have acted immediately.* Obviously, I had either lied about finding them or had neglected to do my duty. Which did Gretchen believe? Was I deceitful or was I incompetent? Was the sentence *Stacy might be able to help with this* a covert suggestion that I should urge my tattling counselee to come up with further allegations? And what about *That one's a troublemaker?* Did Gretchen have it in for Janet? Why? I had read Janet's file, and other than one incident of stark brutality, I'd found nothing to suggest that the label *troublemaker* was appropriate. Indeed, her former counselor had lauded her progress, and I myself, after dealing with the tiny matter of the radio cord, had found her rather charismatic. Was Gretchen basing the label *troublemaker* on that silly instance alone? Or was she confusing an allegation with proof of a crime? And why, if Gretchen did think me either deceitful or incompetent, was she so quick to ignore that and adopt a conspiratorial tone?

It seemed clear that Gretchen was brokering a deal: She would forgive my blunder as long as I participated enthusiastically in a plot to nab Janet. But this struck me as a cynical bargain. I couldn't help wondering whether *Gretchen* had something up her sleeve and where my own real loyalties lay. Why, for example, had I been so pleased to learn that Janet Tremaine was still in residence at Responsibility House? Why was I so aware every evening of where she was sitting at the table? Why did I wait with bated breath for her to say hello to me and keep remembering that illicit touch? Was it possible that I was forming some sort of inappropriate emotional attachment and/or physical attraction to her? If so, how could I bring any enthusiasm to the process of nabbing her? But if I didn't join Gretchen in her apparent vendetta, how could I safeguard my job, as I certainly wished to do, especially now that the prospect of my getting a Ph.D. from Harvard University looked about as likely as adjunct professors being paid a living wage.

My anxiety crescendoed as I pictured several possible outcomes of the situation: Stacy testifying in a courtroom against Janet and me; Janet hauled away in chains as Gretchen sat nearby admiring a sparkling engagement ring; myself in rags, ejected from Harvard University and Responsibility House, pushing that wire cart around Lublin. Only this time, instead of my parents driving by listening to scientific tapes, Bernard Bandolini sauntered by with a starlet on each arm, and I looked down to find that I was wearing a cardboard placard that said STILL A VIRGIN — PLEASE HELP!

The human body cannot endure that amount of stress for very long. My head grew heavy and began to sink. Knowing that a narcoleptic attack was imminent, I fought to keep my eyes open, which resulted in a fluttering of my lids that had a nauseating effect. My favorite chant vanished from memory, so I stumbled to the wall on which Gretchen's phone number was posted and began to enunciate the seven digits out loud, breathlessly but firmly, until I felt the traitorous part of my psyche slink back to stable consciousness. I repeated the cycle of numbers over and over, in an increasingly forceful and commanding tone, until I was sure that I was again the undisputed captain of my soul. By that time I was booming out Gretchen's phone number in the rhythm of a slow march.

"Gillian? Are you all right?" I recognized the dulcet tones of Meg, who resided with Janet across the hall.

"Yes! I'm quite fine!" I yelled, throwing open the door to show what perfect mettle I was in.

"Are you sure?" she asked timidly. Her tiny nose twitched a bit.

I realized that, after my barrage of undoubtedly audible chanting, I owed her more of an explanation, so I admitted that I had received two terse missives in one day. After such an extravagance of bad luck, I explained, it was not abnormal for a person to have a bit of a spell. "But now I'm super-duper!" I assured her. "Responsibility House has a capable leader at the helm!"

She smiled weakly. "Anyway, it's time to eat. We've already started."

The mood in the dining room was somber. Although all

twelve women sat around the table, there was no noise but the clink of stainless-steel utensils on plastic plates. I sat in the only empty chair. The meal was spaghetti. It was always spaghetti. I was handed a bowl filled with pieces of Italian bread much like the one I had been hit with, only these had a yellow garlic-butter paste splattered Pollock-like across their faces. The sauce looked as though it might have meat in it, which raised my spirits.

"Who helped Maria with dinner tonight?" I asked in an effort to be jovial. Janet was sitting three seats to my left.

No one answered.

I waited. "Surely someone here knows who helped cook? I merely want to commend the chefs on a lovely meal."

Florine raised her face an inch or two off her chest. "I helped Maria."

"Wonderful," I exclaimed. "Excellent!"

Chris gave me a pitying look.

I suddenly wondered whether my chanting had been so loud that everyone had heard it. Well, I thought defensively, at least I don't stick unsterilized needles in my arms.

"Our rooms were searched today," Chris said.

"They were?" I acted surprised.

"Janet and Meg's was searched for a half an hour."

"It was?" Now I understood the somber mood, perhaps even the tossed bread. The women didn't like their rooms to be searched. It implied distrust, heralded conflicts of a dire nature in which they would be powerless, and clashed with the universal human need for zones of privacy.

"It feels like jail again," Janet said morosely.

"I'm sorry," I said. And I meant it, too, though the fact that I had helped to instigate the action I was regretting made me feel like a wee hypocrite.

No one spoke.

I pushed the spaghetti around my plate. I realized that the dining room was quiet not only because the women keenly felt the loss of their dignity but because they weren't inclined to be spontaneous around me anymore. They probably suspected that I had been involved in the room searches, even if they didn't know exactly how, and this new and traitorous behavior on my part would have moved me out of the category of Harmless Buffoon and into the dreaded group of Screws with Teeth. I might never again be included as a cohort in their playful banter. The mortuarial silence at the dinner table was their way of telling me this.

I was glad, at least, that Gretchen had searched every room, not just Janet and Meg's, so it wouldn't have looked as if a particular individual was being singled out. However, I realized with a shudder, even this small deception had been unmasked by Chris, who had made a point of informing me that Janet and Meg's room had been searched for *half an hour.* Under the circumstances, I could only assume that the other room searches were carried out more quickly, and that the relatively longer period of time spent in that particular room had alerted the residents to the search's true target, Janet. (It would have been obvious to everyone that the house had no quarrel with Meg, whose only noticeable faults were staggering docility, masochistic passivity, and a truly pathological degree of compliance.)

Someone sneezed, a napkin was passed, but the silence at the table was not broken by so much as a *Gesundheit.*

I tried to eat, but the spaghetti seemed to slide from my fork with more than the usual sliminess. I found myself staring at it. Some weird-looking greenish specks clung to the yellow rubbery shafts. A paranoid thought crawled across my mind: Might they be trying to poison me?

Helplessly, I glanced around the table, looking for some sign of forgiveness or goodwill, but not one of the women looked back at me. Then someone pushed back her chair and took her plate to the kitchen, presumably having already finished her meal.

Stacy chose to glance at me in this moment. She offered me a tiny, secretive smile. I smiled back, glad for any ally I could get, but the acidic taste that quickly filled my mouth may have robbed that expression of authenticity.

More women were leaving the table now. Their chair legs scraped the floor most hideously. I began to feel abandoned as well as ignored, and I could not bear to let the situation continue. I needed to say or do something, but what? Were there any words or actions that would reveal my true character, proving how aligned I was in spirit with them and their interests, without compromising my authority or sounding too infantile? I looked out the window and saw Janet's motorcycle parked on the street. Its black paint and silver chrome glimmered darkly in the twilight.

"Janet!" I yelped. "After dinner, I would like to go for a ride!"

All the women looked at me now. Their faces registered alarm.

"What?" Florine said.

"I would like to go for a ride on Janet's motorcycle. I've never been on a motorcycle before."

All eyes turned to Janet. She pushed back her chair and stood up, holding her plate and frowning with perplexity. She seemed enormous to me in that moment, like a historic monument. I was afraid she would laugh, make some cruel joke about me, or simply pretend she hadn't heard, but she looked around the room slowly and finally drawled, "That can be arranged."

Stacy scowled. "Motorcycles are dangerous, Gillian."

"I'm aware of that," I replied. "But they're fun too, aren't they?"

A few of the women tittered, possibly because my voice squeaked uncontrollably on the last interrogative, which I had meant to be merely rhetorical.

"Oh, yeah," someone said. The flatness of her tone drained the statement of conviction. "Real fun."

"Then we'll go," I said, wiping sauce from the corner of my lip. "I'm in the mood for a ride."

"You can't ride without a helmet," Stacy said firmly. "It's against the law."

Since when have you worried about that? I wanted to ask. But I said, "I have a helmet, thank you. I do ride a bike."

"Bike helmets and motorcycle helmets are two different things," Stacy persisted. "You can't wear a bike helmet on a motorcycle."

I could feel the eyes of the women on the three of us — Stacy intent on her bureaucratic know-how, me uncharacteristically impulsive, and Janet standing at the table but hunched over, listening, not looking up.

"Actually, I believe the law stipulates *helmet* without specifying any particular variety or style," I answered. I didn't know if this was true at all, but would Stacy dare contradict me? The fact that I went to Harvard was enough to make most of the women believe I had encyclopedic knowledge of every conceivable subject.

Stacy pursed her lips, but she remained quiet, and we all filed outdoors.

In the cool air, the idea of flames, which had occurred to me once already that day in reference to the red leaves whirling around the entrance to the Divinity School, returned to haunt me. Only now they were gasoline flames, ignited after an accident involving two women on a Harley-Davidson. I wondered if there was such a thing as a pressurized suit that inflated upon the very nanosecond of impact, causing the wearer, suddenly rotund and rubberized, to bounce harmlessly off telephone poles, bridge abutments, and oncoming vehicles traveling at high speeds. If this suit has not yet been invented, I thought, it should be. Someone should talk to the people at MIT about it. In any case, I did not have one, so, given my reckless pronouncement of just a few moments before, I would have to get on Janet's motorcycle with nothing but some thin layers of shreddable cotton and wool covering the suit of delicate pink flesh in which I was born.

The women gathered on the porch uneasily. I wondered what they had to be uneasy about. That was when it occurred to me that Janet could kill me if she wanted to, that she was, in fact, a violent criminal, and that she might very well want to.

Chris went around to the side of the house and came back with my bike helmet. It was ludicrously flat, and its styrofoam padding had been chewed by use to about half its original thickness. Meg suggested I wear a baseball cap under the helmet, so I knew I was not the only one worried.

Janet wheeled her Harley to the front of the house. Behind the driver's seat there was a very narrow leather area and a chrome backrest. She mounted. I understood that the space between her back and the chrome tubes was where I was supposed to sit. This area was raised slightly, possibly to give the passenger a clear view over the driver's shoulder, but appreciating the friendly design of the vehicle did not make it any easier for me to get on.

"Get on," Janet said.

"Now?" I asked stupidly.

I tried putting one of my legs over the seat, but it was very high up, and I teetered and got stuck in a distinctly unattractive posture.

"Someone help her," Janet said.

Before I could protest, I was picked up under the arms and hoisted onto the bench.

"Put your feet there," Janet said, indicating two chrome sausages that stuck out of the body of the bike.

I did. They were fairly high; I didn't have to stretch.

"You ready?" Janet did something with her wrists that made the engine roar like a sociopathic lion.

Fear made it impossible for me to respond.

"You can do it, Gillian!" Florine called over the revving. "Just hold on tight and don't be afraid!"

We lurched forward, and I was immediately confronted with the problem of where to put my hands. I wrapped them around my own shoulders and proceeded to lean like the Tower of Pisa as we rounded the corner of the driveway onto the street. I grabbed the chrome backrest, but my elbows stuck out like chicken wings and I was not appreciably steadier. I tried holding the sides of the seat cushion, but there were no grips there to aid me, and then I had the wild idea that I might be able to lean down and clutch the pegs that had been provided so thoughtfully for my feet. A sudden stop, however, left me with no alternative but to latch on to Janet herself.

We turned the corner onto Massachusetts Avenue, and the next thing I knew we were accelerating so rapidly that the skin on my cheeks stretched back to my ears. Janet began revving the engine, which seemed entirely redundant. "Hang on!" she called out and, as though we were not traveling fast enough, the motorcycle lurched into the next magnitude of speed. So tight was my grip around Janet's midsection that I feared I was performing an inadvertent Heimlich. With my cheek pressed against Janet's broad back, I watched in horror as the cars parked along the side of the road vanished from view as if they'd been sucked into the cosmos by a nuclear vacuum cleaner. The dashed white lines that marked the lane were a gray, wavering blur.

Suddenly we halted. I picked up my head just enough to notice that we were traveling west, that we were stopped at a traffic light, and that we had advanced only about three blocks from Responsibility House. A little girl in a station wagon was sticking out her tongue at me.

"Howya doin?" Janet called back.

"Not good," I answered, but apparently she didn't hear, because she called out again, impatiently, "Howyadoin?"

And then I could not answer because the light changed and we hurtled forward again, screaming up through the gears, until we were traveling well above the speed limit through the end-of-work traffic, changing lanes indiscriminately and without sufficient warning, jockeying aggressively with passenger cars and minivans and delivery trucks, in a senseless effort to get—where? Wherever we were going.

I fought back tears of fear and outrage. Why this competitive road-hogging? Why this self-destructive belief that every other vehicle on the road needed to be passed and humiliated by clouds of our exhaust? "Slow down, Janet," I moaned. She didn't hear.

Eventually the ride got smoother and there were fewer objects-of-possible-collision in our immediate vicinity. I sensed these changes bodily, as my eyes were tightly closed and had been for some time. Feeling a little safer, I opened one eye a crack. We were on Storrow Drive traveling toward Newton. This was much farther than I had intended to go. The Charles River on our right looked muddy and belligerent, just as, I thought, an intellectual river should. The speed of the bike was still quite sickening. *Why do we have to go so fast?* I felt like calling out, but my voice was somewhere near my knees. Passenger cars and small businesses were flying past and there was a hot dustiness to the air. Highway breath, I thought. Fumes and particles and veering jet streams. The bike between my legs felt like a restless, vibrating animal. It vibrated in a not unpleasant way. The noise of the engine was so engulfing that, even though my mouth was but a few inches from Janet's ear, I was in a world of my own, alone.

The bike swerved to the right. Unprepared for this change in direction, I sat ramrod straight like a modern Ichabod Crane upon a horse that seemed intent on escaping the grip of its master's thighs.

"Don't do that!" I screamed when the bike had righted itself again.

"You mean *this?*" she screamed back, and we swerved to the left so suddenly that I had no trouble imagining how the skin would be torn from my legs on impact and how I would be dragged across the asphalt, breaking in rapid succession legs, pelvis, ribs, arms, jaw, and, yes, finally, the only part of this scrawny body I had ever felt really at home in—my cranium.

"Yes, that! Don't do that!" I cried when she had righted us again.

"Don't be a backseat driver!" she yelled over her shoulder. My fear and outrage drained out of me in exhausted surrender, and my head sank into the warm indentation between her shoulder blades, where for a moment I let myself feel, absurdly, safe. I noticed that she wore cologne of some kind—something mixing moss, dirt, and wet roots—and the effect was pungent and deeply moving, as though the scent had been trained from birth to bypass human olfactory ducts and find an altogether different set of receptors in the middle of a person's groin.

"Oh, dear," I said to myself.

By that time we were on an arborway. The traffic was thin. A clean, cold wind was blowing the smell of burning leaves. It was getting dark now, and Janet put her headlight on.

"Where do you want to go?" she called over her shoulder.

"I have to get back," I answered.

"You're kidding! We just got out!"

"No, really," I answered. "Someone's supposed to be at the house all the time." It was madness that I had not thought of this till now.

"Someone *is* at the house. Eleven women. They're not babies."

"But it's my job, Janet."

"Fuck your job. You wanted to go for a ride, didn't you?"

"I meant a quick ride."

"OK, I'll make it fast."

She accelerated, which, by this time, I was beginning to expect. I couldn't see the speedometer, but I was sure we were over the speed limit. I hoped we would be pulled over, but we did not pass any police cars, only a red sedan stuffed with teenagers, a truck, an old Chevrolet Impala, and a couple in a Honda who wore sedate expressions and quickly became remote in the rearview mirror. I knew I was at Janet's mercy. And what was more, I had put myself there. I sighed with a strange mixture of sensation and emotion. I could feel her arm and shoulder muscles tighten and relax as she steered the motorcycle around curves and along straightaways. Aside from this intermittent tensing of her muscles, she seemed calm and relaxed. She even seemed to slouch comfortably into my embrace. (By that, I simply mean that there was a concavity to her torso in the area over her lower ribs where my hands were clutching each other.) In any case, I somehow got the impression that Janet was actually enjoying taking me for a ride, and this may be what began to give me a modicum of courage.

On a well-tarred straightaway, I lifted my head just enough to observe my surroundings. I saw green fields, stone walls, playgrounds, handsome colonial houses, and trees. I saw a stone mill with a red roof, a mini-mall, a post office, and an old woman in a long scarf walking a small dog. I saw a group of students wearing heavy backpacks, someone trying to parallel park, and a boulder the size of a station wagon in the middle of a rolling lawn. Night was falling, but it was not completely dark yet. It was the magical hour of darkening, the time when substantial objects are transformed into hazy shapes and silhouettes of lavender and purplish hue, when the world, bereft of sunlight but remembering its grace, is suffused with an opaline, ambient light that makes it possible to believe for an hour that things really can be lit from within.

I sighed with deep satisfaction at the beauty of what I saw, and then a startling impulse came over me. I lifted one arm from its safe place beneath Janet's bosom and raised it into the air. The wind whooshed by it on every side. I lifted the other arm and extended it, and the wind whooshed around that one, too.

The wind on my body was an intoxicating mix of soft invigoration—part slap and part caress. I felt wild and a little woolly. I had to smile. I couldn't believe myself. Not three hours ago I had been dressed down by the dean of the Divinity School of Harvard University and had throbbed with self-loathing, believing that my career was over, and now here I was on the back of a speeding motorcycle, my arms stretched out like wings, gulping mouthfuls of wind. Why should I care about deadlines and dissertations? Why should I care about anything when I could feel like this? My smile spread from ear to ear, and I began to laugh. Life is good, I thought, chortling. I don't need a rubber suit; I can bounce back all by myself.

"Yee-haw!" Janet yelled. She was looking at me in the rearview mirror. "Yee-haw!" she yelled again. Her greeny-brown eyes were gazing into mine. I yelled something back—some answering yelp of joy and gratitude—but it was a squawk, a syllable, not even a real word.

Janet smiled. "Yee-haw," she said again, more softly, and we sped through the gloaming with the red leaves swirling and the green grass turning to velvet brown.

five

THE ROAR OF THE HARLEY must have preceded us down the street, because when we pulled up in front of Responsibility House, a few residents were on the porch to greet us. "Did you have fun, Gillian?" Florine yelled.

"It was extraordinarily physically stimulating!" I yelled back.

The women tittered, and I realized they were laughing, not only at my by now well-known ignorance of the common vernacular, but also at the slight (and inadvertent) *double entendre*. I felt a blush feathering my cheeks, and just at that moment, as if on cue, Janet turned to ask, "Was it good for you?" Having seen a few insipid Hollywood films on late-night TV, I knew that this apparently innocent remark was anything but, since it is asked almost ritualistically after the act of intercourse between lovers who lack linguistic inventiveness, and if it is possible for a face to go from pink to maroon, I'm sure mine did. I all but fell off the bike in embarrassed distress and, under the scrutiny of many merry eyes, tried to compose myself, but areas of my gray matter were starting to evaporate, and I knew that a violent storm of sleep was about to whoosh down from my darkening cerebral sky to batter me unconscious.

I began chanting furtively, in a whisper. I made it up the porch stairs without passing out or being overheard, I think, but by the time I reached the front door, which was clogged by a small crowd of curious residents, much stronger measures were needed to keep me awake. I had no choice but to speak out loud, with conviction, "I am not unequal to the task at hand!"

"Of course you're not, Gillian," someone murmured.

But reassurance on this point was not what I needed. I simply needed to keep enunciating the sentence in a commanding manner until I reached the sanctuary of the second-floor office, where I would be able to lapse into dormancy (if that was to be my fate) without either endangering myself or allowing my unwelcome state of complete unconsciousness to come to the attention of the people whose lives I was entrusted to safeguard and protect. However, it distressed me to think that this deeply personal and perhaps silly-sounding aphorism would be overheard, so I translated it into sounds—vowels, to be specific—which followed the rhythm of the original phrase and steadily increased in volume as sleep, my wily nemesis, threatened to topple me. Indeed, our battle became so close and desperate that by the time I was halfway up the stairs, I was yelling at the top of my lungs, "*A-E-I-O-U and sometimes Y!*" The faces I encountered on the stairway and second-floor landing were either frightened or amused and sometimes seemed to be both, and I was never so glad for a room of my own, a room with a door, which I quickly closed, free at last, if only for the time being, from human scorn and pity, hoping that Maria would bring me tea, knowing that she alone among all the residents—whether by virtue of mental disability, of social delicacy, or of damaged vocal cords—would refrain from commenting on my behavior.

As I slumped into a heap on the private side of the office door, the narcoleptic fit passed (please note: I did not succumb!) and the phone started ringing. Given the way my dice had been rolling that day, I figured it would be my boss.

"Where were you?" Gretchen asked. "I called earlier and got the machine."

"I got tied up with something outside." I almost said, *I got tied up by someone outside.* "How's your date?" Deflecting attention from myself was a deeply ingrained habit and a wise move at this juncture.

"Oh, we had a stupid fight. Look, I need to talk to you about this business with Janet Tremaine."

"Shoot," I said, enjoying the cowboy talk.

"I'm very concerned about the drinking."

"Alleged drinking," I said. And it wasn't until I said it that I considered the possibility.

"But you said you found empties in her closet, right?"

"I did. But they could have been planted."

"Planted?"

"Well, it's possible." I could almost see Gretchen purse her small bowed mouth in perplexity.

She decided to ignore me. "Anyway, whether they were planted or not, someone got rid of them between last night and this morning, when I searched the room. I want you to look through the trash."

"The *trash?*"

"Yeah, but don't let them know you're out there. Do it late, when they're in bed. Maybe even after midnight, when Dolly's there."

"You're not kidding, are you?" I almost mentioned minimum wage, no benefits.

"Gillian, we've got to take this situation very seriously. Alcohol on the premises threatens the sobriety of every woman living there. The residents depend on us to keep them safe."

"Even if I found them, they'd be empty," I said.

"The point is, we need to know. I'm worried, Gillian. I'm not sure Janet should even be at the house. I didn't mention this before, but she has a history of violence."

It was clearly provoked! I wanted to scream. But I didn't want to admit I'd read her Confidential File. I was afraid Gretchen would see that action as sneaky, which was what it had felt like to me.

"Normally, I wouldn't have accepted her application," Gretchen continued, "but she came with such good recs from her counselor at Framingham that I thought, OK, I'll give her a try. But something bad happens every time I bend the rules a little. I always end up regretting it. Violent people . . . well, they just don't change. It's like they're hard-wired that way or something. I'm afraid she's a time bomb. And if she *is* drinking, she'll go off pretty soon."

"She seems fine to me. I haven't noticed anything to be concerned about."

"What do you mean? You grounded her on her first weekend at the house. Don't you remember?"

"Oh, that. Right. Well, that was a little dispute over a radio. No biggie." I almost cheered at the way those two words—*no biggie*—tripped off my tongue. My idiom was really loosening up.

"Maybe not. But there must have been *something* going on there or you wouldn't have found it necessary to take disciplinary action. Social work is a lot about intuition, Gillian. Maybe your intuition is better than you realize."

My head was spinning. The logic in this sequence of thoughts urgently needed analysis. Gretchen was giving me unequivocal support for the one act about which I was sure I'd been wrong. What was more, she was suggesting that I'd been *intuitive*. I had always disliked this word: It made me picture a vacuous blond in drippy folk earrings and a tie-dyed sarong. The word I would have preferred was *prescient*. Unlike intuition, prescience at least nods in the direction of empirically based knowledge. Note its component parts: *pre* and *science*. It suggests a gifted telescoping of the reasoning process rather than a complete abdication of it. And yet I could claim to have been prescient in the radio cord incident only if Janet really had been drinking in her room, and that had not been proven yet. It was hard for me to negotiate this conflict between my thirst for any kind of praise, which rose from such deep, ancient caverns within me, and the heavy, dull, tedious burden of fact-finding that is imposed on Seekers after Truth. I am ashamed to admit that I said nothing here, which gave Gretchen license to proceed to her next and even more problematic proposition.

"Believe me, I've seen this kind of thing before," Gretchen was saying. "It's only a matter of time before something else happens, something worse. And we may not have long to wait. I heard she's hanging around with a really creepy guy. A convicted drug dealer. That's definitely not a good sign."

Oh, no. Maybe Janet *was* headed for trouble. Her impulsivity and adventurousness were quite likely to lead her in ill-advised directions. But was she buying drugs? Selling them? Using them? My heart rejected the idea.

"Our responsibility here is to the other residents, the women who are staying sober one day at a time," Gretchen continued. "So from now on I want you to record in the log everything you notice or overhear about Janet—whatever is even slightly suspicious. Having a really clear paper trail will help a lot if we decide to wash her out."

"Wash her out?" The term *ethnic cleansing* came to mind.

"Yeah."

I gulped. "How does one do that?"

"It's easy. We catch her doing something wrong and call her parole officer. He comes to pick her up and we give her bed to someone else."

"What if we don't catch her? Or can't?"

"There are always ways to get rid of people. You have to be really patient, though. Sometimes you have to wait a long time for them to slip up in some small way, on anything. A technicality will do. Then you change the rules so that the punishment for that offense is being expelled. I know it sounds unfair, but sometimes you just have to do what's best for everyone. If you know a person's using drugs, for example. Or drinking."

"If you know it," I said.

"Yes."

The *Handbook of Policies & Procedures* lay on the desk in front of me, a mess of unbound pages. The women were required to read it "upon matriculation"; because of its length, disorganization, and bureaucratic language, I doubted that any of them did. I had to give Gretchen credit for a twisted but elegant idea. It would be so simple to slip in a revised page at any point.

Gretchen continued, "We'd pretend to be deeply sorry, of course, but we'd say we had no choice. The rules are the rules." She uttered this last aphorism with an expert little sigh, as though "the rules" were a natural law, like gravity, that vastly predated man and enjoyed a certain imperviousness to his meddlesome tinkerings, when, as we both knew, they were brought into existence by nothing else.

I wanted to shout, *Don't you realize that if Janet goes back to Framingham she'll have to serve another three years without possibility of parole?* But the same problem concerning my reading of Janet's file constrained me and was coupled, now, with the desire to preserve my employment. "I get it," I murmured miserably.

"Are you all right? Is this upsetting you?"

I assured her I was fine.

"I don't like to be hardhearted, Gillian," she confessed soothingly. Her honeyed tone was designed to disarm and mollify me. There was such natural sweetness in her voice, and such an unquenched thirst for affection in my soul, that it almost worked.

She continued, with more harshness, "But until Janet Tremaine learns some new methods of dealing with her problems, I want her to stay on the top of your watch list. You keep an eye on her, OK?"

"Sure thing," I said, feeling sick to my stomach. Institutions can be so heartless, I thought. And I should know. Hadn't I just been the victim of one myself? How I would have loved to have been a fly on the wall during that Committee meeting. *We've got to get rid of her . . . History of methodological problems . . . Outside the bounds of traditional scholarship . . .* I wondered who had painted me with the killing stroke: *New-Ageism.*

"You know, I was thinking, Gillian . . . It might be a good idea for you to take Janet for counseling. You seem to like her, which is good, and since you disciplined her on her first weekend at the house, she'll know you're not going to let her get away with anything. How about it?"

"Oh, goodness . . . I'm not sure I want to do that."

"Please? At least try it for a few weeks? I really need more time for paperwork during the day and you've got all those hours in the evening free and, Gillian, you're so . . . *good* at it."

"Right-O, darling," I said in a haughty British accent, hoping that my choice of an obviously ill-fitting lexicon would signal my general discomfort.

Gretchen laughed indulgently. "You take a little getting used to. But I *am* getting used to you. I'm so pleased with your work; I wish I could have six of you."

I hung up the phone imagining six plastic Gillians in dork

clothes tumbling clumsily off the end of a conveyor belt, an image that did not improve my mood. Cripes, I'm not even sure they *were* beer cans, I muttered. They might have been soda cans. How often on the streets of Cambridge had I seen those men and women with the fingerless gloves picking aluminum cans out of dumpsters and garbage receptacles. They were redeemable, five cents a can. Who was to say Janet hadn't been collecting cans so she could buy someone a birthday present or sponsor a child in South America for just "pennies a day"?

I threw down the pen I was toying with and stomped around the office. I saw that the plant needed water, and something spiteful in me refused to give it. How could I possibly counsel Janet Tremaine and spy on her at the same time? But why did I persist in seeing it that way? Wasn't close observation exactly what was needed? Hadn't I been hired to do exactly that? Could I really pretend to be outraged by Gretchen's simple request to "keep an eye" on Janet when I had already infiltrated her bedroom with the stealth of an FBI agent?

I sank into the upholstered chair. The ivy beside me drooped. Gretchen was probably right about Janet. After all, there *had* been a bag of empties in Janet's closet. I'd heard them tinkle, seen them gleam. And while I had not scrutinized the labels — I remembered only red and white, I thought — the cans clearly were hidden, and why would anyone hide soda cans?

Then a vexing little question poked its snout up from the mud: Why did I blush so hard getting off the bike? What was the feeling I had when I placed my arms under Janet's bosom and indulged myself in her pungent, leathery scent? Oh, yes, I may have been a (reluctant) virgin, and therefore totally inexperienced in these matters, and I was naturally surprised to find such strong feelings flowing toward another woman (more on that later), but I was not, as they say, born yesterday, and at this point in my cogitation I had no choice but to admit that my feelings for Janet Tremaine were just possibly being colored by an irrational and unpredictable but ubiquitous human hunger that only a handful of people in recorded history had ever been able to eradicate, and then incompletely and (in my opinion) at far too great a cost to their mental health.

Musing anxiously along these lines seemed to make the problem worse. I felt what can only be described as a flowering deep in the center of my loins—a feeling, I blush to admit, as though the tight bud of my uterus was in rapid, rabid, intoxicating bloom—and I found my thoughts flowing (gushing, actually) along a well-worn path that quickly led to an object of many of my sexual fantasies, The Man with Greeny-Brown Eyes.*

I rested my head on the back of the chair and sighed, remembering those eyes. Then I realized that Janet, too, had greeny-brown eyes, that she, too, was manly and handsome, and that her heart, too, seemed true and kind. What did these twin longings mean? Was I bisexual? That would be OK with me. I just wanted the chance to find out.

By this time my evening at Responsibility House was drawing to a close, yet I had not even started to look for the dazzling new dissertation topic I had promised Dean Trubow. More than ever, I needed to be vigilant with my time, so I made several

---

* I met him my first month in Cambridge while falling off my bike. It happened this way: A driver freshly parked on Massachusetts Avenue inadvertently "doored" me. I swerved frantically into a lane of traffic, where I did not fall and was not hit by several passenger cars traveling at high speeds, and, dizzy with euphoria at having survived this brush with death, and perhaps pedaling too energetically given the new direction my bike had assumed, I crashed into a fire hydrant on the curb and was catapulted into a passing businessman. He saw me coming and caught me by throwing down his briefcase and sticking out his arms. He fell to his knees under the weight of me but did not let me go. When we came to rest on the sidewalk, one of his strong arms was cradling me under the shoulder blades; the other circled my waist. His smooth face was only a few inches from my own.

"Are you all right?" he asked.

I couldn't speak. I had never before been embraced by anyone, much less by such a handsome man. In a flash, I saw myself as his bride, being carried across the threshold. Then I was a wee thing in a blanket, being held in the arms of a doting young father whose face, as he gazed down at me, was transfixed with joy.

He helped me to my feet. He even brushed off the stones and dirt adhering to my cloddy canvas pants. He did not seem offended by anything about me and made no comment on any aspect of my physique.

"That was a lucky catch," he said, laughing a little. He waited to see if I could walk. I could, though I wished I couldn't.

When I was standing by the fire hydrant, he picked up my bike and rolled

strict resolutions: All romantic daydreaming, sexual fantasizing, and motorcycle riding would stop immediately. I would find another method for controlling my narcolepsy because the chanting was taking up too much time. It was also getting ridiculous. Whoever heard of a twenty-six-year-old graduate student who ran around screaming *A-E-I-O-U and sometimes Y?* Never again would I let myself act so foolishly in the presence of observers or even alone.

A muffled knock on the door and there was Maria, bearing a tray. She put it on the desk wordlessly. A mug of tea, a small pitcher of milk, a sugar packet, a brownie on a plate, a napkin tucked under the plate. I was supremely touched by her thoughtfulness. "Thank you very much, Maria," I said.

The look I received back said, You're a piece of work, Gillian, but you still deserve some tea.

This blend of tough and tender comforted me. After Maria left, I nibbled the brownie and sipped the tea ceremoniously, and

---

it over to me. "Careful now," he said. But these words were spoken in a neutral tone, without any suggestion that the fall had been anything but an accident, that it had not, for example, been caused by defects in my character.

Then he picked up his briefcase and walked away.

For days I was in a daze. The sensitivity of his eyes, the gentleness of his manner, the warmth and strength of his arm under my shoulder blades, the hand that grasped mine and helped me to my unsteady feet. Dear reader, I cannot explain the effect that the Man with Greeny-Brown Eyes had on my life. I only know it was profound. I walked around in a fog of bliss, thinking that soon he would come for me, that it was fated—certainly, it had to be—for him to arrive at the same café I frequented, or pick up his groceries at the same market I went to, or stroll down the street on which I strolled expectantly, already knowing what he looked like and what goodness lay in the depths of his heart. Just one more accidental encounter was all that was needed to bring us into each other's magnetic orbits, where we were bound to circle each other forever, or at least for a goodly run, secure in our mutual force field, dizzy with the sensual, spiritual delights of our finely tuned, reciprocal energies.

I will not admit how much time elapsed before this spell wore off. I will only say that it was long. I believe the duration of my enchantment may have been proportional to the depth of my longing and the fact that my heart was a pristine snowfield upon which a single footprint could make a deep imprint. I still think of him. The Man with Greeny-Brown Eyes. God bless him, wherever he is. God bless whomever he belongs to, whichever happy man or woman lives in the golden blessing of his benevolent gaze.

when Dolly came I greeted her calmly and respectfully, smiled with equanimity at the stale crumbs of distracted attention she brushed my way, and rode my bike home serenely through a cold Cambridge midnight, having completely forgotten Gretchen O'Neil's directive to look for Janet's empties in the trash.

My first counseling session with Florine, the former Fall River streetwalker and dope fiend, was scheduled for Monday night. I groaned when she knocked on the door. Another hour lost to the pursuit of a new topic! A tension headache began to constrict my frontal lobes. Why was I still bothering to work at Responsibility House when I didn't need interviews anymore? But how could I quit a paying job, now that my halo at Harvard was more than tarnished and my Zephyr was blowing in the wind?

Florine was wearing impossibly tight jeans and a shiny gold shirt with a plunging décolletage. It is my guess that she was also wearing one of those ornately constructed, steel-wired "demi" bras whose purpose seems to be to make the breasts appear swollen, positively tumid, but floating at a much higher altitude than boneless body parts, left to their own devices, would attain. When small-breasted women wear this type of brassiere, their breasts actually appear to be pointing *up*. But Florine was well and generously endowed. Her breasts looked like two about-to-crack, freckle-speckled dinosaur eggs crammed into a robin's nest. The minute she sat down in the chair across from me and I realized that I was doomed to spend the next fifty minutes at eye level (remember my size) with this aggressively presented bosom, I began to worry. I feared that I might begin to squeak or babble or, worse, simply fall into a coma. At the least, I was sure to stare google-eyed, with nowhere near the number of blinks per minute that is average for the human eye. But I came up with a good defensive strategy. I pulled a pad of paper out of my backpack and began jotting down the details of Florine's dishabille.

This took longer than I thought it would. Florine's hair alone—her signature glossy-black ponytail—was a reportorial challenge. It began at the highest point of a narrow skull. From her cranial apex to the midpoint of her spine, it was gathered in a thick braid. After that, it fell loose to her hips and below. In fact, Florine's ponytail was so long that, if she did not brush it aside before sitting, she ran the risk of not being able to nod. (It wasn't until I'd known Florine much longer that I was let in on a little secret: The entire thing was a hairpiece! In fact, Florine's real hair was thin, wispy, shoulder-length frizz that looked a lot like mine!)

She was only thirty-five, yet her neck was lined and her skin was sallow and the cheeks of her face and gluteus maximus were similarly depressed. The other non-breast areas of Florine's body had all the allure of a very bald snow tire, one that had survived many winters of pulling trailers and wearing chains. Yet, as if to dispute this metaphor, Florine herself tottered on two spike heels less than a quarter inch in diameter.

"Lose the pen, Gillian. We're supposed to *talk*," she said finally, snapping her gum.

"Yes, of course." I laid down my implement reluctantly and cleared my throat. "So, um . . . how are things going?"

"Oh God. My boss, what a cocksucker! I'd like to rip him a new asshole," she said.

What tumbled out next was a litany of on-the-job encounters that clearly spelled s-e-x-u-a-l h-a-r-a-s-s-m-e-n-t. Her boss actually pinched her ass, male managers perched on her desk and adopted all manner of bizarre, leaning-over postures, while less refined male workers (window washers, delivery men, and some incorrigibles on the sales force) expressed their fantasies in lusty whistles and leers.

Naturally, the mostly female workers in the secretarial pool assumed that Florine was sleeping with the boss, or soon would be, and they went on to surmise that she would rise eventually to the level of personal secretary to the president, where she would enjoy secret insider-trading deals and in-your-face perks such as a parking space near the elevator and the first choice of vacation weeks, while they, with their years of service, their punctiliously professional manners, their buttoned shirts and nicely clipped and polished nails in ladylike tones like seashell and persimmon, not to mention their proven track records of dotting i's and crossing t's, would be left to wallow unrecognized in the vast clerical pool at wages that would never put their legitimately conceived and arduously parented darlings through the private four-year colleges to which their mothers had never even been told to aspire.

In short, Florine was not fitting in.

One would not have to be especially gifted to discern that the cause of Florine's difficulties lay precisely in the area in which she had a full dose of un-ironic pride—her appearance. On many occasions I had seen her returning from work in skintight T-shirt dresses, leather miniskirts, and precariously high heels. It was painfully obvious that Florine garnered unwelcome sexual attention and the disgust of her peers because she looked exactly like a cheap streetwalker, which happened to be just what she was, or had been until a few months before.

I wanted to interrupt her with *Can you really blame them?* but thought better of making any remark that might injure her ego and damage our nascent relationship. Instead, I waited until she had thoroughly vented her outrage and frustration (this took a very long time). Then, striving for the most positive suggestion I could think of, I asked, "Have you ever considered a makeover?"

"A makeover?" she asked dubiously. "Like they do on TV?"

"Yes, exactly," I said excitedly. "A dress-for-success kind of makeover. You know what I mean."

"Nah, I don't think I'd look good in that traditional stuff."

"Sure you would!" I protested. "Simple styles and classic tailoring flatter every face and figure." I went on to suggest bobbed hair, a scrubbed-clean face, pared nails, suits or shirtwaist dresses in substantial fabrics (wool, gabardine, cotton canvas) or, if she preferred, pants, of the pleated wool trouser variety with a wide, amply covering girth. Warming to my subject, I extolled the virtues of neutral tones, especially beige and gray, and flesh-colored hose.

So engrossed was I in conjuring a career woman's wardrobe that I did not at first notice Florine's reaction. It was only when I was lauding tassel loafers and leather briefcases that I saw what appeared to be a tremble of horror pass across her face. I thought she must have spied a marauder in the window behind me and turned around to look. But there was nothing in the night-darkened pane except my own reflection. That fleeting glimpse of myself may have been what prompted me to remember a personal fiasco from my high school years involving Mrs. Bandolini and depilatory wax.* I was reminded of what I had known all along—that Florine in tassel loafers was about as likely as me in a thong. We were more alike than we seemed, she and I. Outcasts both, though on different ends of the sexual spectrum.

"Do you *like* the job?" I asked, changing tacks.

"God, no. I hate it. Typing, filing, answering the phone. I could fuckin scream."

"Why did you agree to work there?"

"That's what they gave me at the employment office. They said it was the only available opening. 'Here, try this,' they said. And threw a piece of paper at me."

"What would you like to do?"

---

* I have, you see, a very subtle mustache like my mother's. I have had it since I was fifteen, when it grew most unwelcomely on my until-then-downy face. Mrs. Bandolini, who was trying to save me from the social ravages of narcolepsy, kindly thought that she could spare me the embarrassment of facial hair as well, and one day in her office near the cafeteria she applied a hot depilatory wax to my upper lip. I remember the color well—urine yellow. The smell was equally memorable—putrid—and unavoidable, given that the wax was spread directly beneath my nose.

"Now we wait," Mrs. Bandolini said conspiratorially as the wax was hardening. The minutes ticked by. I could hear the raucous caterwaul of teenage banter through Mrs. Bandolini's thin school-counselor door. Soon a kitchen timer on the desk shrieked its alarm, and the school counselor's eyes narrowed to slits.

"Are you ready?" she whispered.

"Ready," I whispered bravely.

But I was not in the least prepared for what followed. Mrs. Bandolini yanked, and it was as though a cement Band-Aid was being ripped from an open wound. I swear that the skin on my upper lip stretched halfway across the room, and for a few hellish seconds it was not apparent which would win—that furiously gripping yellow wax or my face, which had been caught sleeping, as it were, before an enemy's surprise attack.

"Be still!" Mrs. Bandolini screamed as I leapt from the chair to follow my lip across the room. As she thrust me back into the seat, the twenty or so layers of skin that had been successfully commandeered by the tenacious goo were ripped savagely from the underlying tissue.

When it was over, I started to cry. I wept copious tears. "That was my lip!" I protested over and over, blubbering.

The door swung open. An odd assortment of pockmarked, peach-fuzzed,

"Not a fuckin goddamn thing."

"I mean, for work. If you could do anything at all for work, what would it be?"

"Anything?" She seemed suspicious.

"Yes, Florine. Anything at all. Your dream job. What would it be?"

"You mean, besides the street?"

"Yes, barring that one option."

"Hmmm." A dreamy look stole over her face. "No one ever asked me that before." She smiled a little coyly, then looked at the ceiling and let her eyes roam across the peeling paint. "Ha!" she said, laughing a little. "This is fun!"

She seemed content to dream, so I let her.

"Promise you won't laugh?" she said after a while.

"I promise."

"You *really* promise?"

"I promise!"

Her eyes narrowed. "I can break your toes in one stomp."

---

zit-filled, and greasy faces, drawn to the spot by Mrs. Bandolini's indecorous screech, stared in at us. They stared first in curiosity, then in the dawn of enlightenment, and finally in evil adolescent glee. What started with a snicker soon rose to the orchestral swell of full group scorn.

I didn't even care. The wound to my ego was less than the pain and grief I felt over the scraped-raw, throbbing patch of skin above my mouth. It was like a battlefield across which lay scattered the bloody stumps and roots of scores of fallen hairs. And who had led the charge, I asked myself? Who had cried *Onward!* when she ought to have cried *Retreat!* I had. I had sacrificed my skin and betrayed my face. To the god of vanity, no less.

Mrs. Bandolini brought an ice cube wrapped in a handkerchief, and as the area began to numb I was left with the curdling feeling of shame, to which the gibes and guffaws of my fellow students were a fitting soundtrack. But sometimes life is miraculous; sometimes, all unwittingly, we pull a rabbit out of a hat. As I raked the last bits of hardened wax off my lip and shouldered my very heavy backpack, I asked myself a question and came to a decision. The question: Why did I need to humiliate myself when so many others were willing to do that job for me? The decision: Never again would I try to be different than I was.

Waving aside Mrs. Bandolini's smothering arms, I pushed my way through the crush of spectators at the door. "Don't you retarded mutants have anything better to do?" I asked. And it was not my imagination; the snickers really did subside.

"I *promise*, Florine."

She sat back, looked around the room, sighed noisily. "Weeell, I've always wanted to . . . well . . . *bake*." She looked suddenly very vulnerable and stared fiercely into my eyes to cover it.

"Bake?" I was surprised, I must admit.

"Bake."

"Baking's nice. Baking's good," I said.

"I used to bake when I was a kid. My grandmother, Leelee, we used to call her, she grew up in the slums of Paris. Man, that old whore could bake."

I smiled.

"Bread, petit fours, croissants, wedding cakes. All kinds of pastries. That flaky crust, you know what I'm talkin about? That shit is an art, man. It's not just like, bang, mix it up, stick it in the oven, and haul it out when the buzzer goes off. There's a lot more to it than that. It's a fuckin *art*."

"She taught you?"

"She *raised* me. I was raised in a bakery, man. The New Paris Bakery, Congress Street, Fall River, fucking Massachusetts. My shitty hometown."

Yes, it's true: I was charmed. I felt as if Florine was radiating a beautiful light and I was being bathed in it. She must have caught the look in my eye, because she smiled at me. A beautiful smile.

And then we were both laughing, for no apparent reason. Except maybe that life is wonderful sometimes. Sometimes, unexpectedly, you pull a rabbit out of a hat.

"I'm outta there," she said, grinning.

"There must be twenty bakeries in Cambridge," I replied.

"I won't mind starting at the bottom," she said enthusiastically.

"You'll work your way up," I agreed.

"In no time," she said.

"Bring home lemon squares," I pleaded.

Then her face clouded over. "What will I tell my boss? I can't just not show up, can I?"

"No. It's best if you give notice. Two weeks is the norm, I think."

"Oh my God, he'll scream his turd-shaped little head off.

'What do you mean, you're quitting LifeLine, Inc.'" Florine mimicked his nasal voice. "This is the best job you'll ever get. Other companies won't even *look* at someone with a criminal background.'" She frowned deeply, making creases in her forehead makeup. "Do you think he's right?"

"I don't know," I answered. "But I know you shouldn't let anyone prevent you from following your heart." I scanned my memory for a suitable backup quote from Saint Paul, Saint Augustine, Walt Whitman (who seemed more likely), or Confucius, but Florine wasn't waiting for scholarly validation.

"Yeah, you're right. But it's going to be a long two weeks with that jackass of a manager and those vipers in the secretarial pool."

The image of so many uncouth, nonaquatic animals in a pool conjured one of my favorite moments in literature. It's the moment when Alice, having spent twelve chapters being confused, misled, tyrannized, and harassed by various rodents, insects, amphibians, pets, and royalty, and feeling at the end of her very short or altogether too long rope, desperately gambles the last straw of her sanity by blurting out, "You're nothing but a pack of cards!" Which, of course, is true. And with Alice being willing to make just that one tiny nod in the direction of Reality, the Dream ends. She wakes from her nap, picks her head out of her sister's lap, and looks around to enjoy the warm summer sunshine and the company of her (somewhat pedantic) sister, having come to appreciate, through an excess of the opposite, the pleasant ordinariness of ordinary life.

Granted, the more of the story I remembered, the less it had to do with Florine's predicament, but that didn't stop me from relating the vignette as an interesting and perhaps-pertinent-to-her-situation parable.

"Wow," Florine said when I was finished. "I can really relate."

The hour was over (actually, I had generously allowed the session to go a few minutes late). I stood by the office door and fondly watched the various parts of Florine bob, wobble, and bounce down the stairs.

six

I WAS STILL so flushed with pleasure at what I considered to be my success with Florine that I was totally unprepared to find an angry Gretchen waiting for me in the office the next evening.

"You didn't really tell Florine to quit her job, did you?" were her first words, delivered with more heat than I had come to expect from the comely counselor. "You *did?*" she asked incredulously when I nodded very slightly. "Oh my God, Gillian, what on earth were you thinking?"

Although I had always feared receiving negative criticism from someone higher in the food chain than myself, my boss's displeasure left me surprisingly untroubled. Given the way she was clutching a stylish new purse and glancing at her wristwatch, I figured she was anxious to meet her boyfriend and wouldn't waste time on a really thorough diatribe. In this I was mistaken.

"Her boss called after lunch," continued Gretchen. "He was livid! Apparently, after the screaming match she had with him, Florine pulled up her shirt and showed her breasts to an entire floor of office workers, yelling out, 'You're nothing but a pack of cards!' I don't understand it, Gillian. She was doing so well! What could have gotten into her?"

"Hmmm," I proffered gingerly. Neglecting to mention the fictional but nonetheless bloodthirsty Red Queen, and the really deleterious effects similarly toxic characters in the workplace can have on professionally inexperienced individuals, I explained Florine's long-standing ambition to labor in a bakery. I said that Florine and I had agreed that that environment might be less sexually harassing for her as a person.

Gretchen all but erupted. "What are you teaching her, Gillian? She needs to *work through* her problems, not *run* from them! She needs strategies, coping skills, assertiveness training, a toolbox of new behaviors. Running is the *old* way, the *old* behavior. I *know* her boss was coming on to her, but what do you suppose will happen when the boss at the *bakery* comes on to her? Where will she go then?"

"Maybe she'll have a woman boss," I answered weakly.

"Oh, like that's going to make a difference," Gretchen scoffed. "Women can come on to women, Gillian. Or haven't you noticed?"

Well, yes, I had noticed. I had done more than notice. In fact, for several days now, at the outer reaches of my cosmic consciousness, where my psychic matter was no more than a few molecules of expanding gas, there had been smoldering the infinitesimal and remote idea that maybe someday I could use the power of my office to do with Janet Tremaine exactly what Florine's boss had been trying to do with her. The fact that such a selfish and unethical desire could inhabit any part of my gray matter shocked me, of course. So when I first noticed the disturbing speck lingering out there, I had hastened to reassure myself on a key point: I had neither the courage nor the cowardice to turn my fantasy into a reality. This realization had relieved me somewhat. Still, I was far from comfortable with the turn the conversation had taken. It was disconcerting to hear the subject of girl-on-girl eroticized power imbalances, which until that moment had been just a shadowy, almost undiscovered little pip of a longing in my own private universe, being treated like yesterday's hackneyed news.

Gretchen continued, "What's worse, if Florine works at a bakery, she'll make minimum wage!"

What am I making? I wanted to ask.

"How will she be able to provide for her child?"

Once again I was speechless. Her *child?*

"You do know that Florine has a daughter in foster care, don't you?"

I mumbled incoherently.

"When Florine gets out of here, she's going to have to pay for housing, food, clothing, family health care, after-school programs, and a lot more."

"No one can do all that on minimum wage!" I said.

"That's exactly my point, Gillian. Why do you think the employment counselor and I bent over backwards to get Florine that receptionist job? Because they're training her and paying her more than she can get anywhere else and probably more than she's worth. *And* they have company health insurance, which she gets at a discounted rate. *And* they have family-friendly policies that will allow her to take days off when she needs to. And she will definitely need to because her daughter has asthma. So when you see her tonight, be sure to ask whether she would rather bake cookies or be a mother."

"You mean she really can't do both?"

"Maybe not," Gretchen replied. "At the very least, working at the bakery will make it ten times harder for her to get Raven back. DSS has a set of minimum requirements that Florine has to meet before they'll return custody. For starters, she has to have decent housing and a reasonable income. She has to show that she can *provide* for Raven. Even if we helped her get food stamps, Medicare, and low-income housing, it still might not be enough. Besides, there's no low-income housing left in this city. And if there was, it would be the worst place for Florine—it's full of drugs!"

I felt sick. I was clearly unprepared to deal with these women's problems. For starters, I didn't even know what their problems were. "I'm sorry," I told Gretchen.

"Don't be sorry. Just tell Florine to get her job back. Tell her she can't stay at Responsibility House one more week unless she returns to LifeLine, Inc., tomorrow morning, apologizes to her boss, and begs to be rehired—on her knees, if need be."

I had an image of what Florine would be doing on her knees, but I didn't think it was the same as Gretchen's. "What if she refuses?" I asked.

"In that case, you might remind her that she'll *never* get Raven back unless she proves her sobriety to DSS. And the only proof they'll accept is a diploma from Responsibility House, signed by me. That ought to persuade her."

Gretchen flounced her hair across her shoulders with a preening motion that seems to be instinctive to the female of the species. She picked up a belted tweed jacket and slung it over one shoulder. It looked as if she was trying out for a modeling job. I wanted her to go away and give me time to think about Florine, but she brought up another subject. "So, did you find the empties?"

The empties? "Uh-uh," I muttered, which could have meant anything.

"You didn't find them?"

"That's right." I wasn't lying. I didn't find them. I didn't add that I didn't look.

"Well, this whole thing about Janet drinking in her room seems very strange. You say she's not acting weird in the evenings or anything?"

"No."

"Then I'm really not getting something. Usually, if someone starts drinking, you can tell right away. Who told you about the empties again?"

"Stacy."

Gretchen puckered her glossy maroon lips. "Hmm. Stacy's very reliable. I would trust what she says."

Reliable was not a word I would have used to describe Stacy. *Dangerous*, perhaps. *Diabolical*, maybe. *Scary*, certainly. But not *reliable*.

"So what could have happened to the empties?" Gretchen mused.

"Maybe she put them in someone else's trash?"

Gretchen narrowed her eyes at me. "You did look, didn't you?"

"I did. But it was dark," I said, with the idea that letting my lie brush up against a kind of truth would make it less of a lie. "Past midnight, in fact. And, you know, rubbish can be sort of . . . smelly."

"OK, Gillian. I see what you mean. So maybe the empties were there but you just didn't find them."

"Maybe," I concurred.

"Which I guess is something we just have to accept right now. The facts are: We really don't know Janet was drinking, we don't have any evidence, and so far she hasn't done anything really wrong, or, like, drunken, that would mean she has to be thrown out. So I think we should just sit on this one for a while. Although I do want you to keep a close eye on her like I asked, OK?"

I nodded solemnly.

"And please make sure you talk to Florine tonight and really impress on her how important that job is to her future. She seems to be making a very good connection with you, Gillian. Honestly" — and here Gretchen shook her head in what appeared to be perfect bafflement — "she seems to think you have all the answers."

"I'll talk to her," I promised stoutly, glad to let the meeting end on the bright chime of confidence in my abilities.

But as soon as Gretchen was gone, I sank into the chair, moaning audibly, overwhelmed with the difficulty of the task at hand. Send Florine back to her *job?* Was Gretchen *insane?* How could Florine possibly return to that den of convention and conformity, especially after so cogently dramatizing her true feelings to the entire staff of LifeLine, Inc., with the gesture made famous by biker babes at Formula One racetracks in the Midwest? (I don't remember where I learned about this. It must have been a *very*-late-night talk show.) This counseling business was more complicated and potentially discouraging than I thought it would be. Just as one of my clients was moving into a safety zone, the next was careening toward a jackpot.

I pulled Volume 1 of Dawson's *History of World Religions* out of my backpack and laid it in the center of the desk. I had checked all four volumes out of the library a few days before, intending to use the famous compendium to get ideas for a new dissertation topic. So far, I had paged through half of the first heavy tome. Now it stared at me blindly, like the large closed eye of Cyclops, waiting for my hand to open it. For a fleeting moment, I didn't. My eyesight went fuzzy, as if my ocular lens were being jostled out of focus by my suspensory ligament, and my hand hovered a few inches above the black cover, which suddenly appeared, not only blind, but also turgid, vacuous, intractable, and false — three thousand pages of man's attempt to create his own immortality through mass delusions, time-wasting rituals, and plastic figurines. I shook my head slightly to rid myself of this harsh perception; it dissolved quickly but left an emotional trace. I started to pout. Then to whimper. Why did I have to worry so much about the world's religions? Why couldn't someone else do that for a change? And why had I been given the two worst counselees at Responsibility House, Stacy and Florine? Why did I have to worry so much about *them?* Who in this world was worrying about *me?*

Pushing the book aside, I pulled out my pad of legal paper and wrote across the top of it TEN GOOD REASONS WHY FLORINE SHOULD APOLOGIZE TO HER (ASININE) BOSS. The way this headline suggested its own deconstructionist interpretation was interesting, I thought, but it was likely to confuse a streetwalker. So, still pouting a little, I crossed out the word *asinine* along with the postmodernist camouflaging/attention-drawing parentheses. But the word could still be read, so I blacked it out with a really thick layer of permanent marker. The paper looked grievously assaulted and vulnerable after that, so I ripped it off the pad and threw it away.

On a clean page, I printed these words in confident block letters: FIVE VERY GOOD REASONS WHY FLORINE SHOULD APOLOGIZE TO HER BOSS. Yes, this felt better. There was definite authority in the heading, which gave me a nice expectant feeling, as though something really interesting was sure to follow. What followed was twenty minutes of feeling as if my mind had been squeezed into a straitjacket and pushed into an isolation cubicle.

I decided to try the headline again on the next page, this time using the number THREE. Three is such a favorite number in religions, fairy tales, and slot machines that I was sure I would have better luck. However, before I had come up with even one item to put on the list, a totally unrelated and rather vexing question fluttered down from the psychic ether to settle on the nearly virgin paper. The question was this: What kind of person chooses *Alice in Wonderland* as a suitable text from which to draw a moral allegory? What nonsense (literally) had I been thinking? Why hadn't I followed the well-worn path of Western sages by opting for the King James Bible, Shakespeare, Tocqueville, or the Bill of Rights? Were my character and conscience woefully undeveloped? Was I *responsible* for what had happened to Florine? Wouldn't Florine's future be looking a whole lot rosier right now if I had quoted from the Book of Job?

I pushed the legal pad aside and opened Dawson to where I had left off that afternoon, in the middle of a thorough discussion of the dietary restrictions of the Maccabees, at page 756. As I advanced through the pages, my anxiety grew. I had just about a month—a mere heartbeat in academic time—to find a topic of suitable heft and obscurity. Yet nothing was jumping out at me. I was wandering in a wasteland of esoterica. Occasionally scribbling words like *theosis, energeiai,* and *kerygma* on my notepad, I read compulsively for the rest of the night.

By the end of my shift, I had scared up two possible topics—two men, actually. I was greatly relieved. They were just the kind of obscure historical figures graduate students were supposed to write about. As Dolly came through the door, I leaned back with satisfaction, stretched, and executed a truly jaw-breaking yawn.

"You look beat." This was the first slightly kind thing Dolly had ever said to me.

"I guess I am," I concurred, closing my book.

"So go straight home and get some rest!" she barked like a savage dog.

As I hurriedly stuffed Dawson into my backpack, it occurred to me that someone who wasn't me might say, *No thanks, Dolly, I think I'll go to a Hula-Hoop convention and swivel myself into a corkscrew of exhaustion!* But then I wondered whether barking like a savage dog wasn't Dolly's way of being nice.

———

I believed my parents could sense from afar when I was weak. Surely that was why the phone rang promptly at nine A.M. the following morning.

"Making progress, dear?" Joan chirped.

"That deadline's coming up mighty quick," Bertram said heartily.

Even I couldn't carry on the charade any longer. "There's been a change of plans," I said, bracing for their reaction. "My former topic wasn't working out. I had to put it aside, and now I'm starting something new."

"You can't be serious!" Joan shrieked. "Why would you begin a new dissertation now, when you've already invested months in the old one?"

"I've seen this before," Bertram said darkly. "A graduate student runs into a problem with his research and, rather than fix it, he veers to another subject, not realizing it will be just as difficult. Dissertation writing is not for the weak-willed, Gillian. Don't think you can avoid its challenges."

"I am not weak-willed," I protested. "It's just that I've become very interested in Huldrych Zwingli."

"Who?" Bertram asked.

"Oh, Gillian, have you met someone?" Joan said.

"For both your informations, Huldrych Zwingli, 1484 to 1531, was a Swiss theologian who analyzed the social, political, and economic aspects of religion. I am magnetized by his insight into the multifaceted cultural role that religion played in Europe in the early sixteenth century. I believe that my agnosticism, far from being a limiting factor, will complement his practicality. In short, we will make a very good pair."

What followed was the kind of bottomless silence that one experiences only a few times in one's life. It was filled not only with the usual ocean of unsaid things between myself and my parents, but also with the curdling realization that I had just traded one bluff for another—although right up until the moment I betrothed myself to Huldrych Zwingli, I had actually believed what I'd said.

"And what will you do if Huldrych doesn't fulfill your needs?" Bertram asked slyly.

I knew he was setting a trap. "Well, in that case, I might try Denys the Aeropagite," I said, throwing myself heedlessly into it. "Denys the Aeropagite, Saint Paul's first Athenian convert, managed to blend Greek, Semitic, and Christian influences into a seminal mystical treatise in the sixth cen —"

"Enough!" Bertram said sharply. "I was suspicious before, but now I know. You're not going to get your Ph.D. in June. You probably won't ever get it."

"Thank you, Bertram. Your faith in me is touching," I said.

"Now, stop it, you two," Joan soothed. "I'm sure something can be done. Gillian has been one of the most brilliant students in her department for three years. Surely if you spoke to him, dear, the dean would understand your difficulty and find a way to let you continue with that subject you were so interested in — what was it again? — speculative diversion experiences?"

"OK, that's enough for today," I said, just as sharply as my father. "Please be assured that I am fine and my life is under control. Good-bye."

I slammed down the phone, marched to my room, and sat on my bed. There was no winning, I realized. There was only exile or defeat. And what made me think I deserved to win? Bertram was right, actually. I *had* screwed up. And I was still screwing up. Huldrych Zwingli. Denys the Aeropagite. Why, I couldn't even say their names. I deserved my parents' scorn — and my own.

No, I don't! a little part of me shouted. It shouted from a long way off.

The hydrangeas in the wallpaper blurred and swirled together. When they came into focus, they looked like smirking feral cats, waiting to slither into my closet and pee in my nerdy shoes.

I sat and stared at them. I was too disgusted to be cowed. It dawned on me that there was a simple action I could take to eradicate them: I could paint my room. Yes, I could. My excitement grew as the idea took hold. I could smear a lovely color of my own choosing over their smirky little faces. What was I waiting for?

A half hour later I was entering a large hardware store not a mile from where I lived. The paint section was in the back. The first thing I saw was a towering display rack covered by hundreds of long, thin cards, each bearing five or six shades of a certain color and a three-digit number. Altogether, there must have been over a thousand hues, a glorious spectrum of possible choices, not only every color of the rainbow, but every color in creation, and many that in my opinion do not occur naturally anywhere on earth. I coasted through the initial choices with relative ease. I winnowed approximately one thousand down to approximately six hundred, reduced that number to 230, rejected 105 more wannabes, disappointed another 50 contenders, and jettisoned 72 not-good-enoughs. The three finalists looked nervous, but I knew the anxiety was actually mine. They were remarkably similar — indeed, they lived on adjacent cards — and had especially lovely names: Billowy Down, Icy Moon Drop, and Celestial Hyacinth.

That's when agonizing self-doubt took hold. First in the back of my mind, then in the front, and finally from all around, I heard the voices of my parents carrying on about Big and Strong. These words had dogged my childhood; they had accompanied practically every spoonful of runny yogurt, every clump of puréed ham. It soon became apparent, however, that the only thing that would ever be Big and Strong about me was my eyeglass prescription. In a rare display of sensitivity, my parents dropped the injunction of Big and Strong, but the impulse behind it could not be quelled so easily. As I moved sluggishly into adolescence, they pelted me with their increasingly urgent, nearly hysterical philosophy of Up and More. It went like this: *Speak up, sit up, stand up, live up. Do more, say more, learn more, know more, be more. Grow up, be greater. Rise, increase.* All of it underlining, in spirit at least, the original mandate of Big and Strong.

Which is why, if you will follow a logic that is more intuitive than rational, I had such trouble picking from among those three blue hues. I knew which one I wanted, but I could not choose it. Was Celestial Hyacinth, as a color, too weak? Was it frail, wimpish, washed out? Not Big enough, not Strong enough? Not living Up to the promise of More? Was it, in other words, *too much like me?*

Oh, I moaned, why is my eye not drawn to pomegranate, tourmaline, eggplant, or ocher? Why do I take pleasure in something so bland and self-effacing, so boringly Northern European, when I could have anything I wanted, any color imaginable, including lavish Middle Eastern stripes of turquoise and magenta? Why indeed am I not home right now slathering my walls with olive oil or painting a bold erotic mural of my own design? Am I, like Hamlet, afraid To Be?

I slogged to the cash register, card in hand, and waited while the store clerk mixed my color and vibrated a gallon of it in his paint-can orgasmatron machine. As he did his work, smiling benignly and not criticizing me at all, I kept up a steady murmur of pathetic self-deprecations — all, I'm sure, to keep him from exploding with ridicule: This weak, washed-out, wimpish blue is a failure just like you!

By the time I had carried the paint, roller, pan, drop cloth, and brush back to my room, I felt as though I'd survived an ordeal. And I was more worried than ever about my graduate career. What on earth *would* I write about, now that my attractions to Huldrych and Denys had been exposed as superficial? I stuffed my purchases in a corner and opened Volume 2 of Dawson.

Thursday night was Stacy time. Just seeing her name in my appointment book for eight o'clock made me feel like sludge.

"Are you ready for me?" she asked, opening the door a crack.

She sat down and immediately launched into a diatribe against the parents of students at the karate academy. There had been some mix-up in the registration process for a new term, soon to begin, and it had fallen to Stacy to straighten out the mess. The work involved calling a number of parents and asking them to reschedule classes for which their children were already enrolled. Apparently, some of the parents had not been kind, and Stacy had an urgent need to launch vitriolic counterattacks against each and every one.

I listened as best I could. "Well, these things happen," I said finally, hoping to spur her into wrapping it up.

"Shit happens," she said enigmatically.

I did something wobbly with my mouth that could have been interpreted as a smile.

"Manure happens," she added slyly. If she had been my student, her clear enjoyment of scatology would have prompted me to recommend Jonathan Swift. Indeed, I was just about to do this when she said, in a perfectly flat tone, "My father is the father of my sons."

I felt as if the air had been sucked out of me, and out of the room in which we sat, and for a moment I thought it also might have been sucked out of the planetary atmosphere, leaving earth as a rock to hurtle lifelessly through space.

We stared at each other. I was in too much shock to measure out eye contact.

"You heard me," she said.

I noticed her sunkenness, the shallow concavity of her chest, and wondered whether the airlessness in my lungs and in the room was perhaps what she felt, what she lived with, all the time.

"Say more," I ventured.

"What more is there to say?" She laughed hollowly. "He fucked me, I got pregnant, I had his baby, and then he did it again. Not the fucking, I mean. He did that all the time. I mean, he knocked me up again."

There was silence in the room. My core felt leaden; my extremities felt light. How did a person live in skin that had experienced that?

"Now you know," she added blandly, "everything there is to know."

"Who else knows?"

"He does. How could he not? Now he's dying, thank God."

"Do the boys know who their father is?"

"No. Do you think I should tell them?"

"No."

Stacy sighed. "They're nine and eleven. They're staying with my cousin."

"When do you see them?"

"Every weekend. I take them to see my father, their father, then I take them back."

"Why do you do that?"

"Because he's their father. And he wants to see them."

"You don't have to do what he wants, do you?"

"He's their *father* and he's *dying*," Stacy said. She made it sound conventional.

I had the curious thought that, if the boys were girls, and the father impregnated them, he would be mating with people who shared three-quarters of his genes. The resulting progeny would have seven-eighths of his genes. If those children were girls and he mated with them, the issue of those wombs would share fifteen-sixteenths of his genes. And so on. If a man like that lived long enough, he could come close to producing a clone. But fascinating though this intellectual peregrination was, it didn't stop the nausea that was billowing through my stomach.

"Why didn't Janet get kicked out?" Stacy asked, in what I thought was a stupendous change of subject.

"Well, the beer cans were never found," I said, grateful, I must admit, to be on what now seemed like relatively safe ground. (I meant, of course, that they hadn't been found by Gretchen during the room search.)

"They were in the closet like I told you," Stacy said. "Any idiot could have found them."

"Really?" I asked, alert. "You must have seen Janet put them there."

"Yeah. I saw her do it."

"Did you just happen to be peeking in the door or something?"

"The door was open. I was walking down the hall."

"Really?"

"They were in a garbage bag. She hung them in the back of the closet."

"Wow. You saw a lot."

"That's right."

Hmm. Something was wrong here. I wasn't sure what it was. I tried to act nonchalant. "I wonder why they didn't turn up in the room search."

"Janet took them out the next morning, I bet. She must have

put them in the trash." Stacy's eyes slid sideways in their sockets. Her lips pursed disdainfully. "Someone should have looked there."

"You seem disappointed that Janet wasn't caught," I said carefully.

"I am."

"Why?"

"Because she's a cow pad."

I decided that scatology must have more resonance for people who grow up on farms.

"A dung pile," Stacy added.

I raised my eyebrows slightly in mild appreciation of her facility with synonyms. "You don't like her," I said.

"I'd like to inject her with battery acid."

"Oh, my." The nausea in my stomach congealed, and for a moment I thought I might regurgitate the ham sandwich I'd eaten for lunch. I was sensing depths to Stacy I didn't want to plumb. My eyes furtively sought the clock, whose hands had barely moved from the hour. I wondered vaguely if she'd put a hex on it.

"Your time is up. Please deposit eighty cents and then go fuck yourself," Stacy said in a staccato, nasal voice.

With nothing to lose, I looked squarely at the clock again and realized with relief that the hands had, in fact, advanced a full hour, and while it may have been my professional and civic duty to find out just how serious Stacy was about the battery acid, I jumped out of my chair and opened the door.

"Can't wait to get rid of me, can you?" she sneered as she slithered past.

I shuddered into my seat and tried to absorb what I had just encountered. For that was what it felt like—a what, not a who. A force of hatred. A young woman who had been objectified, humiliated, and abominably used by one of the people she most relied on. Who seethed with such understandable rage that she had learned to despise most of the world and lived with atrocities in her head. Why Janet was the object of her ire was anyone's guess. Maybe it was something as simple as the fact that Janet seemed

. . . well, happy. In any case, it was clear to me now that Stacy was capable of anything. I squeezed my eyes closed, opened them fearfully, and glanced around. Why had I never noticed that the office of Responsibility House—earnest, shabby, naively hopeful—was the perfect setting for a scene of horror? I could just imagine the stapler through someone's cheek. The copy machine splattered with blood. The skull of the chair-slumped cadaver (me) adorned with a simple ax. I was very glad that I had nothing more stressful than Dawson to worry about until Dolly came to relieve me.

For the next few hours, pages of Volume 2 slipped through my fingertips. I urged myself to hurry, to focus only on my scholarly goal. I simply could not afford to waste any more time tangling with the twisted inmates of Responsibility House. Huldrych and Denys had set me back enough as it was. As the night wore on, I plowed through the tome, persevering mightily, praying to find the perfect topic. Suddenly I sat ramrod straight, the book fell closed before me, and I felt a cheer gathering in my sternum. Janet was innocent! She hadn't been drinking beer in her room! Stacy had planted the beer cans to get Janet thrown out of the house!

What made me so sure? I had just remembered that Stacy had *not* told me that night where the beer cans could be found. She had said only that she smelled alcohol on Janet's breath and urged me to look for the empties in Janet's room. Yet tonight she not only knew where the beer cans had been hidden but also insisted that she had seen Janet hide them. Since Stacy had obviously been anxious for me to find the empties that night, why hadn't she told me *then* where they could be found? And was it really plausible that Stacy had seen Janet hang the garbage bag in the back of the closet while Stacy was walking down the hallway? Now that I thought of it, Janet's closet wasn't even visible from the hallway! And if by some miracle Stacy *had* seen Janet stash the garbage bag in the closet, how could Stacy have been so sure what was inside it?

To say that Stacy's story was fishy was an understatement. It seemed obvious that Stacy knew where the beer cans were hidden because she had put them there herself. Gretchen would be pleased, I thought. I was getting a pretty clear intuition about the kind of person Stacy was.

I grabbed a pen but, on second thought, decided against recording my insights in the log. Gretchen respected Stacy and had taken a dislike to Janet as immediately and irrationally as I had taken a shine to her. The situation was sticky. I didn't want to make allegations I couldn't prove. But one thing was certain: Stacy could not be allowed to succeed. From now on, there would be more than one resident I would be keeping an eye on.

From outside on the street, I heard a roar that I knew came from the engine of Janet's Harley-Davidson. I went to the window in mild curiosity. Moments later the driveway floodlight, which was activated by a motion-sensing device, switched on, and the motorcycle rolled to a stop in a bright circle of light. It surprised me to see that Janet had a passenger. He slid off the back bench and stood next to the bike, undoing his helmet while Janet removed hers. He was a short, sloppy, somewhat decadent-looking man. His paunch drooped a bit over the waistband of baggy pants that pooled around his shoes. Despite the cold, he wore no jacket, only a tight-fitting T-shirt. He shook his head slightly when he took off the helmet. His hair was impressive—heavy, black, rather coarse-looking curls that fell down to his shoulders. I guessed that the shake he'd given it expressed a measure of pride, but that impression may have been caused by envy. My distance from him and the angle at which he was standing prevented me from seeing his face.

Who is he? I wondered. Then I remembered the convicted drug dealer Gretchen had told me about, the one Janet was rumored to be hanging around with. This man wasn't what I pictured a drug dealer to be (I imagined slick leather, dark sunglasses, and sweat above the upper lip), but he didn't *not* look like a drug dealer, either.

My first impulse was to turn away. If Janet was up to something, I didn't want to know. But how many times had Gretchen urged me to "keep an eye" on her? Surely, duty compelled me to engage in covert surveillance at this point. I switched off the overhead light and sidled to the window. I thought I had a pretty good idea what a drug deal would look like: sly glances in several directions, followed by a casual brush-up and the package slipped from one palm to another, then stuffed into a commodious pocket as the two veered off from each other like billiard balls after a collision.

I watched almost without breathing as Janet and her guest stood in the driveway and conversed. Janet was significantly taller, and her solid, well-defined musculature made the man's body look soft and yielding. Her hair's boyish cut seemed to feminize the man's long curls. I found myself rather fascinated by the pair. Each was somewhat nonstandard in his or her own right, and their proximity to each other seemed to amplify their aberrant traits. As I watched them talking together in that yellow spotlight, it occurred to me that in the 1920s in Boston's notorious Scollay Square, they might have been cast opposite each other in a tacky burlesque skit.

Their conversation went on so long that the floodlight shut off. One of them must have waved an arm or something because it quickly lit up again. I waited attentively.

A minute later they turned and strolled toward the house. Unless it had transpired in the one or two seconds when the light was doused, no illicit transaction had occurred. In fact, the pair seemed pleasantly relaxed and law-abiding. I couldn't help feeling a bit let down, and then I felt ashamed of having been so eager to witness a criminal act. Gretchen, of course, would have approved of my vigilance, but I felt as if I had betrayed Janet for having suspected her so readily, especially now that I was almost certain that the cans I found in her closet had been part of an underhanded plot to get her expelled.

The floodlight switched off again, but a light above the back door illuminated the steps where Janet now stood, apparently about to bring her guest inside. I suddenly remembered a rule tucked in a middle page of the *Handbook of Policies & Procedures*. It forbade nonrelative males to enter the treatment facility without written permission from the director. Janet, who didn't even read the newspaper, would be completely unaware of the rule's existence. But Stacy would know, and she would not fail to raise the alarm if an unapproved man was discovered on the premises. Determined that Stacy should not have an opportunity to catch Janet in a legitimate error, I quickly pushed up the window and raised the rusty storm pane.

"Halloo!" I called down to the pair. "Isn't it a lovely night?"

Janet glanced up and said hello. Then she stooped and spoke in a low voice to the man who stood slightly behind her, his face in shadow.

"So you're the Professor," I heard him say.

"I am not an actual professor," I corrected the man, leaning out my window, "though I hope to be."

I could just see the outline of his head, made large and fuzzy from his thick hair. From the way his face was tilting up, I knew he was looking in my direction, probably trying to see me better in light that, when it reached the second story, was no more than a dim glow. Since I always assumed that people saw me as ugly, foolish, or forgettable, and I figured I would look especially unappealing to a streetwise man like him, I couldn't help feeling that being cloaked in darkness was a tiny boon.

"I think you will be," he said simply.

What a foolish remark, I thought to myself. He didn't know me; in fact, he could barely see me. He had no business thinking anything about me, especially anything about my career prospects in academe, at present a rather sensitive subject with me and one he certainly knew nothing about.

"People should refrain from making predictions when they are uninformed," I retorted.

A small laugh reached my ears, and my paranoia chimed. I couldn't tell whether the laugh was gently indulgent or a malicious snicker.

"So inform me," he said.

That was a brazen request. "Why should I? Who are you to me?"

"Why are you so defensive? I'm just being friendly."

"Are you suggesting that I reveal intimate details of my life to a stranger passing beneath my window whose name I don't even know?"

"Gustave," he said. "Janet told me you're writing a book."

"Hardly."

"It's about recovering addicts. You're interviewing them to learn about their spiritual experiences."

"Hardly."

"*Hardly* could mean *yes, a little,* or *no, not at all.* If you say it enough times, it starts sounding like the name of an English butler in a murder mystery."

"Then I'll stop saying it for fear a corpse will turn up."

He laughed again. It sounded genuine.

"What corpse?" Janet asked. "What are you guys talking about?"

Neither of us answered.

"What's your name?" Gustave asked.

I told him.

"OK, now that you two have met, can we go inside?" She opened the storm door and put her hand on the knob of the inside door.

"No!" I yelled. "Don't go in there!"

"What's wrong?" Gustave stepped out of Janet's shadow and looked up toward my window. Now his face was clearly visible in the powerful outdoor light. He had a high, wide forehead and sunken cheeks. A narrow receding chin worked in concert with his general flabbiness to create a roosterlike set of jowls. These features by themselves might have been considered bland — perhaps even ugly to those inclined to make harsh judgments — but they were arranged around a set of strong, widely spaced, rather luminous eyes that demanded reciprocal attention.

"Nothing's wrong," I answered hastily. I might have quoted the rule forbidding men to enter Responsibility House, but I did not want to be seen as a petty rule monger and in any case I was too flustered just then to remember it. But I had to give some reason for my outburst, so I blurted, "Except maybe . . . you. You're wrong about everything. I am not writing a book. I am not learning anything at all from recovering addicts. And I am not attractive either." A split second later, I realized I had made an ass of myself.

"Why do you say that?" he asked. He put his hand over his eyes to block the glare and craned his neck to see me better.

I had an impulse to draw back and slam the window, but then Janet would take Gustave inside the house. Stacy would be at my door in no time, demanding that I dispense a punishment, and my plan to thwart Stacy's nefarious plot would be foiled.

"You don't look too bad," he continued, squinting.

I swallowed uncomfortably. "Again, sir, you judge without sufficient information."

"Well, lean farther out of the window and give me more."

"Not possible."

"Why not?"

"I am not a confident person."

"Yes, you are."

"I prefer not to. And I do not appreciate being contradicted."

"I could crawl up the drainpipe."

"No!"

"For crying out load," Janet said impatiently. "Can we go in now and have a cup of coffee?"

I knew that nothing would keep Janet from entering the house at that point, so my only recourse was to keep Gustave from following. I got on my toes and leaned as far as I could out the window. "OK, Gustave," I said sweetly. "Here I am."

He moved directly under my window and stared up for several excruciating seconds. "You're not *so* bad," he said finally.

It is one of the great ironies of female psychology that, while expecting a negative review, I was nevertheless offended by a lukewarm one.

"Not *so* bad?" I repeated. "Did you say 'Not *so* bad'?"

"Look, I've had a long day," Janet said bluntly. "We'll talk later, Gustave." She went inside.

I thought Gustave would walk away, too, but he didn't. He just stood there, looking abandoned. A pale moon made shadows next to Janet's motorcycle. In the quiet night, a gentle repeating bird sound could be heard.

"Do you hear that owl?" he asked.

Something was reminding me of *Romeo and Juliet*. I had an urge to start speaking in iambic pentameter, but a deeper desire to appear extremely normal made me resist it. I said "Gosh, it's cold out. Don't you think so?" instead.

"Yeah, but the cold doesn't bother me. I actually kind of like it," he said.

"I might have guessed as much. You're wearing only a T-shirt even though the temperature is in the fifties. You must be warm-blooded."

"Very."

As though in sympathy with the idea, warmth suffused my core like slowly poured liquid. It suddenly felt lovely to be leaning out the window in crisp air on a moonlit night, talking to this man. And even though I had been offended just moments before, it now seemed that being considered not so bad maybe wasn't so bad.

"Would you like to go for a walk tomorrow?" His voice rose and cracked a little on the last word. I took this to mean we had many things in common.

Then it dawned: Was he asking for a *date?* I immediately became painfully self-conscious and stuttered an overly complicated statement of mild interest and harsh refusal that left us both confused.

"OK. Maybe another time," he said.

Maybe another time? Did that mean that he hadn't been deterred by my answer, that he *still* wanted to go on a date? I had an impulse to change my mind about tomorrow on the spot, but my mother's voice, which lived rent-free in my head, told me that I could not possibly accept an invitation from a person I knew so little about.

"Are you a drug dealer?" I asked.

"No," he said. He paused. "But I used to be."

He's probably lying, I thought. People who sell drugs are inherently immoral, so only a fool would expect anything other than deceit to escape their lips. It would be insane for me to go anywhere with him. He would probably offer me heroin and take advantage of my subsequent defenseless state. Still, part of me respected his attempt at honesty and wanted to jump up shouting, *Wait! I'll be right down!*

"I'm very busy for the next week or so," I said.

"Well, it was nice to meet you. Good luck with your book." He walked to the corner of the house and disappeared.

I leaned over the window sash for a few moments longer, but the evening had lost its charm. It was actually quite cold, not even remotely T-shirt weather. The man has average intelligence at best, I told myself as I closed the window. He didn't even remember that I'm *not* writing a book.

A minute later, there was a knock on the door and Janet poked her head into the office. "Gillian, about Gustave. He's a good friend. Been sober a long time. Always around meetings helping people. I really can't think of a nicer guy. But if he, like, starts coming on to you . . . be kind of careful, OK?" She gave me a meaningful nod. "He's probably better than he used to be, but I've heard that in the past he got around a lot. You know what I'm saying?"

I gulped in thrilled embarrassment. "Uh-huh."

"Good." She closed the door.

Wow. Gustave was a womanizer. I couldn't decide whether to be flattered that a man who had such skill and experience with women wanted to spend time with me or disappointed that his interest in me probably stemmed from an inability or unwillingness to make meaningful choices among available female individuals, as well as from a measure of completely impersonal compulsiveness. In any case, now that I knew the truth about him, it was even better that I'd refused. The last person I wanted to lose my virginity to (I wasn't *consciously* allowing that thought in) was a two-timing ex-con with a paunch, sloppy pants, and jowls. But his eyes were riveting. And I loved his hair. And the fact that he knew about murder mysteries meant he must read *some* books. Even genre fiction was better than nothing! I sighed with pleasure. Really, was "getting around" such a terrible thing? Some women might consider it an advantage in the sense that he would probably be very open to the idea of casual —

Slow down! my conscience screeched. Don't let the fact that you want to lose your virginity almost more than you want your Ph.D. blind you to the clear unsuitability of this character and the fact that you will probably never see him again!

OK, you're right as usual, I replied sullenly, and I plunked my posterior right where it needed to be — in the desk chair.

Volume 2 of Dawson was staring at me. I opened the stiff

cover. I'd neglected to mark the place where I'd left off, so I thumbed through the chapters for a while, trying to remember what I'd already skimmed. It was hopeless. All the pages looked the same. Finally I picked a place at random and tried to focus my mind. But the beginning of every sentence I read slid away before I reached the end. Only one idea seemed to matter: Someone had been "coming on" to me. If it could happen once, it could happen again.

seven

G RETCHEN, LOOKING SWEET and fuzzy in a peach mo-
hair sweater, hurried me through the kitchen when I arrived for work the next night. "Come upstairs. I want to show
you something."

A few women were huddled around the stove, solemnly taking turns lighting cigarettes off the gas burner. They raised their
eyebrows as I was pulled along. Of course they would surmise
from Gretchen's harried manner that something was amiss and
would start trying to guess it as soon as we were out of earshot.
They studied our comings and goings at least as assiduously as
we studied theirs, and I'm sure their closed-door meetings included as much on-target, character-assessment activity as you
would find in the best social services agency. I managed a little don't-hate-me-just-because-I-control-your-lives wave, which
they pretended not to notice.

"Did you know," Gretchen asked breathlessly as the office
door closed behind us, "that Florine and Janet are sexually involved?" Her eyes gleamed with an excited light.

I was handed a black-and-white snapshot of Florine and Janet
walking through a park. The photo was taken from behind, but
their idiosyncratic hairstyles—Florine's swishing ponytail and
the crest of Janet's bangs—made the two women easily identifiable. They had their arms around each other: Janet's left arm was

draped across Florine's shoulders, Florine's right arm was looped around Janet's waist. Autumn was dying around them. Withered brown leaves were scattered where there used to be red and gold. Anyone meeting these two women would have assumed they were lovers (even in the 1980s, same-sex relationships were so common in Cambridge as to be unremarkable). There was something in the ease with which they leaned into each other, a slight inclining of both their heads, that indicated a high degree of comfort with each other's bodies, either from long intimacy or a thorough and satisfying introduction.

First I considered Florine. I was glad the ex–happy hooker was finding happiness where she could, but there was something unsettling about her choice, something (I may as well say it) about her being with *Janet*, that gave me a funny twinge on the right side of my lower abdomen, as though an ovary were being tweaked. Then I thought about Janet, and my thoughts grew darker. How could she? How could she possibly hook up with someone as vapid, vacuous, insipid, and inane as Florine? Was she really attracted to the hairpiece, the eyeliner, the tired-looking fringe on the arms of the Western jacket? Had she turned a blind eye to the implants? *Oh, Janet*, I moaned. *You are betraying yourself.* In the outer reaches of my being a tiny voice added, *And me.*

"You know the rule about sexual contact between residents," Gretchen said sternly.

Yes, I knew it. I also realized (now, with sudden panic, much too late) that I had neglected to force Florine to return to her job at LifeLine, Inc. Indeed, an unemployed Florine had spent the last two days pounding the pavement in stiletto heels looking for bakery work.

My heart began beating with alarming vigor. Because rapid heartbeat is a normal response to stress, I actually felt a little relieved. Maybe I was growing out of narcolepsy. When my palms sprouted drops of sweat, I tasted a little, surreptitiously, just to make sure I was really sweating and not just dreaming about sweating after having fallen asleep. Yes, the moisture on the inside of my hand was hot and salty, so the news was good. I was a fully awake person having a completely normal panic attack!

My reaction to the photo did not end there, however. I realized I had found myself in yet another situation that required great diplomatic skill. It was much like the beer can imbroglio, only this time the stakes were higher. Not only Janet, but also Florine, risked being ejected from Responsibility House for a "crime" that was not actually a crime, or anything remotely like a crime, in any freedom-loving country. Sweeping aside my own complex emotions, I realized that I had a patriotic duty to *support* the relationship between Janet and Florine, if in fact it was taking place. The United States Constitution grants certain inalienable rights to individuals lucky enough to live within its borders. Among these are life, liberty, and *the pursuit of happiness.* Janet and Florine were clearly pursuing their happiness, and any obstacle to their right to do so was a threat to our country's values and to freedom itself. Therefore, it was incumbent upon me as a loyal American to protect their way.

You can imagine the difficulty I had in responding to Gretchen's bureaucratic outrage. Since there was clearly no hope for my progressive political agenda, the best I could do was try to direct Gretchen's attention away from Florine per se, away from Janet per se, and away from the idea of actionable offenses to which she was cozying up. I decided to use one of the only weapons in my arsenal: extreme rationality.

"Point One," I told Gretchen, "is that although the women's posture *suggests* a sexual component, it is not sexual *per se.* Point Two: The existence of an *a priori* sexual relationship can not be deduced from it. Everyone knows that in the recovery community, hugs, handholding, and all manner of friendly physical contact are encouraged as healthy substitutes for chemical highs. Point Three: The Responsibility House ban on sexual contact specifically refers to events or episodes occurring *in the state-owned-and-operated treatment facility* or *on the state-funded premises,* a condition that the incident in question clearly does not meet." And here I regret to say that I chuckled at the mutton-headed Gretchen in the most sanctimonious way and wrapped up my little speech with the patronizing phrase "Unless trees and park benches have suddenly sprouted along our hallways!"

Gretchen rolled her eyes. "Whose side are you on?"

I smiled vaguely.

"Look, I'm not *saying* there's a sexual relationship here," Gretchen countered, completely changing her position with the maddening flexibility of the interpersonally astute. "I'm only saying there *might* be. I have to know when the rules of the house are being broken, Gillian. You're on in the evenings; I'm not. I need you to pay attention to this."

I tried but could find nothing to argue with there.

Gretchen regarded me with gracious sadness in her eyes. "I know this is hard. You like them and want to see them graduate, don't you?"

"Yes," I murmured, a little guiltily.

"Well, so do I. I would love to see them doing well. But we can't let our hopes for them blind us to reality. They're two very high-risk cases. Janet with her history of violence, and Florine . . . well, let's just say Florine's chances are less than average. By choosing to enter into a sexual relationship at this time, they're risking everything, and they know it."

"I thought love made people happy."

"No, Gillian. It makes them use drugs. All those strong emotions — the jealousy, the conflicts, the disappointment, even the joy. Think how hard a love relationship is for a normal person. Addicts just getting straight can't handle them at all. They go right back to using. A sexual relationship in early recovery greatly increases the chance of relapse; it's almost a warning sign."

"Aren't there exceptions?" I protested weakly.

"This is a state-funded facility, Gillian. We're not set up to deal with exceptions."

I couldn't refute Gretchen's logic, but I didn't like it. I still thought people should not be jailed for walking with their arms entwined.

Having regained the higher ground, Gretchen let her voice return to a cool administrative temperature. "Fifty percent of the women who come through this house will end up using again. That's half. Think about it, Gillian. Really take it in. Six out of these twelve will be back on the street next year selling their bodies or robbing little old ladies or ripping off hard-working people like you and me. Who will they be? Can you guess? I know you don't want to. But I'll tell you something that in my experience has always been true: The ones who make it are the ones who understand how tough it is and are willing to make temporary sacrifices for their sobriety. They're the ones who show they're serious by *following the rules*. Our job is to give those women the chance they deserve in a safe, supportive environment. You do understand that, don't you?"

"I do," I said. But what good did it do to predict that six residents would be using in a year, even if the statistic was true? Didn't the women deserve our faith and optimism? It seemed little enough to give. Besides, I was starting to think Gretchen *wanted* to weed people out. Having learned in a textbook that addicts' recidivism rate was fifty percent, she unconsciously needed to uphold the value of her education by seeing fifty percent of her residents fail. I had noticed that she formed an opinion about each resident fairly quickly. Usually, by the end of a woman's first week at Responsibility House, Gretchen had put her in one camp or another. The "good" campers, such as Meg and Chris, were docile, earnest, abject, and eager to please. They did everything they were told without causing trouble. The "bad" campers were flamboyant, mildly noncompliant, assertive, or too intelligent. They had better watch their p's and q's. It stood to reason, of course, that both Janet and Florine were on Gretchen's watch list.

Gretchen picked a tiny fuzz ball off her sweater. "Oh, I ought to mention what's going on with Stacy. You know that she was asking to help out in the office, right? Well, the other day I locked the file cabinet and let her sit in the office and try her hand at some easy paperwork. She did a really good job, so I took a chance and gave her all the complicated forms the state sends us — the ones that drive me completely bonkers — and she found a way of getting more money per resident because some of them qualify under corrections *and* addictions treatment!" Gretchen fairly giggled. "I can't believe how detail-oriented she is. She reads all the fine print."

"I bet she does," I said.

"So I offered her a job as an office assistant, and she said yes! She'll be starting in four weeks, right after she graduates. She's already found a place to live. Somebody in AA helped her get a rent-controlled apartment with two bedrooms for her and her sons. It's just down the street. She's going to give notice at the karate academy soon. I can't believe she's willing to leave them for us! I can't pay her nearly as much as she's making there, but she says she doesn't mind. She's so committed to Responsibility House. She seems to really *want* to be here."

"That doesn't surprise me," I said. Of course Stacy would be eager to hide her sadistic pleasures under the cloak of social work.

"I know a lot of people don't like her. I can't say I blame them. She's not exactly Miss Congeniality. But she's got great organizational skills. She even does bookkeeping! I just can't pass that up, Gillian. You do understand, don't you?"

I gave no answer as Gretchen put on her coat and grabbed her handbag. She approached the door with unusual poise, as if she were about to float onto a stage, and I knew that she had left us already, that Florine, Janet, Stacy, and I had faded into a dim memory of workdays past, that her head was swimming with dreams of a bright, love-filled future, a future that would not include the hopeless and the untrained, the desperate and the ignorant, or reams of paperwork. After testing the doorknob briefly, as if to be sure it would open on cue, she made her exit.

I sank into the armchair. Stacy as a colleague? I couldn't possibly deal with that! But four weeks brought us to the middle of December. The semester would be ending; my deadline would be reached. I might be giving notice myself by then.

Wearily, I picked up the photo of Janet and Florine. They seemed refreshingly carefree. People find happiness where they can, I thought. It's a universal human need. But I supposed that for every impulse to create happiness, there was a matching impulse to destroy it, which explained whoever took this photo and how it ended up on Gretchen O'Neil's desk.

The women were almost finished with dinner by the time I got downstairs. Some had already left the room; about five or six were still eating or loitering over their plates. I took my place at a clean setting and helped myself to some congealed spaghetti from a bowl that was passed to me. A wedge of iceberg lettuce, a dollop of bright orange dressing, and a hunk of garlic-stained bread completed the usual menu.

Janet bent over a glossy fashion magazine. She whistled under her breath. "Hey, check this out," she instructed the group, and turned the magazine for us to see.

We craned forward to gape at a full-page image of a leggy blond supermodel in tiny shreds of clothing who appeared to be attempting intercourse with a stool in a tropical hurricane.

"She's, like, wicked skinny," one of the women commented.

"Her legs look like toothpicks," another said.

"But she does have tits!" Janet trumpeted.

It was true. Each breast, fully visible under a rain-soaked white safari shirt that had lost most of its buttons in the atmospheric melee, was as large as or larger than the model's head.

Janet shook her head in what appeared to be awe that such riches did, in fact, exist.

Florine, wiping her mouth with a paper napkin, was not one to let a mammarial challenge go unanswered. Zestfully, she tossed this remark across the table to Janet: "Honey chile, you don't need to go to no jungle! You know there ain't nothin yo mama can't do for you right he-ah!" Florine was white, but she liked to sound black on special occasions.

Chris, a girl from a working-class family who had stumbled into cocaine almost by accident and was riddled with guilt over some petty thievery that had brought her to the attention of the courts, blushed from neck to hairline. She wore earnest Birkenstock sandals with heavy socks around the house and hiking boots to her job as a Head Start worker. Every night before bed she ate half a can of Campbell's tomato soup. She was the only resident who seemed the least bit embarrassed by Florine's suggestive remark. The others at the table merely snickered.

Florine was bringing her plate into the kitchen, but before she passed through the swinging door, she stopped to favor Janet with a very personal, very frank, very lingering look.

Janet sat quite still to receive it. A tiny smile flickered at the corner of her mouth, and I swear that the curl that fell across her forehead quivered like an antenna tuned for subtle frequencies. For several seconds, their gazes interpenetrated. I watched closely and noticed, or thought I noticed, one of the hallmarks of romantic love—an amazingly intense focus that seemed to shut out everyone else in the room.

As the intimate moment continued (time seemed to stretch around them the way light curves and elongates around gravitational objects), my vision widened unaccountably. I seemed to rise above the table until I was able to look down upon the people sitting there. Among them, most especially, was myself—a dry little woman watching lovers enviously, a lonely voyeur in their luscious world, a clumsy interloper, a spy. This was a painful moment for me. It is often frightening to see ourselves as we really are. Fortunately, I was able to end my discomfort by reminding myself that I had no way of knowing whether the interaction between Janet and Florine was what I thought it was. In all likelihood, the photo I had recently viewed was creating an overheated impression.

Florine passed through the swinging door into the kitchen. Janet put her head down and gaped at Hurricane Girl. I stuffed my mouth with a forkful of spaghetti. It was worse than usual. It tasted like rubber shoelaces boiled in ketchup. I was chewing doggedly and trying to cut my wedge of iceberg lettuce with a dull knife when I realized Stacy was watching me through slitted eyes. A chill feathered across the side of my face. How long had she been observing me? Longer than a minute? Had she seen me watching Janet and Florine? If so, had my expression betrayed my true feelings? Had my eyes revealed the longing and envy of my soul? To put it bluntly, could Stacy have guessed that I was just possibly "into" Janet?

No way, I thought sanely. Probably not. With so many vectors of observation crisscrossing the room, and so many conscious and unconscious agendas intersecting so many subjective emotions in what was, to be sure, no more than a few seconds at most, it was unlikely that anyone's True Self was revealed.

So, with more courage than I really felt, I smiled pleasantly at my soon-to-be-a-colleague counselee. Stacy smiled back, but it was not a real smile; it had a faintly supercilious quality, as well as a pinch of confident scorn. Then her lips pursed together and made a little smacking noise, her eyes slid over to Janet and back, and she winked at me with a subtlety one finds only among the best actresses.

With a shudder, I realized that what I feared was true. Stacy was no fool. She knew everything. She had figured out, even before I did, that I was attracted to Janet, who cared only for pinups and Florine. Stacy also knew that I had no real future at Responsibility House. Not only were my social anxieties debilitating, but I had no stomach for the rules, forms, assessments, punishments, and procedures that were the ostensible business of the house. She was going to enjoy watching me pine away for Janet like a pathetic, unschooled rube, just as she was going to enjoy rising above me in the house hierarchy one bureaucratic state form at a time.

Dear reader, have you ever been to the baseline of wretchedness—that place in your soul from which it seems there can be no more down? (In fact, it is an illusion, a false floor. There are basements and subbasements below that point, but people who've been blessed with reasonably good mental health don't bother with further excavations.) If you've been to that place, you know what I felt like as I sat at the dining room table that night. The truth about myself, my awful paltriness, billowed through my soul like a choking gas whose noxiousness was doubled by the sensation of physical inferiority that dogged me on a daily basis. I thought of Kafka, who transmogrified the hero he loved best into a beetle, and felt more identification with that character than anyone should. What bitter poison it is to be least, to be small, to be ugly! Incompetent, easily beaten. Unlovable and unloved. To be excluded not only from the star-bright world of romance but also from the reputedly pleasant act of reproduction that even animals enjoy. Now more than ever before, the true blunt fact of my horniness raised its warty head and clung to me as no person ever had. I was left speechless by the insight that now dawned on me and the bad language that it came in: Even beetles fuck. Even Gregor Samsa, as a beetle, could have found a girl (or boy) beetle and fucked with her (or him). But not I. Not now. Probably not ever. Not once in twenty-six years!

I rose unsteadily from the table. My pile of spaghetti had

never looked so plasticine and yellow, so much like a hopeless parody of nutrition. Although I could not see her face, I was sure Stacy was laughing. It was clear to me now that she had planted the photo of Janet and Florine, just as she had planted the beer cans, not only to get rid of Janet, whom she hated, but also for the pleasure of watching me implode.

As I walked across the room carrying my plate, the feeling of unsteadiness metamorphosed into vertigo, which deepened rapidly. I realized that an attack of unconsciousness was imminent. Putting the plate on the table quickly, I began to mutter, *I am not unequal to the task at hand, I am not . . .*

Out of the corner of my eye I saw Janet leap from her seat and rush across the room. "Gillian—!" she said with care and urgency, and the tenderness in her voice so moved me that I wanted to pour out my heart, to declare my love for her right then and there. But like the heroines of nineteenth-century novels, who swoon into the arms of the always unsuitable suitor, the one who rouses the overwhelming tide of sexual feelings in their frail Victorian bodies, I simply sank into Janet's outstretched arms, my declaration doused by a roaring, rushing blackness that rocked me like a rogue wave and knocked me off my feet.

The next thing I knew, I was looking up at a ring of women's faces. Maria knelt on the floor next to me. She was holding my head in her coarse work-hardened hands, and her ample black-clad bosom brushed my right ear and the side of my face. I had an impulse to turn my face in to the crevasse between her breasts and cry my eyes out, but I resisted it.

"Are you all right?" someone murmured as I was helped to my feet.

I nodded mutely, flushed with embarrassment.

"Are you sure?"

A glass of water was thrust at me, and the ring of concerned faces widened a bit but seemed in no hurry to disperse.

"I've been under some stress lately," I managed to say.

"You're not pregnant, are you?"

I recognized this hardly applicable question as one that is asked routinely of passed-out women in their childbearing years and tried not to let it wound me. "No, it's not that."

"What is it then?" they asked.

I tried to think of something dire and dreadful that was happening in my life, something that would explain my behavior. Of course! How odd that I'd almost forgotten. I tried to look scourged and mournful. "It's nothing, really . . . It's just that . . . *my funding might be cut!*"

Usually, when I have a period of unconsciousness, I hasten to provide myself with a corollary period of restful calm, which I think of as a kind of antidote after the fact. I lie down, or drink a tall glass of water, or meditate upon a chakra, or walk unhurriedly in a cool, rain-spattered garden. That night I did not have time for such healing pastimes. I was scheduled to meet with Janet in our first counseling session. As soon as I woke, I commenced hoping she would forget our imminent meeting, but she reminded me of it as she gallantly helped me up the stairs.

"Well," I said as we took our seats, "I certainly don't want this small spell of mine to become a focal point. I would much rather"—and here I smiled artfully—"hear about you."

"What funding?" Janet asked.

"Of course you are speaking of the funding I mentioned downstairs." I straightened my skewed cardigan.

"What else?"

"Well, that, you see, is my business. It is irrelevant to the task at hand."

"Task?"

"Well, yes. The counseling task."

Janet grimaced.

"In any case, let us proceed," I rejoined quickly to cover the awkwardness. "How are you coming along in all areas of your life?"

But she persisted. "Funding for what?"

So I explained how the Zephyr Foundation Fellowship had made it possible for me to attend graduate school for three years without my parents' help. It included a tuition and fee waiver, I said, and provided me with a small stipend.

"That's cool," she said. "I never heard of anyone getting paid to go to school."

"I'm lucky, I guess."

"So why are they cutting you?" The way she said *cut* made it sound like something done with a switchblade.

I wriggled in my chair like a child who needs a bathroom. "Janet, this hour really belongs to you."

"I want to know," she insisted.

"They're not cutting me yet. But unless I come up with a dazzling new dissertation topic by December fourteenth, they probably will."

"I thought you had a topic. It was . . . ah, something like . . ."

"Yes, that's right. Secular conversion experiences. Actually, I came here to conduct interviews on the subject with you residents. But every time I asked a woman if she'd had a secular conversion experience, she laughed, gesticulated rudely, or walked out of the room before I was halfway through a brief explanation. One woman started telling me about her orgasms. When it became apparent that I wasn't making progress, my Committee suggested I find a more traditional subject to research."

Janet nodded sympathetically. "It's a lot of pressure on you, isn't it? Is that why you're so uptight?"

"Not at all," I bristled. "Oh, I had some trouble with the idea at first, but I have since seen the wisdom of the Committee's recommendation. I'm sure my research will go more smoothly when it is not dependent on the whims of . . . other people."

"Drunks, you mean. Addicts. Fucked-up assholes."

"Your words, Janet."

"Do you want to switch?"

"Switch?"

"To a new subject?"

"It does seem to be the right choice under the circumstances, don't you think?"

"It doesn't matter what I think. What do you think?"

"I respect my Committee's judgment. They are highly qualified scholars of international renown."

"I asked, What do *you* think?"

I sighed raggedly. "I think they're probably right."

"*Probably* right isn't right."

"All right then. They're right. Unequivocally." My shoulders drooped.

"How can they know what's right for you?"

"I don't know. They just do," I said peevishly. My spine shrank.

"Come on, do you really believe that? For someone who's thought about a lot of things, I'm surprised you haven't thought about that."

"I believe they have my interests at heart." My upper body felt too heavy to elongate.

"They probably don't even care about you."

"Of course they care about me, Janet. They're my Committee!" I sat up straight to make my point.

Janet whistled slowly under her breath. "Wow. Are you naive."

"It's clear you know nothing of my world," I said icily. "Unlike people in other professions, academics *do* care about others. Men and women who have devoted their lives to seeking truth cannot help but live according to the highest moral standards."

"You really believe that?"

"I'm sorry you're so cynical. Perhaps your life would have turned out differently if *you'd* had higher standards and loftier ideals."

"Hey, watch what you say. There's nothing wrong with my ideals."

"And they are—?"

"Uh . . ." It was clear that I'd caught her off-guard.

"My point exactly, Janet. Perhaps it would be therapeutic to discuss whatever tattered value system you have."

At first she remained speechless, but she rallied quickly and, to my surprise, delivered a torrential speech. "Well, one value I have is that if I want to do something, I do it. I don't sit around crying because some old farts won't give their permission. Oh, yeah, I know what you're thinking. You're thinking that I did what I wanted and look where it got me—prison and a halfway house. Well, that's right. I did some things that took me down a certain road. Not a pretty road. Not the *right* road. OK. I accept that. I won't even try to defend my crimes. But I'm not going to condemn myself for them either. I'm not going to sit here and say, 'I'm a bad person. Please help me get some values.' 'Cause I know I'm not a bad person, and the good people around me know it, too. And I'm not making stupid excuses for what I did either. Like, oh, I had PMS or a rotten childhood or poor fucking impulse control. 'Cause when I did my crimes, Gillian, I did them on purpose. Yeah, that's right. You heard me. On purpose.

"You probably know everything about me already from reading my file—it's as thick as a city phone book, I know—but in case you haven't done your homework yet, I'll give you the *Reader's Digest* version. I wanted to get fucking high with my fucking girlfriend because that's the only way she would fuck me like she meant it. So I went out and bought cocaine and used it and we both got addicted and our lives turned to shit and she died in a stupid useless car accident with me at the wheel. And I was gonna kill the guy who in my opinion caused the crash, but I thought about it and decided to smash his head with all the fucking force I had instead. So that's what I did. And that's why I'm here. And here's the thing you probably won't ever understand: I know in my heart that I'm not gonna do shit like that again. But when I look back, I don't regret a thing."

I sat there, shuddering. I was sitting not four feet from a woman whose physical magnetism had made me swoon minutes before, and now I could not summon even a dollop of allurement. In my mind's eye I saw Janet's raised arm crashing down onto her victim's skull, the turned-around pistol like a hammer in her hand. What kind of person would do a thing like that and not regret it? Was Gretchen O'Neil right about the futility of trying to rehabilitate Janet Tremaine? Was Janet, just possibly, a sociopath? This fear did not have a chance to blossom into terror because it was balanced by an equal measure of anger that came from a wound to my professional pride. I was the counselor here, not to mention a (usually) competent scholar, and if anyone was going to be giving lectures on morality, it really ought to be me.

Janet leaned back in her chair, clasped her hands behind her head, and looked at me in apparent triumph.

I said, "What does any of that have to do with having standards or ideals?"

She sighed with exasperation. "I was *telling* you my standards and ideals."

"Forgive me if I missed the gist."

"I decide what I want to do and I do it. I take the consequences. If it doesn't turn out good, I don't make excuses or blame anyone else."

"OK. I get it. You take responsibility for your actions. I applaud."

"Not just that. I also *do what I want to do*."

"Fine if what you want to do is beneficial. Not fine if it's not."

"The point is, I think about it. I know when something I want to do is burning a hole in my heart."

Champagne bubbles of admiration crossed the blood-brain barrier and rose to the top of my head. If only I had that clarity, courage, and self-knowledge!

"Look," she continued, "it's obvious you don't want to do what those dildos are telling you to. Why, just now when you talked about finding a new topic, you slumped in that chair with misery all over your face. The old topic was what you liked. It got you all excited. But you're afraid to keep at it just because they didn't think it was good. Or maybe you're worried it's too hard for you or you don't know how to go about it or you're afraid you might have to give up that stupid piece of paper you think you need so bad. Whatever your reason is, it's pathetic. It's time you grew up and just did what you want to do."

"Hmmpf," I said. If I could have ignored what she said, I would have. But the part of me I feared the most was gaining strength under her rough tutelage. Was she right? Had I turned my destiny over to others because I was too timid to risk the repercussions of my deepest desire? Maybe. But my case was compounded by the fact that I wasn't sure what my deepest desire *was*. Did I really want to write about secular conversion experiences or was I just holding on to the idea out of childish stubbornness? Back in September, Dean Trubow had told me that graduate students usually had personal reasons for the topics they chose. He had asked what my personal reason was, and I had told him I didn't know. Well, I still didn't know! Was it possible to have a deep personal reason without knowing it? And if I didn't know it, how could it help me even if it did exist? Haltingly, feeling as vulnerable as I had the night I asked Bernard Bandolini to sleep with me, I explained all this to Janet.

"You're asking how you know what you really want to do?"

I nodded meekly.

"You feel it in your gut."

I clasped my hands over my stomach. "I'm not sure I've ever felt anything other than digestion there."

"Start paying attention. You will."

In silence, I considered the possibility. Could a gut choose and communicate life goals? If it could, should it be allowed to? How much did a gut know anyway? I shook my head in perplexed confusion. This whole conversation was ridiculous. Obviously, I was being intellectually seduced by a woman who had received such an abysmal education in the rural public schools of western Massachusetts that she was actually capable of mistaking stomach acids for ideas.

"We ought to get on to therapeutic issues now," I said.

"I could give you one," Janet said.

"One what?"

"An interview. You never asked to interview me." She looked a little hurt.

"I'm sorry. It was an oversight."

"Let's do it now."

I took a deep breath. It didn't surprise me that Janet was urging me to ignore my professional responsibilities in pursuit of a personal goal. She had a way of leading me to the edge of acceptable behaviors and beyond. Whenever I was with her, or even *thought* about her, I ended up outside my comfort zone. It was time to reassert control.

"Janet, even if I was still looking for interviews, which I'm not, I wouldn't interview you. You're not sufficiently converted for my purposes. You just admitted that you don't regret your crimes, and I think it's fair to say that even the most marginally converted individual would feel deep remorse for actions that hurt other people and themselves. I'm trying—excuse me, I *was* trying—to find true and thorough converts who experienced moments of sudden revelation followed by complete and lasting psychic reorganization. Dramatic, intense moments when the spiritual world became evident to their senses, when it broke through the veil. I am beginning to think that those moments are extremely rare."

"But I have changed *some*," Janet insisted. It was an appeal.

It was touching to see how eager she was to participate in my study in whatever small way she could, so I decided to indulge her whim. "All right. Tell me one way you've changed."

"My vocabulary's improved," she said.

"Really? I hadn't noticed."

"Yup. I'm using better words. Like, the other day when I got to the job site and it was a mess, I didn't swear like usual. I just said, 'Man, this place looks like a *sinkhole* today!'"

I sat back in consternation. I had no idea how to respond. I could have laughed or wept or slapped her a high-five, and none of them would have been wrong.

"Wonderful, Janet. I'm happy for you."

"Thanks."

She swept her cresting cowlick off her forehead in the unconscious gesture that I had seen her perform many times. Only now it looked somehow intimate, as if it was subtly intended for me. Could she be flirting? Did I want her to? Her eyes were friendly and direct.

"We have about thirty minutes left," she said, glancing at the clock. "And I got nothing more to say. Why don't we talk about you?"

She was audacious, that was for sure. But I was worn down with resisting her. How could I be expected to do therapeutic work with someone who seemed constitutionally incapable of playing by the rules, especially when I was untrained, inexperienced, and almost completely unsupervised?

Besides, no one had ever asked me about me before. No one had thought to, not even my parents, who had seemed intent on *not* knowing me, who had greeted my most innocent autonomous declarations (I want to play Chutes & Ladders; I wish I had a hamster; I do not like my hair in braids) with as much shock as if I were announcing that I was wearing a ticking bomb under my jumper or declaring myself to be the missing Romanov, Anastasia. And since my intellect had driven away my classmates and my physical appearance had earned me the rank of the animal usually considered man's best friend (though never his date), I had come all the way to my twenty-seventh year without ever enjoying the experience that is every human's birthright — the experience of knowing and being known, of sharing with another creature of one's own species the joys, pains, and bittersweet insight one has accrued over the years. If truth be told, I had been sorting, classifying, and storing my most precious thoughts and feelings for years in the dull but remarkably persistent hope that someday, somewhere, I would meet an individual who would find them interesting, who would take the time to learn (as I would learn about him or her) how things connected in me and what even the smallest, most mundane incident was likely to mean in the ongoing narrative of my life.

So it was with raw hope that I found myself trying to explain to Janet what being a graduate student was really like. I began by describing the horrible boiling cauldron that is Harvard Divinity School. The immense pressure, the cutthroat competition, the rigorous performance standards, the knifelike bias against short ugly people with squeaky voices. I touched upon the poverty, the isolation, the months and years of tedium. Then I returned to the subject we had talked about before, my rejected dissertation topic. I did not talk about it the way I usually did — too fervently, too apologetically. I talked about it the way a parent might talk about a dying child — the miraculousness of its inception, the elegance of its design, and all the important things it might accomplish in the world, if only, by some miracle, it was allowed to breathe and thrive.

Janet listened with a gratifying look of seriousness.

"You're right," I said finally. "I don't want to give up my topic."

"See?" She smiled. "Just go with it, Gillian. You'll get what you need. I'm sure of it."

eight

I WOKE THE NEXT MORNING with one clear idea in my head: I had surrendered my topic too easily.

I decided not to blame myself for the cowardice I had displayed on that bleak day in Dean Trubow's office. I knew only too well that I had been the victim once again of my own neurotic problems — notably my great gaping need for success and its attendant shadow, the fear of failure. These twin culprits had been my companions since childhood. The need to succeed noisily urged me forward, to higher and better feats of accomplishment, while the fear of failure mutely restrained and paralyzed me, so that I had gone through half my life in a frenzy of purposeful motion and spent the other half hiding under my bed sheets, quivering. The Committee's disdain for Chapter One had fed the latter attitude so heartily that I had not even struggled with its unjust verdict. I had laid down my arms, waved a white flag, and sunk into faithless defeat. Janet was right: I had let a bunch of old farts run me around.

There was only one thing to do: I quickly created a new chant, *You haven't seen / the last of me!*, which I set to the tune of *Oh, when the saints / go marching in!*, and forced myself to sing it in lusty repetitions while imagining the graybeards of the Committee playing croquet in their boxer shorts.

Having thus achieved a more stable, confident mindset, I was ready to confront a second difficult truth: The residents of Responsibility House were completely unsuited to my purposes. Either they were hiding their unconverted states under temporary veneers of social compliance or they were simply too dull-witted to understand and answer my questions. In either case, I would never be able to make a go of the only topic I'd ever really cared about unless I found a richer mine of converted individuals quickly. But where in this eleventh hour of urgency could I hustle up some true believers (lowercase *t*, lowercase *b*)?

Here I was at last in luck. The city of Cambridge, Massachusetts, is stocked with denizens who consider themselves vastly interesting and unusual and are more than willing to attempt to prove it to anyone who will listen. How had I overlooked what was under my nose all this time? By simply taking to the streets, I would probably have no trouble finding people to share their most profound, nonreligious spiritual experiences with me, especially if the venture was called a study and administered, however vaguely, under the auspices of the city's favorite university.

I spent the day in the library excitedly fleshing out a questionnaire. After some deliberation, I decided on a lively mix of true/false and multiple-choice questions, followed by one long essay. I used my knowledge of the salient features of conversion experiences to plant misleading statements about conversion beside the true, a strategy I trusted would allow me to identify imposters as quickly as possible. The directions were child-simple.

For each question, circle one.
1. God has spoken to me.   T   F
2. God's voice sounded like
   a) mine,
   b) my mother's,
   c) Charlton Heston's,
   d) other. *Please describe:* _____
3. I have felt an unnamable presence.   T   F

4. This presence can be described as
   a) oceanic,
   b) the hairs on the back of my neck standing up and cheering,
   c) a caterpillar crawling on my arm,
   d) floating peacefully in an atmosphere of supercharged electrons,
   e) other. *Please describe:* _____
5. To my amazement, I found that I no longer needed to (*circle all that apply*):
   a) depend on the use of chemical stimulants/depressants to control my mood,
   b) support the billion-dollar adult entertainment industry in any way,
   c) visit my family,
   d) return phone calls,
   e) pay the electric bill,
   f) fear death,
   g) take abuse from anyone,
   h) sin as much as I used to.
6. After being an average (Sunday school/Hebrew school/other) student, I found that the entirety of the (New Testament/Old Testament/Koran/other) suddenly made complete and perfect sense to me.   T   F
7. I quote religious texts frequently.   T   F
8. I genuinely (without any reservation) wish to love and comfort my enemies.   T   F
9. On the back of this sheet, write an essay describing one or more life-altering conversion experiences you have had.

After paying a hefty bill at the copy center, I stood outside the MBTA stop in Harvard Square during rush hour under a cardboard placard that read PLEASE HELP ME GET MY PH.D! In less than twenty minutes, all three hundred of my surveys had been snatched from my hands by harried commuters. Cleverly, I had printed my name and address on the bottom part of the back sheet so that the respondent needed only to fold, staple, and stamp the completed survey and drop it in a mailbox for it to find its way back to me. Tossing my placard into a trash can, I mounted my trusty bike and, as horns sounded urgently all around me and brake pads squealed, rode proudly down the middle of Massachusetts Avenue, congratulating myself on a job well done. *They hadn't seen / the last of me!*

The Hindus say, "If you take two steps to God, God rushes to you." As a nonbeliever, I have to say that this phenomenon of feeling as though one is hearing a great big *Yes!* from the universe actually has its origins in the psychic energy released by breaking up negative thought or behavioral patterns. But whatever its etiology, I can personally attest to the phenomenon's reality because my luck seemed to change dramatically that night.

I was seated in the second-floor office, browsing through the *Handbook of Policies & Procedures* to see whether any arcane rules had been added without my knowledge, when I heard a soft knock on the door. I opened it to Meg, Janet's shy, docile roommate, a dental hygienist whose well-laid plan for a completely conventional life had been shattered by unfettered access to laughing gas.

I sensed that something momentous was afoot. "Come in," I said, urging her forward.

Her walk was unusually delicate. She rolled from the balls of her feet to the tips of her toes. There seemed to be something going haywire around her pale gray eyes. It looked as though the lids, both upper and lower, which fluttered plenty on a good day, were packing to depart. But that was not all: In marked contrast to the gymnastic flesh around them, the pupils of those eyes, which rarely settled on anything in earnest, were unusually darkened and fixed. I suspected drugs, of course. In fact, I feared an overdose and was already planning how I would rush her to the emergency room in the Responsibility House van and call her parents and Gretchen O'Neil upon my return. I helped her to the armchair, into which she sank like a crumbling column, and quietly closed the door.

"What is it, Meg?" I whispered fearfully.

"I saw something . . . as I was walking across the yard . . . It was . . . so beautiful," she murmured.

"Meg, are you on something? Did you take something, Meg?"

"Not an *it*, really . . . A *she* . . . So beautiful . . ."

I knelt in front of her, took her hands in mine, and spoke in a clear, slow voice. "Meg, you need to listen to me carefully right now. I am going to ask you a simple yes-or-no question. Are you listening?"

"Uh-huh," she murmured, gazing dreamily out the window. "She was right out there . . ."

"Meg, have you been using illegal substances?"

"Oh, gosh," Meg said, pulling her hands away in pique. "You know I go to meetings every day."

"Yes or no, Meg. That was a yes-or-no question."

"No. I am not using. Is that all you people ever think about?"

"Well," I said, scratching my head. "This is a halfway house." I was greatly relieved that I would not have to drive Meg to the emergency room because I had never driven the van before and actually didn't know where the hospital was.

"I am not high," Meg repeated in disgust. All vestiges of the trancelike aura were gone. Rather matter-of-factly she announced, "I saw the Virgin Mary."

"Well," I said. I walked to my desk slowly, seeking to buy myself time. "Well, well, well." I was caught off-guard, I must admit. Could this be what I'd been waiting for? A conversion event? My excitement mounted in geometric leaps. Yes, it was. Finally! A conversion event! A trifle too Catholic for my purposes, true. But I was in no position to be picky. What should my next question be? I wondered in panic. And blurted, "You're kidding, right?"

"No, I am not kidding," Meg replied with some exasperation. She got up and walked to the window. "I saw her. She was right out there." I joined Meg at the window. We stood side by side — me about eight inches shorter, of course, but still tall enough to see over the ledge. In an admirably businesslike tone, Meg began to describe her experience, and I felt a thrill not unlike what an archaeologist must feel at the first small piece of pottery unearthed at an excavation site. *Please, God, let there be a city here!*

"I was taking some garbage out to the barrels," Meg said, "and on my way back through the yard I saw something, something that was . . . well, glimmering. I thought it was leftover rain at first. It rained a little this afternoon, remember? And then there was this funny lightness and darkness thing happening under the tree, and I thought maybe it was more rain or the dusk falling earlier than usual. Anyway, I just thought it was some kind of weird weather thing. But then I saw blue coming together. Like, pieces of it coming from all around and making something. A blue robe, just like in the statues. And all of a sudden, there was a woman in a blue robe with her arms out—you know, like to hug you or something. I couldn't believe it! I walked over, slowly, because I didn't want to startle her, and as I got closer she raised her head just enough so I could see her face and she was so beautiful! So beautiful!" And here Meg clasped her hands to her chest and moaned a little. "Ooooh! But it wasn't just her face, which was kind of average. It was her soul shining through. The beauty of her soul! And she said my name! She said, '*Meg*—!' and I said, 'Yes—?' And then she said my name again just like that, soft but clear, like she really wanted me to know she knew it. Like this"—and here Meg tried to mimic the Virgin's beauteous tone—"'*Meg*—!'"

"And then," Meg continued in a harsher, down-to-earth voice, "I just couldn't fucking stand it anymore! I said, 'Wait a minute, lady! Like, what the fuck? Like, are you the fucking Virgin Mary or fucking *what?*—'"

Unfortunately, the relatively weak-willed Meg had fully adopted the speech patterns of her comrades as a way, I believe, of fitting in.

"—and I just couldn't fucking believe it!" Meg's voice rose to a peak of shocked incredulity. "Like, I freaked, you know? I fell down on my knees, just like they did at Lourdes. And I said, 'I am so, so, *so* sorry for everything bad I ever did.' And then I said, 'Oh my God, oh my God, oh shit, oh my God!' But she didn't get mad! She *smiled* at me. And she said '*Meg*—!' again in this really sweet voice and then she disappeared." Meg's face fell slack in memory of the sudden abandonment.

"Gone?" I was disappointed, too, I must admit.

"Disappeared. She just disappeared."

"Did you check the ground?"

"I did. Not a trace."

"No footprints?"

"Nuh-uh."

"Nothing that she might have dropped?"

"Nothing."

"And she didn't leave by the gate or anything, you're sure of that?"

"I'm sure."

"Oh, my." A chill ran up my spine. My bowels loosened a bit. I was amazed at the immensity of what had transpired, envious of Meg's good fortune, and terribly chagrined by the fact that I would not be able to use Meg's experience in my dissertation. As I had at first feared, it was all too Catholic. In its placement, its posture, and the style and color of its garments, the apparition was undeniably similar to the classic lawn statues of the Virgin we have all seen. And, of course, Meg herself had identified the figure unequivocally as the Catholic goddess. In her reference to Lourdes, she had even historicized it according to the well-known Catholic tradition. This was by no means a *secular* conversion experience. I felt like weeping. So near, and yet so far. I slumped into my chair, unable to hide my great disappointment.

Meg looked alarmed. "Gillian, you're not going to fall asleep, are you?"

Before I could answer, there was another knock on the door, only this one was strong and determined. Without waiting for a response, Janet Tremaine opened the door and strode into the room.

"Hey, guys! What's up?" she asked rather manically.

"I saw the Virgin Mary," Meg replied. Her tone was slightly bored, which seemed odd, but I reminded myself that addicts have short attention spans and are used to seeing phantasms.

"Hey. Wow!" Janet whistled under her breath. "Gillian, are you writing it down?"

"I can't," I moaned, dropping my head into my hands. "It's too Catholic!"

"What do you mean?" Janet asked.

I snorted derisively. Was it possible that I had not adequately explained the term *secular?* Of course I had. I had explained everything to Janet just a few nights ago. But Janet, like most students, had understood only a fraction of what I'd said and had not bothered to raise her hand to clarify the rest. This made me feel irritable. Very irritable, in fact. In my head I shouted the question my mother had asked me a thousand times when I was growing up. *Why, for goodness' sake, is it so hard for you to listen?* Thankfully, this question echoed in my head only, because the grown-up me, the me that is not my mother, does realize that many sincere people such as children, the elderly, and undergraduates are prone to lapses in attention.

"Sit down and I will explain something to you," I told Janet in what I hoped was a neutral tone.

Meg looked a bit panicked. "Can I go now? I told Varkeesha I'd give her a pedicure." She didn't wait for an answer.

Janet sat obediently in the bedspread-covered chair.

I took a deep breath, ready to launch into my spiel.

"Wait a minute," Janet said, raising her hands as if I were staging a holdup. "I really don't need a lecture right now. I just want to know what went wrong."

"Well," I said testily. "I can't explain that to you *without* giving a lecture."

"But I don't get it. It should have worked. You said you needed examples of people seeing God and stuff like that. I thought the Virgin Mary would be good enough!"

She seemed to be taking my setback rather personally. "The Virgin Mary is good enough at the Vatican," I explained. "But I need *nonreligious* visions."

"Who would that be? Humpty-Dumpty?"

"Ha-ha," I said stiffly. "Really, Janet, this issue is far too difficult for me to explain briefly, and since you refuse to undergo a lecture, I really don't know what else to say."

Janet frowned. "I thought it would help you out."

Help me out? I didn't get it. But certain aspects of what had just transpired did trouble me somewhat. If Meg had really seen the Virgin Mary not ten minutes ago, wouldn't she be praying or moaning or something like that, instead of rushing off to paint toenails? And what had brought Janet to my door so fortuitously? And why hadn't Janet questioned Meg? Indeed, Janet hadn't shown much interest in Meg's remarkable experience at all. However, she seemed unusually disappointed that the event didn't suit my purposes, as if the whole thing were her responsibility. She had thought the Virgin Mary would be good enough!

With creeping dismay, I started to get it. I couldn't accept it at first. It was sad. And stupid. And horribly humiliating. I felt like paper burning from the outside in.

I managed to speak. "I am very upset right now, Janet. You have toyed with me. And with a subject I hold dear to my heart."

Janet's greeny-brown eyes clouded over.

"I know I am an easy mark. Easy to ridicule. But I had not expected that . . . from you."

"I'm sorry. I didn't mean . . ."

Her hand began to cross the distance between us. It was the same hand that had touched me before, and now it was trying to touch me again. Why? She was not my lover, nor ever would be. She was not even my friend. I pressed my palms under my armpits, wrapping myself in a straitjacket of my upper appendages. "You needn't do that," I said, blinking rapidly. "It is inappropriate in any case."

"Gillian," she said softly. "I didn't mean . . ."

I squeezed my eyes closed. "Leave me alone."

"Can I explain?"

"Go away."

I kept my eyes tightly shut until I heard the door swing open, a pause, and the quiet click as the bolt fell back into its accustomed place.

I was extremely busy for the next week and a half. My interest in secular conversion shrank to the size of a wrinkled pea and vanished with a tiny *poof*. Obviously, it was a laughable topic; I needed to find a new one as soon as possible. That was what I'd promised Dean Trubow in any case. I quickly finished the last two volumes of Dawson's *History of World Religions* and checked twenty-seven additional books out of the library. The Gnostic gospels were very interesting, I thought, and the Jewish Kabbalists did leave my mind agog with wonder. But at times it was all just too rapturous for me, and I had to stop reading and clean my room. Not a thing had been done to it since I moved in, and it was high time to clear the cobwebs and rearrange the furniture.

I was dragging my bookcase from one wall to another when I spied the paint, brushes, and roller tray stashed in the corner. There was no time like the present. I rushed downstairs and asked Lawrence if he would allow me to scrape off the hydrangeas (the paper was water-stained near the roofline, I reminded him) and sand, spackle, and paint the room. He looked up from Thucydides and asked with mild curiosity what color I intended to use. A lovely delicate blue, I replied. He nodded and went back to his book. The project occupied me for three long days (one of which was Thanksgiving) and left me physically exhausted. However, Lawrence was so pleased with the result that he gave me a plate of leftover turkey with cranberry sauce and twenty percent off my December rent.

Bertram and Joan telephoned Saturday as I was finishing the job. They had spent a few days at their camp in the Upper Peninsula of Michigan looking for rare fauna and were exhilarated by a sighting of an unusual type of vole. We acted cheerful to prove we'd forgiven each other for the last, painful discussion of my (uncertain) academic future. I made a point of engaging them in long congratulatory discussions of each of their exciting research projects, and we all enjoyed a hearty family moan over the slashing of the NSF budget by our greedy, shortsighted government. Then Bertram asked the question I'd been trying to skirt.

"Sooo, how's the dissertation coming along?"

"Terribly well, thanks."

"Are you finding adequate research materials about your subject—Mr. Swingforth, is it?"

"Zwingli. Huldrych Zwingli."

"I thought it was Dennis, dear," Joan said.

"Actually, I'm not working with either of them."

"Why not?"

"I didn't find them suitable."

"How could they not be suitable?" Bertram asked testily. "They were important people, weren't they? Influential thinkers of their day. Why, men like that *need* to have dissertations written about them."

"They hardly need much of anything," I said. "They're dead."

"Don't get smart with me," Bertram warned.

"Shush, you two." Joan intervened quickly this time. "I'm sure Gillian will tell us what she means by the term *suitable*. Why, the problem she's experiencing could be easy to fix."

"What exactly *is* the problem?" Bertram was using his harsh voice.

I closed my eyes fearfully. I was about to risk more honesty than I believed I was capable of. It felt like stepping off a high dive, not knowing if there was water in the pool below. "The problem is . . . that the minute I turn my attention to their very important ideas, or the very important ideas of similarly influential men, my interest drains away like water through sand, leaving nothing but a small wet mark where my enthusiasm had briefly played."

Silence. Perhaps they were dumbfounded. Perhaps my words had fallen into the chasm between us and never reached their side.

"Well, what *have* you been working on?" Joan asked finally.

"I just finished painting my room."

In the foggy silence that followed, I realized that I had never seen my parents paint anything. The house I grew up in was dingy at best.

"Do you really have time for a project like that?" Joan asked.

"No. But my room looks nice."

Bertram cleared his throat. "Writing a dissertation requires unwavering focus, Gillian. The handful of graduate students who go on to achieve renown are the ones who can push distractions aside."

"Normal people paint their rooms." The words popped out of my mouth like balloons blown up by someone else. I wanted to take them back. I could just see the shock appearing on my parents' faces. They would have no idea how to respond to such a brazen lack of ambition. And the word *normal* was not in their vocabulary.

"You seem a little tense, dear," Joan said woodenly. "Perhaps you ought to get some rest."

"Rest?" Bertram scoffed. "Don't coddle her, Joan. She's obviously been getting too much rest as it is."

Joan lowered her voice to a whisper. "Bertram, she could be taking after your sister Miriam. There's peer-reviewed evidence that those tendencies are genetically coded."

Obviously Joan had forgotten that she'd told me all about Aunt Miriam, who had a nervous breakdown in her mid-twenties, opened a delightful flower shop on a pretty Seattle street, and presumably was never quite right again. "I am *not* having a nervous breakdown," I told my parents firmly.

"Why do you always talk about my family as if *we're* the ones with genetic flaws?" Bertram asked Joan angrily. "Your half brother's autistic, in case you forgot, and the causes of that could be genetic, too."

"Autism is not genetic. Its etiology is unknown," Joan insisted.

"Well, you don't have to worry because I'm not autistic either." I shouted a little to make sure I was heard.

My parents quieted down.

"Look, Gillian. Your mother's right," Bertram said in an initially neutral tone. "We don't want to put excessive pressure on you during what is clearly a stressful time in your career. But for God's sake what are you doing out there besides painting your room?"

"I'm thinking."

"About what?"

"Me. You. Life."

"Talk to her, Joan. I'm not making any headway," Bertram said.

"Honey, I know it must be hard to be at loose ends like this," Joan intervened. "Your academic performance has always been the most important thing to you. So just try to get some rest between study sessions and when you come home at the end of

December—it's only a month away—we can put on some nice Shostakovich and go over your options together. I did think Herbert Swingforth sounded interesting, dear—maybe he's worth another look—and Dennis will always be there in the wings. Sometimes one just has to *decide*, you know. And then one can go on to the next stage of one's life, and everything just moves forward smoothly at the usual pace."

"Right," I said.

"Did you have a nice Thanksgiving?"

"Yes."

"Did you have turkey for dinner?"

"Yes."

"All right then, darling. Now take care and do keep your eye on that finish line! We'll see you soon."

I hung up the phone with dread. If I lost my Zephyr, those days at home would be intolerable. I had to find a new topic, and I had to find it fast. Back in my room, I scanned the stacks of books I had laid out on the floor in a perfect grid pattern. There had to be a topic in there somewhere, sleeping on a page, unaware of its potentially dazzling beauty. I shut my eyes, asked without belief for supernatural guidance, and pulled a random book out of a random stack. It was an anonymous, late-fourteenth-century English mystical treatise called *The Cloud of Unknowing*. I looked into the air in the middle of the room and said sarcastically, "Ha-ha." All that night, through Sunday, and into Monday I read book after book like a desperate knight searching for a lost princess.

I went to work on Monday tired and irritable. With my last particle of naiveté, I cast a hopeful eye on Meg. But her behavior was just as morally middling as usual. In fact, she had added several juicy swear words, which I will not deign to identify, to her growing street vocabulary. It was painfully clear that she hadn't had one dollop of congress with the Mother of God.

Her scurrilous handler, Janet Tremaine, stopped by the office after dinner, trying to make amends. "I have work to do, Janet," I said briskly, shutting the door on her sputtering apologies. When our counseling hour came up later that evening, I feigned a case of pneumonia, of the sudden-onset variety, and taped a clammy cancellation note to the office door.

On Tuesday evening Gretchen O'Neil did not rush out of the house as usual as soon as I came in. I found her seated in the second-floor office.

"Let's you and I have a few minutes of face time for a change," she said pleasantly.

"Sure." I tried to sound enthusiastic, but I felt the way I used to in third grade when the teacher asked to speak to me. Even though I never did anything wrong and had nothing to fear, I couldn't help resenting the fact that so much power was lodged in a single individual. Just the sight of her sitting at her big desk, cutting apples out of red construction paper, was enough to set off torturous fantasies about what she could do to me if she wanted. Gretchen reminded me of her. She had the same aura of superficially benevolent Machiavellianism. She had forgotten about the beer cans by this time, but, as she had informed me several times via logbook, she was still "concerned" about the photograph. It lay just inside the top desk drawer next to a box of ballpoint pens. I knew its exact location because I often took it out and stared at it with a jumble of complicated emotions, mostly envy. So we were both a little obsessed with that photo.

My instincts were correct. Gretchen wasted no time in removing the photo from the drawer and waving it at me. "Gillian, have you looked into this yet, like I asked you to?"

"Oh, for goodness' sake, I really can't be bothered with prying into people's sex lives!" I said airily.

The look on Gretchen's face was peculiar when she heard that. Admittedly, it was an odd response. It contained more candor than is generally advisable in hierarchical relationships, and its off-the-cuff tone was uncharacteristic of me.

She put the picture back in the drawer, frowning slightly. Changing tacks, she asked, "What about Florine's job? How's it going at LifeLine, Inc.?"

LifeLine, Inc.? For more than two weeks I had been meaning to order Florine to return to her job there, but little things kept getting in my way. A light bulb needed changing, the Responsibility House basketball got stuck in a tree, someone took the nail-polish remover that was supposed to be kept on top of the refrigerator — so many demands had been made on my attention that it was a wonder I could remember anything.

"She did return to her job there, didn't she?" Gretchen asked in a low, flat tone. Dubious, I would call it.

"Oh, yes. Of course," I lied, smiling.

"How's she doing?"

"Loving it!"

"Well, good for her," Gretchen said firmly. "And good for you, too, Gillian. You seem to be doing very well with her in counseling."

"Oh, definitely," I said, grinning like an ass. "We're a team! But I am keeping an eye on her"—I lowered my voice—"to be sure she doesn't . . ."—I pointed to the desk drawer—"you know . . ."

"Yes, that situation's been on my mind a lot lately," Gretchen chimed in. She looked relieved to find me finally coming around. "Sexual relationships can be very dangerous in early sobriety. It's a roller-coaster of emotions that takes a woman's focus off recovery. She starts thinking she can find answers in another person rather than herself. And when the relationship ends, as it always does, she feels devastated, cheated, and depressed. It's a very tricky time. Lots of people relapse then. I don't want to risk that for any of our women, and I'm sure you don't either. So the rule about sexuality is one we need to enforce very strictly right now."

"I couldn't agree more," I said with conscientious fervor.

Gretchen sighed. "I'm so lucky to have you, Gillian. You're responsible, organized, observant. I know I can count on you, especially where the logbook and paperwork are concerned."

"Thank you very much, Gretchen," I said. A voice inside me yelled, *Now! Do it now! Ask for a raise, you idiot!* But I didn't. I missed that opportunity, and I'm not going to kick myself. Studies have shown that women as a gender have a hard time asking for raises because they prefer to work toward win-win scenarios that protect the long-term interests of as many parties as possible. And the fact that I had lied through my teeth about Florine's job didn't help much either. Indeed, at the moment when a more assertive person, such as a man, would have been sticking his pecuniary interests front and center, I was praying that Florine, who usually came home from work at just that time, would have a hankering to fly to her room to change out of her flour-dusted, definitely-not-office-worker clothes before Gretchen laid eyes on her.

"When you're working with people," Gretchen continued, "things can get complicated. It's sometimes hard to know what you should do. Do you ever feel that way?"

"Often," I admitted.

"Well, I'd like to help you with those feelings, Gillian. So let's try to touch base more frequently from now on. Maybe we could use Tuesdays at this time to talk about whatever might be feeling kind of hard or complicated for you at the moment. How does that sound?"

It sounds syrupy and patronizing, I wanted to say. But I was glad, I must admit, to think that she wouldn't always be running past me as if the house were on fire. I noticed she was dressed drably in jeans and a not-new sweater. Oh dear, I thought. That's why she's lingering. The end of the affair.

"By the way, how's grad school going?" Gretchen asked as she gathered up her belongings.

"Actually, not too well at the moment," I replied evenly.

"Why?"

"I'm a nonbeliever. I'm beginning to think that religious studies and I are not a very good fit."

Gretchen nodded sagely. "It takes time for people to find where they belong."

"Well, at least I'm doing well here!" I chirped. I was being so cheerful and false, I felt like Doris Day.

"Lucky for us," Gretchen said, smiling.

I smiled back crookedly.

"Oh, I should tell you that I'll be going to Washington, D.C., for a week as soon as Stacy starts. There's a bill before the Senate, and a few of us from addictions treatment are going down to do some lobbying. The bill would provide more federal funding for halfway houses and alternative-sentencing programs. Do you know we're one of only a few halfway houses for women in the state? It's crazy. We've got a waiting list as long as my arm—these are people who are begging to get off drugs—and instead of funding more houses and saving money on corrections costs, the government keeps cutting our budget until we can barely keep our doors open. It's so frustrating. I'm really hoping this trip will make a difference, but I'm afraid it won't."

"Don't be discouraged. I'm sure people will listen to reason," I said. (Back then, I still believed people listened to reason.)

"Thanks, Gillian," she said. Her face crumpled a little, revealing fatigue and a bit of melancholia, and I realized that I had never seen Gretchen look so vulnerable before. That expression soon passed. By the time she had put on her coat and slung her handbag over her shoulder, her professional demeanor was restored. At the door she turned to face me. "Now don't forget. Residents who engage in sexual acts must be automatically expelled. We've really got to be super-clear on that from now on. Bye!"

nine

I FELT AWFUL as Gretchen closed the door. Was I really being asked to punish people for the "crimes" of fondling and nuzzling? No wonder the job paid minimum wage.

But parts of Gretchen's argument made sense. What if Janet and Florine *did* break up (assuming, of course, they were together)? What if, on account of that, they used? It was awful to think of a jilted Florine slumped on the floor of a public toilet with a dirty needle hanging out of her arm. And Janet's history of romantic and murderous passions did not encourage faith in her ability to tolerate frustration. They would be better off alone for a time, that much seemed true. But how to make that happen? Dire warnings? An electric cattle prod? Four-point restraints? And what would be a fair response if they transgressed? Given what they had to lose, expelling them from Responsibility House seemed more barbaric than forty lashes. For Janet especially it would be one step down from execution. *Humans are human*, I wanted to tell Gretchen. *They need each other. They reach out.* But I knew Gretchen couldn't see the issue from a humanistic perspective. Her mind was held hostage by her education in the social sciences, numbed by the stacks of devilishly complicated state forms she was forced to file, and demeaned by the intermittent trickle of income with which she was trying to fill a leaking pail. Was it any wonder that her thoughts came organized in columns? This is acceptable behavior; this is not. If this is the crime, this must be the punishment. Who could blame her for prizing order and conformity? That was how she had created a haven for a dozen vulnerable women.

I went down to dinner. All I could do was hope that I would not encounter a situation that put me to the test.

The food was worse than usual. The spaghetti was extremely *al dente*, and the tomato sauce was pink. At least the residents seemed happy. Having apparently forgotten the room searches and the fact that they couldn't trust me, they joked and insulted each other breezily across the table. I heard some of the humor I had come to love—the bitter, sardonic humor of galley slaves chained to their oars. Sexual innuendoes were as frequent and as blithe as ever. In general, the women treated getting laid as a festive occasion, a little like winning the lottery (the fifty-dollar Lotto ticket, not the million-dollar jackpot). So there was nothing out of the ordinary when purple-robed Varkeesha, jangling her many bracelets, called across the table to modest Chris, "Hey, sweetie, didn't I see you with a *man* last night?"

"Shut up." Chris's blush was so immediate that there was no doubt that the incident had happened.

"Ooooo-ooo, yes'm," Varkeesha continued with relish, "in the parking lot after the meeting. He had his great big hands all over your tiny little b—"

I jumped from my seat with my right arm extended in a Nazi-esque salute. "Please do not speak further of this matter in front of me!"

The women stopped chewing and stared at me in alarm.

"Engaging in sexual acts is completely forbidden! Any resident who comports herself in that manner will be automatically expelled!"

"Oh, now this is too fuckin much," someone groaned.

"You must realize," I fairly shouted over the groundswell of laughter, "that the rule against sexual contact of any kind is clearly stated in the *Handbook of Policies & Procedures*. You were all asked to read this book upon matriculation!"

"Upon a what?" someone murmured.

"Not five minutes ago, Gretchen O'Neil was demanding that this rule be stringently enforced. I understand that some of you may not even be aware of its existence. Therefore, I will review it for you: Residents of Responsibility House may not engage in any kind of sexual activity while they are technically a resident here. The offense is punishable by Immediate Automatic Expulsion. Bear in mind, please, that Responsibility House is not considered part of the state or federal criminal justice system. It is a treatment facility. This means that if an incident occurred that even potentially infringed upon this rule, residents would not be given access to lawyers, juries, judges, or victim advocates. In fact, in the event of a dispute there would be no adjudicating process whatsoever. So don't make the mistake of thinking you can talk your way out of this. Even the appearance of impropriety may be enough to terminate your residency!"

A buzz filled the room as the women reacted to this news. Some of them tittered as though I had been telling prurient jokes. A few of them threw their napkins onto their plates in disgust and started to get up from the table.

"Please sit down!" I commanded them. "I have not finished yet. In order to close all possible loopholes, I want to define my terms. Sexual activity includes but is not limited to the following: kissing, nuzzling, stroking, fondling, or any kind of touching or bodily contact that could possibly be interpreted as sexual by anyone at all, *especially in a photograph!*" At this last phrase, I stared pointedly at Janet, who looked alarmed.

"And there will be no discrimination in this matter according to race, religion, gender, disability, or *sexual orientation!*" I glared at Florine when I said this last phrase and added archly, "if you get my drift." This cunning cliché was fun to say. I couldn't help a small swivel of my hips.

Janet and Florine exchanged wary glances. Then they looked at me. On their faces I thought I saw traces of guilt that they were trying to cover with bland, obedient stares. I frowned from one to the other meaningfully.

Meanwhile, Stacy's head was swiveling. Her position at the table did not allow her to bring the three of us into her purview at once. I was glad for this because I sensed that she alone among all the residents realized that some kind of clandestine message was being passed, and the feverish look in her eye made it obvious that she was eager to intercept it, parse its meaning, and analyze the lines of power it revealed. Luckily, she missed my under-the-radar message by a nanosecond. By the time her suspicious glance came to rest on Janet and Florine, they were twirling forks in pink spaghetti with their heads down, while I was smiling benignly in Stacy's general direction, miraculously recovered from my pique. Stacy ended up scowling into thin air.

"All right then, folks," I finished pleasantly. "Let's just remember that the rules are the rules. And let's try not to break them."

Chris's face was pale and her bottom lip was trembling. "I wasn't doing anything, I swear!"

"No, she wasn't doin nothin!" Varkeesha said. "That was someone else I saw!"

"Yes, I'm sure of that," I told them in an even tone. "I'm quite sure, Varkeesha, that the woman you saw last night in a parking lot with a man's hands on a part of her body that begins with a *b* is not currently and never has been a resident at Responsibility House."

With strange logic Varkeesha blurted, "There ain't no men in here anyway!"

I put down the fork I had been waving for emphasis. "Look, all I really care about is your well-being," I said sincerely. "I hope that from this day forward all of you will refrain from behaviors that could jeopardize your sobriety and threaten your residency here."

"Hey, can I jepperdize when I get out?" This was spoken by Amalia, a gruff fisherwoman who, in the grip of a mysterious oceanic rage, had steered her thirty-foot boat into a wharf piling in Hyannis. Stinking of gin and shrieking obscenities, she had proceeded to pelt the tourists fine-dining on a nearby deck with putrefied herring guts wrapped in baseball-sized pouches of nylon twine (a.k.a. lobster bait).

"By all means," I answered. "With your diploma from Responsibility House firmly in hand, you may jeopardize anyone you like."

For the first time since I had come to the house, I saw Maria smile. Her teeth were brown and crooked. She put a hand over her mouth to hide them.

I took my plate to the kitchen and, forgoing a lime gelatin dessert, proceeded to the second floor. Confrontations drain me dry, and as I sank into my desk chair that night, I felt like a squeezed rag. But another, less familiar emotion was also flickering in my breast. I had a hard time identifying it. I think it was pride. I had managed to speak entire sentences and paragraphs to the residents without squeaking like a mouse on helium. What was more, I had progressed through all the necessary stages of a stressful interaction without once falling asleep. I felt the two ends of my mouth ascend in a tiny but genuine smile. The way I had walked the fine line between the requirements of my job and the dictates of my conscience had been rather elegant, I thought.

With my anxiety somewhat attenuated by this small success, I emptied my backpack onto the desk. Several books and eight completed questionnaires tumbled out. I had almost forgotten handing out the questionnaires at the T stop in Harvard Square. These were the first to be returned. All eight had arrived that day, filling my untrammeled little graduate-student mailbox with a delightful profusion of blue. Although I had twice vowed to abandon the topic that the questionnaires addressed, I was curious to learn what they said, so I had stuffed them into my backpack, knowing that I would have plenty of time to peruse them during my long evening at Responsibility House. I sliced open the first one with my pen.

Dear Fruitcake, it said. *The world doesn't need another asshole like you, jambing* [sic] *your stupid ideas down people's throats. If I wanted to have a spiritual expereince* [sic] *I wouldn't fucking check something off on a fucking form, you stupid fucking asshole. There is no god anyway, that's my quote unquote expereince* [sic]*. The world is run by money, six* [sic]*, and power. The men in black, and I mean black suits, you racist pig, claim there is a god to scare everyone shitless so they can make money off the backs of the peasants as in me. Jesus sucks. Buddha is a fucking statue. If you want a quote unquote spiritual expereince* [sic]*, go ride the monster rolla* [sic] *coaster at Coney Island if they haven't sold it. You'll be scared shitless and for, like, ten minutes you'll be glad you didn't die. But you don't deserve that much redemption. Asshole.*

Oh dear, I said bravely, refolding the survey. That one's clearly an anomaly. Best to ignore it, I think. I opened the next blue sheet.

An advertisement fell out: *Enhance the size of your penis by several inches with my new foolproof penile enlargement technique! No tools required, no messy chemicals! Just a safe relaxing series of stimulating exercises performed in a private or group setting with me, Jo-Jo, your cross-gendered guide. I have twenty years experience in sexual function techniques and have personally handled hundreds of clients in your area, taking them to the peaks of satisfaction and beyond. Ask about my home tutorials. Go ahead! You know you want to! Call 1-900-SAY-GROW today! P.S. Works for the clitoris, too.*

Several *inches?* I thought in amazement. How many *is* several, exactly? Could these techniques possibly be modified to address issues of *height?*

Stop it this minute, Gillian, my superego scolded. You know nothing can change your stature. Oh, sure—maybe growth hormones would have helped when you were younger. But your parents wanted you to have character, so that window of opportunity got slammed shut and bricked over before you even knew it existed. Now there's nothing that can be done. You're four feet nine inches tall and you're going to stay that way. It's not that bad. It's not a disease. So stop feeling sorry for yourself!

OK, OK. I read the advertisement again, this time more carefully. Hmmm, *works for the clitoris, too.* I wonder if . . . given my virginal . . . I could possibly . . . and it's completely private!

Oh, now you're really going too far! my superego screeched. This Jo-Jo is nothing more than a common hooker-gigolo. If you even *think* about calling that number, you will get AIDS, syphilis, gonorrhea, and genital warts. You are probably getting all that just from touching the paper. So what are you waiting for, you perverted weakling? Unhand that advertisement immediately!

Cowed by the authority of this voice, I let the glossy insert fall onto the desk. I tried to improve the atmosphere in my crowded cranium with a bit of cheerful back talk. Nevertheless, we must admire Jo-Jo's flair for marketing! I told my conscience. Then I ripped the damp-seeming paper into minuscule shreds, scattered half the shreds across the top of the brimming wastebasket, and buried the other half at various depths of camouflaging refuse.

The third survey was totally blank. Not so much as a pencil mark. Could this mean my luck was about to turn? I opened the next one.

Dear Sir, it began in cramped, tiny handwriting that covered the top third of the page, winding its way carefully through and around, but never over, the printed lines of the survey questions, which had been left unanswered. *I found your paper on the floor outside my apartment and read it with interest. You must be a good person to have so much curiosity about G-d. I wonder if I might ask you a small favor? A few days ago my cat, Rodin, passed on. Rodin was my friend and companion for more than ten years. I would like his body to go to the vet, whom he loved and who will give him a good burial. But I am in a wheelchair, and my neighbors are very busy. Would you be willing to help? I ask this with urgency as the days are going by. Sincerely, Anna Friedlander, 36 Linnaean Street, Apt. 4B, Cambridge.*

What an absurd request, I thought. I can't possibly do that. I grabbed a piece of paper and the phone book, intending to jot down the phone number of the Animal Rescue Society, which is known to handle problems of this sort, and send it to Mrs. Friedlander. Then I thought, She seems like an intelligent woman; why didn't she call them herself? Maybe she doesn't have a phone. Then why didn't her neighbors make the call for her? Maybe she didn't ask them. She said only that they were busy, not that they refused. I suddenly had a vision of Mrs. Friedlander, a stooped, balding woman slumped in a wheelchair, parked on her landing for hours and hours, waiting for a neighbor to bound up the stairs past her, only no one comes, and the next day she isn't well enough to wait on the chilly landing, and the next she is so sad from missing Rodin that she just rolls out to the landing, not even hoping to intercept someone, and somehow she finds my survey instead, imprinted with a dusty footprint, wedged between the elevator doors where she can reach it. Poor Mrs. Friedlander, I thought with a sigh. Who knows what prompts the human cry? I put away the paper and phone book. In the morning I would bicycle to Linnaean Street, stuff Rodin in a garbage bag, and swing by the vet's. It wasn't too much trouble at all.

Three of the remaining surveys were exactly what I was looking for. They described spiritual experiences that I would classify as "secular." One occurred at a beach at sunset, another after a violent thunderstorm, and the last on a "perfect" June day. This gave me a new question vis-à-vis my rejected subject: Did weather play a part?

The last survey also described a conversion experience, but it was useless to me because of its traditional Christian symbology. The respondent, walking on a country road, deeply agitated by a thorny personal problem, had looked up to see a shimmering gold cross suspended in the sky. As if to prove the religious validity of his vision, the respondent had sprinkled several New Testament quotes throughout his long description. He ended with a famous quotation that is attributed to Jesus but appears in no other gospel but the book of John: "I am the way, the truth, and the life. No one comes to the father, but through me."

This quotation saddened me, perhaps because I pictured Mrs. Friedlander as Jewish. And who would tell my other respondents that the sunset or the thunderstorm was not also a way?

Mrs. Friedlander was livelier than I'd imagined, though not, of course, quite sane. She said she needed help with Rodin because her visiting nurse was on vacation, and the substitute had not shown up. She wanted me to stay for tea, but I couldn't afford to waste any more time, so I bundled the cat in newspaper, stuffed it in a garbage bag, and carted it off to the address she supplied.

I arrived at the Divinity School later than usual to find five more questionnaires sitting in my mailbox. These roughly followed the pattern of the original eight: three were crank responses, two were sincere and thoughtful accounts of the spiritual cataclysms of nonreligious people, one was what I was coming to think of as Christian propaganda. Not that I doubted the revelation described therein (it seemed perfectly authentic if a bit conventional), but that I took exception to the way biblical quotations were splattered like buckshot all over the page, as though to imply that the revelation had been stamped with God's own seal of authenticity, when it was clear that the respondent himself had selected the vaguely relevant verses and scribbled them with a dull pencil.

Thirteen completed questionnaires—of which only five were usable—convinced me that I had been right to abandon the topic of secular conversion experiences in favor of something more traditional. But I was still having trouble finding the right topic. So far, I had read sixteen of my twenty-seven books, to no avail. My eyes were red-rimmed. My nerves were frayed. I turned page after page whenever I could, at every possible moment, feeling as though I was fighting for my life.

Stressors at Responsibility House added to the pressure I felt. I had yet to straighten out the mess with Florine, who was happily situated in a famous French bakery in Harvard Square, and despite my stringent warning to the residents, I was still worried that I might catch any one of them, but especially Janet and Florine, in *flagrante delicto* and be pressured by my job description into taking actions with which I did not agree. Unsettling suspicions about Stacy intruded on my consciousness as well. I had no direct evidence that she had planted the beer cans in Janet's closet, but I was still convinced that she had. Had she also snapped and planted the incriminating photo? If so, what was her motive? It was obvious that she hated Janet. But why?

It may seem that I had bumped into the subject of Janet inadvertently, but let's face it, there was a kind of homing instinct involved. And it was hardly a bump. Actually, I felt like a besotted pigeon flying smack into a wall of bruised feelings and vexing questions. Why, I wondered for the umpteenth time, had she gone out of her way to ridicule me with that horrid Meg-sees-the-Virgin thing? I thought she had truly been interested in my work that night, that she'd listened, felt my passion, felt my pain. It was excruciating to think that I'd revealed so much, only to be made the butt of a dumb, slapstick joke.

Of course, my pique over the incident was just the latest layer of frosting in the wedding cake of feelings I had for Janet Tremaine. Ever since I'd been shown the photo and witnessed the personal look that passed between them, I had been asking myself the same questions: Was Janet really "with" Florine? If so, did she care about Florine "as a person" or was she simply impressed by her measurements? Why did I so desperately want to know? Why did I spend precious minutes every evening, minutes

I should have spent saving my career, staring at a photo of two lesbians from the back? *Was I in love with Janet?* Does visceral rumbling added to mental fascination equal sexual attraction? Is sexual attraction the same as love? Why didn't I know the answer to these questions? Would I ever figure them out?

No psychoanalyst would blink at the way my fevered mind had driven straightaway and at full throttle into the Nubian Desert of sex (so much heat, so little rain). Having found myself in that desperate territory, I couldn't help posing one last self-referencing question: Since I was a twenty-six-year-old virgin, which meant that I was old enough to make these decisions and had a reason to do so, why had I allowed my superego to talk me out of calling Jo-Jo?

My life these days didn't slow down enough to let me ponder such questions for long. As I was staring at the photo, which I had slipped almost unconsciously from the top desk drawer, someone knocked. I opened the door.

"You got me like a dog's got heartworm," Stacy said.

"Come in," I said, realizing that it was eight o'clock on Wednesday and therefore Stacy's counseling hour. I smiled as best I could.

Stacy plopped into the armchair. Her hair was tied in short drooping pigtails slightly above and behind each ear. Stiff denim overalls encased her like a suit of down-home armor, and she wore the kind of blond suede work boots with the reinforced toe that the residents called shit-kickers.

Stacy prepared to light a cigarette just as she had before, while I, as before, pointed to the little sign.

She slipped her pack of Newports into the high center pocket on the overalls' bib and whined, "Same old double standard. You won't let me smoke, but Janet and Florine can fuck whenever they want."

My eyes widened. Almost simultaneously I admonished myself, Why be surprised? This is just what she did last week. You should have seen this coming. (Maybe they will write that on my tombstone: *She should have seen this coming.*) Gathering my wits, I asked, "Um, what makes you think that Janet and Florine are doing that?"

"Everyone knows. It's obvious."

"Do you have evidence?" I felt slick and cagey when I said this. I was setting a trap.

"I could get some."

"How?"

Stacy shrugged. "I have my ways."

Aha! I thought. That's almost an admission.

She looked me in the eye. "Do you really need any more?"

A chill ran down my spine. Stacy was admitting she knew about the photo. If I was careful, I could probably trick her into admitting she had planted it. "More? That implies we have some."

"You know you do."

"Yes, Stacy. *I* know we do. But how do *you* know we do?"

She said, "Because it's on the desk."

I swirled around in my chair. To my chagrin, the photo of Janet and Florine was lying in plain sight on top of my questionnaires.

"Well," I said, turning back to Stacy. "Well, well, well."

"You should kick them out."

"It's just a photo," I said. "It doesn't prove anything."

"Hypocrite!" The word exploded into the room. "You read us all the riot act last night. You said anything that even *looks* sexual *is* sexual, even if it's in a photograph. In fact, you said, '*Especially* if it's in a photograph.' Those were your exact words. And there's the photograph right in front of you, and what do you do? Nothing!"

"Well . . . uh . . ."

"God, I hate this place. You're such an asshole, Gillian, just like every teacher, priest, counselor, lawyer, and judge I ever met. I swear, you people get a little power, you immediately start playing favorites, playing with people's heads. Double standards everywhere. Rules for some people, not for others. It's disgusting."

Stacy got up, strode across the few feet that separated us, reached behind me, and grabbed the photo off the desk. She waved it between two fingers, close enough to my face that I could feel the wind of its fluttering. "These two should be expelled, and you know it! Do it right now!"

Stacy's face was flushed and perspiring, which made the freck-

les on her cheeks darken and conjoin into brown melanotic puddles. She was right, of course; she had the moral high ground.
But what is rightness, really? At the least, a layered thing.

I plucked the fluttering photo from her fingers. "I adamantly
refuse!"

Before my eyes, Stacy's entire demeanor changed. She
slouched to the armchair and seemed to squirm her way into its
embrace with a newly gelatinous body. Her mouth grew slack;
her voice turned brown and syrupy. "I know why you're protecting them. It's because you're hot for Janet. Like a dozen other so-
called straight women I could name." The tone in which she said
so-called straight women made me think of leprous scabs.

I sucked a ragged breath. My moral high ground was tainted
now, perhaps not undeservedly. But even worse was the wound
to my ego: If I had to go through the ordeal of having an illicit,
not-so-secret, homosexual attraction (if that was what it was), the
last thing I wanted to know was that I was one of many.

"Vroom, vroom," Stacy purred with a glinting eye. "Vroom,
vroom."

I admit to being dumbstruck at this point.

"You want to fuck her, don't you?" This in a soft, enticing
voice.

I pursed my lips, pushed my glasses onto my nose.

"It's true!" Stacy shrieked delightedly. "Oh my God, it's true!"
She threw her head back and laughed as if she'd heard the joke of
the century. Maybe she had.

I got that billowy, vacuous feeling I knew so well. I felt like I
was a rag doll being thrown into the basement for dogs to chew
and mice to pull the stuffing from. One advantage of deep famil-
iarity with an emotional state is that one knows its architecture
so well. Here were the broken-down stairs, the laboring immensity of the furnace, the dirty webbed corners, the sour-smell-
ing pipes. I made my way through the mold and shadows rather
quickly and climbed out the bulkhead, into the light.

"No, Stacy, you've got it wrong," I managed to say. "I don't
want to fuck Janet. And I'm not protecting anyone. I'm simply
concerned with what goes on in this house. One thing I'm concerned about right now is how this photograph got here. I would

like to know who took it, and why. Can you shed any light on that?"

"If I said I took it, then you'd think I put the beer cans in Janet's closet too."

"Did you?"

"You'd love it if I did."

"I just want to know."

"You hate me, don't you?" Stacy said sweetly. "You've always hated me."

I thought it odd that she seemed so happy. Perhaps she deeply wanted to be hated, or it pleased her to think that she had reduced me to such a primitive state.

"I don't hate you, Stacy," I said, aware that I lied. "I simply want to know who took the picture, that's all."

Stacy rolled her eyes like one oppressed beyond endurance. "Oh my God! Why do you keep asking me that *same question?* You're asking it *over and over again!* Don't you *trust* me?"

I sat back. I rubbed my forehead. I knew I would not be able to get any studying done that night.

Stacy went on bitterly, "You guys like to pretend this place is perfect. Everything's fair, everyone's nice. That makes it easier for you. You can come in here and close the door and read your stupid books and think you know something. But you don't have a clue what's really going on. You see what you want to see, that's all."

"What am I not seeing, Stacy?"

"How badly run and hypocritical this whole place is. How some people get treated like royalty, and some are the fucking slaves."

"Who's a fucking slave, Stacy?"

"Me. I do everything around here! I do the grocery lists, most of the shopping. I wipe down the bathroom every night and rinse out the tub, which is full of pubic hairs. I help Gretchen with bookkeeping, filing, paperwork. Filling out those stupid forms. Why do I do it? Because I want to better myself, that's why. Some of us really do want to better ourselves, Gillian. Isn't that what we're supposed to want when we come to a place like this?"

"Is that why you want to work here too?"

"Yes, it is. For once in my life, I want to do good for society. And I can't stand that asshole at the karate academy who can't even get the address right on his own fucking letterhead. We got a three-hundred-dollar print bill last week, and we have to pay it, because they showed me the form *he* filled out. And it was completely wrong! The karate academy is at three-five-seven-*eight* Madison, not three-five-eight-*seven* Madison. The idiot doesn't even know where he works! And he makes forty thousand dollars a year. But I'm the one who does all the work, and I get seventeen. So I say, 'Eat shit, asshole! Here's your two-week notice. Cause I got a new job that's a lot better than this one! So fuck you, fucker!'

"Then I come home, thinking, OK, I'm OK now. This place is cool. This place runs right. And the first thing I see is fucking Janet fucking Tremaine strutting around like she's Bruce Springsteen with a hard-on—never helping with anything, never doing her share, not picking up a sock, just drinking, smoking weed, riding her motorcycle, and fucking anyone she wants to fuck whenever she wants to fuck them. And you guys look the other way! Like the rules don't apply to her. But to me you say, 'Stacy do this, Stacy do that, Stacy file these folders, Stacy fill out these forms.' I'm fucking sick of the double standard in this place, Gillian, and I'm warning you, when I work here, I'm gonna make this place run right!"

"Hmm," I said, taking as much cover as I could get from those two runny consonants. Smoking weed was a new allegation. A month ago I would have jumped all over it, begging for details, but I was starting to realize three things: (1) what I didn't know wouldn't hurt anyone; (2) there was a speck of truth in what Stacy was saying, which made me feel guilty; (3) I was up to my eyeballs in her noxious resentment and could barely speak.

Stacy was staring at me aggressively, waiting for a response.

"Well," I iterated for the sixth time since the start of the hour. It would have been nice if I could have found something funny to say just then, but one is never funny when one wants to be. The remark that came out of my mouth was a horrible cliché: "You seem really angry right now."

Stacy offered a frozen, sick smile. "Fuck you, Gillian."

I grimaced back and resisted saying *Ditto*. "OK. What do you say we start over? We have a half hour left. What do you want to talk about?"

"How I killed my sister," Stacy said, deadpan.

The blood drained out of my hands.

"I injected her with battery acid. She died squealing, like a pig."

If I'd had any saliva, I would have swallowed it. But my mouth was dry as rubble, and the area behind my forehead felt bombed. I remembered Stacy's last pronouncement: My father is the father of my sons. This one had the same epic simplicity. It occurred to me that Stacy was either a pathological liar or the scariest person I'd ever met. For once in my life, I was grateful to be sitting inside my own unattractive skin.

"Why don't you confess?" I managed to ask.

"I just did."

"To the authorities," I said.

"Everyone's corrupt, like I said. The cops, the judges. All corrupt. Especially you."

"Me?"

"I know you hate me. And now you're going to do everything you can to get rid of me."

"I don't want to get rid of you, Stacy." But, in truth, just then I did.

"Liar. Hypocrite. What did I say? You're a liar. You lie." Stacy slid out of her chair. Her movements were both oily and childish. "See you next week," she said with sour pleasantness as the door closed behind her.

I felt like London after the blitzkrieg. The index card bearing Gretchen's phone number (and the phrases FOR USE IN TRUE EMERGENCIES ONLY and DON'T FORGET 9-1-1) had been ripped off the wall, leaving a few random bits of graying tape to mark its former location. But I'd chanted those seven digits so often in my first weeks at Responsibility House that the absence of the card was no obstacle to me. I picked up the phone.

"Gretchen," I said urgently when she answered, "I'm sorry for the inconvenience, but I can't possibly see Stacy in counseling one more time."

"Yeah? How come?" Gretchen was munching something that snapped and crunched. A raw carrot stick, perhaps.

I tried to describe the horrible experience I'd just had, but it was not easy. I hemmed and hawed quite a bit. The problem was, I didn't want to get anywhere near the subject of wanting to fuck Janet Tremaine, for fear that I might be asked to affirm or deny it, and I didn't want to repeat Stacy's accusation that I was protecting Janet and Florine, for fear that I might have to admit that I had given the women a strict public warning against having sex in photographs. The description of the double standard that presumably prevailed inside the walls of Responsibility House needed to be avoided also, I thought, as I feared Gretchen might too willingly agree and use the opportunity to take drastic steps against certain residents. This was a lot of material to censor, but luckily there was still plenty to discuss. I described in detail the confession Stacy had made about her sister and what she had confessed the week before about her father. I said that Stacy had all but admitted planting the beer cans and the photograph and that she seemed to be on a bloodthirsty vendetta against Janet Tremaine.

"Stacy has a very troubling personality!" I concluded breathlessly. "She even resents doing the housework and office tasks that she herself chooses to do!"

"Her sister lives in Chelmsford," Gretchen replied. "She's not dead."

"Could it be a different sister?"

"I don't think so."

"Then why—?"

"She's testing you. To see if you'll run away."

"Wha—?"

"People with trust issues do this all the time. They tell you something horrible about themselves, which half the time isn't even true, and then they see how you react. It's important to stay calm. Did you?"

"I think so."

"Then you're OK."

"And the allegation against her father? What about that?"

"Probably the same thing. Just listen and keep good session notes, Gillian. And then don't worry about it."

"But Gretchen, you don't understand. Her statements are deeply upsetting. If they are true, they are horrifying. And if she is merely being manipulative, as you suggest, then she is the most appalling person I have ever met. In either case, I don't like her, and I have no idea how to interact with her!"

"Look, if she's staying sober, getting to her job, and abiding by the rules of the house, that's all we really care about. We're a halfway house, not a psych unit. She's going to graduate in two weeks anyway, so I'd say, just stick with it, you're almost off the hook."

"Good. Because I can't endure much more." I felt a little calmer, if not exactly relieved. "But what about the beer cans and the photograph—this vendetta she's on?"

"Are you sure that's what it is?"

"Well, it seems like that. I mean, *someone* planted the photograph, right?"

"Mmm. Someone. But we don't know who. I don't think we should jump to any conclusions. Just because Stacy's being difficult in counseling doesn't mean she did it. And frankly, even if she did, there's no rule against that. We might even thank her for it."

"Thank her! For what?"

"For alerting us to a possible situation."

For being a snitch, I thought.

Gretchen continued, "It seems like Stacy's just trying to help out, doesn't it? I mean, in the last few months she tried really hard to get me to hire her, and she's made my life a lot easier. You wouldn't believe how much she's done and how competent she is. The fact is, we need people like her around. To keep an eye on things, you know? I'm really excited about her starting as house manager."

"Wait a minute. I thought she was going to be an office assistant," I said.

"I thought so too, at first. But Stacy has a managerial-level job at the karate academy, and she'll be bringing those skills with her to the house, so a higher title seemed more appropriate. And besides, she really wanted it."

No surprises there. My title was staff counselor. The *Handbook of Policies & Procedures* was missing an organizational chart, so I had no idea which of us would be farther up in the hierarchy.

"You know, I actually think it was Varkeesha who planted the photograph," Gretchen continued. "I saw her with a camera the other day. I'd like to know how she could afford that little item. You know what I mean?"

Oh dear, I thought tragically, *now Varkeesha.* I could hear the jangle of her bracelets as she was pushed onto Gretchen's watch list, and I wanted to stop the process. "She could have brought the camera with her from home."

"This was not the kind of camera she would be likely to own. It was big with a zoom lens. It was *expensive.*"

"Oh."

"Look, I know you're kind of upset right now after this bad session with Stacy. You're probably not thrilled about her coming to work at the house. So I just want to reassure you. She'll be working days, so she's not going to get in your hair. In fact, when I get back from D.C., I'll probably give her mothers' hours so she can be home when her boys get out of school. Then she won't even be around when you come on. I'll still be the one waiting for you at five. You can handle that, can't you?"

Well, yes, I could handle it, but I didn't want to. Stacy was right, I realized. I did hate her. But Gretchen was boss, and she had obviously made up her mind. The question to me was merely a workplace formality.

"Sure. No problem," I said.

December 1 dawned pale and chill, with the watery, monochromatic light of a New England winter. I lay in bed, hopeless. The four volumes of Dawson's *History of World Religions* occupied the middle of my desk. The twenty-seven additional books I had checked out of the library were arranged in pygmy skyscrapers around its base. I had spent every free moment of the last week reading them, arranging them, writing notes about them, and sorting the notes into different configurations of figures, eras, and trends. It wasn't easy. I had muttered, cursed, and made up speeches. I had given up sleep, meals, and rudimentary hygiene.

All the while I'd been convinced that, with a proper level of dedication on my part, the perfect topic would jump out at me, something to which I could willingly devote a year or more of my life. But nothing had jumped. Nothing had hopped or even twitched.

The deadline for filing a new prospectus was less than two weeks away, and I was beginning to think it could not be done. Or, if it could be done, it could not be done by me. Something was holding me back.

As I lay in bed, taking shallow breaths, my eyes roamed the slanting walls of my room, walls I had recently painted blue, and I thought to myself, *I like this color. I really do.* I remembered wandering into the hardware store and being overwhelmed by choices. I remembered wishing I was drawn to tourmaline or ocher, waiting in self-conscious misery while the clerk mixed my color, and slogging home with my gallon and a sense of defeat.

But now the light was playing across the planes and angles of my walls, and the color was tranquil and comforting. It had soft depths, quiet confidence, and it was not hydrangeas. I decided to let myself in on a little secret: The Real Me always knew I wanted Celestial Hyacinth. The Real Me had made the right choice.

I had no idea whether these thoughts were distracting me from my academic dilemma or helping me to resolve it.

I pulled my body out of bed, put on a roomy red sweater and stretchy tights, got a cup of tea and some Ritz crackers from the kitchen, and sat down at my Macintosh. I had received two more questionnaires I could actually use, which brought the total to seven. This was not the response I had dreamed of, but it was what I had. The experiences described therein were, in fact, strange and wonderful. It took more than five hours of intense labor to categorize, compartmentalize, and break down the components into suitably dry academic prose. By midafternoon, I held in my hand a twelve-page essay simply titled "Seven Secular Conversion Experiences." Despite its admittedly turgid style, I believed it to be the best paper I had ever written. It was honest, humane, and almost moving. I knew there was an overwhelming probability that the Committee would reject it, but I decided to give it to Dean Trubow anyway. What else could I do?

ten

I WON'T GO BACK," Florine said. "You can't make me."

She was dressed in batter-crusted jeans and a tight T-shirt, on which the outlines of the apron she had been wearing at Château de Gâteau were marked by a dusting of flour. A webby white hairnet appeared to be covering her hair, but that, too, was flour. There was a smudge of brown sugar on the side of her nose.

"Florine," I said, trying to quell my impatience. "You won't be able to support yourself, much less a child, on a minimum-wage job. Even subsidized housing will be out of your reach, never mind electricity, telephone, clothing, transportation, and after-school programs. And you'll never be able to pay for the health insurance you desperately need for Raven's asthma. LifeLine, Inc., gives you salary plus benefits and family-friendly policies. Don't you get it? Working there would make your life so much easier!"

"I'll never go back. I hate that place. And what makes you think they'd take me back? Don't you remember? I showed them my tits."

"They could probably be convinced that gesture was a small behavioral regression you deeply regret."

"I don't regret it."

"You could *pretend* you regret it."

Florine rolled her eyeballs around the heavily penciled rims of her eyes. "You don't know me very well if you think I could do that."

Anger clotted in the lower half of my esophagus. We'd been at this for half an hour, and clearly Florine hadn't heard a word I said. "Look, I hate to be the one to tell you this, Florine. But Gretchen says if you don't go back to LifeLine, Inc., you can't stay at the house."

"What? That's ridiculous! I'm clean and sober and giving you guys one-third of my income for room and board just the way I'm supposed to. What more does she want?"

"And if you don't finish the program here, she won't vouch for your sobriety, which means you'll have a hard time getting Raven out of foster care."

Florine glared suspiciously. "What's that supposed to mean? Are you saying they won't give Raven back?"

"It's possible."

"But she's my daughter! They can't not give her back!"

"I'm afraid they can, Florine."

Florine's face turned red, then white. She started to sweat. "I don't believe you, Gillian. DSS can't keep Raven for good. It's against the law!"

"No, actually it's not. Remember that we're talking about a state agency here, one with clout in the courtroom. The fact is, they make the rules and you have to play by them. It's their game, Florine."

"But I put Raven in foster care voluntarily! Just so I could come here and do this stupid program. I told them the placement was temporary, just the six months I'd be in this halfway house. And they told me, 'No problem. We're here to support you. When you're clean and sober, you can get her back'!"

"What they didn't tell you," I said sadly, "is that you have to meet a set of minimum requirements before your daughter will be returned to you. You have to have decent housing and a decent income, for starters. You have to prove that you can *support* Raven at a level the court deems satisfactory. Making minimum wage, you'll never be able to get an apartment around here. Forget all the other requirements. And if you've *also* been kicked out of Responsibility House, you'll have no way to prove to them that you're really clean and sober. What do you suppose will happen then?"

"That isn't fair!" Florine wailed. "I'm doing everything I said I'd do! I'm staying clean and working at an honest job! I'm trying to be a better person!"

"Florine, that may not be enough."

"Well, fuck you!" Florine bellowed, rising from her chair like a nuclear mushroom cloud. "Fuck Gretchen! Fuck DSS! You all lied to me! You're all a bunch of stupid cunts! Fuck the whole damn world!"

"Look, I know you're feeling really ang—"

"Oh, shut up, bitch. I swear, if you say one more word, I'll smash your face."

I took a deep breath and made a mental note: Stop using the I-know-you're-feeling-really-(fill in the blank)-right-now line. "Florine," I said gently, "isn't there some way you could go back to LifeLine, Inc.?"

"No," she said morosely, sinking back into the chair. "I can't possibly go back. You have no idea what it's like. It's a sick, disgusting place—"

Yes, it was strange to hear this judgment coming from the mouth of a woman who gave unprotected blow jobs to pool-hall scumbags behind dumpsters in oil-slick alleys in a drizzling Fall River rain. But I sort of understood her point, which she went on, in any case, to clarify.

"—The people there are so fucked up. One morning a lady complained for an *hour* because a family on her street painted their house a color she didn't like. And the color was yellow! I'm not kidding! And at the end of the day, she was still mad about it! I mean, how can people *live* that way? They just hate and hate. And judge and judge. And they couldn't get enough of hating and judging me. I felt so out of place there I thought I was losing my mind. I'll never go back there, Gillian. It's just not possible. I don't care what Gretchen says. I'd rather go to jail."

I blinked rapidly a few times. I was in a bad jam. I had told Gretchen that Florine had *already* returned to LifeLine, Inc. What was I going to say now?

Florine was in a world of her own, muttering. "I'll get Raven back. One way or another. They can't keep her. They don't own her. She's my kid, the bastards. They have no right."

"OK, Florine. I'll do whatever I can to help." I felt horrible. I hadn't asked Gretchen nearly enough questions. I hadn't found out, for example, what the hell she was even talking about. Did she really *mean* it when she said DSS might not give Raven back? Could they really *do* that? Why had I told Florine a very upsetting thing that I didn't actually know to be true?

Florine mumbled, "I'll kidnap her if I have to."

"That would not be wise," I said sharply. "That's a very bad idea. No, no, no. You don't want to do that."

Florine gave me a look of pitying disparagement, as though it were patently obvious that I had, as she might say, "the *cojones* of a pussy" and was therefore not even remotely equipped to give advice on desperate matters. I felt the last drops of my power over her (had I ever had any?) drain away, and there rose in my imagination a technicolor film strip of Florine and Janet in spats and leather holsters, kicking down the door of a split-level ranch in the suburbs, Janet splattering rounds of ammunition everywhere, shooting up the kitchen cabinets and the plaid upholstered couch in the family room, with all the little hearts and homey things jumping and popping off the end tables and the entertainment center's veneer shelves. Eight-year-old Raven tears away from the terrified foster mom and dives into her prodigal parent's outstretched arms. Raven and Florine weep and clutch; their black ponytails commingle. "I always knew you'd come for me, Mommy," Raven says. Florine takes Raven out to the driveway, where Janet's huge Harley is pointed westward, humming like an eagle. Janet shoots up a few more things because she feels like it, spins her revolvers on her index fingers, shoves them into thigh-high holsters, and, tipping just the brim of her leather hat to the foster mother, says, "Sorry for the damage, ma'am. Send the bill to DSS." Then they all jump on the bike and disappear in a cloud of exhaust.

When I came out of my reverie, I noticed that Florine's face wore the most sober expression I'd ever seen on it. "I can make money, if that's what they want. Back in Fall River, I got plenty of johns. Rich ones, too. They love me to death, the poor babies. I'll raise my rates."

"No!" I protested. "Please don't even think that way! Fall River is bad for you. All your drug friends are there. There'll be pressure on you to use and, more to the point, you can't list income from prostitution on a state custody form. They'll lock you up!"

"Oh, get real. Hookers don't go to jail. They blow the judge."

"Stop it, Florine."

Her red lips settled into a wobbly dash. Her face looked gray and slack. She stared glumly at the window, which was pitch black and reflected only us. Two women with nothing in common. One who made sex a business; the other who couldn't get laid.

"This is your fault, Gillian," she said at last.

I looked miserably at my ink-stained hands. "You're right. I urged you to quit. I should have talked to Gretchen first. I'm sorry, Florine."

She stared at the window for a few more moments. Finally she sighed. "Look, my DSS caseworker never said anything about any minimum requirements, and I can't believe she wouldn't have told me something as important as that. I know Gretchen's trying to do some good here, with this house, but I also know she's totally prejudiced against me; she has been since the day I got here. A lot of women hate prostitutes, you know. And Gretchen also hates gays. I can see it in her face. Why do you think she passed me off to you for counseling? Me and Janet? She's giving you what she can't handle, her queers. Maybe she thinks we're the only ones, but we're not; we're just more out than the others who are here.

"Stacy's a different story, of course. She's not a lesbian; she's a Nazi. Gretchen would rather hire her than help her. Because if she had to help Stacy she might have to face what a fucked-up, sadistic little prick Stacy is, how totally psycho. And I'm a hooker, Gillian. Believe me, I know psycho. That's why Gretchen gave Stacy to you for counseling. So you could be the one tortured by her personality while she gets all the glory of Stacy's anal ways."

Florine took a long, ragged breath. This speech was obviously coming from down deep. "So you just tell Gretchen two things for me, OK? Tell her I'm not leaving my job at the bakery. I'm going to stay there and learn how to bake. She can kick me out if she wants to, if she's got the balls. And tell her she's got no business even mentioning my daughter anymore. If I want advice from someone, I'll call my caseworker at DSS. And you better believe I'll be on the phone with her first thing tomorrow to find out how much of this shit is really true."

I gulped. "Is there anything I can do?"

"You can start by admitting you don't know shit. You're in over your head."

"I don't know shit. I know I don't know shit." Gretchen wouldn't want me to admit that, but it was the honest thing to say. "I'm really sorry, Florine."

"All right. You've apologized. Now don't make things worse by feeling sorry for yourself. Working at a bakery was a good idea, Gillian. Actually, it was a very good idea. I like my job. I feel good when I get up in the morning, which for me is a fucking miracle. You *helped* me, OK?"

"OK."

Florine got up and moved to the door. She suddenly looked older and burdened and dignified. She looked me right in the eye. "Next week then. Same bat time."

I don't know what I had really thought of her before, whether I'd cast her as a character in a comic strip or merely some kind of featherbrained, Dolly Parton wannabe. But it was time to change my opinion of Florine. She had put her daughter in foster care so she could get off dope, and she had Gretchen's number right down to the extension. On several occasions during the last few weeks, when I had attempted to obey Gretchen's orders by prying into the subject of her and Janet, she had blown me off as if I were the paper wrapper on a straw. In short, she was not the booby floozy I thought she was. It made me a little jealous to think that maybe she deserved Janet's love, that maybe Janet wanted her love in return. Maybe it went deeper than I'd thought, their clandestine affair. Maybe it was the real thing.

———

On the night of Friday, December 7, I pedaled to work musing about Maria. Some of the residents thought that her persistent silence and nonstop appliance cleaning were strange. They had asked whether the house intended to take any remedial actions. I had discussed the situation with Gretchen, who explained that Maria had been diagnosed with moderate depression and put on medication. Beyond watching for signs of a worsening of that condition, she said, there wasn't much the house could do. Maria was staying sober and working on her GED. (This was why she was usually home early enough to begin making dinner before the others got there.) Most likely, Gretchen said, Maria would speak when she had something to say.

I told the concerned residents that the house was taking a wait-and-see approach to Maria's odd behavior. They were unimpressed. Amalia, her roommate, said that she felt spooked by Maria and sometimes couldn't sleep. Others insisted that Maria was making them feel crazier than they already were.

It seemed important to address the problem somehow, but it wasn't until I saw the tiny smile that crept across Maria's face while I was reminding the residents of the no-sex-while-in-residence rule that a strategy took shape. Obviously, Maria heard what was being said around her, and she was intelligent enough to discern subtle strains of humor. Thus, it made sense simply to keep talking to her — loudly, cheerfully, without invitation or apology — with the goal of provoking another reaction. So, each evening for the last seven nights, when I arrived for work, I had made a point of spending a few minutes in the kitchen, regaling Maria with robust sound bites of information — the day's weather forecast, political updates of a decidedly liberal slant, or whatever amusing newsy tidbits had come to my attention during the day. I was sure that Maria would eventually respond to my steady verbal assault with a bit of her own free speech, and that when she did, something of true significance would be revealed.

On that particular evening, I was eager to share a human-interest story I had found that morning in *The Globe*. It was about the wife-carrying contests that are staged annually in the Finnish countryside.* The minute I read about this blithe folkloric custom, I knew it was just the thing to tickle Maria's fancy, but when I entered the house I encountered something so unusual and noteworthy that the whole idea of wife-carrying made a bee-line out of my brain.

The kitchen was filled with the smell of garlic. Red and green peppers and yellow-skinned onions, clumps of fresh parsley and oregano, were strewn across the counter. Maria in her black dress, one small dimpled hand wrapped around a knife and the strong sausage arm it was attached to moving in an energetic rhythm, was chopping and tossing vegetables into a simmering pot. After months of the watery bottled stuff, she was making real tomato sauce.

"Whoa!" I cried. "What's this?"

Maria said nothing. She did not even turn around.

"Garlic has numerous health benefits!" I crowed. "In fact, plants of the genus *Allium* are used medicinally in many parts of the world!"

Maria's knife paused, so I knew she heard me. I couldn't help squinting for a moment, fearing a wet slap of lettuce in my face perhaps, but no disrespectful edible gesture was forthcoming. Relieved and gratified by the happy turn of events, I proceeded to the second-floor office, whistling a jaunty tune.

I was recording the miracle of Maria's tomato sauce in the log—waxing on about the positive ethnic identification clearly symbolized by her choice—when someone knocked. I opened the door. Janet stood there, grinning with submissive hope. She

---

* Wife-carrying, for those who need to be told, is a feat of marital athleti-cism best carried out by a burly husband and a tiny, birdlike wife. The wife is cradled like a bundle of kindling in the husband's arms, or slung across his back like a sheaf of arrows, or hung on his body in any number of strange ac-robatic postures, which change regularly to relieve stress on his muscles, so that watching one of these contests must be a little like thumbing through a fully-clothed-for-cold-weather version of the Kama Sutra. Busily rotating and revolving his pliant spouse, the husband jumps over logs, bounds through thickets, and, if necessary, paddles across freezing lakes. The wife does ab-solutely nothing, the husband does absolutely everything, until finally they come, twig-whipped and burr-bedraggled, to the finish (ha-ha) line.

had made several more attempts at rapprochement since she'd tried to make a fool of me by goading Meg into reporting fake Catholic hallucinations. On each occasion, although my slow heart had wanted to forgive her, my nimble pride had scrambled to its feet first and I had put her off, either by shutting the office door in her face or patronizing her with icy cold professionalism. I probably would have done the same again but for one thing: Beside her stood Gustave. His presence was so unexpected and created such a nervous reaction in me that my eyes lost focus and saw nothing but gray fuzz.

"Would you excuse us, please?" I said with sweet clumsiness as soon as I could see right again. I grabbed Janet's forearm, pulled her into the office, and shut the door. "What do you mean by bringing this person into this house?" I hissed.

"What's the matter?"

"He's a man!"

"What's wrong with that?"

"It's against the rules!"

"Being a man?"

"Don't get smart with me," I warned. It was horrible to find myself using my father's horrible phrase. "Men are not allowed inside Responsibility House without special permission from the director. You should know that, Janet. It's on page one hundred twenty-seven of the *Handbook of Policies & Procedures*."

Janet frowned thoughtfully. "I don't get it. Why not?"

"I'm not exactly sure," I admitted. "But it probably has something to do with promiscuous sex."

"What if I tell him to keep his clothes on?"

"No! You have to get him out of here right now!"

"OK. But he isn't here to see a resident anyway. He wants to see you."

"*Me?*" My heart screeched to a stop. "Why me?"

"He said he wants you to interview him for your book."

"For the last time, I am *not* writing a book! I am *supposed* to be writing a dissertation, but I am no longer writing the one I told you about. In fact, at the moment I'm not writing *any* dissertation at all and may never write one as long as I live!"

"Maybe you should tell him that yourself," Janet said.

"You tell him." I felt like a child who, facing a frightening obstacle, says to her friend, *You go first.*

"He came to see *you*, Gillian. Specifically." She cocked her head playfully and raised one eyebrow a quarter inch.

I took a few steps back as the possible implications of this statement dawned. Was Janet insinuating that Gustave wasn't here as a spiritually converted person, that he was here as a notorious womanizer *posing* as a converted person? Had she brought him to my door *knowing* that? "For shame," I told her bluntly. "Isn't it bad enough that you sent Meg to pull that stupid stunt? Does your treachery know no bounds?"

"No, really. I'm serious this time. He's been asking me questions about you ever since I told him you were a professor. He's really interested in the kind of stuff you were telling me about—you know, people seeing God. What can I say? He's a weird guy. He reads poetry and shit."

I decided to let her obviously willful misunderstanding of my title go by just this once. Pulling her down by her shoulder to my level, I whispered in her ear, "And what about that other attribute you mentioned the last time we discussed him? Do you think that some of his supposed 'interest' may spring from a nonintellectual source?"

"Hell if I know. I didn't ask him. Look, he comes with a warning label. So what? You're a big girl, aren't you?"

Maybe it was being called *big* that gave me courage. I took a moment to compose myself and then opened the door. "Hello, Gustave. How are you?"

He was leaning with a hint of insolence against the wall, and his face wore a look of faintly amused uncertainty. His hair, which had appeared impressive in moonglow, looked a bit stringier in indoor light. But the coarse, shoulder-length curls still struck me as provocative. His eyes were deeply, truly blue and were looking right at me.

"I-I appreciate your interest in my work," I stammered. "Unfortunately, I am no longer involved in the project Janet described and must ask you to vacate the premises immediately."

He frowned and shifted his weight slightly. Stubble on his chin and long sideburns gave him a rather thrilling air of debauchery.

Noises were coming from downstairs. The women tended to mill about in the kitchen after work, swapping the day's anecdotes. Those who had been brought up poorly (*all*, I might as well say) filched before-dinner snacks. This was also a time when many residents changed their clothes. As I finished speaking to Gustave, I heard footsteps on the stairs. A resident in need of a new outfit was en route to her room! In a matter of seconds, she would walk directly into Gustave standing in the hallway. His presence would instantly become a subject of curiosity and discussion for all. In short order, the news of it would worm its way to Stacy and from there to Gretchen O'Neil.

"On the other hand," I said brightly, "why don't you come right in?" I gripped his wrist, yanked him into the room, and shut the door so fast it almost knocked him over. Then I spun quickly on one heel and leaned against the door frame with what I hoped was a certain *je ne sais quoi.*

"I won't bother introducing you," Janet said. "I remember you did a pretty good job of that yourselves a while ago."

"I hope you don't mind me coming by," Gustave said, briefly massaging his wrist.

"Oh, no. I'm glad you're here!"

"You are?" He looked confused and hopeful.

"Absolutely."

"What I have to say won't take long."

"I insist that you stay at least an hour." I figured it would take that long for the residents to finish dinner and disperse.

Gustave, looking very bewildered now, motioned for me to take the desk chair. I motioned for him to take it. After several rounds, he sat down in it, and I perched on the windowsill, my back to the draft. Janet was occupying the bedspread-covered armchair.

"I was thinking about your book," he said.

I saw no point in correcting him.

"If you're still looking for people to interview, maybe I could help."

"How? Do you know converted people?"

He bobbled his head a bit. Was it embarrassment? "I was thinking of myself."

"You consider yourself converted?"

"I think so. I mean, I used to be different. I did some bad things."

"Yes, I know. You said you were involved in drug trafficking."

"That's pretty bad, isn't it?"

Did he really need confirmation? "I think it qualifies."

"I did some other bad things, too."

"Really?"

"Yeah. Pretty bad." He shrugged as if weighing the options. "Really bad, I mean."

I gulped. What did he mean by *really bad?* I raised my eyebrows very high to indicate continued interest and hide an upsurge of fear.

"I guess you could say I had a bad life," he concluded.

"Well, then. OK."

"But I changed, you know? Now my life is good."

"Aha." I smiled broadly, signaling great happiness.

"I thought maybe you could put my story in your book."

A pulse of naked vulnerability passed across his face. I could see him harden his cheek muscles and jaw against it. Then his eyes softened, and he looked at me a little sadly.

How could I refuse?

I took a pen and pad of paper out of my backpack. "Let's start with your name and address," I said.

His first memories were of breaking glass. He remembered other noises, too, of course—his father yelling, his mother yelling, the blare of the TV. The breaking glass was different, though. It was a high, clear ripple of sound that seemed to come from far away. It could have been a bell trying to signal something. To him it always meant that whatever was happening should end.

Soon he was old enough to follow his brother out to the playground. The sounds on the street could be dull or roaring, but they were always impersonal and therefore easier to endure than the sounds of home. The graffiti around the playground were the words and pictures of rage. Rage was on the streets, too, in the carjackings, break-ins, holdups, and muggings. Even old women who had lived in the neighborhood since their immigrant days were not exempt. Locals called the place Lynn, Lynn, City of Sin.

As a teenager he occasionally found refuge in the cool, impersonal library. He liked to read books now and then, but mostly he needed a place to sit and examine his thoughts. He thought a lot. He wondered why he had been born. He wasn't depressed; he just wanted to know. He figured there could be many answers or one or none. It seemed that to find out, a person would have to be able to hold a lot of things in his mind at once—everything in the library maybe. In any case, more than he could ever know.

Sometimes he filched paper from the library copier and doodled the way he had as a child. With little effort he produced detailed, pencil-drawn comic strips full of angry men with fists in the air and shrieking fat women and old men with stooped backs and mouths filled with insincere pleas. All around them would be people running, climbing out of windows, falling from fire escapes, being flung from crashing cars. The stories were of madness and survival.

Once he went to the reference desk and asked the librarian for something to read. His dark tight curls and burning eyes must have reminded her of desperate genius because she handed him Allen Ginsberg's book of poems written around the time Gustave was born. Gustave read about the chaos he knew and had known, but the book gave no solutions. He handed it back to the librarian, unimpressed. What he wanted was the opposite of Allen Ginsberg. He wanted clarity. To be able to look at the world and know what he was looking at. Not to own it or control it, just to be free of it.

On the beach he saw girls walking under leaden winter skies, their hair whipping their faces. They walked together in a tight clump like nervous zebras that didn't want to be separated from the pack. He watched the way they swept their hair off their necks and off their wet lips where tendrils had stuck. He noticed their clothes, their cheap jewelry, and the things they did to their faces to be attractive. He wanted to get close to the laughter and emotion that bubbled through their bodies, but they didn't pay much attention to him then.

His grandfather owned a boxing gym, and Gustave—five feet five inches and one hundred thirty pounds—started to train there as a lightweight. His grandfather had come from Germany and didn't talk about the past. The advice he gave Gustave on boxing was the most he had said to anyone in his family for years. Gustave was eighteen; he wanted to please his grandfather. It seemed that history demanded of him that he make something come out right.

He started boxing in amateur matches that forty or fifty people would attend. Invariably, in the seventh or eighth round, when the sounds and lights faded in his consciousness and all he could feel was the pounding of muscle, bone, and blood, an image of his father's face would slide over the face of his opponent, and a fury that seemed to come from hell would rise in Gustave's chest. The bell would clang, and it would be time to stop. But his father never stopped at the bell, and neither would he.

Gustave would have to be pulled off his opponent, and he would strain in the arms of his handlers until the signal was given to begin again. But just when he was about to take the victory he'd earned—when his opponent was reeling away from him, gloved hands covering his face, and the entire audience was yelling for Gustave to finish the job—a memory would come to him of a morning a few years before when he had been awakened by an unfamiliar sound and had gone into the kitchen to find his father slumped over the table, sobbing, while the sun rose outside the window in a watery pinkish glow. Gustave had not been able to speak to his father or even to wonder why he was sitting there. Gustave had simply gone back to bed. And yet the memory, which seemed to mean nothing, would make him lose the will to fight.

"A veakling you are. Not with the heart of a boxer," Gustave's grandfather said.

Gustave had finished high school. He was not interested in most of the employment he could get. Someone offered him a waiter's job. It meant decent tips, a cheap dinner, and the freedom to do what he wanted during the days. But he found out that he didn't know what to do with his days, and in any case the job soon became unbearable. It was the details that got to him: the chefs cursing in the kitchen, the clanging pots and clattering dishes, the smell of frying beef and butter and boiling vegetable oil. The high false laughter of people eating expensive meals. The balled cloth napkin into which a diner had spit olive pits, the smear of garish lipstick on the rim of a half-filled cup. Clearing plates that people had eaten from made him feel weak and faithless. He started to avoid eye contact with others, lost muscle tone, and put on weight. He grew his hair for reasons he was not aware of and was told to get it off his face. His ears rang with a silent scream that started in the morning and didn't end until he was asleep.

Two friends worked at the restaurant, Lisa and Kim. He liked them but felt crowded by them. They wanted him to make love to both of them, one after the other, and he did. Then he would let them be and not go back till he was ready, till he could be with them on his own terms, and this seemed to make them want him even more. He became absorbed by sex. He learned that it was exalting and demeaning. It could feel as if the history of the world and all its art and music were filling and overflowing his body. At the same time, he knew that what he was experiencing was just the play of nerve endings and the firing of visual receptors in the male brain.

He was too old to run away (he'd done that a few times before) and too honest to fall in love. He was not the type to enlist. Lisa and Kim started finding fault with him. He kept seeing one or both of them longer than he should have.

His brother asked him to hold six pounds of marijuana, which was nothing. All he had to do was drop it off at a certain place. He took money for it, money that was supposed to go to his brother, but when he saw how much it was, he cut himself in to the upper level of the fledgling business with a sibling's natural leverage and a veiled blackmail threat. That was how it started. It wasn't long before he was involved in other illicit substances. First he acquired material trappings that brought him into debt despite his earnings, and the next thing he knew he had women, a twitch, and enemies. He still went to the library on occasion to find out what he was thinking, but the inner voice was either dull and sluggish or an angry, manic rant. It was like listening to a telephone connection that became increasingly broken and scrambled until, finally, it went dead.

From then on, he lived his life the way so many people he knew did, as though it were happening to someone else. He had always secretly believed in destiny; now he realized it was a joke. The course of a person's life was beyond his ability to shape. This way of thinking was primitive, he knew; it was probably nothing more than a way of distancing himself from his acts. But believing it was sometimes the only thing that kept him from putting a bullet through his own or someone else's head.

Eventually he entered a police station and pled guilty to a crime less serious than the ones he had actually committed. The sentence was light because the police were negligent, and the lawyer was better than he'd had a right to hope for.

The man who came in twice a week to run the prison library was a priest. "Has anyone read all the books in this place?" Gustave asked him one day, knowing that the question was gibberish. The priest said that Nathaniel Hawthorne had set out to read all the books in the Salem library. He thought he needed to know everything so he could write a masterpiece. But he soon discovered that the job was too big and all he would ever have was a few drops of knowledge and fewer of wisdom, which nevertheless turned out to be enough. The priest said that a person is like a cell in the collective heart. We each contribute what we know and feel and believe, and the cataclysms of history are the forces for good and evil that we have created as a group. The priest gave Homer, Shakespeare, and Yeats to Gustave. He read them and was moved. He went back to Allen Ginsberg and saw that the poet had depicted truthfully all the chaos Gustave had known.

Sitting in a jail cell, he had come to the place he had wanted to be in all along.

Gustave stopped talking. He and Janet exchanged a quiet smile.

I put down my pen. The whole time he talked, I had been scribbling notes. Now I looked at him, really looked at him, and thought how impossible it would be to describe him on paper.

Janet shifted in her seat, leaned forward to get my attention. "Does that do it for you, Gillian? I mean, is that what you had in mind?"

"Yes, but I have a few questions if Gustave doesn't mind."

"Go ahead," he said.

"It's clear that reading great works of literature over a period of months or possibly years made a favorable impression on you," I began.

"It was a couple of years. And it wasn't just that—"

"Fine. But did you have an epiphany?"

"What do you mean?"

"A brief, dramatic, spiritual-seeming event when your life was completely changed."

"Well, no. Not exactly."

"I mean *inside*, Gustave. In your soul. Was there a moment or moments when you repudiated the destructive course you were on and reached out, willingly, with conscious intent, to grasp the path of light and sanity?"

Gustave frowned, which made his eyes as dark as the ocean in winter. "I don't think so."

OK. I was disappointed, but I didn't push it. I tried another tack. "What was it like, inside you, during the bad years?"

"It was gray. No color, no shape. I was barely alive."

An artist would say it that way, I thought. "Did you believe in God?"

"I didn't not believe."

"Have you ever experienced a divine or supernatural presence?"

"What do you mean?"

"Visions, voices, apparitions, or the like."

"I ate magic mushrooms a few times and saw some really strange shit."

"Did you see God?"

"Not that I remember."

I sighed in frustration. Clearly his conversion had not been dramatic. At least it was secular.

"I wouldn't want to see God," Gustave continued.

"Why not?"

"I don't know. I just wouldn't."

Hmm. There had to be some way to crack him open and get at the essence of this thing. "To what besides great literature do you attribute your remarkable turnaround?"

"I always wanted something, I guess. I don't know." He shrugged and looked uncomfortable.

"That's it?"

"Yeah. That's it." Folding his arms across his chest, he looked around the room with mild curiosity. Janet was untwisting the fringe on the hem of the bedspread. The air in the room had gone a little flat.

The interview had not been particularly useful, I thought. Here was the best example I'd had so far of a secular conversion experience, but there seemed to have been no specifically spiritual galvanizing force. Was he lying, I wondered, or embarrassed to talk intimately, or, like so many people, simply incapable of articulating his deepest, most profound experiences? Yet I was not as disappointed as I could have been. I felt a strange sort of privilege in his presence, which may have been caused by nothing more than the fact that he had favored me with his life story. And, of course, I was impressed by the way his hair caressed his relatively broad shoulders when he turned his head ever so slightly.

"I'm glad," I told Gustave.

"For what?"

"That you came. That you're OK."

He smiled, and his eyes seemed especially friendly. "So am I."

Janet walked with him to the door. I wanted them both to stay longer, but I didn't know how to hold them. They left together, a strangely attractive pair—Janet in leather and a boy's unruly cowlick, Gustave in a T-shirt and curls.

My world felt unreal for a moment. Who was I, really? What subject was I toying with? Did I want to sleep with one or both or neither? Why hadn't I remembered to say either thank you or good-bye?

———

"Gillian, was there a *man* upstairs?" Gretchen was waiting for me in the office on Monday, wearing a camel twin set that was not cashmere. She looked irritated.

A *man?* For a minute I couldn't grasp the meaning of this word. She made it sound like a newly discovered unstable element, one that could blow up in your face. Then I remembered the rule. "It was just Gustave," I said.

"Sounds like a man."

"I guess he is."

"Men are allowed in Responsibility House only with permission from the Director. And they are never allowed on the second floor!" Gretchen said in a snappy, commando voice. "Who is Gustave and what was he here for?"

A month before, I would have blurted that he was a friend of Janet's, but a newer, more sophisticated impulse made me lie. "He's a friend of mine. We were just talking," I said.

"About what?"

"Religion."

"Oh my God, Gillian. You're not supposed to have colleagues over when you're working!"

"No, I understand. He stopped by to pick up a book, that's all."

"OK, well. Don't do it again, all right? The women get flustered when men come into the house. Some of them are walking to the bathroom with bathrobes on, you know?"

"Sure," I said. "Sorry." But what she had said didn't ring true. The women I knew didn't give a hoot if a man walked into the house. In fact, they'd probably like it and if he was at all good-looking would soon be trying to seduce him. So who was telling Gretchen about a sinister male? My grasp of interpersonal intrigue was coming along so nicely that I was able to translate my suspicion into a question right then and there. "Was anyone in particular flustered?"

"Stacy was really upset," Gretchen said. "She talked to me about it this morning before she went to work. She said she thought the man was selling drugs. And she said *Janet* brought him in."

"Oh, no. Janet may have come home at the same time, but she

didn't bring him into the house. And Gustave doesn't sell drugs. He's clean as a whistle. In fact, he's a Seventh-Day Adventist!"

"Well, maybe you can reassure Stacy if you see her. Sorry if I sounded kind of bitchy just now, Gillian. I'm having a terrible week. The state budget crisis is unbelievable. If the governor has his way, we'll be closing our doors soon." Gretchen sighed. "I'm thinking a lot about going into private practice. All my friends tell me I should. They say I'm getting depressed working here. And they're right, in a way. I'm more exhausted and pessimistic all the time. But I can't bear to let Responsibility House go down the tubes. I'm really hoping this Washington trip will make a difference."

"When are you going?"

"I'll be leaving as soon as Stacy comes on board, and I'll be gone until just before Christmas. Stacy will be in charge during the days, and you'll be in charge at night. I'll leave the hotel number."

"We'll be fine."

"When I get back, I'm planning to transfer a lot of the paperwork and managerial stuff to her and dedicate myself to lobbying and fundraising. There may be no other way to keep this place afloat. But I have no experience in fundraising. I don't know where to begin!" She seemed ready to cry.

I reached up and patted her soft camel shoulder. "Go home and get some rest. And try not to think about it any more today."

Responsibility House isn't the only thing about to go down the tubes, I thought after Gretchen left. I had received a note from Dean Trubow earlier that day. He wanted to see me in his office that Friday, December 14, my deadline for becoming a well-behaved scholar. He'd had my paper entitled "Seven Secular Conversion Experiences" for almost a week, plenty of time to read it and confer with the Committee. There were two possibilities: (1) The members of the Committee were so impressed that they wanted to shake my hand and shower more stipends upon me. (2) They were going to give me the ax.

Anxiety flooded my body. My breath grew shallow, and my cranial neurons began to singe. Sensing a narcoleptic attack, I sat down, put my head between my knees, and took deep breaths.

When the spell had passed, I picked up my head and looked around. The room seemed unaccountably different. There were the battered file cabinet, the institutional metal desk, the flattened armchair where residents poured out their mostly prosaic troubles and the occasional splatter of rot-gut spleen, the dirty braided rug, the walls plastered with notices, official state licenses, and fire escape procedures, the cheap bookshelves, sagging with conference proceedings, textbooks on addiction, and pamphlets about STDs, the brittle ivy on the windowsill that refused to die. It was a messy, ugly, hardworking room. It suited me somehow. For the first time I thought, I care about this place. I don't want it to go down the tubes. I don't want me to go down the tubes either. I don't want Janet, Florine, Maria, Meg, Varkeesha, Chris, Amalia, and the other four residents (Stacy conspicuously excluded) to go down the tubes. I want us all (OK, Stacy too) to thrive.

All weekend I'd thought about Gustave. I kept remembering the way his eyes slid away and then back to my face as he was talking, the way his irises were circled by a dramatic rim of darker blue. Had I written off the interview too hastily? Maybe there *had* been a specifically spiritual galvanizing force that I simply wasn't aware of. He had given me his name and address at the start of our interview, and I had committed them to memory without even trying. Now I found myself slipping the telephone directory from the shelf and locating his street on the map inside the back cover. I skimmed the phone listings, too, but his number wasn't there, and then I quickly closed the book, embarrassed by the acuteness of my interest in him. He hadn't asked me to go for a walk or anything like that after our interview, and I hadn't had the presence of mind or the courage to ask him. The only way I could imagine being brave enough to contact him was if I could say that I needed a more thorough interview with him for my dissertation. So now there was even more riding on what Dean Trubow would tell me on the fourteenth.

I pushed the telephone directory back into its place on the bookshelf, sighing. Then I drew a deep, surprisingly happy breath. Clearly, it was time to forgive Janet. In bringing me Gustave, she had paid the debt she'd incurred with that awful talking-lawn-statue thing. I was glad that I hadn't expelled her when I was supposed to and that on several occasions I'd thrown Gretchen off her scent. My faith in her had proven justified, I thought. There'd been no whiff of suspicion surrounding her sobriety since my discovery of the beer cans and Stacy's hostile remark about weed, and no further evidence of a sexual liaison between her and Florine since the incendiary photo surfaced a few weeks before. It seemed possible for me once again to speak to her about my work, especially when she seemed so eager to be a part of it. There was no reason to put off a reconciliation. I tucked my button-down, pinstriped shirt into my nylon athletic pants, smoothed my sticking-out hair, and walked across the hall.

I knocked. No answer. There was noise, however, coming from the room. It sounded like distant bleating, as if a sheep were lost on a moor. My first instinct was to go away, since the inhabitant of the room was choosing not to answer. But neither was she choosing to stifle her cries, and it would be cruel of me to leave a fellow human in that quiet distress. I knocked again, gently, to communicate how much I wanted to be sensitive and non-intrusive, but persistent in offering solace nonetheless. The moan continued; in fact, it rose in pitch. It could not be Janet. The voice wasn't hers.

"Meg?" I called with concern. "Meg, dear, may I come in?"

The moan gave way to a warbling sound. There was a scrambling noise, the sound of furniture being moved, and I had the awful thought that poor sweet Meg was tying her neck with a bedsheet to the ceiling fan and was just now about to kick away the chair, so I threw open the door, on which for purposes of surveillance there was no lock, and took two steps into the room.

Florine was naked as a jaybird, lying spread-eagled on Janet's bed. Janet was perched on the end of the mattress, gently holding Florine's curved right foot. She was fully clothed in flannel and denim, but her shoes and socks were off, her back was oddly stooped over, and there was a vulture-ish hang to her plumed head.

If I'd had more time, I might have wondered why my image of them in that moment contained five bird allusions, but I could not process anything just then; I was experiencing a mental tsunami, an electrochemical crash.

"Ah," I gasped. Black clouds billowed down the corridors of my mind. I smelled singed wires, hard metals, and asbestos dust. I groped for a chant, but it had been several weeks since I needed one. I had the impression they were stored in a faraway attic of my mind. There was movement around me—perhaps Janet leaping from the end of the bed. But she was not in time to catch me. I was unconscious before I hit the floor.

When I came to, my head was lying near the center of the office rug. My feet were lying a short distance away, pointed toward the door. Janet and Florine were kneeling side by side next to my body. They looked anxious, guilty, and uncomfortably erect, like a pair of Catholic penitents.

I fluttered my eyelids to let them know I was conscious.

"Thank God. You're back," they said, clasping hands.

The waistband on my nylon athletic pants was not of good quality, and, presumably during the process of my being dragged out of Janet's bedroom, across the hall, and into the office, the fabric had slid a few inches down my hips. I awkwardly pulled up one side, then the other, and was gratified to find that I had feeling in all four limbs.

I tried to rise to a sitting position, but some dizziness remained from my spell, so I let my head and upper body fall back onto the rug. "You two are in big trouble," I said, noticing the yellowed ceiling paint.

"Please don't tell Gretchen!" Florine whispered urgently. She had wrapped herself in a sickly pink bathrobe with bunnies on it. It must have been Meg's.

"The rules are the rules," I said sternly.

"Easy," Janet said. "You're too weak to talk."

"I bet you wish I were," I said sarcastically, trying to rise again. This time my head was more willing to be vertical. I sat cross-legged on the floor for a few seconds, breathing as mindfully as humanly possible, then crawled onto my legs, which held up long enough for me to take a few steps and flop into the desk chair.

Janet and Florine were still kneeling together on the rug. The look on their faces was unlike anything I'd ever seen, even on my own. Terror. Trembling. Abject fear. As I regarded them from my superior position, which only moments before had been subservient, I realized how easy it would be to get drunk with power, to justify convincingly whatever way I used it, and then, having abused it a few or hundreds of time, how nearly impossible it would be ever to give it up.

I didn't want that much power. I didn't want to rule them.

They were adults, after all, though they didn't always act that way. Two strong, flawed women who had made good and bad choices, who, though just a few years older than myself, had already won and lost more than I'd ever had. I couldn't deny the fact that I admired them, that I longed for some of their lust and courage to rub off on me.

"Get off the floor," I said.

They rose. Janet sat in the flowered chair and Florine sat, of all places, in her lap. Janet put a protective arm around her lover, her chosen one. The one with big breasts, cheap makeup, and a hairpiece. The one who wasn't and never would be me.

"So, am I going back to prison," Janet asked casually, as if my power in that moment meant nothing to her, as if prison meant nothing, as if it were a lark.

Florine said sadly, "I probably *will* lose Raven now."

"Why do you take such foolish risks?" I asked them.

They looked troubled. They didn't answer. It was obvious they didn't know.

"All you had to do was wait a few months," I continued coldly, "until you graduated from this house. Then, Janet, your parole restrictions would be looser, and Raven would be living with you, Florine. You could screw all day and night, if that's what you wanted, without risking your freedom or your children, which, by the way, are important things—or haven't you noticed? They're the kinds of things you can't always get back."

Both heads pointed down. Both sets of shoulders slumped. The wail of a siren came through the window. Florine must have thought it was coming for Janet, because she laid her ear on the top of Janet's head and whispered, "I'll always love you, babe."

Janet rubbed her cheek into the curve of Florine's neck. "Yeah, same here."

I couldn't have stood this scene much longer. It wasn't just jealousy; it was confusion. I didn't know who I was. Was I really supposed to be policeman, judge, jury, and executioner? If so, why had I agreed to play such a monstrous role when all I really wanted was to say, "Go in peace, my sisters"?

I managed to utter at least part of what I felt. "Go."

Janet glanced up quickly. Her greeny-brown eyes registered surprise. "You're letting us go?"

"I don't know what I'm doing. I'm just asking . . . if you would leave."

Florine slid off Janet's lap with alacrity, pulled the bathrobe tighter across her big chest and skinny hips, deftly cinched the terry-cloth belt. "Um, OK," she said.

Janet stood up, and I was struck once again by her size and strength, by the sense I got, from just being near her, of opportunity all around. She frowned at me. "Hey, are you OK?"

She was probably referring to my bout of narcolepsy. I looked frankly into her eyes. "I'm going to be fine."

They left. I heard them go into Janet's room. Florine, I supposed, was putting on her clothes.

My gaze instinctively traveled to the window, but this was December in Cambridge, and the pane was totally black. As I had so often before, I saw my reflection in it, and for once I wasn't disappointed. There was something different about me, something stronger in the outline of my face, something level in my eyes. Then I realized that I wouldn't be able to see myself if there weren't light inside the room. Yes, of course there was. There was light inside. There had always been light inside. And this made me happy, the way funny thoughts do sometimes.

It took me about four minutes to decide what to do. I would bring the matter of risk-taking behavior to each of their attentions in their counseling sessions. I would make them promise that they would not take foolish chances for the duration of their stay at Responsibility House. I would hold them accountable for everything they did. I would argue with them as if I were their conscience, just the way I argued with myself. I would kick them when they needed it, just as I kicked myself, and show them kindness when they deserved it, as though showing kindness to myself. I would be with them, on their side. I would let them make their promises (*No, really! We'll never do that again!*), knowing what promises are made of, and what people are made of, too. After all, I was dealing with two addicted criminals here—people who, like everyone else, needed all the chances they could get.

In the meantime, I would stay away from closed bedroom doors.

It was close to midnight when I opened the logbook, preparing to write my usual observations. I had several items of interest to report: Chris's parents had called to say they would be visiting over the weekend; I had left a note to her to this effect; the kitchen drain was clogged; raccoons had gotten into the trash cans and made a mess in the driveway again; the two newest women had cleaned it up. As I was ending my entry for that day, I heard Dolly's car pull into the driveway. I grabbed my backpack, which was rather light these days, and headed down the stairs.

eleven

DEAN TRUBOW PERCHED on the edge of his desk. He was wearing a buttery yellow cable-knit vest, worn corduroys, and sloppy loafers. His thin gray hair stuck out all over like Einstein's but retained some of the curliness that must have made him an adorable child. "Seven Secular Conversion Experiences" lay tossed upon his blotter.

He got to the point. "I'm not sure what went wrong here, Gillian."

"I take it you didn't like my paper."

"I don't know why you even submitted it."

I took a deep breath. This was going to be tougher than I'd expected. "I thought if you saw some examples of real secular conversion experiences, you might be ... moved." *As I was*, I could have said.

"Hmm." He stroked his chin. "In this paper you describe a banker looking at a sunset and a housewife talking to her plants. Could you please tell me what contribution you think you are making to our discipline?"

I was prepared for this question. "I'd be happy to. In his *Varieties of Religious Experience*, William James takes a journalistic approach to the study of what religionists would call spiritual transformation and psychologists might call extreme or intense mood states. He doesn't feel the need to make a distinction between these two fields; he simply uses case histories and general reporting skills to convey what appears to be a rare but persistent human phenomenon. I think that my work would fit nicely into the scholarly tradition he created and perhaps develop some of the themes and ideas he raised."

"You intend to improve on William James?"

"Not improve, exactly. More like *develop*."

"William James was a psychologist."

"Yes, but he certainly made a contribution to the field of reli—"

"He was also a genius."

"Without a doubt." I faltered. Was I being arrogant? "But aren't geniuses the very people we should try to emulate? His approach was so simple and straightforward, virtually timeless. I think his genius lay in the use of narrative for—"

"Now which department are we in? Literary Studies?"

"No, sir. Absolutely not!" Dean Trubow's opinion of literary critics was well known. He thought of them as scholars in search of a subject.

"Yet you seem to have less focus now than ever," he said.

"On the contrary, I have a clearer sense of mission than ever before. I want to use a straight, journalistic approach to record some of the ways in which people with no religious affiliation nevertheless come to a full appreciation of—"

He was giving me a cold, blank look. He had heard it all before.

I felt a small sob growing in the back of my throat, but I managed to swallow it. "My paper can't be *that* bad, can it? I mean, you must have found *something* in it interesting."

"A banker looking at a sunset and a housewife talking to her plants are not interesting. What you describe in this paper are overly emotional—indeed, at times sloppily sentimental—psychological states that not only are outside any religious tradition but have almost no overlap with the subject of religion at all. Your arrow missed the target, Gillian. It didn't even come close. While I'll admit that your idea in its broadest terms has a certain appeal, the execution of it is, as evidenced by this paper, remarkably mundane."

Dear Dean Trubow, I thought, how he loves those M words. I spoke bracingly through a brittle smile. "Well, sir, at least we've moved from *monstrous* to *mundane*. That's a speck of improvement, isn't it?"

He wasn't amused. "I'm worried, Gillian. I don't see how your future here is going to unfold."

OK, there it was. The hooded executioner stepping to the block, the glimmering blade unsheathed. It was time to let out all the stops, to fight as hard for my beliefs as Thomas More did for his. I suddenly got that surge of adrenaline the drowning are said to experience.

"Dean Trubow," I said, with a degree of calm yet forceful equanimity that surprised me, "you know as well as I that the one theme that has dominated our century is loss of faith. Doubt has been cast on everything—our political and economic systems, our social structure, and human nature itself. Science disproved Genesis; it is now widely recognized that the Bible is not literally true. Religions everywhere have tried to keep up, by becoming either more rule-bound and fundamentalist or more open and undefined, so that religion in our time either has hardened into a set of strictly required beliefs requiring medieval fealty or has degenerated into wishy-washy, anything-goes, relativist, feel-good pablum. It's high time we cleared away the mess and looked at how ordinary people like the banker and the housewife somehow manage, without any texts or middlemen, to perceive, experience, and worship the divine. That not only overlaps the subject of religion; in my opinion, it is the *essence* of religion." I took a deep breath. "What is in that paper is the truest and most honest work I know how to do at this point in my life."

To his credit, Dean Trubow listened to every word. He didn't rush me or interrupt me, and he didn't look away. When I had finished, he allowed a few seconds to elapse. Then he said, "I admire your gumption, Gillian. You've got passion and imagination. And you're an eloquent speaker when you want to be. I'm sure those qualities will be of great use to you wherever you go."

He handed me my paper. When I took it, our fingers brushed. I will always remember that his felt chilly.

He walked to the back of his desk and tapped a Salem out of

its pack. Facing the side wall, he spoke very clearly, "Starting next month, your Zephyr Foundation Fellowship will be awarded to another student. Don't think of this as a failure, Gillian. There's a place for you somewhere."

So that was it. The ax had dropped; my head was rolling.

If anything else was said that day, I don't remember it. I don't remember leaving his office or walking down the corridor. I only know that when I emerged into the biting wind I felt deaf, dumb, and blind. I couldn't remember where I'd put my bike and wandered around the building for the longest time, looking for it. After all, it was just where I'd left it, leaning against a tree. I was glad to get my hands on the cold, stiff handlebars. I needed something to hold me up.

A gust of snow whirled around me as I got on my bike. It was just before noon, but the sky was darkening. I pedaled slowly away from the Divinity School. What was the rush?

It had always been my habit in times of great distress or elation to buy myself a very good meal, so I did not turn west down Massachusetts Avenue toward my small, lonely room. I went east, toward Harvard Square, that famous neighborhood whose smug trendiness always made me feel uncouth, but which did have some good ethnic cuisine. Maybe Ravi, the handsome waiter, would be working at the Indian Pavilion, and I would sit at a table there all afternoon, ordering course after course despite the cost, just for the chance to stare at him longingly and wonder about love. Or maybe the Man with Greeny-Brown Eyes would step off the curb directly in front of me, throw down his briefcase, haul me off my bike, and say, "You thought I'd never find you again. Why so little faith?"

A loud horn sounded behind me. I came out of my daydream to discover that I'd drifted into a lane of traffic. Quickly, I swerved closer to the curb. The car spewed slush as it passed me. A wet hunk landed on the side of my face and dribbled down my neck.

It was now quite cold. A strong wind blew cyclones of snow around my bent body. My hands turned red from windburn and damp from melting snow. I stopped to rub them when I got to the square, and stamped my feet to keep my toes from going numb. I had not expected this weather. I had no hat or gloves. At least my backpack was light.

To my right was a tall wrought-iron fence; each baluster ended in a little spear. Its ancient, rusty gate was partly open. A nurse was passing through it, walking briskly in white clogs, clutching a thin raincoat closed at the neck. I watched her cross a small courtyard and approach an imposing stone church. Three black doors with iron hinges spanned its dark façade. The nurse did not go in one of the front doors, I noticed. She walked around to the side of the building, descended a few steps, and disappeared through a small, low entrance there.

As I stood there astraddle my bike, my leaky-booted feet in slush, a laborer in an open barn jacket and steel-toed boots passed through the same gate and entered the basement of the church through the same little tucked-away door. Next came a pair of office workers, then a woman wearing a tailored wool coat and elegant leather gloves.

I remounted my bike and had pedaled no more than a few yards when the badly stooped bag lady in purple sweatpants, the one I had glimpsed so often rooting in dumpsters and picking through trash, hobbled down the sidewalk in front of me. She was pushing her wire cart with one hand and pulling, with her other hand, a trash bag filled with clattering aluminum cans. I was so surprised that I stopped pedaling and again stood astraddle my bike. How often over the last few months had I worried about becoming a bag lady? I had been sure that getting kicked out of Harvard would lead to that despoiled fate. Now that I *was* kicked out and she was so close that I could see the bungee cords securing her paltry belongings, I realized that I had been thinking like a melodramatic child and felt ashamed. I looked away and waited for her to pass by me on the sidewalk, but she, too, crossed the courtyard and vanished inside the church.

What's going on in there? I wondered.

The wind had died down, leaving the snow to fall in a fine, dense mist. About fifty feet up the sidewalk, out of an ethereal fog, Meg and Chris emerged. My heart lurched with happiness. It was good to see people I knew. "Hello there!" I yelled.

"Hey, Gillian. Are you going to the meeting?" Meg asked as they came abreast of me.

An AA meeting. That was what it was.

"Oh no, not me!" I sputtered. "I don't drink to excess. I had Sazerac once at a party to honor my mother's Guggenheim, but I didn't like it at all."

"Sazerac?" Chris said.

"Bourbon, bitters, absinthe, and sugar, stirred or shaken with ice."

Meg and Chris exchanged a glance. "Anyway, you should come," Meg said. "Just to see what it's like."

"Yeah. As long as you're working at a halfway house, you ought to go to at least one meeting," Chris said.

"Oh, no. I don't have time for that sort of thing," I said without reflection.

"Why not?" Meg looked a little hurt.

I could have told her that I urgently needed Indian food, but I actually wasn't very hungry, and I was devastated enough by what had just happened to me that the prospect of spending a brief amount of time in the company of other people, whoever they were, did not lack appeal. I looked up and down the street warily. Would someone from Harvard see me go in? Then I remembered that I didn't go there anymore.

"Do they let . . . uh, normal drinkers attend?" I wasn't sure whether one needed a special ID card or a notarized diagnosis from an accredited detoxification unit.

"It's an open meeting," Chris said.

Presumably that meant open to nonalcoholics. Pushing my bicycle, I followed them through the gate and across the courtyard, past a hoodlum with a shaved head who had entered after the bag lady and now sat rather desolately on the wet church steps.

When we got to the door, I asked nervously, "What about my bike?"

"You can leave it here. If you lock it, it will be all right."

There were, to my amazement, about sixty people inside. The air had a friendly buzz as members greeted each other and found their seats and sipped coffee from styrofoam cups. A lectern was set up at one end of the room, and a tweedy academic type with half glasses (I was quite surprised to see a kindred spirit there) held a gavel and smiled delightedly in all directions. I was too nervous to follow Meg and Chris to the front of the room, so I found a seat near the back. I was hoping to remain unnoticed, but as soon as I was settled a wolfish man came up to me. Six feet tall at least, craggy black brows, a severely bent nose, thick brown lips that seemed to sneer. "You're new," he said accusingly.

I cringed. Did he think I was an alcoholic? Could he tell I wasn't?

He went away, walking with one shoulder slumped and a funny rolling limp, and came back a minute or two later with an over-filled styrofoam cup of coffee loaded with a floating yellow pile of unstirred Coffee-Mate. I knew I couldn't possibly drink it, but I took a sip to be polite. It was so bad I nearly choked.

"Thanks," I said, wiping my mouth on my sleeve.

He seemed satisfied and loped away.

The meeting started. There was some organizational mumbo-jumbo, some ritualized verses, and then a speaker was called. To be honest, I couldn't understand a lot of what he said. He had a terrible lisp. And I couldn't figure out why he insisted on giving out certain pieces of deeply personal and certainly irrelevant information, such as the number of children in his family (seven), his father's disciplinary techniques (petty, conventional humiliations not worth mentioning), his great desire to be a high school football player (unfulfilled), the reason he didn't go to college (which I forget), the girl he got pregnant and married (fifteen years now, three kids), and his surprisingly successful career as a mechanic specializing in Porsche, Audi, and BMW.

There was polite laughter at some points; at others there was sad commiseration. I found it all rather leaky and embarrassing and thought maybe I'd have been better off getting botti kebab at the Indian Pavilion after all.

After a while the mechanic's voice faded into a muted, some-how comforting drone, and sitting alone in that row of quietly attentive, coffee-sipping people, I tried to comprehend the reality of what had just occurred. I had been kicked out of grad school. In my fourth year, no less. I was still having trouble believing it.

Me? Gillian Cormier-Brandenburg? Kicked out of grad school? Not likely! But if I hadn't been kicked out, why was I sitting at an AA meeting in the middle of the day?

I tuned in the mechanic. He was describing a horrible binge in which things were broken and his wife was slapped. She told him to get out. He said that at the time he did not fully appreciate the logical sequence of these events. In any case, he moved to a seedy apartment, where he drank greedily like a guilty rat. Which, in my opinion, he was.

I tuned out again as fast as I could. What was the point of such confessionalism and wallowing? Life cut you, and you bled. Maybe you cut yourself. Whatever. You couldn't change the past. Besides, how could I be sympathetic to someone else when my own pain was sitting inside me like a pile of broken glass? I felt as if I had to move my body very gently so as not to be torn by it any more than was necessary. Then an awful thought occurred to me: I would have to tell my parents. No matter how I explained it, they would never see me in quite the same way again. I would stop being Gillian to them and would become Gillian Who Got Kicked Out of Grad School. Their disappointment would probably last for the rest of their lives.

The mechanic found AA. He stopped drinking. He called his wife. Hooray, she still loved him! And the kids still loved him! Hoopla and happy times!

I could barely stand to listen. Nice to have a happy ending, I thought. Nice to have a problem that can be *fixed*. What about the children who die in car accidents, the starving, anguished millions, the slaughtered, maimed, and tortured? What about *them?* And what about *me*, I suppose I was also thinking. What about people who don't fit in?

The next speaker was a sixtysomething woman in a boiled-wool cardigan and pearls. She said she came from a privileged family and went on to describe a lovely, distracted mummy, an indulgent Irish nanny, summers on the ocean with shrimp salad, macaroons, and lemonade. Wooden tennis rackets and terry-cloth beach robes. *Blah, blah, blah* . . .

I drifted again. What would I do now? Now that I was—what should I call it?—*free*. Well, for starters, I would have to take all those library books back. And after that? Despair crawled over me. How could I plan a future when there was so much to rue in the past? I had worked hard. I had thought my ideas were good. I had believed in them. I still did! How could Dean Trubow not have seen the value of what I was doing? Had he no soul, no imagination? Why did they always make graduate students write turgid, anal things? Did they *want* dissertations to be boring and incomprehensible? Why? What were they afraid of? Something that might *interest* people? Something people might *read?* I flexed my fist, but my anger had no time to build before it dissipated strangely. Maybe Dean Trubow was right. Maybe I was just an immature, all-over-the-place kind of thinker. No map, no Big Picture. No talent, no brains. Hadn't I always felt slightly fraudulent? Wasn't I more ambitious than skilled?

Privilege Lady went to posh rehabs. Everyone covered up. She kept up her public image but lost all dignity in her marriage. Why would he want to sleep with her anyway? Well, she'd been beautiful once. Money was solace of a kind. Not as good as pills, though. She liked Percoset best, but she'd settle for any opiate, even Tylenol 3. Pills weren't as much fun as alcohol, but they didn't make her smell bad, but she still fell down. The stairs, in fact. Rehabilitation followed. From then on she was able to wrangle drawerfuls of pain prescriptions. They kept her foggy for another decade, until her husband spent the last of her money and filed for divorce.

Really, I thought impatiently. Have these people no pride? Isn't it bad enough to *be* pathetic without *advertising* it? Still, I was curious to see how her happy ending would come.

One day, she said, as she was lying in bed, a younger and more attractive version of herself left her body, moved across the room to the French provincial chair next to the vanity, sat down, crossed lovely legs, and gently informed her that she was insane. Deeply distressed by the news, which she recognized immediately as true, Privilege Lady vowed to kill herself, but soon forgot to. She just got dressed and hobbled out of the house.

By then she was old and spectacularly lonely and unwanted by anyone. She got the house, but the bulk of her money was gone. She goes to a lot of meetings and hasn't used alcohol or drugs now for several years, which is long enough to know what she had, what she didn't have, and what she lost. Among the things she didn't have are love, children, and a career. That is a lot to mourn. Among the things she's gained are friends and dignity — the most precious things she's ever had. She would like to be able to say that all is well with her now, but it is not. She has some serious medical problems. But she is ready to face whatever comes.

The people stood up and said the Our Father. I mumbled along with them, though I didn't know the words. I wandered out with the others and met Meg and Chris by the door.

"What did you think of the meeting?" Chris asked me.

"I thought it sucked." I was as shocked as they were by my choice of words.

Meg giggled. "You sound almost normal, Gillian."

Chris said, "You get used to them."

"I have no intention of getting used to AA meetings," I answered, bristling. "In fact, if only to be spared them, from this day forward, I won't touch a drop."

Chris threw an arm around my shoulders and squeezed.

The storm had let up some. Leisurely flakes drifted down from the sky. I brushed a covering of fresh snow off my bicycle seat. The bag lady's wire cart was parked nearby, and the garbage bag of empty aluminum cans was lying next to that. She passed by me on her way to the cart. Stooped as she was, she did not have to lean far to pick up the bag. I watched as she piled it on top of her other belongings and tried to secure it with one of her many bungee cords.

"Hi," I said.

She turned and appraised me with small brown eyes, a ferret's eyes, slightly jaundiced. Hepatitis C? I wondered. She did not speak.

"Tell me, do you have a room to go to?"

She shrugged. No consequence.

I had a ten-dollar bill in my pocket. I pulled it out. "Would you take this, please?"

It left my hand in an instant and disappeared into one of the folds of her bulky coat.

We walked across the courtyard together—her with her cart, me with my bike—in a moving throng of people who seemed generally high-spirited in spite of the weather and the nature of their bond.

The fact that I'd been expelled didn't sink in completely until I saw the crumpled papers and scribbled-on index cards covering my desk and the twenty-seven library books strewn across the floor. All that scholarly work had gone for nothing. An angry, defeated sob rose in my throat, but I choked it back, remembering that Yahweh had told suffering Job to "gird up his loins." Being a woman, I wasn't exactly sure how to proceed with that operation, but I think I did the next best thing by shoving my affairs into ruthless order.

Every last book was returned to the library. (This took several trips.) My recent jottings on the Rosicrucians, Carpocratians, and other early Christian esoteric groups were balled up and catapulted into the wastebasket. Questionnaires completed by the banker, the housewife, and other hopeful innocents were torn with exacting patience into minuscule white flakes that gradually became a four-inch mound of paper snow on the edge of my desk. Coldly, I blew it into the wastebasket. I destroyed those questionnaires, not just because I wouldn't be using them to write a dissertation, but because, at four o'clock that afternoon, with a winter night descending, I understood all of a sudden and with perfect clarity that asking people to answer true/false and multiple-choice questions about their spiritual experiences is a really stupid idea. As I watched the white flakes settle among the paper chrysanthemums of my foreshortened Christian esoteric period, I knew in my bones that Dean Trubow was right. As a scholarly contribution to the field of religious studies, my work was a horrid farce.

How had I managed to delude myself so badly? The answer to this question was long and complicated and filled with many a whining turn. In fact, it was so long and complicated that I didn't dare begin it. Also, I dimly sensed that however thorough and complex I made the answer (and I was confident of my abilities here), it wouldn't come close to expelling the thorny ball of frustration and self-loathing that was lodged like Snow White's apple in my throat. I actually thought about killing myself. I was hunched over the wastebasket, swaying maniacally, when this idea insinuated itself, and the bottom of a wastebasket seemed a particularly fitting focus of my attention. But suddenly what I saw inside was snow and chrysanthemums, not a wasted past and lost future. In this way did a vivid, naturalistic imagination thwart the impulse to self-annihilation. How strangely we are saved.

I straightened up, turned away from the wastebasket, and looked around my sad, nude room. I had no professional reason to call Gustave now, and I knew I was not brave enough to call him for any other reason, especially when I was no longer becoming the professor he mistakenly thought I was. There seemed no choice but to add his name after Ravi's and the Man with Greeny-Brown Eyes to my list of lost potential loves.

I sighed and looked hesitantly into the small mirror above my dresser. A pinched, miserable face looked back at me. Come now, I told my face in an attempt at consolation. Keep in mind that romantic love is almost never what it's cracked up to be. Indeed, you know as well as I that every novel you've ever read portrays it as a vexing and regressive state of affairs that causes otherwise mature people to sniffle petulantly, gush nonsensically, and stomp their feet like little babies. It's entirely possible that, relationships between the sexes (and within a sex) being what they are, you are actually fortunate to be an independent operator with few expenses and the sudden freedom, albeit unasked for, to do whatever you wish.

I turned away from the mirror and began to toss dirty clothes into my laundry basket. Privilege Lady came into my head, though I felt ashamed now of having designated her thus. Well, I said to myself dryly, I guess shrimp salad, macaroons, and a doting mummy (where was dad, by the way?) don't mean much after all. Yet the woman had managed to pull herself out of an appalling miasma of dysfunction. It occurred to me that with good health, energy, and a long span of years still in front of me, I was in a far better position, existentially, than she had been. If she could rescue herself from oblivion, why couldn't I? As I carried my basket down to the washer and dryer in the basement, a soft but nevertheless stirring rendition of "When the Saints Go Marching In" escaped my lips.

It is always nice to experience such a mood swing—from the depth of suicidal ideation to a form of happiness. It was not true happiness, I hasten to add, because it was laced with an acute sense of the dangerousness of life. But it was clearly a positive emotional state—an attenuated happiness, a frayed but grounded contentedness. For the first time ever, I appreciated the fullness of my participation in life. It did not seem unreasonable in that moment to compare myself to Janet. In the sense that I, like she, had risked and lost. Had put my chips on a roulette table and seen them swept away by the croupier's fast hand. What did it matter if the only goal I ever had was gone? At least I'd done something vivid and interesting. I'd gotten myself kicked out of Harvard—an act that may not be as full of Shakespearean flavor as, say, love, obsession, or murder, but that was, for me, a start. And wasn't there something deliciously ironic in the fact that this particular fate had befallen me, Gillian Cormier-Brandenburg? Those who thought they knew me would be shocked. Some would be appalled. I couldn't help feeling a few sparks of pride in having stepped out of my costume for once.

At five o'clock I showed up at Responsibility House as usual. And as usual, Maria was the first person I saw. She was on her knees, scrubbing the oven with a putrid pink foam cleanser. I sat on the floor next to her scrubbing rubber glove and announced the forecast: accumulations of four to six inches with flurries tapering off by midnight, no moon, temperatures in the teens tomorrow, partly sunny for the next few days.

Then I noticed something new in the kitchen—a mint-green sheet taped to the center of the refrigerator door. It looked official, so I went over and peered curiously. It was a most ingenious affair—an elaborate grid of boxes and columns that managed to bring nine household chores, seven days of the week, and twelve residents into dynamic relationship. Despite its complexity, however, the notice was easy to read. Any literate person with a steady finger could see that if you were Meg and it was Tuesday, you were supposed to dust. If you were Varkeesha and it was Saturday, you were required to empty wastebaskets. And if you were Florine and it was Sunday, it was incumbent upon you to scour the tub. Right away I recognized the handiwork of Stacy and perceived a cruel irony—this historic day, my last day as a graduate student, was her first day as house manager.

It was clear to me that the notice would cause a riot. My hand reached out to tear it down, but, out of deference for Stacy in her new position, I decided to go upstairs and talk to her instead. As far as I could tell, none of the other residents were home from work yet, and Maria gave no indication that she had seen the posted paper. Her head was in the oven in any case.

By the time I got to the bottom of the stairs, I was agitatedly composing my argument in my head. The residents of Responsibility House had been getting on very well without such a schedule of chores. While there was occasional squabbling over dishes left on the coffee table or undergarments draped over the shower rod, there was also a spirit of camaraderie as the women divvied up tasks according to their talents and inclinations and swapped them back and forth like so many trading cards. Now household chores were being removed from the free-market system of preference, luck, and bargaining and placed in a complex, non-intuitive, overly bureaucratic holding pattern that would give anyone but Stacy one of those tight little tension headaches. What's more, they had been added to. Vacuuming was supposed to be done not once a week but twice, and was scheduled rigidly for Mondays and Fridays, so that women who might have wanted to enjoy a certain Friday laxness were now required to come home and vacuum rugs that had been vacuumed not four days before.

The office door was closed. I took a long breath and pushed it open. Stacy was filing papers, looking better than usual in drab green cargo pants and a gray sweatshirt.

"What's going on?" I asked.

"Nothing much."

Now that Stacy had graduated from the house, our relationship was on an entirely different footing. Rather than being my counselee, she was my colleague, and since I didn't know whether the organizational chart placed house manager or staff counselor on the higher rung, I was not entirely sure how to communicate my concerns.

"I saw the schedule of chores," I said open-endedly.

"We've needed something like that for a long time," she said.

"Have we?"

"Yes."

"Oh." Oh, dear. Some residents had come home. I could hear their voices in the kitchen. The decibel level was rising quickly. "Do you hear that?" I asked Stacy.

"What?"

"Those angry voices coming from downstairs."

Stacy didn't bat an eye, which indicated to me that she knew full well what effect the schedule was likely to have. "So? What about it?"

"Well, do you really think we need a new way of assigning chores? Things seem to be going along pretty well."

"No, they aren't. This place is a pigsty."

"It looks reasonably clean to me."

"You don't live here, do you? If you did, you'd know. It's horrible, disgusting. A pigsty, a trough of slop, a goddamned stall."

"You must be referring to metaphoric slop. Because I can't say I've ever seen any actual slop in the house."

Stacy gave me a disgusted look and slammed the file drawer on purpose. *Bam!*

I blinked several times—too rapidly, I'm sure—and told the neuronal elves that live in my brain to start humming a good chant, but my consciousness merely quavered for a second or two, then settled down. "I'm just wondering out loud here, Stacy. Maybe we ought to slow down with this chore reorganization scheme. What do you think?"

"No."

"The women are really going to hate it. They're going to rebel. And who can blame them? It's rather infantilizing."

"*Ra*-ther," Stacy said in a hollow British accent. "In-*fan*-tiliz-ing. I mean, who talks like that?"

I looked over my shoulder. "I guess I do."

"You." The word had an opaque quality in her mouth. Hard to decode.

"Me."

Stacy stared at me with eyes as dead as marbles. After a few moments she emitted a tidy, practiced sigh. She had decided to indulge me. "Look, Gillian, what you're not getting here is this: The only reason this place looked halfway decent before is because I was doing all the work. And I do mean *all*. Not one of those bitches helped me. Now I can make them do what they should have been doing all along, and they can't say anything. Because if they don't obey me, I'll kick them out!"

"Did Gretchen say you could kick people out?"

Stacy primped. "Yes."

"But you can't kick people out for not dusting on a certain day, you know."

"Can't I?"

"Of course not, Stacy. That would be ridiculous. Unfair. Sadistic."

Stacy smiled.

The cartilage behind my kneecaps loosened a bit. I felt as though I had stepped into the zone of a dangerous, nonhuman force. Rather tremulously, I spoke. "It's important to keep an eye on the Big Picture, Stacy. There are much larger issues at stake than dusting, you know. Like people's lives. Our purpose is to give residents stability and support while they maintain sobriety and find suitable employment and housing, not to impose arbitrary standards of cleanliness and hygiene." It would have been better if I'd stopped there, but with a curled lip I continued, "And we certainly don't want to engage in petty power trips. Or personal vendettas."

"Vendettas," Stacy said in a flat tone. "Really. What about affairs?"

"Affairs?"

"Like your affair with Janet."

I faltered, confused. "I'm not having an affair with Janet."

"Only because she won't have you. You're a dog, that's why. Face it, Gillian. You can't even give it away."

I should have expected this, I know. I should never have walked into that room without having first donned a bulletproof vest at the very least. But in addition to a few other confounding personality traits, I have this streak of infernal optimism, which makes me believe that the human race is due to improve soon, possibly today, so I rush about thin-skinned and festively clad, psychologically speaking, with the happy intention of being among the first to clap and dance on the grassy knoll when the snipers have laid down their arms. A lovely idea, but not good in practice. One always ends bloodied and bruised.

Interestingly, what hurt far more than the savage indictment of my physique was being unjustly accused. Yes, I had been attracted to Janet. That much was true. But over weeks and months, as desire, denied an outlet, had pooled inside me and turned first cloudy, then brackish, I had swallowed my hopes, rubbed down the jagged edges of my libido, accepted the circumscribed role I was fated to play in Janet's life, and mourned the passionate affair I would not have. I had not engaged in the petty retaliations of the rejected and unloved (whining, pleading, stalking, and snide comments, to name a few), nor had I abused the power of my largely unsupervised office. I knew what it had cost me to renounce my attraction to Janet Tremaine, and I wanted that amount credited to my account, even if the bookkeeper was only Stacy.

"You are correct on one point, my friend," I said, after clearing my throat. "I am physically unattractive. There may be a human being somewhere who would want my body. I do not foreclose that possibility. At the same time, I do not hold out hope. I simply live as best I can the way I am and experience various mood reactions to my physical state. Sometimes I look in the mirror and despair; most of the time, I feel painfully self-conscious and inferior; on rare occasions, I am convinced that I am lucky, that pronounced unsightliness is going to spare me the greatest time-wasting debacle of human life—i.e., romantic love—which in the last analysis may be nothing more than trumped-up, psycho-biological trickery or the narcissistic hankering for half clones. So yes, Stacy, I will agree with you on that one point. Many sexless years undoubtedly stretch in front of me."

Stacy blinked a few times.

"However, you are sadly mistaken if you think I ever had an affair with Janet Tremaine. Though I must, in fairness, give you half credit. Because I did want to. Yes, to be sure. Many nights, lying in bed, I imagined her coming through the door of my narrow garret and taking me in her arms. But this desire would finally pass, and I would fall asleep and get up in the morning and go about my day."

Stacy stared.

"Emotions are so changeable. Have you noticed, Stacy? They are like birds that alight for a brief time and fly away. Some you meet only once, and if they are lovely, you wait years for their return. Others come home to roost at the same hour every day, whether or not you invite them, whether or not you even think of them as yours. The hurt you inflicted on me a moment ago with your crass insult was just another passing emotion, Stacy. I felt it, but it quickly faded."

Stacy began to say something, but I held up a hand. "Now before you start describing pig feces or the ingredients of slop, I would like to suggest that we hold off posting the new schedule of chores until we've had a chance to discuss it with the residents. We all need to have a say in it, I think."

"Go ahead, take it down," Stacy blurted. "But you'll get in trouble if you do. Gretchen OK'd it. It was her idea, really. She put it up."

"It was her idea?" Maybe, but I doubted it.

"Uh-huh."

The noise from the kitchen was getting louder. More women had come home.

"Stacy, are you telling the truth?"

She handed me the phone. "Ask her yourself. Call her in Washington. The number she's staying at is on the desk." She grabbed her parka and slipped past me.

I was left holding the phone, with a tough decision to make. Did I really want to bother Gretchen with a thorny but mundane problem on her first day in Washington? Would she think her staff incompetent and feel pressure to come back? Oh, I thought, sighing, why did Stacy and I have to have a conflict on Gretchen's very first day away? Maybe I was blowing this whole thing out of proportion. Maybe it was no big deal. Stacy was just obsessive-compulsive, that was all. How could that hurt anyone? Why, she'd already done a wonderful job on the office. The cobwebs had been swept out of the corners, the windowsill was dusted, the desk was washed and organized, and the bookshelf had been purified of trash. Even the bulletin board on the far wall was remarkably purged and immaculate, with only one item tacked in its very center. At first I could not make out what the item was. I had to take a few steps toward it. Then I froze. It was the photo of Janet and Florine, pinioned by a long needle, slashed from corner to corner with a red, aggressive *X*.

Eleven digits flew off my fingers. The concierge connected me to Gretchen's room. I had to endure twelve or thirteen rings before I was bumped to the hotel operator. I left a three-word message. *Call me back.*

twelve

I HURRIED TO THE KITCHEN, where a group of emotionally labile women were gathered in a tight knot in front of the refrigerator, complaining violently. Their favorite phrase — "Fuck this shit!" — careened around the crockery more than once.

"Please, ladies, please," I said. "We're talking about chores here. Nothing big, nothing earth-shattering. Relatively unimportant things!"

I was aware, of course, of how quickly I'd become an apologist for the regime. It was my concern for the residents' safety if an uprising were to occur that guided me, I think. And there was always the chance that the new notice really was Gretchen's idea, and I didn't have the courage then to oppose the person who controlled what had just that day become my only paycheck. In any case, the women did not appreciate my point of view and began pelting me with angry words.

"It's not fair."

"Fuckin Stacy. That's who did this."

"There's no way I'm cleaning the bathrooms on Tuesday. That's my hardest day."

"The bitch wants to fuck with us, that's all."

"Even if we did everything the way she wants it, she'd still find reasons to start throwing people out."

"It says I have to go food shopping on Friday, and I just realized today's Friday. Does that mean I have to go right now, even though I just went yesterday?" Petite Cortina had been with us more than a month, yet she still kept asking for directions on how to behave.

"Fuckin Stacy."

Denise and Letitia, two newer residents, came home. The others immediately started to explain the frightful injustice being visited upon them. Just as I had feared, the women began feeding off one another's frenzy as the crowd got bigger, and a highly unpleasant thing was said.

"I'd like to shove a broomstick up her cunt."

"Ladies, ladies!" I shouted in alarm. I waved my arms to get their attention, but since my arms, when raised, did not extend beyond most of their shoulders, I had to pull a chair from the dining room and stand on it.

"Ladies, I know you are gravely disappointed," I yelled over the din.

"Oh my God, Gillian's giving a speech."

The volume of chatter lessened a little, and I repeated my remark. "I know you are gravely disappointed."

"You said that already," Chris reminded me.

"Yes, I know." They quieted some more. "But it bears reiteration, because grave disappointments are hard to manage."

"Oh jeez, here we go."

"Pass out the Dramamine."

"We might feel that we are being marginalized by a blind, unfeeling power structure intent on chipping away at our personal liberties," I continued.

"What's she talking about?" Cortina asked Denise.

"I'm talking about the occasional abuses of power that are an unfortunate fact of life in any society and that we must learn to deal with through proper, nonviolent means."

Janet strode impatiently across the room. "I'm talking about ripping that fuckin list right off that fuckin door and shoving it up Stacy's ass!" She reached out to grab it.

"Wait!" I screamed.

Janet paused, arm in air, and turned a darkened face to me.

"Wait, Janet! Don't do it! Don't act out of anger. Think first. There are better ways."

She looked confused. She let her arm drop. "Yeah? Like what?"

"Like . . . like composing a Declaration of Responsibilities! Yes! A group document putting forth a simple, fair-minded policy regarding chore distribution. A policy that springs from the experience of its participants, that is shaped through discussion and compromise, that reflects the values of the majority while respecting the legitimate needs of the minority, and that successfully achieves its aims. The kind of policy, in other words, that no rational person could find a reason to argue with. Not even Stacy."

About ten blank faces, mouths agape, answered my rousing speech.

"Do I still have to go food shopping?" Cortina asked.

The women looked at Janet.

She sighed noisily, then shook her head in weary surrender. "OK, Gillian. We'll give it a try. But what's it going to *say?*"

"Oh, that's easy," I said, chuckling. "All we have to do is describe the current policy. You know, just write down how you residents have been doing chores all along. Then each person signs it, and we put it on Stacy's desk, and tomorrow you all act nonchalant, while you do whatever chores you would normally do just the way you normally do them. That's all."

"Does that mean I have to go food shopping?" Cortina wouldn't let it rest.

"No, OK? So shut up," Denise said.

"Will Stacy really fall for that?" Chris asked.

"Think of it this way. Stacy can't *make* you do anything. She can only request it. If you are united in a polite refusal to do chores the way she wants you to, what can she do about it? Even if she becomes quite angry, she can't expel *all* of you. Especially if the house is clean!"

Silence followed. The women looked puzzled.

"Don't you see?" I continued. "You have more power than you realize. If you stand together, you're a force!"

Janet's strong arms dangled at her sides. "I don't know. I'd rather just rip that fuckin thing off the fuckin icebox."

"Janet, you told me your vocabulary had improved," I said with sternness.

She looked a little embarrassed.

"Oh, come on! What's wrong with you, girl?" Varkeesha pushed her way past Janet to the refrigerator. "I don't care what word gets used. That thing's coming *down*."

The women closed around Varkeesha, eager to witness her defiant act.

"Wait!" I cried again.

Varkeesha rolled her eyes. "What's your trouble now, sister? You don't like my words?"

It was obvious to me at this point that the notice would not last the night, that even if I talked Varkeesha out of doing it, someone else would rise up in her place. I took a deep breath. "Let me do it."

Varkeesha's eyes narrowed. "You?"

"Yes. I should be the one to do it. You people have too much to lose." Of course, since I was a staff member, my decision to perform this act could hardly be considered mutinous. But even if it were, I would have done it anyway. Being kicked out of grad school had somehow brought acts of rebellion within my reach.

Varkeesha shrugged.

Janet said, "You sure, Gillian?"

"I'm sure."

A few women stepped aside, and a clear path to the mint-green notice opened before me.

I got down from the chair, walked to the refrigerator, and took the notice off the door.

The women cheered. A few slapped me on the back. I laughed a little. I felt kind of fizzy inside. The women started to disperse.

"Not so fast! We have work to do," I said.

They looked disgruntled as I herded them into the dining room and bade them take their places at the table.

I had the romantic notion that composing a Declaration of Responsibilities would be a joyous group effort that I would merely witness. But after a quarter hour of stop-and-go, dead-end nondiscussion, it became clear that my role needed to change from group amanuensis to chief policy architect. I started by asking obvious questions about the present chore-distribution system. Its most salient features were readily agreed upon, but there was a great deal of argument on the specific processes involved. I wondered guiltily if there wasn't a speck of truth in Stacy's allegation that the house, for those more intimately acquainted with it, was a pigsty, because the women really didn't have a clue as to how certain important chores had been getting done and finally admitted that they hadn't been getting done at all. There was no point in lingering over the holes in the system, however. I filled them in as best I could, using common sense. By then an hour had passed, and we were tired but happy. I think we all felt satisfied that the building blocks of a coherent policy had been laid.

Spaghetti was served. While the residents were eating, I went upstairs and composed the first draft of the Responsibility House Declaration of Responsibilities on the office computer. I brought it downstairs and read it to the women while they were enjoying tea and Oreo cookies. A very long, completely futile argument on the subject of yard maintenance ensued. Several residents became unreasonably heated—in my opinion, they showed signs of clinical paranoia—but nothing really came of it. They argued until they seemed to forget what they were arguing about and finally drifted off to clean the kitchen, go to an AA meeting, or watch the Celtics game.

I went upstairs and composed a second draft, which included a new section on yard maintenance (while listening to the women argue, I had figured out how it should be done). I worked hard to develop just the right dignified, self-governing tone.

Proudly I brought Draft #2 downstairs to show the women, but they seemed to have completely lost interest in the subject of chore distribution. Cheering with gusto or moaning miserably in chorus, they sat in front of the TV, rapt by ten men and an orange ball on a parquet court. I tried several methods of getting their attention, but none of them worked. Finally I was able to snatch the remote from an unguarded lap, which allowed me to douse the game with the slightest finger push. I then stood in front of the darkened television set (without surrendering the remote) and read Draft #2 in a high-pitched, yet unwavering voice. There was no dissent this time. Unanimous agreement was quickly reached. A pen was produced, and it wasn't until every woman had signed her name on the numbered lines I had provided at the end of the document for just that purpose that I slipped the remote from under my shirt and flung it, like a bride's bouquet, into a welter of upstretched hands.

When the residents who had gone out to meetings came home, I had them sign, too. By ten o'clock that evening, all twelve signatures had been obtained. As I placed the Declaration of Responsibilities on the office desk, I fondly remembered the Declaration of Independence, but that document had united thirteen participants against oppression, so, with a funny sense of historical echoing, I signed my name, too.

Gretchen returned my call shortly before eleven.

"How's it going?" I asked.

"Oh my God, Capitol Hill is a madhouse. Did you know that practically every profession and industry in America has lobbyists in Washington? So why don't social workers, huh?" She took a slurp of something. "So what's up?"

"Oh, not much," I said. "There was some debate about the best way to do chores. Stacy had an interesting, rather elaborate idea that I think she deserves a lot of credit for. But the women discussed it and found it to be unworkable. They came up with their own method, a modification of the present system. They wrote it all down, just to be extra clear. You'll see when you get back."

"Wow," Gretchen said. "They really did that?"

"Yes. It was an inspiring group effort."

"Wow. Is it . . . good?"

"I think so. It provides freedom and flexibility while clearly defining areas of responsibility."

"Well, as long as things stay clean, I don't care."

"So you didn't OK Stacy's idea?"

"OK it? I never even heard about it."

"Hmm, just wondered. In any case, I think you'll like what

the women did here. Their behavior was really sensible and mature."

"I'm sure you helped, Gillian."

"A bit."

I woke the next day to a howling snowstorm. It was the first day of the rest of my life as a failed scholar, and I wanted to spend it in bed feeling sorry for myself, but the mail brought an unexpected Christmas card (one of the few I'd ever received), which Lawrence slipped under my door. The picture on the front was a schlocky imitation of a Currier-and-Ives New England covered bridge topped with the usual pristine dusting of snow, only this bridge was also laden with Santa, his sleigh, and eight reindeer, and in the night sky all around it, the faces of rosy-cheeked children were lit by glowing stars. I snorted derisively as I opened it.

Dear Ms. Cormier-Brandenburg, it read, *I cannot thank you enough for the kind service you performed for me in taking poor Rodin to the veterinarian's office to be cremated. I am writing now to ask you another favor. I know you are a busy young woman, so I hope my request will not be an imposition. I am very lonely without Rodin and wonder if you would find a new cat or kitten to be my companion. I would prefer an animal from the Animal Rescue League or city pound because I feel a special bond with the unwanted. You are a very kind person, and I trust that whatever cat or kitten you select will be the perfect companion I am fated to have. Yours sincerely, Anna Friedlander.*

I groaned. All I had wanted was one little day to myself to be thoroughly and completely miserable, but no, that simple pleasure was to be denied. Obviously my guardian angel was taking the week off. In my opinion, she'd been doing pretty shoddy work for the last twenty-six years as well. In a fit of self-immolating bitterness, I flung the card across the room, did not shower, did not brush my teeth, did not comb my hair, and dressed in the very same clothes I had worn the day before. If a pathetic, rejected animal was what Mrs. Friedlander wanted, a pathetic, rejected animal was what she would get.

The storm was a real ripsnorter. In addition to heavy precipitation from the sky, the wind whipped stinging cyclones of snow off the roofs of houses and hoods of cars. What yesterday had been messy slush on the roadside was today a treacherous shelf of corrugated, gray-white rock. It must have been twenty below with windchill. When I grabbed my bike, the cold of the handlebars immediately penetrated my wool gloves, and when I threw my leg over the seat, an arctic gust nearly knocked me over.

"Not so fast, bully," I told it through a clenched jaw. I mounted and pushed hard against the pedals in a slanted, shoulder-to-the-elements position. My eyes became slits; my teeth turned brittle. As I pedaled through the ghost town of Cambridge, my lips lost feeling, and I started to drool. By the time I reached the uninspired concrete cube of a building that served the city's animals, the skin on my face was a chafed-raw mask, and each of my two hundred and six bones was shivering.

I do not enjoy the pound. Not only is the light and ventilation usually bad in these places, and the temperature almost always poorly adjusted for the season, it is filled with the mewings and woofs of sensate beings destined for the gas chamber. Oh, sure, one or two will be adopted into ostensibly loving homes, but the vast majority will soon number among the nameless, unsung legions of the dead. Choosing from among them can never be anything but a joyless process, because once the happy selection is made, one confronts the dour faces of the many creatures still unclaimed, creatures who may very well have become, thanks to one's salvationary meddling, even more cognizant of their impending doom.

The cage I was shown to harbored a disturbing, hollow-eyed crowd of cats and kittens. I quickly averted my eyes. I did not want to be prejudiced by any physical characteristic, especially what some would call beauty or the lack thereof. I knew only too well how I would fare if subjected to that criterion of selection, and suddenly, having started thinking in these terms, I went on to imagine myself and everyone I knew *as cats*, sitting together furrily in a big cage, meowing.

Well, I thought wryly, I guess I know how this story will unfold. Lovely, plump Gretchen O'Neil would be snatched in a moment, and shining, black-skinned Varkeesha would follow right along. But the rest of us would be left to yawn and fart together, eating cheap kibble out of a trough and getting on one another's nerves. Maybe in time Janet would find a home with that rare person in the market for a square-jawed, short-haired female tom, and Florine might get picked up by an oily male looking for any kind of pussy. But Meg would be totally overlooked in her tabby plainness, Maria would be considered too old and fur-matted for anything, and Stacy's blank face and robotic movements would throttle the enthusiasm of even the most ardent feline fan. It was hardly worth noting the obvious fact that the biggest loser in the cat pageant would be me.

"Sometime today?" the Animal Control employee drawled, lazing against the open cage door.

I reached inside and, squeezing my eyes shut, scooped the first bundle of fur my hand landed on. It happened to be a tricolor tabby with watery blue eyes that widened in shock as it found itself squeezed by a giant fist and lifted through the air. I stuffed the kitten in my coat — it hung by tiny claws to my sweater — and left a five-dollar donation at the desk.

Mrs. Friedlander answered the door. As she was seated in a wheelchair, we were nearly eye to eye. "You came," she said simply, with delight.

I placed the tabby in her lap.

"And look who you brought! Oh, my! Oh, my!"

The kitten stood and stretched its legs in the most luxurious manner, as if it sensed it had landed on Easy Street.

A cup of tea was again pressed upon me, and since I no longer had to tear out the door to pursue a career, I accompanied Mrs. Friedlander into her narrow kitchen, where I was forced to witness the arduous process of a person in a wheelchair making tea. There were a number of things to collect — an assortment of tea bags, milk, sugar, Sweet'n Low, lemon (but she was out), and spoons. All this had to be transferred to the small table as the water boiled in the kettle, then the water had to be poured perilously into cups. Here's a question for anyone who dares confront it: Should one sit by passively and watch? Or should one urge the disabled person to step aside (in a manner of speaking) so that one can take over the whole painstaking process oneself and get it done before nightfall? I opted for a clumsy combination of the two—first smiling blandly with my hands folded in my lap, then grabbing cups and saucers before they shattered on the floor, and finally leaping to get hold of the kettle, which from my vantage point—slightly *above* the cups—I could pour more easily. Finally Mrs. Friedlander and I were settled across from each other, smiling politely, ready to sip.

Over the course of the next twenty minutes, I heard the history of every cat Mrs. Friedlander had ever owned, from sensitive Aloysius to mischievous Rugby. To be congenial, I shared a few pet stories of my own, leaving out the hamster found dead on his treadmill and the goldfish I flushed. Finally, after many blandishments, I was able to leave.

Outside in the freezing air, I wrapped my six-foot scarf several times around my neck, mouth, and nose. Then I got on my bike and pedaled down Linnaean Street, trying to avoid potholes and fallen ice chunks as I squinted into a howling wind. When I turned onto Massachusetts Avenue, I began working my jaw in an exaggerated yawn to keep the scarf I had bunched around my lower face from creeping up over my eyes. But the scarf was soggy from my condensing breath and refused to stay where it had been put. In frustration I stopped under a street sign to rewrap it. Hudson Street. Where had I heard that name before? Oh, yes. My blood grew a little warmer, and a funny fluttering occurred in my chest. Hudson was Gustave's street. Of course, I had no professional reason to contact him and I was much too debilitated by social anxieties to try to reach him for some vague personal reason that I could not possibly explain, but there was no harm in riding my bike past his apartment building, was there? It was highly unlikely that I would run into him, especially when the weather was so harsh, and the fact that just the day before I had given up hope of ever seeing him again somehow made a chance encounter seem even more remote.

I rode down Hudson Street without sighting a single person. I turned and rode back up the street. Ignoring the numbness in my extremities, I pedaled down the street again and up it again. I did this a number of times and eventually saw three people leave his building and scurry to ice-covered cars and one person enter it carrying a bag of groceries. It was a large, five-story building with, I estimated, as many as sixty inhabitants. Having seen a measly four in about forty minutes of back-and-forth bicycling, I was reasonably sure that there would be no embarrassing accidental encounter in my future, so I saw no harm in taking a much-needed rest on the steps leading up to the building's main entrance. The fact that I was almost frozen to death added to the tiredness I felt, and I ended up sitting there for rather a long time. Indeed, the number of residents I noticed either entering or departing the building slowly rose from four to seven to ten and finally to fifteen, one-quarter of the estimated total inhabitants, when, completely out of the blue, a voice behind me said, "Gillian? Is that you?"

"Oh!" I jumped up and turned around. He was standing in the doorway.

"What are you doing here?" he asked. He had his hair pulled back, and his face looked especially clean.

"Why, I . . . I was just in the neighborhood delivering a cat."

"I looked out my window and saw you there. I wasn't sure it was you."

"It's me," I said, smiling brightly, hoping to make him see this as a happy fact.

"Why are you sitting out there in this weather?"

"Well, ah, I was just passing by and these steps looked so . . . inviting."

He looked down. I looked down. They were concrete covered by mud-streaked slush.

"Next time, buzz me," he said.

"Oh! Is this *your* building?"

He frowned. "You didn't know that? I thought I gave you my address."

"Oh, right! Yes, in fact you did. And I guess I just wanted to see you to, um, to talk to you some more!"

"Good. Because I want to talk to you, too." He opened the door and let me into the foyer. "Come on up. I've got some coffee brewing."

His third-floor apartment had a sharp, masculine smell—old sneakers, burnt scrambled eggs, and something that made me think of wooden boat decks in the rain. There was a whiff of steam from a recent shower. His hair was damp, I noticed. A bath towel was draped over a kitchen chair.

He began speaking immediately. "It was so weird talking to you the other day. I've never told my story to someone who wasn't in recovery. Afterwards, I kept wondering what you thought of me. I mean, I did some stuff I shouldn't have." He glanced at me a little shyly. "I regret that," he said.

I sensed that he was asking me for something. Exoneration, I supposed. "Most religious systems, except for those of a few ancient South American tribes, grant forgiveness when there is sincere contrition," I said.

He smiled slightly. His eyes twinkled.

I noticed a dimple. Just one.

I don't think I'd ever noticed a dimple before. In fact, it was possible I'd never thought the word *dimple* in all my life. That lonely dimple, that dimple with no companion, had a curious effect on me. It made me feel playful, a little devilish. I raised one eyebrow and a corner of my mouth. I sniffed the air discreetly. Was it just me, or was there some kind of funny electrical impulse in the room?

We were standing in the kitchen. Gustave was pouring coffee into mugs. "That talk we had really got my head going," he said over his shoulder. "I've been thinking about spiritual experiences for the last few days, and there's a lot more I want to say."

He looked at me with some hesitation, as if asking for permission to trespass on my subject.

I nodded encouragement.

"I don't have a good education, Gillian. Not like you. But I read a lot in prison and I remember reading somewhere that Carl Jung said that the only thing that would cure addiction was a spiritual experience. And, you know, the more I thought about it, the more I realized that I know a bunch of people who've had one—a spiritual experience, I mean. But most of them don't talk about it—except in, like, a whisper late at night—because it's usually some pretty strange shit."

I knew about Jung's theory; it was what had pushed me toward the subject of secular conversion in the first place. It was odd to hear Gustave spouting one of the ideas for which I'd gotten no support at school.

Gustave opened the refrigerator. I glanced inside and saw five or six sauce-stained boxes of Chinese take-out and not much else.

"I hope you don't take cream, because I don't have any. Milk either," he said.

"I love moo shi pork."

"What?"

"Just black, thanks."

He tried to keep from smiling, but the dimple reappeared and gave him away. When he handed me my mug, our fingers brushed. I followed him into the living area, dazedly admiring his ample girth and the slight bow in his legs.

"I have a friend you should meet," he said, settling on the couch. "She had an amazing spiritual experience. I'm talking mind-blowing, fourth-dimension stuff here. You should get her story for your book."

I perched on a chair and found myself staring at his hands. They were square, short-fingered, muscular, and rough. I felt wattages in my palms and fingertips, and my duodenum twitched.

"Then there's this other guy, Ernie. He's schizophrenic, but don't let that scare you away, because he's a real nice guy and very normal when he takes his meds. He draws birds for a living. Goes out to the Berkshires, way into the hills, and sits in a tree. When the birds come, he draws them. Unbelievable pen-and-ink stuff. He's got a lot to say about the Higher Power. And it's not crazy at all."

I nodded appreciatively and, in a spectacular non sequitur, asked Gustave how old he was.

"Thirty," he said proudly. "A week ago."

To my great embarrassment, I blushed. Sitting in his chair, knowing his birthday — these were such intimate things!

He turned toward a cassette player on the table next to him, saying there was something I should hear. Then he pressed a button, and jazz notes floated into the air. "Listen to that saxophone," he said.

I leaned back. So did he. The notes swirled around us — they were surprising, yet made perfect sense—and I became so delighted that I giggled like a schoolgirl and saw him crack a smile. It occurred to me that we were both remarkably relaxed—he because he had divulged the worst about himself and believed I had come to visit him anyway, me because I had been expelled from Harvard University and had nothing to live up to anymore.

Suddenly I sat bolt upright. I had to tell him. "Gustave, there is something you should know."

"What?"

"That interview you gave me? It was all for nothing. My Committee rejected my paper, they rejected my topic, and they rejected me!"

"What do you mean?"

So I explained it all—my fellowship, the Committee, my topic, my writer's block, the reason I went to Responsibility House, my failed research, my long boring paper with the tortuous footnotes, my near expulsion, my frantic search for a new topic, my heart-to-heart with Janet, my defiant decision to stick with my old topic, the questionnaires, the paper I was proud of and handed in, and Dean Trubow's reaction to it. By itself, it was a long and convoluted story, but I'm afraid that the emotional manner in which I conveyed it made it even longer and more convoluted.

"I'm sorry," I panted when I came to the end. "Strunk and White would not approve. That was hardly brief and clear."

"I understood it fine. Your deal with them fell through." He shrugged noncommittally. "It happens."

I had expected sympathetic horror, or at least commiseration. Not a cavalier tone. "You don't seem to understand," I said heatedly. "All my work for the last three years is wasted! My future's ruined! Why, I don't even have a defensible reason for sitting here talking to you. Is that all you can say?"

He turned to the window, frowned, and took a slow sip of coffee from his mug. When he finally turned back, his eyes were rather sharp. "You want some advice?"

"I do."

"Move on."

Move on. Two words. I felt as though the boat I was sailing in had suddenly run aground. My anger and hurt pride deflated like windless sails, and tears rose in my eyes. "Where to?" I asked.

He didn't answer, but his eyes softened and kept looking into mine. It seemed that there were many words between us waiting to be spoken, but that it was better not to speak them then.

"We can still talk about spirituality," he said finally as a clarinet played a high, mysterious phrase. "If you're really interested in it."

"Am I?" Everything seemed topsy-turvy. I really wasn't sure.

He laughed. "Are you?"

I laughed, too. "I must be."

"Let's have dinner."

"Dinner?" My jaw gaped. I'm sure all my fillings showed. I couldn't believe it. I had lusted after many men since puberty, and not one had ever asked me for a date. But maybe Gustave didn't *mean* a date. Maybe he meant a buddy-colleague thing, because he didn't like to eat alone, and it was my own imagination, superheated by sexual deprivation, jazz music, and the Caribbean blue of his eyes, that had supplied the romantic piece.

I managed to close my mouth. Then, with horror, I remembered my (lack of) morning toilette. Fiendishly I tried to smooth my rumpled clothing and pawed my unwashed hair. Of course he's kidding, I thought. Surely he isn't willing to be seen with me.

"Um . . ." I said. "Ah . . ."

His face clouded over. "Is it my past?"

"Oh, no! Most certainly not!"

"Then meet me," he said genially, naming a restaurant and a time.

And I waltzed clumsily out the door.

That afternoon I did something I'd never done before: I shaved my legs. I also conditioned my hair, plucked my eyebrows, cut my toenails, and cleaned the lint out of my bellybutton. At six o'clock, choked with panic, I rushed to the drugstore and bought an eyelash curler, mascara, eye shadow, eyeliner, a lip pencil, and some other things I didn't know how to use. I applied it all to my face and, when I looked in the mirror, saw a truly frightful sight, so I washed it all off and arrived at Szechuan Pagoda wearing nothing but deodorant and ChapStick, in addition, of course, to my clothes.

Gustave wore a long leather coat over his T-shirt. He had added some jewelry, too: a gold chain and a heavy gold ring with a large red stone. Any one of these items by itself might have been natty; in conjunction, they were a little too Godfatheresque for me. But I brushed aside our fashion differences. I was hardly an Oscar-night starlet myself; besides, it was intoxicating to think that he had dressed up for me.

We were shown to a huge booth with vinyl seats. I folded my coat and sat on it to be a little higher.

He asked for soda water with lime. I usually stayed away from caffeine, especially in the evening, but I wanted the night to be different and special, so I ordered Coke. We decided on Kung Bo Three Delights and more appetizers than two people really needed.

Gustave asked about my family, and I answered as briefly as possible. Given what I already knew about his life, it seemed unnecessary to turn the question around.

Gustave took the paper umbrella out of his drink and tossed it on the table. There seemed to be nothing to say. The silence stretched out uncomfortably until I thought to ask, "What's your favorite book?"

"*Siddhartha.*"

"Oh, yes. Hesse. German. Early twentieth century. Nobel Prize."

"Did you read it?"

"I haven't gotten to it yet."

"You should. You'd like it."

"I'm sure."

Silence again. It grew like an invisible balloon being slowly inflated until it seemed to occupy the entire room. Finally, he looked up and asked, "What's *your* favorite book?"

"Better ask me what my favorite library is," I said, chuckling. "I do have one. But I've only been there once." I paused—a little coyly, to be sure—to give him time to probe my secret if he wished. But he was pouring tea into a tiny porcelain cup, so I went ahead and divulged the name. "The Library of Congress. It's magnificent. Have you been there?"

"No. Maybe someday."

"Oh, you really must go if you have the chance. It will absolutely stun you. It will change your life. How clearly I remember the day I sat in that exquisite reading room. My spirit positively soared. I thought, Here I am in the very heartbeat of civilization. In the veritable Soul of Man!"

Gustave nodded thoughtfully and brought the cup to his lips.

The silence this time seemed a bit easier, more contemplative. I looked out the window and analyzed passing strangers. He seemed to take an interest in them, too. But soon what had felt companionable became awkward. I realized that I had always relied on others to make conversation, having no small talk of my own. But this night would be an awful flop unless my social skills improved rapidly. "So, what did you like about *Siddhartha?*" I asked.

That turned out to be the key. Across the next two hours, as dish after dish appeared on our table (Gustave was not shy about eating), we talked about Hesse and other authors he'd read, the many conversations he'd had with recovering addicts, his sense of how deep inner change happened in the lives of the people he knew. I listened closely, nodding frequently. Then I passionately shared everything I cared about: classic conversion experiences, the Rosicrucians, inner knowledge, the role of secularism in the coming global world.

It was thrilling to be having a deep, serious conversation with a man, and I wanted more than anything to give it my full attention, but at regular intervals the sentence *I have been kicked out of grad school and my life is completely ruined* floated across my mind like an advertising banner pulled by a single-engine plane across the sky. Also at regular intervals the word *Sex!* popped into my head like an insistent jack-in-the-box. These two very different thoughts twisted around each other confusingly and called up distinctly different physical responses. One one hand, my body felt deadened by the bottomless angst of purposelessness while, on the other, incipient lust was whipping all my nerve endings into a premature Dionysian frenzy. I quelled this inner chaos as much as I could, so as not to let our discussion of profundities waver.

After dinner we strolled through the snowswept square. The plows clattered down the narrow streets, but the night seemed quiet nevertheless. A few inches of snow covered everything—fence rails, the high rims of lampposts, even the gently curved tops of mailboxes. People walked more slowly in the hushed, crisp air. Strangers looked each other in the eye and said hello.

I usually would have walked through Harvard Yard, but that night we went another way. I told Gustave that I didn't want to be there as a tourist. He took me to a deserted park, and we sat on a bench and looked across a field of deep, unbroken snow. It was cold; he put his arm around me, and I fit easily under the crook of his shoulder.

"Look up there. Can you make out the Big Dipper?" He traced its outline with a gloved finger.

"Of course I can," I said with a bit of impatience. Did he really think I needed to be shown the Big Dipper? I pointed deep into the northern sky. "Now look there. Between Ursa Major and Perseus, there's a really lovely little constellation called Camelopardalis, a.k.a. The Giraffe." We were far enough from the city lights that it was faintly visible. I sighed happily. "That's my favorite."

Gustave gave me a funny look. "Do you ever listen to old-style rhythm and blues?"

"I'm not familiar with that musical genre. But I'd enjoy hearing some examples of it." I took a deep breath. "So why don't we go back to your apartment?"

We did.

Dear reader, I have thought long and hard about how to reference what transpired there after the Blind Lemon Jefferson and the Bessie Smith. Many writers employ the ellipsis. Others rely on a single asterisk; still others, more ebullient, use three. After prolonged consideration, I have decided to break radically with tradition and utilize six ampersands. Are you ready? Here:

&&&&&&

So, what do you think? Don't you agree that the sensuous, interconnected nature of the symbol is remarkably well suited to what it signifies, while its exact denotation—*and*—corresponds with happy serendipity to acts of joining, coupling, and the rest? And isn't the whole aura of the ampersand round, playful, and gorgeously fulfilled—which is exactly how I felt when I fell out of Gustave's bed on Sunday morning, giggling and more sweet-tempered than I had ever been.

For those of you who want to know the significance of *six*, I will say only that that is a private matter between my guardian angel (back from vacation) and me.

thirteen

I ARRIVED AT WORK on Monday in an unusually bubbly mood, but palpable tension inside the walls of Responsibility House sobered me immediately. It felt as if the atmosphere were infused with super-heavy neutrinos that had passed through a miserable, subjugated planet on their way to Earth. Maria was on her knees, pushing a scouring pad over the scuffed linoleum floor. An extra measure of stiffness in her back made her look more like an indentured servant than a recovering alcoholic trying to scrub away her blues. I glanced at the refrigerator and was relieved to see that Stacy's mint-green chore reorganization scheme had not reappeared. But everything else that had once been there was gone as well—the festive announcements of sober dances and sober cruises, the encouraging postcards sent by recent graduates embarked on fulfilling substance-free lives, the exuberant children's drawings that the mothers in the group acquired during visits with their families, and all the stupid cartoons.

I squatted on the floor close to Maria. The tomato sauce that she had made ten days earlier had convinced me that my strategy of loud, cheerful banter was working and that soon she would speak to me in words.

"Sunshine and thawing temperatures for the next few days," I announced proudly, as though I personally had wrought the improvement just for her.

She raised her gray head and stared at me with burning eyes. The long furrows on either side of her arching nose quivered with intense emotion. A hard tremor passed across her face. "Do something," she said.

It had happened! Maria had spoken—to me! *Do something.* Two words, or three if you included the implied subject, *you.* Meaning me, of course. Me do something. OK, Maria. But what?

She turned arduously, like a tanker in narrow straits, to clean under the kitchen table, presenting me with a close-up of her wide-beamed, black-clad rump. That, as well as increased vigor in her wiping arm, made it clear that those were the only two words I would be favored with that day. I scurried upstairs—excited, mystified, eager to share the news.

The office was neat as a pinprick, which made it seem smaller somehow. Stacy stood in the middle of the floor, 1982 Demolition Derby cap on head, purse on shoulder, coat over arm. "You're late."

"Only a few minutes. I was talking to Maria," I said nonchalantly, anticipating the pleasure of watching Stacy's face brighten as the stunning import of this breaking news seeped into her mind.

But she didn't seem to hear. "I know you were behind this, Gillian," she said, pointing to the Responsibility House Declaration of Responsibilities, which lay just where I had left it, in the center of the desk. "And I talked to Gretchen, so I know why she approved your idea instead of mine. She seems to think the residents worked on it together like the mature people we both know they're not. So here's the score: Gillian one, Stacy zero. But don't worry; that will change."

I blinked with stupefaction. Why could I never remember what kind of person she was?

"Now before I leave I want to bring you up to speed on a few of the changes I made. Starting today, residents are absolutely forbidden to have any food in their rooms. They are not allowed to leave laundry in either the washer or the dryer for longer than five minutes after the machines have stopped. Anyone who is caught overloading the washing machine or dryer will lose weekend privileges. And from now on, people who take granola bars, yogurts, and fruit out of the house to eat on their way to work will have to pay for them."

"Oh."

"As house manager, I'm making it my business to enforce rules and cut expenses. That's my *job*, Gillian; that's what Gretchen hired me to do. So don't try to interfere. Do you have any idea how much waste there is around here? Have you even noticed that the bathroom window is left open all day sometimes, allowing heat to escape?"

"Can't say that I have."

"We spend nearly half our budget on gas, electricity, heating oil, and food," she said darkly. "I intend to bring those costs way down. I've calculated that if the residents were allowed to eat only five dinners a week here, instead of seven, if we got rid of snack foods like brownies and cookies, and if we substituted a large pot of porridge for expensive boxed cereals in the mornings, we could save a lot."

"I'm sure," I murmured.

"And I got rid of Chris."

"You what!?"

"She left yesterday morning."

"Chris *left?*" Yesterday morning. Sunday morning. While Gustave was making me a huge breakfast. "Why?"

"She was caught making out in the parking lot during the Saturday night AA meeting. Not only is sexual contact forbidden, so is skipping meetings."

"Who caught her?"

"I did."

"But you don't even work Saturday night!"

"I was at the meeting, Gillian. I saw her go outside with lover boy at the break. I knew just where they were headed, too." A simpering smile—lips stretched without parting, a quiver at each end.

I wished I could have said something brilliant and devastating just then, but I could not. The look on Stacy's face disabled me. I had seen it so many times before on the faces of playground bullies, phys ed teachers, girls in cliques, and children passing on the street. It was the look of pleasure in power over another, in power to make another suffer—the look of sadism. You might think that repeated exposure would have inured me to its ugliness; instead, the opposite was true. Like a finely tuned instrument, I was more keenly sensitive to it, more aware of its many subtle and dramatic guises, more distressed by its arch ubiquitousness and horrible destructive power. Indeed, the ugliness of that look was so familiar to me that when I saw it on Stacy's face that day, I felt like I was melting, like it was *me* who'd been found arbitrarily unworthy, *me* who'd been told I wasn't wanted, *me* who'd been ordered to leave.

I slumped into the armchair and managed to choke out these words: "There was no reason to expel Chris. Chris wears Birkenstocks and works for Head Start, for God's sake. Chris is as straight and decent as a junkie can get."

"The rules are the rules," Stacy prattled. And went smugly home.

I sat in that chair for a long time, rolling my head in my hands. What was I still doing in this harsh, unforgiving place? I didn't belong here. I hated it! Back in September, all I'd wanted was to snag a few proofs of secular conversion. Now that my vaunted academic career was cremated, what on earth was keeping me here, at a job I'd never really wanted, doing work I wasn't suited for, friendless, unguided, not sure whether I was helping or hurting, pierced through with agonizing moral dilemmas I didn't know how to resolve?

And of all the moral dilemmas I'd encountered, this one was by far the worst. Because Stacy was right. Chris had been warned; she knew what the score was. Yet she'd stepped out of bounds—*colored outside the lines!*—and been caught red-handed. What recourse could there possibly be for her? What idiot would even try to argue her case? Armed with free will, Chris had made the choice to disobey. And, as she well knew, the rules were the rules.

But isn't that the ultimate in tautology? I muttered huffily. With so much circular reasoning going on, we'd surely have butter soon. It was like saying blue was blue, red was red. But would saying that make either of those colors *right*? Would it make either of them *good?* No, of course not. I knew full well that Stacy knew full well that the rules as we employed them were much more than rules. They were a means of coercion, a form of crowd control; they were the way we wrested social order from chaos, by binding those below us, hands and feet. But here was the secret dilemma, the one Stacy probably didn't know. Weren't we, sitting in this little office, as terrorized as any of the residents, as shackled as they? Could either of us *close* the rulebook? Did we know how to rely on our own wisdom, justice, and mercy, provided we had any to rely upon? Did we have the courage to stand up for *people?* Would either of us risk our job?

I didn't know how to answer these questions. I only knew how I felt. Sickened by my association with Stacy and this heartless place, ashamed of my own power-loving obedience, wishing I could finally decide either to come or to go.

I looked up to see the photo of Janet and Florine, still tacked in the center of the otherwise empty corkboard, still slashed through with a bloody *X.* They were far from discreet lovers, so it wouldn't be long before Stacy got ahold of them, too. Suddenly I realized what Maria meant. *Do something about Stacy!* Before she turns Responsibility House into a gulag. Before she kicks everyone out.

Yes, Maria. I will.

I got up, crossed the room, and pulled the photo off the corkboard. Just as I had ripped up my questionnaires, but with an entirely different feeling of steady conviction in my gut, I tore the photo into quarters and tossed them into the wastebasket. In the drawer I found the same red permanent marker Stacy had used. I got out a sheet of paper and quickly scrawled some fat words across it. Without thinking, I tacked my passionate message where the photo had been:

Death to tyrants! *Vive la liberté!*

The slogan was good, but it was only a start.

I scurried down to the kitchen, where five or six residents were chatting and snacking after a day of work. The minute they saw me, their mouths clamped shut and they stared at me with hostility. It was obvious they were lumping me with Stacy under the general heading, Management.

"Does anyone know where Chris went?" I asked anxiously. I feared that turbulent emotions might be leading her back to drugs.

"Ain't none of your business anymore, bitch," Varkeesha said.

"I had nothing to do with her getting kicked out!" I protested.

"Yeah, right." Florine elbowed past me roughly to get to the refrigerator. A quick clutch of the counter allowed me to remain upright. She grabbed a plastic quart of Diet Coke off the refrigerator shelf, unscrewed the top, and swigged from the bottle a good long time, all the while keeping her left eye trained on me. When her thirst was slaked, she screwed the top back on the bottle, burped extravagantly, and took three giant steps in my direction. Standing about eighteen inches from where I was backed up against the counter, she swung the Diet Coke bottle slowly and deliberately between two fingers until it managed to resemble a clublike weapon.

"Come on, Florine," I pleaded weakly. "You know I'd never . . ."

Florine advanced to an even more uncomfortable proximity, bringing her tremendous bosoms to within inches of my eyes. "You sit up there night after night writing in that logbook. Don't think we don't know. What are you writing, Gillian? What's so fuckin interesting about us anyway? Our sex lives? The way we piss and shit? You knew Chris was seeing someone. And since Gretchen isn't here, you're the only one who could have ordered Stacy to kick her out."

"I didn't!" I said. (Secretly, it pleased me that Florine assumed I had been given power over Stacy.) "Why, Florine, you of all people ought to know I wouldn't do that! Certainly, you remember . . . you remember . . ." What I wanted to say was, *How I found you and Janet in bed and didn't report it,* but I couldn't refer to that incident without admitting in front of the group (1) that I, as a staff person, had been aware of their relationship for some time, and that the expulsion of Chris was therefore an egregious example of the double standard, and (2) that Florine's prior characterization of me as a mercenary voyeur had a particle of merit because on one occasion at least I'd barged through a closed bedroom door. (I also had a personal qualm: I think it is churlish to discuss one's own or other people's sex lives publicly, even in self-defense.)

Florine smirked and turned to the others. "She's lying."

Janet closed ranks. She stood at Florine's left shoulder like a totem, thick arms folded across her chest, so near that I could smell the cheddary Cheez-Its on her breath. Varkeesha moved to Florine's right side, muttering something sharp and aggressive. I stood there trembling, cornered like a fox by a triumvirate of hounds, my egress to the office blocked. Meg huddled by the back door, her lips puckering nervously around a lollipop stick. Maria was watching everything.

Janet, Florine, and Varkeesha moved a few inches closer. My back arched over the hard edge of the counter. "Please, friends. Hear me out. I didn't order Stacy to do anything. I wasn't given power over Stacy. I don't even *like* her."

Janet shook her head sadly. "That's pathetic."

The Diet Coke bottle, dangling from Florine's fingers, resumed its pendulum swing. In my mind's eye, I saw it battering my skull, turning my bones and tissue into splinters and bloody pulp. Could a person really be killed by a Diet Coke bottle? I asked myself. Of course, I replied. In the olden days, innocents were slain with stones.

"Wait, I just thought of something. I can get Chris back!" I said.

Janet narrowed her eyes. "How?"

"Gretchen said Stacy's in charge in the daytime and I'm in charge at night. So it doesn't matter what Stacy did when she was here. I can take Chris back right now!"

"What about Gretchen?"

"I'll handle things with her."

Florine shook her head. "Chris wouldn't come back to this shithole if you sent her a fifty-percent-off coupon."

"Why not?" I asked stupidly.

"Would you?"

Meg pushed her way into the middle of the group with surprising assertiveness. With a big smacking suck, she pulled the lollipop out of her mouth. "Leave Gillian alone. Chris wouldn't want you to hurt her."

Meg was Chris's best friend, so her opinion carried weight. Janet, Florine, and Varkeesha took a few steps back.

I took my elbows off the counter, where they and they alone had been supporting most of my weight. "Where's Chris now?" I asked Meg, rubbing my sore triceps. "Is she OK?"

Meg sighed. "She's at her boyfriend's, Gillian. She's fine. She doesn't care that she got kicked out, and she doesn't want to come back. She was going to graduate in a few weeks anyway."

In the silence that followed, the women regarded me distrustfully or disgustedly, I'm not sure which. That's when I realized that Responsibility House and all its services had little to do with their success. What saved them was the love they had for each other.

"I'm sorry. It shouldn't have happened that way," I said.

Florine snorted and got a glass out of the cupboard. Janet ran her fingers through her short hair. Maria wiped her hands on her apron and turned back to the stove. The others disappeared into the living room, which quickly filled with the crisp, detached voice of a news announcer.

I retreated (where else?) to the office. To my surprise, I didn't feel any narcoleptic tremors. I felt restless, useless, frustrated. I sat at the desk. The calendar said December 17. As usual, the ivy on the windowsill was dying and the windowpane was dark. I had nothing to study anymore—nothing, really, to do. How much time had I spent in this room since September, I wondered, reading books whose chapters I could not recall? What had the residents been doing with those hours? I tried to picture them going about their lives—cleaning up after dinner, washing their clothes, taking care of half a room, surfacing slowly after the wasted years of their addictions, thinking of family, jobs, and each other, dreaming of someday sleeping in somebody's arms. It bothered me, now that one I cared about was gone, how little I actually knew them, how poorly I could imagine what it felt like to be one of them—ashamed, prideful, guilty, fierce, with so much to long for and regret.

I missed Gustave suddenly, with an awful pang. It seemed miraculous that he had been willing to love me, if only for a night. In gratitude and fresh desire, I relived every word and caress. I wasn't good at falling in love, having never done it before. But I did what I thought was called for by attempting a re-gendered version of a Shakespeare sonnet, "*My mister's eyes are nothing like the sun . . . ,*" and humming my favorite Sinatra tune, "*Is your figure less than Greek . . .*" It was impossible, of course, but I felt as if I'd known Gustave forever, as if the touch of dampness at his hairline and the sudden bloom of sweat across his chest were lodged in Pleistocene-period amygdala memories I never knew I had. The office, which had seemed small a minute before, shrank to the size of an airless closet. The metal desk felt as hard and constricting as an animal trap. It was surely not a piece of furniture one wanted one's body to be in contact with for long periods of time, especially when one could lie on a big soft mattress covered with warm white sheets infused with a lover's sultry pheromones.

For the next two hours I waited by the phone, willing Gustave to call. I believed he couldn't possibly want to see me again, which is why I didn't call him. But eventually my romantic longing, spiked by hot shots of lust, overcame my insecurity, and I dialed his number. I held my breath through four toe-tingling rings, then was lulled into a stupor of pleasure as his voice told me he wasn't home. Then a beep screeched in my ear.

Hi! This is Gillian! I blurted. *Um, Saturday night was great—I mean, really, really great! It was the best thing that's happened to me in a long time! Maybe my whole life! Do you foresee any time in the future when we could get together again? I hope you don't think I'm being too forward! But we did have a lovely evening, not to mention sexual intercourse, and if you called me, which you haven't so far, I wouldn't think you were being too forward at all! So I guess I won't worry about being too forward either. Hey, do we even know what that word means? Anyway, as you've probably figured out, I am only agonizing over my possible forwardness because I want to be deeply respectful of your privacy and personal boundaries. I am acutely cognizant, as you also must be, that despite our totally satisfying (I speak for myself only, of course) episode of physical intimacy, we remain staggeringly unknown to each* *other and that it is entirely possible—indeed, <u>probable</u>, if statistics are to be believed—that in the future, provided there is one, we will discover many good reasons to break off contact with each other entirely. If that unfortunate circumstance were to occur, I want to promise you right here and now that I would not do any of the spurned-lover things that I've read about in books or seen on late-night TV. I would not stalk, harass, or seek to intimidate you. I would not slander your name, boil your pet, damage or withhold your rightful property, throw your clothes and old trophies in a heap and set it on fire, or call you in the middle of the night sobbing while holding a razor blade over my wrist. I would not even do things you wouldn't know about, such as staring at the rain for hours with smudged eyeliner on my cheek or staggering around my apartment in a flimsy nightgown sloshing gin everywhere. My only hope at this point, Gustave, is that we give ourselves all the time we need to deeply experience whatever the causes of our probable breakup might be. I hope I'm not being too nihilistic here! If I am, I'm really sorry. I never know what to say. What do people say when they leave messages like this? Maybe this is what they say! Oh, gosh. I just know the beep's coming. Please please please call me the exact second you get in!*

It was spur-of-the-moment honesty, completely unrehearsed. Over the next silent hour, and the next, I wondered with increasing desperation whether I'd made a mistake. Most evolutionary psychologists would agree that, despite what some fringe elements might say, the human female is never supposed to let on that she's as sexually eager as men happily admit to being. Indeed, to ensure her reproductive success (this to be measured by the amount of resources allocated to her future offspring), she's supposed to act as if she would never sleep with anyone but her True Love (this to reassure the chosen one that he won't be raising a rival's offspring) and she's somehow supposed to get Mr. True Love either to stick around until the kids are grown or, if he must be off, at least to provide generous child support. These are not easy tasks. But the human female has adapted well. She learned that it's in her best interest to treat sexual contact as a nearly sacred transaction, intimately entwined with sensitive emotions and complex interpersonal responsibilities (a.k.a. guilt). In extreme cases, she may even go so far as to deny having any interest in the animalistic rutting behavior with which the randy male's rustic imagination is tirelessly obsessed.

By that logic, I had left a very unfeminine message on Gustave's answering machine. I had acted like a man by letting my enthusiasm *show*. The more I thought about it, the more mortified I was by my faux pas. As the minutes crawled by and no phone call came, I became convinced that I had totally discredited myself *as a woman*, not only on the answering machine, but also in Gustave's bed, which I had jumped into without needing an ounce of persuasion and where I had cavorted shamelessly.

You might be saying to yourself that I really did not have to sit there and analyze this situation as much as I did. I could have watered the gasping plant or changed some burnt-out light bulbs or gone downstairs and watched Dick Cavett. But you must remember that I was new to the dating game, and spectacularly eager, hopeless, and confused, and filled to the brim with elaborate sexual/romantic fantasies that I was nowhere ready to give up, so there really was no other recourse for me but to hunker down with a face as droopy as a basset hound's and stare at my silent tormentor, the phone.

At eleven o'clock I was listing all the legitimate reasons Gustave might have for not calling (including the possibility that he'd died) when the phone rang shrilly. I pounced on it like a famished lioness. "Yessss?"

"Hi, Gillian. It's Gretchen. You sound kind of funny. Are you OK?"

"So kind of you to query," I said, swallowing a granite slab of disappointment. "I'm perfectly better, couldn't be fine."

"Hmm. I guess that's good! Anyway, sorry for the late hour. I just got back to my hotel room. I had the most wonderful dinner with Steven—He came down to join me in Washington! Isn't that incredible!—and thought I'd call to see how you're doing. I got a really weird message from Stacy this afternoon on my voice mail. She said—I *think* this is what she said—she said you sent her a death threat."

"What?"

"A death threat."

"A *death* threat?"

"Mmm."

"For goodness' sake, that's ridiculous!" Then my eyes popped. There on the corkboard was my red scrawled message: *Death to tyrants! Vive la liberté!*

"Gillian? Are you there?"

"Well," I hedged. "Weelll, ummm . . ."

"You mean you *did* send her a death threat?"

"I wouldn't call it a death threat *per se*."

"No?" Gretchen chirped in a very high octave. "What would you call it?"

There are moments when you wonder whether the world's perceptions of you are correct — whether you are so far outside the mainstream that you might as well be insane. I had one of those moments then. I felt as if I were simply dropping out of reality, down a rabbit hole like Alice's, and, like all the characters scurrying around me, had lost any claim to sense or understanding. If anyone had handed me a hookah emitting queer, pungent smoke just then, I would have tried a puff or two to see if it made me feel normal.

I didn't mention hookah-smoking to Gretchen. Instead, I described what had been going on at Responsibility House in her absence — the extra rules, the atmosphere of oppression, the callous expulsion of gentle Chris.

"Chris did break the rules," Gretchen said matter-of-factly after she had heard the details. "Stacy had to kick her out."

"Why?" I shrieked in a fairly deranged voice. "For *kissing*, for *making out?* It's not like she was doing any *harm.*"

Gretchen sighed. "Well, you've got a point. If it was me, I probably would have just looked the other way."

"We need to revise our *Handbook of Policies & Procedures*, Gretchen. I mean, we really do."

"Well, OK. Can you and Stacy work on it together?"

"Together? Me and *Stacy?* Are you mad?"

"Come on, Gillian. Can't you at least *try* to get along with her?"

"We are oil and water, fire and ice! We are not compatible!"

"Well, I don't think that's very nice of you. Sure, Stacy's a little hard to take sometimes; I can see that. But have you ever thought that the reason she bothers you so much is because you're a lot alike?"

"Alike?" I nearly gagged.

"Think about the two of you for a minute. Don't you see any similarities?"

I thought about it. "Yes, I guess there are a few. We're both insecure and perfectionistic; we both have low self-esteem and poor social skills. Our gender identifications are wobbly, our sexualities are undeveloped, and we both tend to be paranoid and histrionic."

"Right! But that's just the bad stuff. The good stuff is that you're both smart, responsible, and really hard-working. Now don't you see how much you have in common? How important *both* of you are?"

"It's a nice idea, Gretchen, but it's not going to work. The bottom line is this: The day/night division of power is ineffective. You need to put one of us completely in charge while you're gone. And I think it should be me."

Gretchen sighed. "Look, we're getting into a sticky area here, so I guess I'll just be blunt. Gillian, I'm wondering about your plans for the future. You haven't said anything about your research lately, which gives me the feeling that things at grad school are not going the way you hoped. I need to know how long you're planning to be with us. I can't afford to invest in a person who's not committed to the house. If you'll be leaving, I'll put my eggs in Stacy's basket. If you'll be staying, I'll put them in yours."

I felt as if Gretchen had looked right through me. "I don't know what to say."

"Then don't say anything. There's more. I just found out we're not in the supplemental budget that's supposed to undo the governor's veto of our line item. At this point, all we can do is muddle through '85 underfunded and try to reinstate our line item in fiscal year '86. I need talking points and statistics, and I've got to get a grass-roots letter-writing campaign under way. It's a ton of work. I can't possibly do it all myself. I'm not good at this stuff, Gillian. I'm a social worker, a people person. I'm not a good writer and well organized like you."

"You want me to—"

"Work with me on the lobbying effort. We also need to start hunting up private fundraising sources. There are books in the library that tell you who to contact and how to write the proposals. I'll find you some more money somewhere, I promise. But it won't be much. And you can give yourself any title you want."

"What about me and Stacy?"

"That depends. Are you going to accept my offer?"

I answered blindly. "Sure."

"Great! I'm so glad! In that case, you can be in charge of Stacy. We'll tackle that handbook and do an organizational chart when I get back. And Gillian, one more thing. I might take a few extra days off next week. Steven's family lives in New Jersey and he wants me to meet them over Christmas! We're going to drive up and stop in his hometown. Isn't that exciting? Do you think you can handle a few more days on your own?"

"No problem," I said. "Now that I'm in charge."

I woke the next morning knowing I had agreed to do something large and difficult, but I couldn't remember what it was. Finally it came back to me. Lobbying. Fundraising. Who knew?

But first there was the matter of the *Handbook of Policies & Procedures*. I had brought it home with me the night before, and now it lay in the center of my otherwise empty desk. I got some tea and Ritz crackers from the kitchen, and settled down to work.

The job was easier than I expected. I simply went through the handbook page by page, crossing out any rule that did not relate directly to sobriety and simplifying the few policies that needed to stay in place. Gone was the rule forbidding radio play during dinner, the strictures about gang-related clothing and colors, and the prohibition against new tattoos. The forbidden parts of the city, the denial of dating, and the strict ban on sexual contact were stricken from the record. The type of job a resident could accept was left to her discretion. After giving the house its percentage for room and board, a free and sober woman could use the rest of her money as she chose. Weekends were unstructured; children were allowed to visit anytime. Guests were permitted in one's room and could stay for dinner for a small fee if the cook agreed. The phone limit was scrapped, use of the laundry room was expanded, residents were allowed to open or shut the doors and windows of their rooms at whatever times and to whatever degrees they wished. The ingestion of snacks was not monitored, the number of meals was not counted. The curfew was moved to eleven, and Lights Out occurred at twelve. No medications ordered by a board-certified physician were prohibited, and the women were allowed to keep these medications in their rooms. Individual files would be kept locked but would be made available to residents on demand under the Freedom of Information Act. The house's fiscal information (income and expenditures) could be obtained by anyone who wanted it.

I typed up the new handbook. It was considerably shorter than the last. For no reason whatsoever, I called it *The Pink Book*. When I sat back and looked at it, I realized that everything the residents really needed to know could be boiled down to two basic rules:

1. Don't drink or drug. If you do, you'll be expelled.
2. Don't be an ass. (You know what this means.)

I printed these rules in big block letters on a piece of paper, folded it, and put it in my coat pocket.

If *The Pink Book* was ever adopted, some chaos was likely to follow. There would be errors of judgment, unimagined consequences, and the occasional serious mistake. The residents would have to communicate their needs and wishes; they would have to learn to listen, too. There would be more bickering, more complaints, more negotiation, and better solutions to the conflicts that inevitably arise when twelve impaired women try to live in the same house. However, I firmly believed that a freer, less bureaucratic society would achieve greater therapeutic results. Only freedom, after all, allows for choice, and free choice is what makes us human in the mixed-up way we are — sometimes weak, sometimes strong, and mostly a changing combination of the two. In my opinion, whatever the residents lost by losing so many rules they would gain in dignity, self-knowledge, and trust in the goodness inside themselves that had brought them to Responsibility House in the first place.

I suspected, of course, that Gretchen O'Neil would have a few things to say about the liberties I had taken with the *Handbook of Policies & Procedures*. But as harried as she was and as strong as I intended to be in pursuit of my ideals, I didn't expect her to put up much of a fight.

I had one more thing to do that morning. I wrote a letter I hoped I wouldn't have to send. I looked up an address in the phone book, addressed the envelope, and slipped it into my desk drawer.

At about 11:30 I switched off my Macintosh, yawned, stretched, and pulled my earlobe a little to make sure my ear was working. All morning, I'd been listening to the phone not ring. Gustave and I had slept together Saturday night. I had left a message Monday night. Now it was almost noon on Tuesday. Was it so wrong to expect a call?

The quiet deepened, unbroken by anything but my beating heart. I decided I would not, could not, spend another chunk of hours tethered to a mute telephone. It wasn't healthy. It wasn't wise. As I pulled on my worn boots and favorite vest, I was filled with sorrow that this, my first real hope of love, so recently born and therefore still young enough to be soaring, greedy, and naive, was already being sent to school. Despite this feeling, I managed to comb my hair and apply ChapStick. Then, with nothing more in my heart than a desire to escape the silence I was living in, I went outdoors.

The day was sunny, bright, and cold. Icicles sparkled and dripped. I decided to leave my bike on the porch and walk through my neighborhood and across a quiet, snow-shrouded park where boys and girls would be playing baseball in the spring. I saw a brown, abandoned nest high in the branches of a tree. The sky was sharply, brilliantly blue; the snow had a crust that gleamed.

I turned toward the square. I'd never had the ethnic lunch I'd promised myself on the day I was expelled, having given the ten dollars in my pocket to the bag lady. I decided to have it now and headed to a new Thai place that had received decent reviews. But when I got to the corner I had stopped at before and saw people again going through the rusted iron gate into what I now knew was an AA meeting, I followed. I had recognized Wolf

Man, who'd given me the bitter coffee, and I was mildly curious to hear what was happening with the Mechanic and Privilege Lady. Listening to their stories had brought some perspective to my own problems, and I suppose I wasn't averse to having some small portion of that benefit repeated. The fact that Gustave might be there was an added incentive to which I was trying to be completely indifferent. After all, I had promised that I wouldn't stalk.

To my surprise, neither Privilege Lady nor the Mechanic was there. Two entirely different speakers were featured that day, although I heard only one. She was a woman of indeterminate age, ordinary height, and shoulder-length hair. Her facial features were as close to average as you could get, and her body carried just enough fat to muffle whatever individual nuances it might have had. Her voice was so quiet and bland that it seemed to fall through one's ears like water through a sieve. I heard something about high school, something about beer, and something about Kmart before I lost interest and started looking around.

That was when I saw him. Sitting halfway down on the far aisle, his black curls pulled into a ponytail. My adrenaline gushed like a plume of crude from a newly drilled oil well. I craned my neck to get a better look—my eyes longed to caress his arms and chest, or even, if they could find them, his lovely large waist and slightly bowed legs—but I was sitting too far back. I had to be satisfied with glimpses of his profile whenever he turned his head, but even that view was blocked occasionally by leaning bodies or heads in the intervening rows. I sighed in frustration and turned back to the speaker.

She was a whiz at inventory and stocking, so her boss at the biggest Kmart in the Boston vicinity (I thought they were all big) gave her keys. Her mother had emphysema and no health insurance. Think about it. What would you do? Of course she used the keys to open the pharmacy door, and the pharmacist's keys, left in the drawer so they'd always be there, to open the medicinal storage area, and of course since she was young and stupid (these two terms treated as synonymous) she forgot about the pharmacist's passion for inventory and the surveillance cameras, so she was caught and immediately fired.

She got off on probation for a first offense and might have learned her lesson had she not met a small-time cocaine dealer in court. He thought she was unique and beautiful and did not judge her for what she'd done. He understood how it affects a person to hear her mother coughing herself to death. She didn't plan on moving in with him and using the drugs he brought home. Her first pregnancy miscarried, but perhaps that was for the best because soon the battering started. Cheap wine to numb herself when he was gone.

I felt terribly uncomfortable. Why had I come here? Obviously, I'd forgotten that listening to these stories was like falling through a trapdoor into hell. I should try to be compassionate, I thought. But I couldn't stand it and wanted to leave.

Gustave was turning to talk to the woman beside him. She was a big-haired blond who appeared to be of higher-than-average height. There was a garish metal ornament in her hair, and even from a distance her earrings looked ornate. I remembered Janet's warning about Gustave: *He gets around.* Then I remembered his gold necklace and heavy gold ring, and my intuition leapt far ahead of where it had a right to go. Had this jewelry-loving woman picked them out?

To stop these thoughts, I returned to Fired from Kmart. Drinking and drug use have a way of taking over, she explained. "You don't notice what's happening until you are lying on your kitchen floor, bloodied by the madman you are living with, swimming in your vomit." Those were her exact words. I found them utterly painful, so I tuned out. Gustave was smiling at the big-haired blond. She was smiling at him. They were sharing a private joke.

I found that painful too, so I tuned back in to Fired from Kmart. She didn't get into treatment for five more years, during which time her nose was broken seven times, her pancreas was damaged, her shoulder was dislocated twice, she had scores of debilitating panic attacks, she drank about a gallon of Boone's Farm a day, and she lost another child.

I shut my eyes against the horror. When I opened them, Big-Haired Blond was walking down the aisle to refill her coffee. She was about forty, probably strong and well-proportioned years ago, but now thickening at the middle and spreading at the hips. She wore a tight, button-down denim dress with a red scarf tied at the waist, and cowboy boots. Her false eyelashes spanned a western mile and made her eyes look as big and empty as highway billboards. She walked as though she hoped everyone was watching and gave cute little fluttering waves to several people as she came down the aisle. She passed within a foot of me, leaving a too-sweet floral scent in her wake, possibly camellia.

One day Fired from Kmart left the emergency room and went to detox. She sat in the waiting room for ten hours until they found a bed. She moved away from her abuser and got a job at a supermarket chain. Is assistant manager now, after seven years. Goes to meetings. Bowls on weekends. Can't have children. Dates a man with a motorboat on Sebago Lake in Maine.

But what *happened?* I thought with some annoyance. What transpired between the floor of vomit and the detox waiting room? What caused the sudden psychic shift? I cursed myself for paying such close attention to Big-Haired Blond when I should have been listening to Fired from Kmart. In all the stories of addiction and recovery I'd heard (five so far, including Gustave's and what I had gleaned from Janet's file), I kept missing the conversion fulcrum, the point of radical change. Obviously, there was something here I wasn't getting. Was anyone else not getting it too? I glanced around furtively, but the faces in the rows behind me seemed quietly content, even serene, and I got the spooky feeling that either I was sitting among a throng of programmed robots or I was completely out of touch with the mainstream of society (if one can call an AA meeting that) than I realized.

The emcee called an intermission and people got up and started milling about. A line formed at the coffee urn. I saw Gustave stand up, straighten his sweater, and look expectantly around the room. He didn't see me. I wondered, Should I wave? Did the fact that he had not returned my message mean that he wasn't interested, that he was brushing me off? Maybe he really *did* want to talk to me, but his answering machine was broken, or he hadn't played his messages yet, or (and this almost made my heart stop) he had been staying someplace else. He was walking down the aisle now, not the middle aisle, but the one on the side where the coffee table was. He looked relaxed and confident. His chest (the hair on which was familiar to my fingers) took deep breaths; the true blue of his eyes was visible from across the room.

"Gustave!" I called out, waving. I couldn't help myself.

At the same moment, a crash was heard. Someone in the back dropped a folding chair. Big-Haired Blond made her way to Gustave's side, holding two styrofoam cups. She handed one to him. He took it. She bent down, and just as her mouth got close to his head, he looked up, and her hair fell like a curtain across their faces. They seemed to freeze in that awkward position—him craning up, her bent over, each with a styrofoam cup outstretched like a holy chalice that could not be spilled—as they . . . yes, as they kissed.

It didn't last long. They pulled apart before anyone noticed. As they walked back to their seats, Big-Haired Blond brushed her fingers along Gustave's arm.

I sat back in utter amazement. Where had I been when they passed out luck? There were so many reasons to get out of there—the crowded hall, the stuffy air, the bad coffee, the sordid lives. But what made me run like I was turbo-charged was the bitter knowledge that I longed for the company of a recovering criminal who kissed trashy women suggestively in public while not returning my call.

I passed the bag lady on the way out. She looked at me expectantly, but I did not respond.

fourteen

W HEN I GOT TO THE HOUSE that evening, Maria was at
the counter mincing onions, and a simmering pot was
on the stove. It was nice to see her making tomato sauce again,
but my mood was so low I couldn't manage any conversation. I
just slumped against the counter alongside her.

Stacy whirred through the kitchen and out the back door
without so much as a nod. I hoped this meant that there was no
new conflict between us on the docket and no new crisis among
the residents to resolve.

I turned back to Maria and watched her practiced hands. I had
no sound bite or weather report to offer her, having forgotten
to check the newspaper. But Maria was facing the window, I noticed, so she hardly needed to be told that a white sliver of moon
was rising in a clear cold sky.

My heart was breaking; it had been breaking all afternoon. I
longed to confide in someone who was old and wise and would
not talk behind my back. I knew that Maria fulfilled two of these
criteria. And if she ever spoke more than two words, I might
find out that she was wise as well. Besides, I had grown fond of
Maria, or the person I imagined her to be, and had come to depend on her steady presence in the kitchen, which at times had
made me feel primordially mothered.

"I fell in love over the weekend," I began gingerly. "With a long-haired, possibly dangerous man of average intelligence." I half expected some food to be thrown or a great guffaw to escape her lips. When neither of these things happened, I continued. "On Saturday night I lost my virginity to him. It wasn't at all the messy, painful affair that bad movies and old wives' tales had taught me to expect. It was glorious and freeing. A peak experience for me. Then he didn't return my call, and just a few hours ago I saw him kissing another woman — a *cheesy* woman — in public. Now I feel used and cheap and rudely abandoned, and what's worse, Maria, far worse than this, is that I am beginning to suspect that all my favorite sexual/romantic fantasies, all the lovingly embroidered chimeras that have been sustaining me across so many lonely years, are nothing more than childish wishes for a perfect Candy Land of love that never has and never will exist. So deflated am I by this dawning realization, and so trounced and humiliated do I feel in my spurned state, that I am not sure I can carry on."

Maria slowly put down her knife. Her jawbone shifted slightly. When she turned to face me, her eyes were stern but not entirely unkind. "Get a Christmas tree," she said.

I reared back. Four words! Double what I got last time! And weren't they doubly wise? Yes indeed. The holiday was fast approaching, and for the women's sakes if nothing else, something festive ought to be done. I rushed into the living room, presently dominated by an old twenty-eight-inch Sony. That could be pushed to the side, and the couch could slide a few inches toward the far wall, and the coffee table could be stored temporarily in the basement, which would clear the lovely space in front of the double bow windows for a good-sized tree. I sighed in relief. The pain of my broken heart was being temporarily displaced.

The sound of banter and slamming cupboards rose in the kitchen. Several residents had come home. Varkeesha entered the living room, snapping open a soda can, and slumped onto the battered sofa, simultaneously scooping and clicking the remote. Her eyes glued to the popping screen, she managed to enunciate, "Whazup?"

"We're getting a Christmas tree," I said.

"Decorate with what?"

"Why, ornaments, of course. Popcorn and cranberries and tinsel and shiny balls."

"Ain't got none."

"We'll get some, then. That's easy enough."

"Who pay?"

"For goodness' sake, I don't know, Varkeesha," I said with some annoyance. "Maybe I'll get the money out of petty cash or we'll take up a collection or we'll have a craft fair and sell hand-made goods. I haven't thought that far ahead. And now that we're on the subject of thinking, why do I have to do all of it around here? Why don't *you* make a suggestion sometime?" It wasn't premenstrual syndrome; it was that cheesy woman who'd made me this irritable, I think.

Varkeesha brought the soda can to her lips. Her eyes were dead level on MTV.

I went out to the kitchen, where several women were standing around, gorging on the snack foods that Stacy wanted to ban. A couple of them went upstairs, and some more came in the door, and soon Responsibility House was the clanging, banging fortress of sound that it would be until Lights Out. I dragged a dining room chair into the kitchen, which added to the din.

"Oh, my God," someone said. "She's doing it again."

I stood on the seat. "Ladies, may I have your attention!"

Slowly they quieted down.

"Christmas is coming," I said. "We need a Christmas tree."

"Yeah, something for the cat to piss on."

"No, a real Christmas tree. With tinsel and holly and—"

"—And lights! Colored lights!" someone chimed in.

"I hate colored lights. I want white," another said.

"I like blue. My family always used blue."

"Blue sucks. Whoever heard of blue Christmas lights?"

"Blue is for Hanukkah. We used to put blue lights on the Christmas tree because we were, like, religious mongrels."

"Wha—?"

"That's it!" I shouted over their arguing. "It's been decided. We'll have red, white, and blue lights on our tree."

"What about green?"

"Green too."

"Oh, gag me," someone said. "This is all so cute. Can we move on now? I'm starved."

Varkeesha sauntered in. "It's Kwanzaa," she said. "Kwanzaa. Come on, ladies, get out your money. Put it in this sock." A clean sock was lying beside the toaster. It had probably been found on the floor of the laundry room and brought upstairs to be claimed by its owner.

Varkeesha held it out to a new woman, Charlotte, a washed-out, middle-aged coffee-shop waitress with blotchy skin and a rumbling smoker's hack. Charlotte looked nervously around the room. She hadn't been with us long. She seemed to be debating whether this was an elaborate group holdup designed to pirate her tips.

"Make a fucking donation, bitch."

Charlotte blanched so dramatically that the brown spots on her face stood out like chocolate Necco wafers. Her fingers scrabbled in her coat pocket and emerged with a wad of small-denomination bills. She stuffed the entire thing into the sock.

Varkeesha sighed, put her hand into the sock, and pulled out the wad. She rolled it open and counted it slowly, with the sock pressed under her arm. A few bills came crisply off the top; she handed the rest back to Charlotte. "You give ten percent to Santa. You keep the rest for your cigs."

The others crammed their hands into tight jeans pockets or pulled wallets out of the purses that still hung from their shoulders.

"Be generous now," Varkeesha warned.

"Yeah, be generous or she'll fuckin shoot you!"

A laugh rippled through the group.

From the corner came a soft, strangled cry. It sounded like *grow* or *row*.

The women stopped laughing.

"What was that?" someone asked uneasily.

We turned to the source of the sound, and some women stepped away. There, in front of the stove, stood a red-faced, weeping Maria.

"What is it?" someone asked her gently.

"Ro — roast turkey?" she implored.

Meg, who was standing closest, put an arm across Maria's heaving shoulders. The women made a tight circle around her. They touched her hands; they stroked her hair.

Yes, Maria. We will.

The next morning, as I was about to head out to the library to find the fundraising book that Gretchen O'Neil mentioned a few days before, there was a knock on my door. Lawrence had never known me to entertain a guest, which may explain the worried look on his face when he announced, "You have a visitor." Or maybe it was Gustave himself, striding into my room in his long leather coat and wind-tousled hair, who incited anxiety.

"I didn't think you knew where I lived," I said as Lawrence, despite being reassured that my visitor was known to me, suspiciously closed the door.

"I have my ways." Gustave winked.

But I was hardly in the mood for that. "I'm sure you do. You've got lots of ways, don't you?"

"What's that supposed to mean?"

"Oh, don't toy with me. I saw you with that big-haired woman at the noon meeting yesterday. Don't try to deny it."

He plopped on the bed. "I can't believe you're talking like this. Do you mean Eileen? My sponsor?"

"Call her whatever you like. I know what she is."

A playful light appeared in his eye. "You sound like a jealous wife in a soap opera."

"Far from likely. I have never watched a soap opera, only late-night TV."

"Still, you're jealous, aren't you? Ha!" The dimple twitched a bit. It was obvious that he was trying not to laugh.

"I have been mocked enough in my life. Please leave now, if that's all you can do."

"Hey, I didn't mean it that way. Don't be mad." He patted the bedspread next to him. "Come on over and sit down."

"I shall do no such thing. How dare you treat me like a child." I sat at the other end of the room, in the desk chair, my legs crossed and my arms folded stiffly across my chest.

"Gillian, please. Let me explain." He said Eileen was his sponsor, which meant a kind of recovery drill sergeant/therapist.

"I see. Do you usually kiss her on the mouth?"

"What are you talking about?" He appeared perfectly confused.

"At the break. Standing in the aisle near the coffee pot. The two of you holding out your styrofoam cups so stupidly."

He frowned and seemed to be searching his memory. Then his face relaxed. "Oh, I remember now. We were whispering, not kissing!"

"Well, it's your word against mine now, isn't it?" I wasn't going to let him buy me off with that sly substitution. Although it was true that I had been at a distance, with a number of people obscuring my line of sight, and her hair had been in the way.

"Since I'm the one who was doing it, I think my word should carry more weight," he said.

I turned away, pouting, unwilling to give up my indignation just yet.

"Look, I wasn't kissing Eileen, OK? We were talking about what we're going to get a friend of ours for Christmas." His voice grew tender. "Gillian, I like *you*."

"Then why didn't you call?" I shrieked, turning back to show him my fury.

"I'm here to see you, aren't I? It's only been three days!"

"Three days with no phone call! *Three days!* And what about that horrible, revealing message I left on your answering machine more than twenty-four hours ago? How dare you not answer it!"

Gustave dropped his head into his hands and groaned. "I wanted to call you, but you sounded so . . . intense. I didn't know what to say. I thought it would be better if I just came by."

"I know why you're here," I told him darkly. "You thought you would surprise me in my bed. You didn't know how early I rise. You thought you could just drop by for some free, unencumbered sex without so much as a phone call first."

"Yes, but I thought it would be romantic," he said.

"Ha! What do you know of romance?" I scoffed.

"Gillian, please. Can we start over?"

"There is no starting over, sir. The damage has been done. I was transported, I was set on fire Saturday night, and now I'm hopelessly in love."

"With me?"

"Who else, you idiot."

He managed a little smile.

"And I have a few more things to tell you, Mister . . . , Mister . . . What is your last name, anyway?

"Feinstein."

"Oh, sure. Fine Mr. Feinstein who goes around breaking hearts. Well, listen up, my plump friend, and listen good. I am not a floozy. I am not a tramp. I slept with you wantonly on our first date. But that's not the whole story. There's much more to me than that. Because, try as I might, I find that I cannot separate my sex drive from my affections, my libido from my heart. Why, it's unnatural! It's like trying to separate one's body from one's soul! The only place that happens is in death. Don't you see that? Don't you see who and what I am? Yes, go ahead, call me a woman if you like. *Woman.* Call me that."

Gustave had a curious look on his face. A mixture of emotions, one of which was pain. "I'm no good at promises."

"Hmmpff. I thought not."

"Only honesty and respect. That's all I can offer."

I turned away — agitated, strangely moved. Honesty. Respect. Should I believe him? I wanted to.

He walked across the room and took me in his arms. He hugged me, rocked me like a baby, and I started to cry.

"I'm sorry. I don't know what's gotten into me," I said after a few minutes, smearing tears off my cheeks. "I usually don't act this way."

"It's just me, Gillian. You can act however you want."

We made love for the second time that morning, more tenderly than we had on Saturday night. When it was over, I lay with my head on his shoulder and my hand on his warm chest.

"Look, I'm sorry if I was kind of hard on you when you told me you got kicked out of school," he said. "I know being there meant a lot to you."

"I'm not sure it did, really. Sometimes I think I never wanted to go to graduate school at all."

He drew his head back and looked at me in a funny way. "You're a pretty complicated person, you know."

"What does that mean?" I asked warily.

"I don't know. It's just that my life seems so simple compared to yours. I stay clean and sober, I wait tables, and I go to art school. Simple."

"How did you know that going to art school was what you really wanted to do?"

He shrugged. "I like to draw."

"Don't you worry about whether that skill will translate into a career?"

"Not really. I figure I'll be a graphic artist someday. Maybe a book designer. I don't know. I think I'll always cartoon." He cocked an eyebrow at me. "What do you like to do?"

"That's the problem. What I like is so amorphous. I like to think."

"Think?"

"Yes. Think."

"Maybe you could be in a think tank," he said, attempting humor.

"Frankly, it would suit me well. But usually you have to be invited, and that means having a doctorate, an area of specialty, a faculty appointment, published books, papers—in short, a renowned career."

"Oh."

We lay quietly. I spread my fingers through his chest hair and observed the rising and falling of my hand as he breathed.

"You can still write your book, can't you?" Gustave asked. "Even though you're not in school."

I sighed. "I could, I suppose. But I don't think I want to anymore. The truth is, I never really understood why I was so interested in secular conversion experiences in the first place. I gave my dean some good reasons when he asked me a few months ago, but they were all merely intellectual. When he wanted to know what was motivating me on a personal level, I didn't have an answer. And now the whole project just seems dumb to me. Like a child's silly game."

"Wow. When did that happen?"

"When I went to that AA meeting—the one I saw you at—I listened to a woman describe something that I knew was really deep, true, and profound, and I had no idea what it was. I felt like there was a sheet of glass between me and everyone else in the room, and they were on the inside, understanding all the important things, while I was on the outside, without a clue."

Gustave stroked my shoulder. "The glass isn't real. It's in your mind."

"It's real, Gustave. I know because I've always felt it—not just at the meeting but at different times my whole life. I hate it. It makes me feel alone and pointless. Now I'm beginning to think that it will always be there. That it's just part of who I am."

I thought I could feel his chest grow a little warmer. He cleared his throat. "I can't tell you what happened to that woman. But I can tell you what happened to me."

I got up on an elbow and looked at him intently. "I want to know."

He shook his head slightly with what appeared to be embarrassment. "It's just that . . . when you put it into words, it sounds so . . . corny."

"I won't laugh."

"Well, it wasn't like an angel came down from the sky one day. It was more gradual than that. I was living in a nightmare—selling drugs and using drugs and hanging out with people who used each other, especially women, in the worst ways you can. And I didn't give a shit about anyone, least of all myself. All I wanted was to score, and after a while that didn't mean anything either. I didn't care if I died. I used to drive by bridge abutments and think, What the hell."

I gulped. This might be more then I bargained for.

"Every once in a while I'd get this weird feeling that there were things moving next to me. Like, people I could almost see. And animals. They were just walking around with everyone on the street. I'd see something, a glove lying on the sidewalk maybe, and I'd think, That belongs to one of them. I figured I was going crazy. You'd think that would have scared me, but it didn't. I didn't really care. I started paying attention, and eventually I got a few good glimpses. Once I walked past a basketball court and there was a guy sitting at the foul line in a rocking chair, staring at me, just rocking back and forth. Another time a girl about twelve years old walked through my living room and went out the open window down the fire escape. I began to realize there were a lot of them. It was like they were living in a world that was happening at the same time as ours but was completely different. They'd come around a corner and look right at me, and I felt like they knew me and were waiting for me to do something. I wanted to meet them, only I was afraid to, because I didn't want to have to beg or bawl or crawl and I thought that was the only way you could approach them. But all this was buried so deep inside me that most of the time I didn't even remember it was there.

"I felt change coming from a long way off, long before it happened. It was like a silent rumbling at the edges of my mind. Little things that I barely noticed at the time seemed to be making a path. It's like if you're outside digging a hole, say, and all of a sudden you see a butterfly and a wasp, and then you forget about them right away. But the butterfly and the wasp were there, and they entered you like things being dropped down a very deep well, and you're walking down the street days later, and suddenly the echo of them is with you, in your ear. Or it's like the way night falls. You look around and notice that things are different. You know the change is coming by itself in its own time and has nothing to do with you, yet for some reason it's letting you in on the secret of its existence, just like the people and the animals did. And the next thing I knew the people and the animals were walking right beside me, close enough to touch. I could see the expressions on their faces—their suffering, their smiles. I didn't need to beg or cry for anything after all. I just walked along being part of them. It was a while before I realized I'd finally gotten well. My mind was the last thing to catch up.

"My life was still a mess, of course. I had a lot of things to get untangled from—a lot of people, too. I turned myself in to the police so I could get off drugs. But that's the boring part. It's not the point. It's just what I had to do." He laughed a little. "See? It's fucking weird."

I turned on my back in the narrow bed and looked at the ceiling. "I envy you."

"Why?"

"Nothing like that will ever happen to me."

"What makes you say that?"

"My symbolic imagination isn't that strong. Oh, sure, I saw weird things in my wallpaper a while ago, but that was anxiety-based. I think it's pretty safe to say my soul's not going to be saved by real or imagined apparitions in the street."

"You don't need them. You can save your own."

"How?" My life so far was in that question.

"I don't know. You'll only know yourself by looking back."

"I don't get it, Gustave."

"You don't have to get it. You just have to want it. And you do."

I rolled over and rested my arms and chin on his chest. "Can I ask you a really stupid question?"

"Sure."

"What do you see in me?"

"Courage, passion, curiosity."

"Really?" I hadn't expected that.

"Sure. How many people with college degrees are brave enough to work at a halfway house and take a chance on a recovering addict like me? And as far as passion goes, I've got all the evidence I need."

"And curiosity?"

"That one's easy. Have you ever stopped learning?"

I flopped back onto the bed, amazed. Did those words really describe me? Could I in good conscience lay claim to them? An unfamiliar sensation spread throughout my body. I think it was happiness. Maybe Gustave really cares about me, I thought. Then a dark idea bloomed and rose in the form of a dangerous question to the tip of my tongue. Every cell in my body told me not to ask it, but it popped out anyway.

"Please select *never, occasionally, usually,* or *often* in response to the following statement: I date more than one woman at a time."

"Come on," he joshed, nudging me with his shoulder. "You're not still upset about Eileen, are you?"

"Not just Eileen . . ."

"Oh, I get it. You heard a rumor about me."

"Yes."

"Tell Janet I said thank you, would you?"

"Is it true?"

"Yes, I've been with a lot of women. But that part of my life is over."

How many other women? I wanted to ask. My mind was speeding through a list: gonorrhea, chlamydia, herpes, syphilis, genital warts. At least we'd used condoms.

He turned on his side so he could see me better and softly stroked my cheek. "You're not like any of them."

"I don't imagine that I am," I said with stiff self-consciousness. I was imagining ballrooms full of sexy women with shining curls, Rubenesque figures, and mysterious clothes.

"I never talked to any of them about the things we've talked about," Gustave said. "Do you think they cared about *Siddhartha?* Do you think I could have told even one about my hallucinations, if that's what they were—the ones that saved my life? You don't need me to be tough, Gillian. You look beneath the surface. And you already understand me better than anyone ever has."

I didn't answer. I was remembering a line from a poem I'd read.

"What are you thinking about?" Gustave asked.

"Rumi, thirteenth-century Sufi mystic. *I was a hidden treasure, and I desired to be known.*"

"I'd like to read that book."

"You can take it home."

There was a sharp rap on the door. It opened a crack, and Lawrence peeked in at Gustave and me in bed. He closed the door quickly—in acute embarrassment, I presume—and spoke through the wood in muffled alarm. "Gillian, someone's on the telephone for you." I would have been angry at the intrusion had I not felt so sorry for him. He was clearly very worried about me. Not only was there a man in my bed, I was also getting a phone call—both on the same day!

I pulled on some clothes and followed Lawrence down the stairs to the second-floor landing, where the phone rested on a little table.

"You're not going to believe what's happening here," said a husky, whispering voice.

"Who's this?"

"Florine."

"Oh, dear. Is someone sick or hurt?"

"Worse. Stacy's on a rampage. She's kicking out Janet and Varkeesha."

"What on earth for?" Just last night we had all been together happily, decorating our tree.

"For driving the van."

"What?"

"Don't you remember? You let them take the van to get the Christmas tree."

"Yes, of course. Tell Stacy I gave them permission."

"It doesn't matter. Neither one has a valid license or insurance. It's against the law for them to drive, and even if it wasn't, it's *against house rules*." Her voice grew harsh. "Stacy says you ought to have known that, Gillian."

"Which one was driving?"

"First Varkeesha said she was, then Janet said she was. They're trying to cover for each other, and they actually started fighting over it. That's why Stacy's expelling them both."

"All right. Be calm, Florine. Tell Stacy I'll be right there."

"No! I don't want her to know I told you! I got your phone number from Information and I'm sneaking this call from the kitchen."

"OK. Then just hang on as best you can. I'll be there in fifteen minutes."

Gustave gave me a ride. It was nearly two o'clock in the afternoon on December 19. High cirrus clouds floated in a bright sky above the shops and businesses on Massachusetts Avenue. The sidewalks were thronged with shoppers.

When we turned the corner onto Summer Street and I saw

Responsibility House sitting there among its dry, thorny bushes, in its thin coat of pink paint, I thought it looked forlorn and traumatized. I told Gustave to wait in the driveway. My boot heels echoed strangely across the linoleum. (For the first time ever I did not see Maria in the kitchen; she was probably at school.)

Florine was sitting in the living room, wringing her hands. Her bakery was most likely open. Janet must have called her home.

I went to the second floor. The office door was closed. Janet's room was open, though, and I looked in. She was folding her plaid blanket. Her duffel bag lay open on a stripped, antiseptic-looking bed. All across the floor were piles of folded clothes—a pile of sweatshirts, a pile of T-shirts, a short pile of clean carpenter's jeans, socks and work boots, a nylon jacket, a few bandanas that she used as handkerchiefs. There were far too many clothes to fit into the duffel bag. With some embarrassment, I recognized the underwear I had peeked at months ago when I searched her room.

Janet saw me taking everything in. "Now look, Gillian, don't make this worse by getting upset and passing out. This is my own fault. I have a Class M license; it's only good for motorcycles. I knew that, and I knew you didn't know it. So I took advantage of you, see? All because I wanted to be the one to bring home the Christmas tree. That's typical of me, isn't it? I always have to be the star."

I couldn't speak. I had done it again. Through my own ineptitude, I had put her at risk.

"Stacy's just doing her job. That's what she's got to do. Her job." Janet laid the blanket on the floor next to her jeans.

Still, I didn't speak.

"I actually like prison," she said, starting to fold a sheet. "I got friends there. This place is nice, but prison, you know, it's kind of like my real home."

When I didn't respond, she looked at me appealingly, as if willing me to be convinced.

"This was bound to happen sooner or later," she continued. "I've always been on the edge here. You of all people know that. Yeah"—she nodded sagely as she put the last fold in the sheet—"prison's the best place for me."

Finally I found my voice. "Make your bed again, Janet. You're not going anywhere."

I walked across the hall to the office and opened the door. Stacy was on the phone. She put her hand over the mouthpiece. "What are you doing here? Can you wait outside? I'm on the phone with Janet's parole officer right now."

I crossed the room, elbowed her aside, pulled the desk a few inches away from the wall, and got down on my hands and knees. The phone jack was back there, a few inches from the floor. I pulled out the cord.

"Hey, what's the big deal?"

I crawled backwards, stood up, and dusted myself off. *The Pink Book* was on the shelf where I had left it a few days before. I tossed it on the desk. "Read this book and tell me what it says about driving the van."

Stacy picked up the book and thumbed through it briefly. "This isn't our handbook."

"It's our new handbook. Authorized by Gretchen, written by me. Now look through it and tell me what it says about driving the van."

"Where's the old handbook?" I could see her eyes roaming the shelves of the bookcase.

"It's gone. You won't find it there."

"You got rid of it, didn't you? But it wasn't yours."

Tricky Stacy. She always found a way to put me on the defensive. But I was waging war now, and I was prepared to lie.

"If you turn to page three of *The Pink Book*, Stacy, you'll see an organizational chart."

"So what? It doesn't mean anything."

"In fact, the entire book was approved by Gretchen. You'll find her signature on the first page."

"Gretchen's in Washington with lover boy."

"She signed it before she left. I just never got around to mentioning it till now."

Stacy sighed. She chewed her lip.

"Go ahead. Open the book. Gretchen approved it all."

Stacy's fingers crawled to the cover. She peeked inside and

glanced back at me quickly with an odd, slightly vulnerable expression. Was it hope?

"Go on," I urged. "Don't you want to see where Gretchen put you on the totem pole?"

Stacy sighed again noisily, sat down in the chair, and pulled the book onto her lap. She turned to page three and held the book sideways so she could view the organizational chart in its correct orientation. A second later she cried out, "Hey! This isn't fair! I'm on the bottom. I'm below *you!*"

I smiled and pulled a folded paper out of my pocket, opened it to its full size, and tacked it in the middle of the corkboard. "Here are the new rules in simplified form. The only offense punishable by Immediate Automatic Expulsion is the proven use of alcohol or drugs. The second rule applies to everyone, especially you. Now, if you'll excuse me, I'm going upstairs to tell Varkeesha that she'll be spending Christmas in this house, admiring her tree."

Stacy beat me to the door. She stood with her back against it, barring my way. "Wait a minute. Not so fast. It's not just house rules we're talking about here. Janet and Varkeesha *broke the law.* In Janet's case at least, we have a legal obligation to report that to her parole officer; that's what our contract says, Gillian. Here, I'll prove it to you. I'll show you *another* form Gretchen signed." Stacy yanked open the file drawer and pulled out Janet's folder. She held it aloft, then slapped it down on the desk, right on top of *The Pink Book.* "Take a look!" she said excitedly. "It's in there."

I sat in the upholstered chair, leaned back comfortably with my elbows on the arms, and made a pyramid with my fingers. "You make an interesting point. I've seen the form you're referring to, and I think you may be right. We probably do have an obligation to report Janet's little misdemeanor to the authorities. But it would be a shame, don't you think, if through our actions she had to pay an excessive price?"

Stacy's eyes glittered in triumph. "The law is the law."

"Hmm. I seem to recall a counseling session you and I had. I believe it was on Thursday, November twenty-ninth. Yes, I'm sure that was the day because I recently made a copy of my very thorough counseling notes and put it in an envelope addressed to Jack Kazmierczak, Homicide Detective, Cambridge Police Department. All it needs is a stamp."

The color drained out of Stacy's face. "Was that the time I—?"

"Yes."

"You don't think I really—?"

"Injected your sister with battery acid and watched her die squealing, like a pig? Those were your exact words, I believe."

"Gillian, I'd never do—"

"Then why did you say it? Why did you lie?"

"I don't know!" she blurted. "I really don't! I just, well, sometimes I just say stuff. It's not real. I don't mean anything by it. It's just to . . . to get on people's nerves, I guess."

"You succeed very well at that."

"Gillian, I didn't mean it, I swear."

"If I mail that letter, there will be an investigation at the very least. You would be very inconvenienced, I'm afraid. Family members would be drawn in. Of course, I would have to mention the incestuous relationship you had with your father and the actual paternity of your sons—"

"But that's not true either!"

"Oh, dear. What a mess! Well, no matter. I'm confident the police will sort out everything. And don't worry, Stacy, I'm sure your fitness as a mother will be established in the long run, after all the facts are known."

Stacy moved away from the file cabinet and slumped into the desk chair.

"Put Janet's file back, Stacy."

She did.

"There. We'll all have a nice Christmas now, won't we?" I said.

I couldn't put off calling Bertram and Joan any longer. I had to let them know that I wouldn't be coming home between Christmas and New Year's as I usually did. Since Gretchen was taking most of that week off to be with Steven and his family in New

Jersey and I was the most senior remaining staff member, I didn't feel comfortable leaving Responsibility House. But the real reason I needed to call my parents, which was also the reason I had been postponing calling them, was to break the news that I had lost my Zephyr Foundation Fellowship and would not be returning to Harvard to finish my degree.

"But we've been invited to the observatory," Joan protested when I explained that I intended to stay in Cambridge for the holiday week. "Professor Vander Hueven—you met him once—is going to show us how spurts of plasma are emitted from the rotational poles of protostars."

"Tell him I regret not being there."

"Oh, Gillian. Will nothing change your mind?"

"I'm afraid not."

"I see . . . Well, I am disappointed. But I suppose it can't be helped. You probably need all the time you can get to make some headway with your dissertation. Have you found a suitable topic yet?"

Bertram had been silent this whole time. I had the feeling that he was waiting to hear my second piece of news—that, in fact, he already knew it.

"Not exactly. Actually, I have something else to tell you two." My heart seemed to rise to the top of my rib cage. I was afraid my voice would tremble, so I tried to make it firm. "I'm not in grad school anymore."

"Did you say—?"

"I'm sorry, Joan. It's true."

Joan cried out as though she'd been shot. Several echoing seconds elapsed; then she started to weep. Bertram remained silent. I imagined his fury building like compressed steam.

"Surely you can *talk* to them," my mother sobbed.

"I talked. It made no difference. The Committee didn't like my work. They said it was nontraditional."

"But you were *changing* it, weren't you? You were making it better!"

"I didn't, though. I stuck to what I'd been doing all along. And they still didn't like it. I guess you could say that the deal fell through." I didn't even notice that those were Gustave's words.

At this, Bertram found his voice, and it was angrier than I'd ever heard it. "What *deal* are you talking about? There are only *deals* between equals. You were not an equal. You were a student, and your job was to fulfill the requirements of the program as the faculty saw fit. A renowned faculty, I might add. Scholars whom many students would give their eyeteeth to work with. It's galling! Who would do such a thing? No daughter of mine!"

The last phrase pierced like an arrow. Tears sprang into my eyes.

"You were more than capable of fulfilling their expectations," my father continued. "You *chose* not to. Less than one year away from receiving a terminal degree from a prestigious university—and you . . . you threw it away! Good God, you're a stubborn young lady. A lazy, lazy girl."

The second he said those words I realized how often I'd heard them before. Stubborn. Lazy. But I was not! I brushed away my tears before they had a chance to fall. "You can't say those things to me anymore, Bertram. I'm an adult. I'm not anyone's girl."

"Oh, stop, you two! I can't stand it when you fight," Joan broke in. Those words, also, were familiar. For years Joan had tried to keep peace by insisting that Bertram and I were equal when I had never been equal to him. Until now.

"I wouldn't go back now even if I could," I said angrily, knowing it was true. "In fact, if I'd been a stronger person, I would have chosen to leave."

"But *why?* What could make you choose a thing like that?" Joan cried.

If I could have answered her question, I would have. But I didn't know how to put any of what I was thinking or feeling into words. It is a shame to be struck dumb at exactly those moments in one's life when one ought to be saying something truly meaningful and profound, but that is often the case.

"Gillian, answer me. Are you there?"

I heard Joan's anxious question and Bertram's angry silence as if from a distance. And the next thing I knew I felt my soul expanding like a widening blue sky that would not be coerced by anything. There was no one I had to answer to, I realized, and no answers that would suffice.

Joan was weeping quietly, so her next remark was punctuated by little hiccups and snorts. "Oh, Gillian. All we ever wanted was what's best for you."

"I know that," I said.

"Do you resent us?"

"No."

I heard a gruff noise coming from the receiver. Either Bertram was coughing or he was trying to speak. "What do you intend to do now?" he asked finally. It was hard to read any emotion in his voice.

"I'll keep working at the halfway house in the evenings, and I'm going to do some fundraising there too."

"You're making quite a commitment to . . . that place," he said.

"There's real social value in these institutions, Bertram. And I find the work rewarding."

Silence. Long. Longer. I could sense my parents' terrible struggle. I hoped for their acceptance, but I didn't need it anymore.

Joan finally responded as heroically as she could. "I just read a study that reports some suggestive findings about the biochemical pathways of addiction. It seems that GABA may play a part, not just serotonin and dopamine as was previously thought."

"Hmm. Interesting," I said, feeling a slight smile play at the corners of my mouth.

But Bertram wasn't able to follow Joan's peacemaking lead. "I just hope that a year from now you don't look back and realize that you made a drastic mistake."

"At least it would be *my* mistake," I said.

Stacy took her boys to their grandfather's for Christmas, so I filled in. The house was hushed and spacious when I relieved Dolly at nine; about half the women had left the day before to visit family and the other half were still sleeping. We had put names in a hat for a Santa exchange, and I had pulled out Stacy's, so I went into the living room to put my small wrapped present for her under the tree. It was a 5½" x 8" organizer book with Daily, Weekly, and Monthly sections that I hoped she'd like. Then I put on the coffee and slid some pastries I'd brought with me into the oven to warm.

I didn't know what to do next, so I went back into the living room and sat down on the battered couch. I'd never been at Responsibility House in the morning. It was nice to see sunlight pouring through the window, making the ornaments sparkle and the tree look deeply green. A cat that some of the women had adopted jumped up next to me and purred under my petting hand for a while, then lay down with its spine against my thigh and fell asleep. I grew so heavy and relaxed in the warm sunshine, with the smell of coffee and cinnamon drifting in from the kitchen, that my head fell back against the cushion, and I soon followed the cat's lead. Sometime later, in a deep dream, I felt people all around me, bodies moving and hugging and giving gifts, but I did not open my eyes and see that it was real until something heavy and solid landed in my lap.

"Merry Christmas," Janet said. She had pulled a chair close to the couch and was leaning toward me with her elbows on her knees. Several residents in bathrobes were picking presents from under the tree and shaking them delightedly.

I looked down. The object was square, about 1½" deep, and wrapped in emerald-green paper with a silver bow. For a moment I thought it was a real gift, something Janet had freely chosen to give, but then I remembered the Santa exchange. "Oh," I said. "You got my name."

"I got Charlotte. Florine got Denise. But we wanted to get something extra, something from the two of us, for you."

Florine came up behind Janet and smiled at me. She was wearing a slinky red bathrobe and puffy Cookie Monster slippers with pink tongues sticking out. Her face looked longer and more normal without makeup.

"Aren't you going to open it?" she asked.

The bow untied easily. The paper was secured without an excess of tape. In a few seconds I was holding in my hands a framed watercolor of a pink Victorian house. Words handwritten in calligraphy ran around the edges of the picture. I could feel Janet's and Florine's smiles widen as I read them: *Remember Eliza*

—You're nothing but a pack of cards—Death to tyrants—Vive la liberté.

"Florine did it," Janet said proudly.

Although I had always wanted to see my words immortalized, my heart did not leap with joy. In fact, I felt embarrassed. It was not flattering to be reminded of several of my most trouble-provoking pronouncements or to hear in them my signature grandiose tone. I smiled weakly in their direction. "You shouldn't have."

"Janet and I have been talking," Florine said, "and we've decided to play by the rules from now on like you told us to. We really want to graduate."

I looked up then and saw two faces I had come to love, both of them smiling sincerely, both of them looking with respect and kindness . . . at me.

Just then Varkeesha pushed her way into our circle and plopped down next to me on the couch. She pointed a camera at Janet and Florine and squinted into the eyepiece. "Hey, sweetie, scoot down a bit, so I can get both of you in." Florine sank obediently and managed to poise herself on a piece of Janet's chair. The two women leaned close together and looked with fresh, open faces into the lens.

As Varkeesha adjusted the focus, I knew I would ask for a copy of that photo. Yes, I would keep the watercolor, but the photo was what I really wanted. Or, to put it more precisely, what I wanted was to treasure the memory of those two happy faces and tuck inside myself the knowledge that I had helped.

"Say cheese," Varkeesha instructed the pair.

I suppose emotion overwhelmed me. "Wait," I said with a thick voice. "The tinsel's coming off the tree." I got up to fix it, and a second or two later, when my back was turned, I heard the shutter close.

epilogue

GRETCHEN O'NEIL returned from her vacation with a diamond engagement ring sparkling on the appropriate finger. She gave no sign of her intentions vis-à-vis Responsibility House, but a June wedding was planned, and starter homes in the suburbs were being looked at, so it wasn't hard to imagine what would come next. Indeed, in August she announced that the commute from Sudbury was taxing, and with a child on the way and her husband working long hours in his downtown law office, it was time for her to move to easier pastures as a part-time addictions counselor at a group practice not a mile from where she lived. "But I'll miss this place," she said, sighing not altogether convincingly, I thought. Her departure at the end of the summer was a rather limp affair that I think we both realized should have been carried out months before.

Before she left, Gretchen had recommended my promotion to the Board of Trustees, and, there being no other candidates for executive director in the wings, they approved. Stacy stayed on as house manager, and I learned that Gretchen had been right. Not only was Stacy hardworking and loyal, she had a savvy business sense and excellent office skills. Together we mounted extensive grass-roots lobbying efforts, but they were not successful. Our funding was cut by fifteen percent each year in fiscal years '86 and '87. Those were hard times for Responsibility House. We had to put many of Stacy's cost-cutting tactics into operation, and even small raises for staff members had to be deferred. The residents, no longer forbidden to fraternize with the opposite sex, helped out by staging benefit sober dances at local meeting halls. The most famous, the Addicts' Sudden Personality Change Halloween Party (come as yourselves!), is still going on and has become a rather famous Cambridge fete.

Through all this taxing work, I did not forget my interest in secular conversion and the book Gustave finally convinced me to write. He had introduced me to a number of recovering people who were willing to talk about their spiritual experiences. After a while, I knew exactly what questions to ask, and I believe I conducted my research well and thoroughly. By the fall of 1986, I had compiled twenty interviews, which I put into narrative form. I called my book *The Courage to Change*, made six copies, and sent them out hopefully.

Not one of the fifty literary agents I contacted would agree to represent me, and the publishers didn't even read it. The box would come back unopened; only the fact that it was smashed and battered showed it had been anywhere. Eventually I gave up trying to publish it and stowed the manuscript under my bed. But the scholarly impulse inside me would not be quelled that easily. To understand my clients better, I had begun reading about the dynamics of addiction, and it was not long before I was immersed in the fascinating field of human psychology. A few years after failing to publish my book, I applied to Harvard's Department of Psychology. My tenure at Responsibility House helped my application, I'm sure, as did a generous letter of recommendation written by Dean Trubow from the Divinity School. But what the Admissions Committee really liked was the excerpt from my manuscript and my proposed dissertation on the subject of personal change.

I kept up a part-time schedule at Responsibility House through my graduate school years, as I busily observed mice and learned how to measure statistical variations and memorized the numerous bizarre manifestations of human psychic pathology. When I became an assistant professor at Simmons College, my work schedule was just too demanding, though, and I had to quit. By the time I received tenure, I had all but forgotten Responsibility House and the struggles and triumphs I had experienced there. The significance of that whole period of my life had shrunk to one small artifact—the framed photo of Janet and Florine, Christmas 1984—which I keep on a high shelf of my bookcase between *The Varieties of Religious Experience* and the *Gale Encyclopedia of Mental Disorders.*

It's actually not a very good photograph. The background is blurry, and Florine's pupils are red. But it captures their happiness as they lean into each other, their faces relaxed and softly smiling, with Christmas lights winking behind their heads. It's only now, after telling the story, that I remember how much trouble transporting that tree in the van caused us all. And I find it a little amusing, as I hold the photo in my hand, to recall that it was Varkeesha who snapped the picture with her expensive camera, just as she had taken many other pictures of her friends from many other angles, even the back.

Janet and Florine graduated within a few months of each other. They moved to New Hampshire, where Raven joined them. Janet worked on a construction crew and later at one of the last wooden boat factories in the United States. Florine started a bakery, working out of their house at first, but she found the work too isolating and was glad to accept a job as pastry chef at one of the large tourist hotels in the Washington Valley area. Her battle with cervical cancer began shortly after that and ended a few years ago as Raven turned eighteen. Janet sent a letter to Responsibility House with the sad news, and Stacy, now executive director, passed it on to me. In it was a picture of Janet and Raven. Janet has the same boyish haircut, blunt jaw, and square hands, but her hair is grayer, her face is gently lined, and she has lost most of her previous bulk. She looks like the kind of ordinary tradesman or woman one passes on the street a dozen times a week. Raven is very like her mother—black-haired and flamboyantly dressed. But there is something different about her—a freshness and simplicity that I would not have expected, given her lack of a known father and at least one stint in foster care. I suppose she's had a steadying influence in Janet, who obviously looks after her just as a father would, or a mother, or simply a person who cares.

The subject of love brings me, of course, to Gustave. How many hours we spent lying in bed, discussing the world and life and how to be ourselves! Our romance was long and sweet—far sweeter than anything I even knew to hope for—but it was fated to dissolve. Gustave was always restless and began to travel extensively, and I was (and still am) a compulsive worker. Across the years we drifted apart. The last time we spoke he was starting a new job in the Southwest. I have not heard from him now for several years, and there are no replies from the e-mail address I write to. Even so, I often sense him near me, sometimes walking close beside, just as he sensed those mysterious people years ago.

As for me, I look almost the same as I did back then. Indeed, my body seems strangely impervious to time. This is not as wonderful as you might think. It is annoying when new waiters at the Faculty Club mistake me for an undergraduate or when conference coordinators look down their noses, treating me with rude dismissiveness, until I tell them rather sharply that I, in fact, am the scholar they invited to speak.

But I don't have time to fret about my appearance. I am too engrossed in my work. My fall course called "Religion and Psychology" is one of the most popular on campus, and graduate students have to register early to get a seat in my seminar, "The Artistic Temperament." When I am not teaching, I am writing. My first book, on personal mystical experiences, received kind but tepid reviews in a few scholarly journals. My second, on the shared cognitive patterns of paganism, monotheism, and certain mental disorders, was very well received. With the bit of notoriety I gained from it (as well as the fundraising skills I picked up at Responsibility House), I was able to start Icarus: A Foundation for Interdisciplinary Study in the Humanities. We support scholars with nontraditional approaches to age-old questions and sometimes publish groundbreaking books that have been turned down by the usual array of presses. My work gives me great satisfaction.

Living alone didn't really bother me until about six years ago.

I started walking by the extra bedroom in my condo and pausing. The room was empty save for some cartons of books I hadn't unpacked, a few extra reams of printer paper, and an iron and ironing board I had bought one day because I thought I ought to have them and had never once used. It took me a while to realize what kept drawing me to the threshold of that room. The space that was there, ready and waiting to be filled, was also in me.

I eventually started adoption proceedings and brought Emily home from a Chinese orphanage when she was six. She sat very straight on the airplane, I remember, clutching in her tense little fingers the shred of blanket she had slept with for years. Certain details of that day will never leave me — how she regarded the pretzels we were served with suspicion and spit out the ginger ale. Yet she seemed to know we'd been joined because, although she would neither touch me nor allow herself to be touched, she shadowed me across the concourse like a duckling and put one foot, then the other, carefully on the escalator just as she saw me do.

During her first months in Boston, she seemed to make no progress. She remained withdrawn, and her language acquisition was unusually slow. Several well-meaning friends, including a nationally recognized education specialist from my department, took me aside and gently told me not to expect too much.

How she surprised those doubters! It was the soccer that did it, I think. I took her out to a field thronged with little girls one Saturday morning and watched as they were split into teams. The coach yelled and gesticulated, demonstrated dribbling, kicking, and stopping the ball, pointed out the goal demarcated with orange cones at either end of the field, then let the girls have a go. Emily somehow got to the front of the pack, dribbled the ball up the field, scored, dribbled back, and scored at the other goal, too — all while masterfully evading a swarm of petite opponents with bobbing ponytails. After consulting his roster to find out who she was, the coach boomed "Go, Emily!" several times thunderously from the sidelines. The parents cheered, I flushed with pride, and afterward a few teammates with well-developed social skills clapped her on the back. As we walked across the parking lot at the end of practice that day, Emily clasped my outstretched hand for the first time ever, looked me in the eye, and smiled.

She tackled challenges after that. It wasn't easy to figure out dolls and their clothes, but Emily persisted. The cold of ice cream came as an unwelcome shock that she did not let deter her. She traveled the Internet like it was a kingdom she was heir to, left- and right-clicking with increasing verve. Her language skills, which had continued to lag, rocketed nearly to grade level after she learned the dactyl "hot dog with ketchup and fries." She drank in love, hope, and knowledge like a plant that had needed only watering to thrive. Now eleven years old, she plays tuba and hockey in addition to soccer and beats me nine times out of ten at Dogopoly.

I am going to meet her now. We will stop at Bartley's for a burger and make our way home through the violet dusk of a New England autumn. She will do her homework while I prepare my classes, and then we will sit down together to play a fast game of Battleship or watch a little TV. After checking that she brushes and reminding her to floss, I'll help her pick up the clothes she has strewn all over the floor and tuck her into bed. Then I will settle into my pale blue room at the top of the house and take a few moments, as I do every night, to go to my window, gaze at the stars, and marvel at the practical causes and mysterious forces that make us who we are.

ACKNOWLEDGMENTS

Warm thanks to friends and readers Holly Robinson, Amy Callahan, Terri Guiliano Long, Virginia Smith, and Bonnie Cunningham for their time, intelligence, and good advice. I am indebted to Robert Preskill, Adair Rowland, and the late Andre Dubus for generous encouragement in the past and to the Dorset Colony House for giving me a quiet place to work on several occasions. This book wouldn't have happened without Maria Carvainis's faith and wisdom and Heidi Pitlor's enthusiasm and editorial vision. Most of all, I am grateful to Robert for his unwavering love.